Best wishes ~

Chas !!

Mih A Gill MD, JD

Marvin Eling

Prelude to GLORY

THE LIFE & TIMES
OF A TEXAS RANGER

Michael J. Gilhuly, M.D. J.D.
Marilyn Gilhuly

Stroud & Hall Publishers
P.O. Box 27210
Macon, Ga 31221
www.stroudhall.com
©2007 by Stroud & Hall Publishers
Printed in the United States of America.

The paper used in this publication meets the minimum requirements of
American National Standard for Information Sciences—
Permanence of Paper for Printed Library Materials.
ANSI Z39.48–1984. (alk. paper)

Library of Congress Cataloging-in-Publication Data

Gilhuly, Michael.
Prelude to Glory : The Life & Times of a Texas Ranger
by Michael and Marilyn Gilhuly.
p. cm.
ISBN 978-0-9745376-8-9 (alk. paper)
1. Texas Rangers—Fiction.
I. Gilhuly, Marilyn.
II. Title.
PS3607.I435P74 2007
813'.6—dc22

2006039616

Published works by
Michael J. Gilhuly, MD, JD
Marilyn Gilhuly

"Call to Glory, The Life and Times of a Texas Ranger"

"Ride to Glory"

To the usual suspects, our daughters, Tiffany and Jennie.
We would also like to add a special thanks
to our editor, Julie Saffel.

To the men who died at the Alamo...
All Texans acclaim both in song and story...
the days of youth, the days of your glory...
May they also remember wherever they go...
The men left behind at some far Alamo.

—*From a monument to the Texas Militia in San Antonio, TX*

CHAPTER 1

In all of his seventeen years, Leroy Wiley could not remember a year as exciting as 1857. He was now a member of the Texas Rangers. He had dreamed of being a Ranger ever since he was a small boy, but because it was only part-time work, he still had to spend much of his time working on the farm, helping his father and older brother, Clayton.

Leroy was a handsome young man, not quite six feet tall, with features that were already turning rugged. He had squarely set shoulders and piercing blue eyes that quickly turned to steel gray when he was angry. His sandy brown hair had been bleached lighter by the sun and had a windblown, tousled look. But it was his smile, more like a devilish grin, that people seemed to remember.

When Texas entered the Union in 1845, the federal government promised to control the various Indian tribes, especially the fierce Comanche. Since then, neither a half a dozen scattered forts nor the assignment of a special Indian agent for Texas had succeeded in keeping the peace. When the people of Texas demanded more and better security, the powers that be turned to the Texas Rangers.

As if the Rangers weren't stretched to their limits trying to keep the peace, the cattle ranchers began demanding help defending their livestock from rustlers, as well as marauding Indians and hostile farmers. Governor Hardin Runnels responded by ordering the Rangers to protect the herds.

Fifty-two thousand head of cattle and several herds of horses were driven to market during 1857. Most of these cattle were driven from south Texas up to Missouri, Kansas and as far north as Illinois. One of

Leroy's first missions as a Ranger was to guard a large herd of cattle that was following the Shawnee Trail from Lockhart through Dallas. The Shawnee Trail split from the Chisholm Trail just north of Waco and that's where the Rangers joined the herd.

"This herd's going through the Indian Territory to Fort Gibson. From there the trail boss says he intends to drive the herd on over to Baxter Springs. That's way up by the Kansas-Missouri state line," Sam Benson said as the Rangers rode across the grasslands south of Dallas. Sam Benson had been a Texas Ranger for more than five years. Leroy made a point of listening to men with experience like Sam.

"How far north do we ride with the herd?" Leroy heard one of the other Rangers ask. "I'm getting tired of son-of-a-gun stew. Seems like that cook can't fix nothing else."

"The captain told me we go as far as Preston's Crossing up by the Red River," Sam replied, then added, "I hope that's right 'cause I sure don't have much of a hankering to ride up into the Indian Territory. There's a reason they call it the badlands."

Sam looked at the eager young faces around him and wanted to make sure they realized what it meant to be a Texas Ranger. "You boys have a lot to live up to," his voice carried a serious tone. "During those thirteen days when the defenders of the Alamo were asking for help, the only reinforcements they got was a company of Texas Rangers from Gonzales. When those men rode past the Mexican Army they knew they were probably facing certain death because Santa Ana had the Alamo surrounded, and old Sam Houston was way over by San Jacinto, too far away to be of any help." Sam saw that he had each and every one of the young Rangers' undivided attention. He took a deep breath and continued, "What I'm trying to say is that since Texas gained it's independence in 1836, the Texas Rangers have had to take care of things along a frontier that stretches over a thousand miles, and we've done a pretty good job." Sam clinched his fist and added, "The important thing is that we are honest lawmen doing the best we can to protect the decent people who want to live here in Texas. Whether it's chasing bandits back across the Rio Grande or running down murdering Comanche, we don't give up." He shook his head and looked each young man in the eye. "When you're a Texas Ranger people expect a lot of you, so do whatever it takes to make this a safe place for law abiding people to live."

The young Rangers looked at each other, and then back to Sam. "That's all I got to say. I hope you remember my words because there's gonna be times when you'll need all the backbone you got and then some," with that, Sam spurred his horse and rode away.

No one said a word but Sam's speech had made a deep impression on all of them, especially Leroy. He made a silent promise to himself, *I ain't never gonna never let the Rangers down.*

The herd covered between eight and twelve miles each day. Leroy was surprised to learn that cattle drives didn't follow a straight line. The trail boss would ride out before daybreak to look for places to water the herd. The location of water would determine in which direction the cattle would be driven that day.

The Rangers mostly stayed with the herd, watching out for rustlers or any signs of Indians. One day just before noon, Sam Benson rose up in his saddle and pointed to a small rise several miles ahead. Leroy could barely pick out the trail boss who was riding towards the herd as fast as his horse could run while vigorously waving his hat from side to side.

"Haven't seen them cowhands waving their hats like that before," Benson said in a quizzical voice. "Wonder what it means?" The cowboys had their own set of signals using their broad brimmed hats. By the end of the first week on the trail, the Rangers thought they understood all of the signals. As Leroy looked toward the horizon, he saw the trail boss suddenly drop from his saddle followed by the sound of a rifle shot echoing through the valley.

Captain Mallory immediately shouted, "Rangers, follow me."

The Rangers hit their spurs against horseflesh and rode off in the direction of the fallen trail boss. The cowhands stationed around the herd immediately began to slow the cattle.

Indians? Leroy thought as he rode up behind Captain Mallory.

No sooner had they cleared the rise where the trail boss had gone down when thirty Mexican bandits wearing big Sombreros and carrying rifles rode toward the herd from the west. Mallory led his Ranger

Company as it raced toward the Mexican bandits. Riding with the other Rangers, Leroy drew his Colt revolver and prepared to fire.

As the two opposing forces closed the distance between them, sounds of frightened Longhorns filled the air. The drovers had all they could handle trying to keep the cattle from stampeding. Mallory knew that it would be up to the Rangers to deal with the Mexican bandits. The Mexicans had planned to stampede the cattle but apparently they were unaware that there were Rangers guarding the herd. Suddenly, the bandits turned away from the herd and charged into the approaching lawmen.

Leroy's heart was pounding in his chest while the wind blew in his face so hard he could barely see. He heard a rifle being fired off to his left followed almost immediately by the buzzing of a musket ball as it missed his head by inches. When Leroy looked in that direction he saw the Mexican who had fired the shot at him desperately trying to reload his rifle. Before the man could finish reloading, Sam Benson rode up beside the bandit and shot him in the chest.

The young Rangers, most of them hunters and expert marksmen, found that aiming and firing a rifle while riding at a full gallop was a difficult, if not impossible task. As the two sides came crashing together a heavy cloud of dust and smoke covered the entire area. For a moment Leroy was disoriented and unsure as to what was happening. The Rangers and the Mexicans seemed to be scattered all around him. With all the dust, Leroy lost sight of the Mexicans so he stopped firing his pistol. More than one bullet whizzed by him as he continued to ride in search of the Mexicans.

Leroy searched in vain for a target and suddenly became aware of a loud, roaring noise that reminded him of rolling thunder. The gunfire was soon completely drowned out by the sound of the stampeding cattle. Leroy's horse stopped short, snorted out of fear, then without warning, it reared up on strong hind legs and in an instant was racing away from the herd in a panic. It took all of Leroy's strength to stay in the saddle and get control of the frightened animal.

He finally brought the horse to a stop near a steep, rocky mound where he paused to get his bearings. From the high ground he could see in the distance that the Mexicans were retreating with about a half dozen Rangers giving chase. Leroy spurred his horse and headed in their direction. *I've got to catch up,* he thought.

The Mexicans dismounted and took cover behind a cluster of rocks near a creek. Just as Leroy caught up with Captain Mallory and the small group of Rangers, Sam Benson was shot in the face. His whole head seemed to explode in red. For Leroy time seemed to stand still as he watched Benson's faceless body fall from his horse. Captain Mallory shouted for everyone to take cover and Leroy followed him to the shelter of a few scattered hardwood trees.

Outnumbered, with shots pouring in on them, Mallory yelled, "Where are the rest of our boys?"

His son, Billy, answered, "Some of 'em got hit during the gun-fight. The rest were scattered by the stampede."

Captain Mallory quickly took stock of the situation. "We can't count on the cowhands for help. They've got their hands full with the stampede. It's up to us to flush 'em out."

"Captain," Leroy said. "They've got us at least two, maybe three to one."

Mallory made no reply. *Can't be indecisive around the men, especially the young ones. I've got to take control of this situation. They've got the creek to their backs. What if we get behind them? They can't move without giving us a clear shot at 'em.* "We need to get 'em now before they get settled and have time to regroup. I don't want to give 'em time to come to the same conclusion you just did, Leroy." Mallory turned to his son who was crouched down beside him. "Billy, I want you to take two men across that creek and come up behind them. Move as fast as you can and try to keep low. The rest of us will pour on the lead and keep 'em pinned down. When we hear you boys start shooting, we'll come at them from the front while you take 'em from the back.

Billy nodded.

Leroy tapped Billy's arm and grinned. "Bet I can out run you, Billy."

Billy smiled.

Mallory looked around, "Who else?"

"None of the other new fellows made it," Willis said. "I guess I'm the youngest one of this bunch, after Leroy and Billy, so you can count me in, Captain."

Mallory grinned. "You're not that old, Willis. I bet you can keep up with these two." Then his expression turned deadly serious. "Boys, I want you to reload and get ready. When we start firing, count to three, then high tail it for the creek. We'll keep it up until you clear the other side."

Leroy checked both his revolver and his rifle, only the revolver needed reloading. He barely had time to catch his breath when Mallory gave the order to open fire. Four men raised up and started firing at the rocks. Leroy didn't take time to see if the Mexicans were returning fire. He was off and running, splashing through the creek alongside Billy, with Willis following closely behind. Just as they reached the far side of the creek, Billy slipped and fell into the water. Leroy reached down and grabbed Billy's arm while Willis took hold of Billy's shirt, and together they dragged him up the bank toward cover.

"I dropped my rifle," Billy hollered.

"Well we ain't got time to go fishin' for it," Willis snarled. "Use your pistol or throw rocks at 'em. I don't care."

"Billy, you stay here and wait," Leroy said as he motioned for Billy to stay low. "You can't hit 'em this far out with a hand gun. Willis and I will try to get close enough to get a clear shot. As long as the captain and the others keep firing, we stand a chance of sneaking up on 'em."

"The firing ain't gonna last much longer, so let's go," Willis said.

"I'll keep watch from here," Billy said in a low voice. "If one of them raises his head, I'll take a shot at 'em with my pistol."

Willis and Leroy took off their hats and started moving through the high grass, keeping as low as possible.

"He ain't gonna hit no Mexican with that pistol," Willis said. "Not at that distance."

"If we can get a bit closer without being spotted," said Leroy, still out of breath from racing across the creek, "it won't matter what he does."

A few minutes later, Leroy turned to Willis and grinned. Just ahead, he could see a dozen Mexican vaqueros crouched down low

behind a cluster of rocks, reloading their weapons and waiting for the
firing coming from the Rangers to stop.

"You ready?" Leroy asked Willis.

"As ready as I'll ever be," Willis answered. "It's just you and me, so
we've each gotta drop two or three and hope there ain't many more."

Before the two Rangers could make their move, Leroy heard the
bushes rustle behind him. He drew in a quick breath and turned to
fire.

"Don't shoot," Billy whispered. "It's me."

"What the heck are you doing here?" Willis asked. "You almost
got yourself shot."

"I can't do no good from back there," Billy whispered. "You fellows need my help."

"Billy, I swear, I ought to shoot you for your own good after we
take care of them darn Mexicans," Willis whispered back.

Leroy, who had remained silent up until now, grinned at Billy. "Ah
shucks, Willis. I wouldn't have wanted to miss the fun either." He
turned his attention back to the Mexicans. "Let's get 'em now before
they see us."

Leroy had already picked out his first target. "Willis, you take the
ones on the right. Billy, you take the ones over there on the left, and
I'll go for the ones in the middle."

"I ain't too sure about your plan," Willis said, shaking his head.

"On three?" Billy asked, his voice barely a whisper.

"On three!" Leroy answered.

"I'm out here with a couple of squirrel hunters," Willis groaned.

"One, two," Leroy gripped his rifle and raised up on one knee
before adding, "three!"

Leroy and Willis each squeezed off a round from their long rifles
before reaching for their pistols. Billy took careful aim with his pistol,
waited, and fired at a Mexican partially hidden behind the rocks on
the left. Billy's aim was true. When the bullet tore into the man's stomach. Billy heard the Mexican scream out over the sound of the gunfire.

When the firing finally stopped, Leroy gave the signal that it was
safe to come forward. Captain Mallory and the Rangers who were

able, walked through the brush down to the cluster of rocks to view the dead bandits.

"You men did a fine job," Captain Mallory said when he reached them. "I couldn't be more proud of you. This was your first time under fire and you all acted as if you had been Rangers for years." He turned to Leroy. "And remember to tell your Ma that I didn't ask you to do nothing that I didn't ask of Billy. I don't want her after me when we get home."

Leroy chuckled. "I don't blame you for being leery of my Ma. She scares me too, Captain." *Mama even has a captain in the Rangers buffaloed,* he thought.

"We're all a bit scared of the womenfolk," Mallory replied, a smile filling his face.

"Look at them spurs, Leroy," Willis said as he pointed to a pair of spurs on one of the dead bandits. "I ain't never seen nothing like 'em. I'll bet they're pure silver."

"We'll flip for the spurs, if that's all right with you, Captain," Leroy said. "I sure do like the looks of 'em."

"First, gather up the weapons, then you fellows can decide who gets the spurs," Mallory said. "You boys have definitely earned them."

"Willis," Billy said. "If it's all the same to you, I'd like Leroy to have them spurs."

Willis nodded. "I don't really want nothing from no Mexican. I had kin at Goliad."

After they finished picking up the weapons, Billy walked over and unbuckled the dead Mexican's silver spurs. The man's eyes stared into the bright afternoon sunlight. Without saying a word, Billy handed the spurs to Leroy.

"Now let's go see what has happened to all them cattle," Captain Mallory said. "I got a feeling they're halfway to Missouri by now."

CHAPTER 2

As stampedes go this one turned out to be minor—if any stampede can be considered minor. No one was killed and only a dozen or so head of cattle were lost. By the time the cowhands had managed to turn the herd, they had run in a wide circle and ended up not too far from where the stampede started.

Leroy could see that the drovers were exhausted. "I guess fighting Mexicans is easier than herding cattle," he said to Billy. As they got closer he smelled a strange odor about the cattle. The odor was so strong that being near the herd made Leroy's stomach queasy.

"It's because of the stampede," one of the drovers explained. "All that clashing of hoofs and horns causes the smell. But don't you never mind, after awhile you'll get used to it."

They buried Sam Benson and the trail boss on a gentle rise by the creek. Captain Mallory and Sandy Clemmons both said some words over the graves. As the top hand, Clemmons would take over for the dead trail boss. Tall and with a no nonsense attitude, he commanded respect from the other cowboys. Everyone seemed to agree that Clemmons was the best man for the job if they were going to drive the herd all the way to Kansas City.

Immediately after the service the cattle drive continued on up the Shawnee Trail. Several Rangers had been wounded in the gun battle. Some were patched up and continued with the herd, but the ones with more serious wounds were placed in a wagon and sent to the nearest town, hoping to find a doctor and get medical treatment.

After the run in with the Mexican bandits the Rangers had very little contact with the drovers. Captain Mallory had the Rangers scouting the trail ahead and on either side of the herd to make sure they didn't run into any more surprises. The loss of Sam Benson had deeply affected the Ranger Captain. He pushed his men hard. By the time they had reached Preston's Crossing, located near the Red River, the Rangers were exhausted and eager to head back to Smith County.

Leroy sat on his horse and watched the cowboys drive the Longhorns across the muddy Red River. Clemmons had his most experienced drovers up front directing the cattle across.

"Dad says we can head home when the rest of the herd gets across the river," Billy said as he rode even with Leroy's paint.

"You mean Captain Mallory, don't you, Billy?" Leroy chuckled. "He ain't supposed to be your daddy while we're on duty."

Billy laughed, "You know what I mean."

At the end of the day, they rode toward home with a slight breeze to their backs. Once the Rangers were away from the heat and the foul odor created by the herd, it turned into a nice day. The three young Rangers were tired but riding home with their heads held high.

Look at 'em, Captain Mallory shook his head and smiled to himself. *I bet they think they're ready to take on the Comanche.*

CHAPTER 3

During the spring of 1858 Leroy's mother received word that her sisters, Mary and Gladys, would like to come out west for a visit. To say the least, Verlinda Wiley was overjoyed. When the Wileys had left Georgia, Verlinda didn't think she would ever see her sisters again. After much discussion, Taylor and Verlinda decided to send their youngest son, Leroy, to Columbia County, Georgia, to escort Mary and Gladys to Texas. With his son's experience riding with the Rangers, Taylor felt sure that Leroy would be able to watch over and protect his aunts on the long journey.

By the time Leroy returned home from Ranger duty, his parents had already worked out the plans for the trip.

Leroy spoke with Captain Mallory and was granted a leave of absence to take care of family business.

Verlinda wrote to her sisters that their nephew, Leroy, would be on his way to Georgia very soon and she assured them that they would be perfectly safe making the long trip in his company—Leroy being a Texas Ranger.

Verlinda suggested to Leroy that he should rest up in Augusta for a few weeks before coming back Texas. "You don't know when you'll ever get the chance to visit with your relatives in Georgia again."

"Don't worry, Mama," Leroy said with his usual mischievous grin. "I'll be fine, but I've got to get back to Texas as soon as I can. Someone has to look out for Willis and Billy."

Leroy packed his saddlebags with his best clothes and his Bible. He then slung two large pillowcases full of food his mother had cooked onto either side of the saddle. After checking his bedroll to make sure it was secure, Leroy climbed on his horse and rode east into a bright and beautiful sunrise.

"A morning like this is God's way of telling me that Leroy is going to have a good trip and bring Mary and Gladys safe and sound to Texas," Verlinda said as she watched Leroy pause and wave goodbye from the gate.

"I wish I could have gone with him," Clayton sighed as he returned Leroy's wave.

Taylor reached over to place his arm on Clayton's shoulders. "I sure am sorry son, but there's too much work around here to let both of you go."

"The ground's got to be cleared so we can plant corn and wheat at the end of the month," Verlinda added. "Remember, Clayton, you promised to put in the garden right after Easter Sunday so we'll have enough vegetables this summer."

"I know," Clayton said sadly. "But still, I sure would like to have gone with Leroy."

CHAPTER 4

Leroy made good time as he headed east across the Texas prairie. He was riding one of the cutting horses from the cattle drive. The paint was frisky and loved to run. The horse reminded Leroy of stories he had heard about Indian ponies.

Leroy was in good spirits as he paid his fare and prepared to cross the Louisiana Red River on a ferryboat. He had never been on a boat before and stayed by the railing looking down river while holding his horse's reins.

Leroy stopped in several Louisiana towns and found the people to be very much like his neighbors in east Texas. They offered him food and lodging and he repaid their kindness by telling them stories of his adventures as a Texas Ranger. His listeners, including some pretty Louisiana belles, sat spellbound. Leroy decided that this trip might turn out to be more fun than he had thought.

Crossing the mighty Mississippi was certainly not like crossing the Red River in Louisiana. Leroy stared wide-eyed at the broad, rushing river. He caught glimpses of both steam and keel boats making their runs down river to New Orleans. It was while he was on the Mississippi River, just before he landed in Vicksburg, that Leroy first heard about the growing movement in the south to leave the Union. Although they had southern roots, Leroy's family had thought of themselves as Texans since the day they arrived in Starrville. He had never really thought about being "southern," as the folks in Mississippi called people who lived south of the Mason-Dixon line. During the past year he had heard tales of violence in "Bloody Kansas" and about a wild abolitionist named John Brown who murdered five pro-slavery settlers along Pottawatomie Creek. But now he was hearing people talk about forming a militia to march into Kansas as part of a crusade for states rights. Leroy tried to remember as much of what he heard as possible so he could tell his father when he returned home. *Wait until Papa hears about this,* he thought. Leroy smiled as he imagined what his Pa would say when he heard such talk.

Across much of Mississippi, Alabama and the western part of Georgia the countryside looked more or less the same. He stopped at a village called Tallapoosa soon after crossing into Georgia. There he learned that the town was named after the Tallapoosa River, which was famous for the gold that had been found in its rushing water.

"It's name," the proprietor of the Tallapoosa General Store told Leroy, "means River of Gold."

Leroy wasted an entire afternoon looking for gold in the riverbed, coming up with only rocks, mud and mosquito bites.

A few days later Leroy treated himself to dinner at a hotel next to the Western and Atlantic railroad tracks in the small town of Marietta, twenty miles north of Atlanta. After finishing his meal, he rode past the Georgia Military Institute. He stopped to watch a company of cadets all dressed up in their gray coats with three rows of shiny brass buttons and gray pants with a wide black stripe running down the side of each leg doing close order drills on the parade grounds. *Rich boys playing soldier,* he thought. *Wonder how many of those fellows would last more than a month in the Rangers?* He smiled to himself as he pictured the cadets being chased by a band of Comanche.

When Leroy went to check into a nearby hotel, he couldn't believe how much they charged for a room. After he explained to the man at the desk that he couldn't afford to pay that much, the desk clerk suggested that he ride back to the Georgia Military Institute to see if they would allow him to stay in the cadet barracks.

Leroy stopped and asked a passing cadet if it would be possible to rent a room for the night. The cadet took him to the orderly room near the front gate, where he talked to the cadet on duty.

"You'll have to go over to the headquarters building," a tall cadet with thick red hair said with a pronounced southern accent. He walked over to the window and pointed toward a large brick building in the center of the compound. "Ask for Mr. Roberts."

Leroy thanked the young man and started to open the door.

"Hey, Cowboy," the cadet said with a big grin, "Mind if I have a look at your hat."

"Well," Leroy said with a serious expression. "In Texas we're mighty particular about who handles our hats but I reckon you'll be careful with it."

The young man reached out and took the hat with both hands. "How much did a hat like this set you back?"

Leroy thought for a moment. "Oh, about a month's pay plus a few dollars I borrowed from my brother."

"I'll bet that was a lot of money," the cadet carefully handed the hat back to Leroy.

"More than I got on me right now," Leroy grinned. "That's why I'm looking for a bunk here instead of the hotel in Marietta."

"I'm sure Mr. Roberts will find room for you," the cadet smiled and held out his hand. "My name's Matt Brown. I hope I'll be seeing you again, Cowboy."

"My name's Leroy Wiley," Leroy said as he shook Matt's hand. "And if that war ever-body's talking about starts up, we'll be fighting on the same side."

As Leroy made his way across the empty parade ground he heard Matt call out, "We'll probably have all the Yankees whipped before you get back home."

"We've got just over one hundred and fifty cadets enrolled, but not all of 'em are in residence now so I guess I can put you up for the night," an older gentleman with thin gray hair and sharp features said. The man was dressed in a gray uniform and even though he was obviously past fifty, he still had the carriage of a soldier.

"I'd be most grateful," Leroy answered. He looked around the room filled with uniforms, as well as, swords and muskets, all hanging in their proper place. "I don't think we have schools like this back home," he said.

The gentleman nodded but didn't offer a response.

"I need to take care of my horse," Leroy said as he tilted his head toward the door. "Can I buy some hay and rent a stall for him?"

The gentleman smiled. "I'll make sure your horse is taken care of young man," he said as he closed his writing tablet he'd been scribbling on and slowly stood. "You're from Texas, you say?"

"No, sir," Leroy shook his head. "I didn't say where I was from."

"Well," the old man patted Leroy on his shoulders as they walked out the door. "We don't get any boys from Texas here, but I've spent enough time in your part of the country to hear Texas in every word you speak."

Leroy laughed. "I reckon that's a compliment."

"What's your name son?"

"Leroy Wiley, sir."

"Well, Leroy Wiley, you'll find everything you need in here," the kind old man said as he led Leroy into a small room containing four cots. He pointed toward a chest of drawers and a small table. "Wash basin is over there and I'll send someone by around five o'clock to bring you to supper. Be sure and get to bed early 'cause breakfast is at six in the morning." Then he turned to Leroy and asked, "By the way, where are you heading?"

"Columbia County, sir," Leroy reached into his pocket and pulled out a letter of introduction his mother had written for him. "I'm to bring my Aunt Mary and Aunt Gladys back to Texas for a visit."

"I'll draw you up a map that'll get you to Augusta. It's dangerous crossing the rivers unless you can afford to pay for the ferry boat."

"I believe I have enough, sir," Leroy frowned. "But I've got to save my money for the trip home."

"I expect you are going to take your aunts as far as you can by train coach?" the gentleman rubbed his beard in deep thought. "You could ride from Augusta to Atlanta on the Georgia Railroad, then to Selma on the Alabama-West Point line. From there you could hire a team and wagon to take you to the next junction, which is located over in Mississippi. That would be much easier for the ladies."

"I'm leaving all the travel plans up to my Aunt Mary and Aunt Gladys," Leroy grinned. "My aunts have everything planned. I'm just along to make sure nothing goes wrong."

The old man gave a hearty laugh as he left Leroy. Before he closed the door he called back over his shoulder, "I'll give you directions that will get you as far as Augusta, then it might be best to let the women-folk figure things out."

Leroy raised his eyebrows. He considered the duty given to him by his parents to bring his aunts back to Texas as one of extreme importance. He wasn't sure, but he thought the old man might be making fun of him.

Supper that night was full of talk about states rights and the movement toward secession.

"Back in Texas," Leroy explained between bites of sugar-cured ham and sweet potatoes, "we all heard about what's happening in Kansas but I never did hear any talk that the whole country was about to go to war."

"Oh, but the country is seething with trouble," the old gray haired gentleman explained. "Around here people are itchin' to get into a fight."

Leroy shook his head and frowned slightly. "I'll wait and see what Texas decides to do. If Texas fights, I'll be the first one in line to sign up."

Early the next morning Leroy was awakened by the sound of a bugler playing revile. He hurriedly dressed and walked to the mess hall where he was served more sugar-cured ham along with scrambled eggs. He had barely finished his meal when he heard the bugler playing a different tune.

"That's the call for the cadets to come to breakfast," the old gentleman said. "Better be on your way before you get run over. The boys come racing in here hungry and ready to eat a bear."

Leroy smiled and nodded his head. Within minutes he had gulped down what was left of his coffee and made a few biscuit and ham sandwiches for the road.

"Better get out of the way, Cowboy," one of the cadets said as he ran past Leroy.

Just as he had been warned, Leroy was almost run over by swarm of boys dressed in gray jackets with bright brass buttons and crisp white pants.

Leroy thought they looked pretty funny. He pushed back his hat and started for the door.

"Take that hat off while indoors," barked an officer as Leroy passed through the dining hall.

Leroy's eyes widened. *Who the heck does that fellow think he is? This ain't a friendly place 'cept for the old man. I sure wouldn't want to be stuck here all the time like these fellows.*

Leroy walked to the stable, saddled his horse, and rode quickly out the gate into the streets of Marietta. The old gentleman had left an envelope for Leroy. Inside was the money Leroy had paid for his room and board, along with a hand drawn map with directions to Augusta. As he read the note written in a strong and legible penmanship, Leroy said to himself, "Well, that was mighty nice of him.

Leroy,

I am returning the money you paid to me yesterday.

It will help to pay the fees for crossing the rivers between here and Augusta.

When you reach Washington, Georgia, take the enclosed letter to a friend of mine,

Mr. Toombs. He will put you up for the night.

With every good wish for a safe journey for you and your aunts back to Texas.

And, May God Save The South and your fair State of Texas,

William M. Roberts,

Steward,

Georgia Military Institute

CHAPTER 5

Leroy followed the road that ran parallel to the Georgia Railroad tracks from Atlanta on his way to his Aunt Mary's home near Augusta. He rode from sunup to sunset pausing only to rest his horse and buy some food. Despite his fatigue he had to admit that the Eastern part of Georgia was some of the prettiest country he had ever seen. He passed rich farmlands and a few large plantations with slaves working the fields.

Leroy was anxious to get to Aunt Mary's farm in Appling, Georgia. The talk of secession was in the air at every stop and he was beginning to wonder if he'd make it back to Texas before war broke out.

He arrived late one afternoon in the town of Thomson. Both he and his horse were tired after having ridden through a series of rain storms most of the day. Leroy paid for hay and a stall for his horse then went to look for a place to eat supper and spend the night. He read a sign in a store window that offered the blue plate special for fifty cents. *I don't care what the Blue Plate Special is,* Leroy thought. *I'm hungry enough to eat anything that's put on my plate.*

A small lady with light brown hair pinned high on her head smiled and pointed Leroy toward a table near the front window of her dining room. After he was seated, Leroy couldn't help but overhear several men at the next table speaking in favor of Georgia leaving the Union.

While the men argued Leroy ate a heaping plate of meat and vegetables and two slices of pie.

They never take time to eat, he thought. *Seems like they're gonna be mighty disappointed if the war doesn't happen.*

He paid his bill and asked Mrs. McGee, the owner of the cafe, where he might get a room for the night.

She smiled and said in a kind voice, "My friend, Mrs. Sandler, owns a boarding house down the street and I know she'll have room for you," Mrs. McGee gave Leroy a pat on the back and pointed toward her friend's place. "You just go tell her that I sent you."

Leroy wanted to ask the price of the room but was too embarrassed. He wasn't shy about many things but money was one of them.

"Folks get mighty serious when they talk about money," his father had warned him many times in the past

Leroy walked the short distance to Mrs. Sandler's boarding house. On the way he passed three boys playing in front of the general store while they waited for their parents to load their wagon with supplies. *Farm kids,* Leroy thought as he fought off a sad feeling of homesickness. *Just like me and Carter and Clayton.*

Mrs. Sandler reminded Leroy of his teacher back in Smith County. She was short and round and wore her hair piled up on top her head. "Of course, I have a room for you," she smiled. Her face creased into a circle as she spoke.

The boarding house had a large parlor where several men were speaking in loud, demonstrative tones about states rights and leaving the Union. Mrs. Sandler put Leroy in a small room away from the parlor so he didn't have to listen to the "oratory," as Mrs. Sandler described the talk about war. Leroy couldn't believe his ears when he awoke early the next morning. The men were at it again, discussing when and why Georgia should leave the Union. After listening to the war talk for almost a month, Leroy couldn't wait to get back to Texas.

It was late afternoon when he finally arrived at his Aunt Mary's farm in Appling. The farm was just as his mother had described it. A picket fence separated the yard from the road. Crape-myrtle bushes bloomed beside the chimney and a small maple tree was growing near the front porch.

A large black man was busy splitting wood over by the barn. When Leroy rode up to the farm the man looked up and smiled.

Without saying a word, the man put down his ax and began walking towards the approaching rider.

Leroy nodded but before he could explain to the man that he was visiting his Aunt Mary, a woman opened the front door and cried out, "Oh, my goodness!" Mary rushed out the door with both arms opened wide to embrace her nephew. "Gladys, come quick! It's Verlinda's boy. He's already here." She threw her arms around Leroy's slender frame and hugged him close. Not giving him any time to speak, she continued calling her sister and walking Leroy to the front door. "Gladys, come on out here right now and meet Leroy."

She took a good look at her sister's youngest son, and said, "We didn't expect you for another week or two." Turning to her farm hand, Mary said, "Clarence, would you please see to my nephew's horse?"

Leroy tried to assure her that he was used to taking care of his own horse. He also wanted to get his saddlebags and Sunday clothes before the man took the horse away, but he still hadn't been given a chance to speak. He had been brought up not to ever interrupt his elders. Just when he thought his Aunt Mary was going to slow down to take a breath, his Aunt Gladys burst through the door and added another bear hug. For a full five minutes Leroy listened to the ladies nonstop talk. *It's gonna be a long trip back to Texas,* he thought. *Maybe that old fellow at the Military School was right. If we take the train, we'll get home a lot faster.*

"Oh, we've been waiting for you, Leroy," Aunt Gladys said. "Your bedroom is just past the parlor. There's a nice cross-breeze that comes through the windows every night. It cools things off so you should get a wonderful night's sleep. How are your Mother and Father?"

Before Leroy could reply, his Aunt Mary began telling him about the relatives she wanted him to meet while he was visiting Appling.

Clarence carried in his saddlebags and the one remaining pillow-case, which now contained his Sunday clothes. When the women left to get supper on the table, the big man smiled and said, "I'll bet you ain't been able to get in a word edgewise."

Leroy smiled and shook his head. "You're right."

The man carefully placed Leroy's belongings on a small table near the bed.

"Maybe by tomorrow," he said as he left the room.

Leroy took in a deep breath and enjoyed a few moments of silence before he heard Aunt Gladys walking quickly down the hall toward his room

Leroy's aunts were very active in the Appling Presbyterian Church. Bright and early every Sunday morning Clarence had their carriage cleaned and hitched to Annabelle, their favorite mare, so the ladies wouldn't be late for the service.

Leroy quickly dressed and washed up to make sure he would have enough time for a bite of breakfast before riding to church. Sunday sermons on an empty stomach didn't sit well with Leroy. Clarence handed him the bridle and Leroy climbed up on his horse to wait for his aunts. The morning was almost crisp in its coolness with a gentle wind blowing from the east.

"Sure is pretty country, Clarence," Leroy said. "Everything is so green and smells so good." Leroy sniffed the sweet smell of honeysuckle and early blooming bushes and trees.

Clarence nodded. His big straw hat bounced as he moved his head and shoulders.

When they arrived at the church, Leroy followed his aunts up several stairs and into the sanctuary. It was a large whitewashed building with fancy scrollwork. Just as he was about to sit in the pew next to Aunt Mary, he saw the door near the alter open and a tall, thin man with a goatee that matched the color of his glasses walked toward the pulpit. Leroy was about to glance out the window when his eyes caught sight of a slender girl with long brown hair who had followed the preacher through the door. She walked quickly to the harpsichord bench and sat quietly waiting for the service to begin. Leroy was sitting several rows back, but he could still clearly see the girl with the pretty brown hair. She was wearing a light blue dress decorated with yellow ribbons. It wasn't a fancy dress but it sure looked pretty on her.

When the minister gave the signal, she began to pluck the harpsichord and play the hymns. Not the usual loud harpsichord playing that would wake the dead, but instead, she played the hymns with a light touch that produced the prettiest music Leroy had ever heard.

"What's her name, Aunt Mary?" he whispered.

"Shush," came the reply. "Don't talk during church, Leroy."

"I just wanted to know her name," Leroy whispered louder.

Aunt Mary was visibly annoyed. "Who are you talking about?"

"Her name is Mindy," Aunt Gladys leaned over and whispered. "Now be quiet or I'll tell your Mother that you don't know how to behave in church."

"Oh," was all that Leroy could think to say.

Both aunts frowned at him, then turned their attention back to the church service. Meanwhile, Leroy kept his attention on the harpsichord player. He was suffering from the first pangs of love.

To Leroy it seemed as if the service dragged on for an eternity but in reality it was only two hours before the preacher passed the collection plate and the last hymn was sung. After the service, the parishioners gathered in front of the church to visit and catch up with the news of the day before returning home for Sunday dinner.

Leroy was standing next to his aunts holding his cowboy hat in both hands, when he saw Mindy leave the church with her parents. *I just gotta talk to her,* he thought. But try as he may, his feet stayed planted firmly in place.

Just as he thought he was going to make a total fool of himself, Aunt Mary took mercy on him and said, "I'll take you over to meet her."

Leroy swallowed hard. Aunt Gladys gently touched his arm and said, "Leroy, go on over there with Mary and meet her. Now's your chance."

The Lowry family stopped as Leroy and his Aunt Mary approached them. Leroy noticed Mindy's sparkling brown eyes and sweet smile. He stood next to Aunt Mary and tried his best not to blush.

"This is my nephew, Leroy," Mary said. "He's come to take Gladys and me to Texas to visit Verlinda and her family." She hesitated before asking, "You do remember my sister, Verlinda?"

"Yes, of course, I do." Mr. Lowry said as he reached over to shake Leroy's hand. "That's an important job especially for such a young man."

"Leroy, this is Mr. and Mrs. Lowry and their daughter, Arminda," Aunt Mary smiled.

"We call her, Mindy," Mrs. Lowry said, and then asked. "Will you be visiting Appling for long or are you in a hurry to get back to Texas?"

Mindy smiled sweetly and nodded to the young man from Texas.

"I'm not sure, ma'am," Leroy replied with a sheepish grin. "It's up to my Aunt Mary and Aunt Gladys."

"Better not wait too long," Mr. Lowry spoke, his voice filled with concern. "The war might start any day now."

"We hope not, Daniel," Mrs. Lowry frowned, then asked, "Are you sure you should be leaving on such an extended trip now?" she looked to Mary for an answer, and then to Gladys, who had by now joined the group.

"We've been planning this trip for two years," Mary said. "No war is going to keep us from visiting our sister and her family in Texas. Besides," she reached her arm through Leroy's. "My nephew is a Texas Ranger, that's an important lawman in Texas. I'm sure he can protect us."

Mr. Lowry raised his eyebrows and looked at Leroy. "I've heard of the Texas Rangers. Why don't you come by our house for Sunday supper and tell us all about Texas and the Texas Rangers?"

Leroy glanced at his aunts for approval before answering. Although he tried not to stare, his eyes kept wandering over toward Mindy, who was standing off to the side in her pretty blue dress.

"Gladys and Mary, why don't you come to supper along with your nephew?" Mrs. Lowry smiled.

Leroy remained silent waiting for either Aunt Mary or Aunt Gladys to answer. *Never known those two to be so quiet,* he thought. *Now when I need 'em to say something they don't say a word.*

Mary glanced at her sister, then nodded in agreement. "We'd love to come share Sunday supper. I'll bring a pie I baked yesterday."

The issue decided, Leroy walked with his aunts back to their coach. The whole time he was unfastening his paint's bridle, he never took his eyes off of Mindy as she climbed into the wagon next to her mother. Just as he thought she hadn't noticed him, she looked back over her shoulder and smiled. Leroy couldn't believe it. He felt like jumping on his horse, giving a wild Texas yell and taking off after her but figured that might not be such a good idea, given the circumstances.

"How long until Sunday supper?" he asked.

Mary looked at him with a quizzical expression, "Why Leroy, we haven't even had dinner yet." She shook her head and tapped the mare's back with the reins. Annabelle turned toward home and began pulling the carriage.

CHAPTER 6

Leroy rode in silence, looking straight ahead while his aunts chattered away in their carriage. His mind was not on his aunt's conversation as Annabelle trudged along toward home. All he could think about was the pretty girl with long chestnut colored hair dressed in the prettiest blue dress he had ever seen. Blue had always been his favorite color.

When it was finally time to visit Mindy's home, he gathered all the courage he could muster. "This is worse than fighting Indians," he said to himself. "What if she just ignores me?" He paused, then said in a resigned voice, "I guess I'll go fishing or something."

Leroy was surprised when Mrs. Lowry opened the front door. Several other visitors were already in the parlor, including the preacher and his family. In a corner of the room he saw Mindy in conversation with a tall young man. Leroy's eyes squinted and he frowned. Somewhere in the background he heard his Aunt Mary talking nonsense about how happy she was that she had baked two blackberry pies instead of one. Normally, blackberry pies would have been the focus of Leroy's attention, but not today.

Mrs. Lowry spoke to him. Leroy tried to be polite and say all the right things, but he found it difficult to concentrate while Mindy was talking to another man.

Before he had an opportunity to talk to Mindy, the preacher blessed the food and talked for a few minutes about the possibility of war. Leroy was aware of people serving food and the smell of ham, fried chicken and fresh baked bread made him realize that he was hungry. But there was Mindy, the real reason he was at the Lowry's house for Sunday supper, chatting away with someone wearing a Sunday-go-to-meetin' suit and a white shirt with lace on the sleeves. *Lace?* Leroy thought. *Why, I'd be laughed out of the state of Texas if I wore a shirt like that.*

Finally, without caring what kind of impression he was making on these strangers from Georgia, he stood and slowly walked over to the table where Mindy sat. He swallowed hard, trying to figure out what he was going to say to her. She looked up, ran her fingers through her hair and blushed. She then smoothed her dress and looked away. For some reason she was embarrassed that the young man from Texas was staring at her.

"Wanna go for a walk?" he asked.

Surprised, she gathered her thoughts for the right reply, "I'd like to, but I haven't finished my supper yet."

"If she wants to go for a walk, I'll be glad to take her," the man wearing the shirt with lace on the sleeves looked straight into Leroy's eyes, a deep frown creasing his brow.

Mindy bit her lip in annoyance and nudged the man with her elbow. "What do you mean 'if she wants to go for a walk'? I don't need anyone to answer for me, Martin Reynolds." She abruptly rose from her chair and reached for Leroy's arm. "I just now realized I'm not hungry any more. But I am in the mood for a nice walk."

In spite of himself, Leroy couldn't keep a smile from filling his face. Mindy stopped at the door and said over her shoulder, "I'll be outside if you need me, Mama," she said proudly. *That will teach Martin a lesson,* she thought.

"Don't go too far," her mother called out. She was surprised to see Mindy leave Martin Reynolds sitting alone at the table.

"Bet Leroy is tickled pink that Mindy's paying him some attention," Gladys whispered to Mary. Mary returned her smile and winked. Then the ladies turned their attention to coffee and pie while talking about Mrs. Lowry's new window curtains and the quilting bee scheduled for next week at the Lowry's home.

Daniel Lowry cast a glance in Mindy's direction and quietly moved to the door. *He seems like a right nice young man,* he thought. *Still, I think I'll ask the Reverend to move out to the porch.*

"Reverend," he called over his shoulder. "Come with me out on the porch. I've got some new smoking tobacco from Charleston that I'd like you to try."

Looking intently at Leroy, Mindy giggled.

"What's the matter?" he asked. He hoped she wasn't making fun of him. After all, he sure wasn't anything like her beau, Martin Reynolds.

"I just left the house with you and I don't even know your name."

Leroy studied her arms and hands, they were thinner than he had realized. *She sure is a tiny little thing,* he thought.

She hiked up her skirt and walked down the steps. Even though he knew he shouldn't, he couldn't help leaning over to catch a glimpse of her ankles.

"Well," her voice tensed up. "Are you going to tell me your name or not?"

"Not," he grinned.

"What did you say?" she stopped and laughed.

"My name is Leroy Wiley," he said. "I thought you knew my name and was just putting me on."

"You're right," she smiled. "I heard you tell Papa and Mama your name outside church this morning."

Suddenly, Mindy felt a twinge of anxiety because of the way he was staring at her. *Those blue-gray eyes seem to look right through me,* she thought. She unconsciously glanced back to the porch where her father and the other men, including Martin Reynolds, were engaged in conversation. Martin was staring straight at her. Right now his eyes looked dark and angry. "How long will you be here in Appling?" she asked, finding her voice.

"Not too much longer," he said. "When my aunts get everything packed up, we'll leave. Probably next week."

"Oh," she said.

Leroy wondered how much of a "city girl" she was. They continued on with their walk. Mindy decided it was up to her to bring him out or this could turn out to be a long walk with little conversation.

"Tell me all about Texas," she said.

He laughed. "Too much to tell. Texas is a mighty big place with lots going on."

"Is it the same as here?" she asked. "With everybody talking about war with the Yankees."

"Nope," he shook his head. "Out in Texas, we're more worried about the Indians."

"Indians?" she smiled. "You mean the Cherokees?"

"Nope," he replied. "Comanche. They're meaner than a hungry rattlesnake."

"You live near mean Indians?" her eyes grew wide and darkened.

"Not right next to 'em. But they roam all over north Texas, mostly in the western part. My Ranger Company has to deal with 'em and Mexican bandits too."

"Oh, my goodness," Mindy sighed. She stopped and leaned against a tree filled with pink and white blossoms.

"Wanna go for a ride tomorrow?" he asked hopefully.

She thought about it for a moment before answering.

Nervously, he added, "Georgia is such a pretty place. I'd like to see all that I can before going back to Texas."

Whether it was the springtime getting into her blood or just maybe she was curious about this stranger from Texas, she wasn't sure, but she knew that she definitely wanted to go for the offered ride.

"Well, I should ask Mama before saying yes," she said thoughtfully. "But on second thought, I'm sure she will say it's all right if I go." That wasn't the truth and she knew it. She looked up at him and smiled. "What time will you call, Leroy?"

He wanted to ask how soon she could get out of the house but instead he asked, "What time would you like me to come by?"

"I'll pack a picnic," she said, excitement showing in her voice. "If you come to my house about ten-thirty tomorrow morning, that would be perfect."

He couldn't believe she said yes. How was he going to wait until tomorrow? "I'll be right on time," he said with a wide grin on his face.

CHAPTER 7

If Leroy had been home in Texas, he would have talked to his brother, Carter, or maybe to his father about Mindy. But he was in Appling, Georgia, and he felt alone. He certainly didn't feel comfortable speaking with his aunts about his feelings for Mindy Lowry. His heart ached because he knew that he would never meet another girl like her. But Texas was a heck of a long way from Appling, Georgia, and his life was centered in Texas. Mindy's face seemed to blur everything. Before seeing her plucking that harpsichord in the Appling Presbyterian Church, he thought of nothing except getting his aunts to Texas as quickly as possible so he could get back to his Texas Ranger Company. But now things had changed and he wanted to stay in Georgia for as long as possible. He knew that when his aunts took the trouble to travel a thousand miles for a family visit, their visit would probably last for months. *When will I have the chance to see her again?* Leroy asked himself. *She could be married to someone else by the time I get back to Appling.* He grimaced at the thought of her with that fool Martin Reynolds.

At nine o'clock on a Monday morning that was filled with sunshine, Leroy hitched Annabelle to his aunt's carriage, waved goodbye to Aunt Mary who was watching from the porch, and ignored Clarence's complaints about him taking the carriage instead of riding his horse. He was dressed in his Sunday clothes, had polished his boots to a shine, and even combed his unruly hair.

"Wait, Leroy!" he heard his Aunt Gladys call out. "Take Mindy this bouquet of pretty irises and greenery I just picked for her."

Leroy smiled and shook his head. *I should have thought of that.*

Even though he had never gone courting, he knew that he was supposed to bring something. The fact that Leroy could out ride and out shoot most anyone his age didn't add to his confidence as he brought Annabelle and the carriage to a halt in front of Mindy's home. Just as he was planning exactly what to say to her and whether or not to take her arm, she opened the front door.

With a smile on her face, Mindy called out to her mother, "Leroy's here. We're going on our picnic." Then she skipped down the steps and met him by the carriage. Seeing her gaze up at him, Leroy's shyness vanished and he reached over and touched her hand. When he spoke, she noticed that his voice was gentle.

"You look mighty pretty, Mindy. I brought you some flowers. I hope you like 'em."

"Why Leroy," she smiled. "Did you pick these iris for me?"

Leroy shook his head in disappointment. *Wonder why she asked that? Who else would the flowers be for?* He decided to tell the truth. "Nope, my Aunt Gladys caught me before I left and gave 'em to me to give to you."

"Well, *you* brought them to me and that's what counts," she said as she reached for the flowers.

He managed a smile.

"Aren't you going to help me get into the carriage?" Mindy asked.

He took her arm and helped her reach the carriage step. Mrs. Lowry waved good-bye from the front door. "Put your bonnet on, Mindy. The sun's awfully bright today."

As Mindy tied on her bonnet, Leroy walked around, climbed into the carriage and tapped the reins. Annabelle started her usual slow gait and the carriage began moving forward.

"Wait," Mindy laughed. "We forgot the picnic basket. It's back there on the front porch."

"Hold up," Leroy said as he pulled back on the reins. "I'll be right back."

When he reached the front gate, Mrs. Lowry met him with a raised eyebrow and a skeptical expression. She handed the picnic basket to him and said, "Don't be too long. Mindy has chores to do."

He doubted if that was the case but he tipped his hat and said in a polite voice, "Yes, ma'am," then ran back to the carriage carrying the picnic basket.

"It wouldn't have been much of a picnic without the fried chicken and biscuits," Mindy said.

Leroy nodded, then tapped the reins again and hurried Annabelle down the tree lined road. Off to one side of the road sat a sturdy barn and a grove of pecan trees. The Lowry family hound came racing out of the barn and began running alongside the road while barking at the carriage. Mindy hardly noticed. Her eyes were studying the Texas cowboy sitting beside. *He sure doesn't say much,* she thought.

Mindy told Leroy that she knew a nice place to picnic. "It's not too far," she said. "If we go down this road about a mile and a half, we'll come to a pretty spot by Green Briar Creek."

Leroy turned Annabelle down the narrow road. "Sure is pretty here," he said.

"What about Texas? Is it pretty, too?" she asked.

"It is, but in a different way," he looked down at her and smiled. "There ain't nothing as pretty as a Texas sunset. At least I thought so before I saw you playing the hymns at church yesterday."

Mindy was taken aback by the compliment, but before she could reply, Leroy started talking about the Texas Rangers. She breathed a sigh of relief for that. *At least he's talking now,* she thought.

Sheltered by trees on both sides of its banks and a small rise on the east bank, Green Briar Creek was the perfect place for a picnic. When they arrived at their destination, Leroy reached up to help Mindy down from the carriage. As she turned to meet his outstretched arms her foot missed the carriage step and she fell. He swept her up against his chest and for a moment her cheek touched his. Embarrassed, Mindy quickly stepped back and smoothed her rumpled dress.

"You lost your bonnet," he laughed and reached behind her to retrieve it.

"Thank you," she spoke, almost in a whisper as they moved on toward the creek.

Leroy carried the picnic basket over to Mindy who had settled down near a cluster of rocks under a spreading willow tree. After handing her the basket, he went back to the carriage to get one of Aunt Mary's quilts. When he turned to look at Mindy, she was smoothing the full skirt of her green dress. The dress, with a hoop skirt, wide sleeves and white lace cuffs, wasn't like any dress he had ever seen Texas girls wear.

It was such a perfect day to be outdoors. Mindy wished that she had dressed in riding clothes so she could wade near the rocks. The creek water was so clear and cool she slid a little closer to the rocks by the bank. Suddenly, she saw a large cottonmouth water moccasin curled up between the rocks. The snake's tongue flickered back and forth, then it opened its mouth wide and prepared to strike.

"Mindy, don't move," Leroy said in a calm, deep voice as he dropped the quilt and drew his six-shooter. "This is gonna be real loud but just close your eyes and sit tight."

Mindy could hardly breathe much less move. She tensed and waited for the snake to strike. Leroy, standing a good twenty feet away, aimed, then squeezed the trigger. The snake's head instantly disintegrated into mush.

Mindy clasped her hands together then covered her mouth, unable to speak. Leroy was close enough that she could smell the gun smoke. Leroy put the Colt back in his gun belt and hurried to her. The next thing Mindy knew, Leroy's arms were around her, gently lifting her up and pulling her close to him. She felt slightly dizzy, drained and out of breathe.

"It's all right now," he said softly. "I hope I didn't scare you too much but that moccasin was about to strike."

Mindy nodded.

"Maybe we better find a place not so close to the water," he said. "In Texas, water means snakes. I guess it's the same here in Georgia."

He took that snake's head off with one shot, calm as can be, she thought. While she was still quivering, Mindy noticed that his grip around her was firm. "You saved my life," she said, still shaking. She lowered her face in hopes that he wouldn't see her start to cry.

"Not really," he reached down and lifted her chin. "Now let's go enjoy our picnic and talk about something else. Wanna hear about where I live in east Texas?"

Mindy stayed in his arms while she began walking toward the carriage. "Where there's one cottonmouth water moccasin, there's bound to be another," she said in a trembling voice.

He laughed. "I've got five shots left before I have to reload. That's a lot of snakes, even for a creek bottom."

His manner astonished her. He acted like nothing had happened. Then she remembered that *she* was the one almost bitten by a poisonous snake, not him. Her hands began to shake.

"Now, don't you worry, Mindy," he covered her shaking hands with one of his strong ones. "Nothing's gonna bother you while you're with me."

They sat in the carriage. Leroy covered her dress with a large dinner napkin then handed her a chicken leg and a buttered biscuit.

"There's cookies in the tin," she smiled. "I thought you might like some sugar cookies so Mama helped me bake a dozen for you."

"I reckon a dozen might be just enough," he said as he opened the lid of the cookie tin.

Mindy looked up into the blue sky covered in fluffy clouds. "Thank goodness I wasn't with Martin today. Papa says he can't hit a thing he shoots at. Papa and Martin's daddy go hunting every year during Indian summer. They quit taking Martin along because they said all he did was scare away the game." Mindy quickly looked away so Leroy wouldn't see her embarrassment. It had just occurred to her that it wasn't a good idea to mention Martin while she was in Leroy's company.

Leroy grinned and took a bite out of a still warm cookie. *Can't hit anything he shoots at,* Leroy thought. *That's always good to know.*

CHAPTER 8

Leroy had put off the return trip to Texas as long as he could. He knew it wouldn't be long until his parents would start to worry. He thought of asking his Aunt Mary to send his folks a telegraph telling them that their trip had been delayed, but as much as he was enjoying his time with Mindy, he knew he was needed back in Texas.

Before he left home to come to Georgia, the Comanche had begun attacking settlers and wagon trains in northwest Texas. The Rangers were continually under-manned so his absence would be a burden on his fellow Rangers.

During a quiet Sunday supper, he told his aunts that they needed to be ready to leave for Texas early on Tuesday. That would give him one more day to be with Mindy.

Monday morning was cloudy and overcast. Leroy looked out the window thinking how pretty the springtime had been. It was beginning to get warm in Georgia. He could only imagine how hot it was in Texas. His thoughts shifted to Mindy. He was anxious to get back to Texas, but on the other hand, he didn't want to be stuck a thousand miles away from her. *If I make good time taking Aunt Mary and Aunt Gladys to Texas, I might be able to get back here before the end of summer,* he thought.

After giving himself several minutes to gather his courage, he walked to the barn and hitched Annabelle to the carriage. It was time to tell Mindy that he was going back to Texas.

There were two forest-covered hills west of Appling. The road ran between them then dipped into a pleasant valley covered in apple orchards and pecan trees. Surrounded by farmland that was located in the center of the valley, the Lowry home was a peaceful sight. Parts of the land had been cleared leaving bright red clay soil to add splashes of color to the landscape. Camellia bushes among southern pine trees made the Lowry's front yard beautiful during springtime.

How am I going to talk her into leaving her beautiful home and family to head out west to Texas, a place she has never been, Leroy worried.

"Well," he took a deep breath. "Let's go see her, Annabelle. Maybe between the two of us, we can sweet talk her."

As Mindy's house came into view, Leroy saw two people sitting on the porch swing.

"Darn it," he said as if speaking to someone other than the horse. "There's Martin Reynolds sitting right there next to Mindy."

Leroy clicked his tongue and tapped Annabelle's back with the reins. "Let's go, girl," he said. "We might as well see what's going on over there."

He quickly drove the wagon past a row of tall, graceful Carolina poplar trees. Leroy barely noticed their pointed leaves with wavy edges. During an earlier visit she had shown him their small greenish flowers that filled the trees with color. The trees reminded him of those moments spent with Mindy. *That gal sure does love flowers,* he thought, a smile crossing his face.

As if she could read his mind, Mindy stood up and waved. "Oh, look, Martin, it's Leroy Wiley, the lawman from Texas.

"I see him," Martin frowned. "Wonder why he's coming here?" Then he added the words that conveyed his true thoughts. "Isn't it about time for him to go back to Texas?"

Mindy looked at Martin and frowned. "Why, I haven't the slightest idea." Recognizing the irritation in Martin's tone of voice she smiled and continued to wave at Leroy.

Leroy halted Annabelle at the gate and jumped down from his aunt's carriage. "Forget that ride we were supposed to take this morning?" he asked as he opened the gate.

"Gonna be a little crowded, what with the three of us," Martin said.

Leroy ignored the remark. "Howdy, Martin." Then he tipped his hat to Mindy. "I'll wait right here if you need to get a shawl and bonnet."

Mindy paused, looked at Martin, then back to Leroy and said, "I'll be just a minute."

Martin waited until the screen door closed and Mindy had started up the stairs to her room before stretching up to his full height and walking across the porch to confront Leroy. "You got some nerve coming over here unannounced. If you think you're fooling me, you're badly mistaken."

Leroy slowly walked up the steps, never taking his eyes off of Martin. "I'm not the one who's mistaken." He used his hat to point toward the screen door. "The way I see it, she's gone to get her bonnet and shawl."

Martin brushed past Leroy on his way to his waiting horse. "This isn't over between us, *cowboy.*"

Leroy chuckled. "Anytime, any place, Mr. Reynolds."

Martin climbed onto his horse and quickly rode away just as Mindy called out, "My Mama says she wants you to take Miss Mary and Miss Gladys some preserves. She's putting the jars in a basket." Mindy leaned through the door and smiled. "Won't be but just a minute." Looking around the porch she asked, "Where's Martin?"

Leroy shrugged his shoulders. "Don't know, but he seemed in an awful hurry."

Mrs. Lowry came out onto the porch and handed Leroy a basket covered in calico cloth. "Tell your sweet aunts I said to write us a letter as soon as they reach Texas. We'll all be on pins and needles 'till we hear that they have arrived safely."

Leroy nodded. "Yes, ma'am."

"Mindy, don't be long, you've got chores and lessons to do today. You should have told me you were going riding with Leroy."

Mindy giggled. The truth was, she hadn't known herself until just now.

A few minutes later Leroy was helping her into the carriage. *This is going to be a mighty fine day,* she thought. *Wonder if Martin's gonna stay mad very long?*

"What's so funny?" Leroy asked.

Mindy hadn't realized she was laughing. "I was just thinking about Martin," she said.

Leroy shook his head. "I was hoping you had forgotten about him."

"How could I forget about someone I just saw ten minutes ago?" she laughed.

"Oh, I don't know," Leroy said as Annabelle started to trot down the narrow road. "He just seems like someone who is kind of forgettable. I know it wouldn't take much for me to forget all about Martin." Mindy turned her head and tried to keep from giggling.

After a pleasant morning spent telling Mindy about Texas and how much he wished she could visit Tyler someday, Leroy squeezed Mindy's hands tightly and said goodbye. As he helped her down from the carriage, he felt a knot growing in his throat.

"I'll see you when you bring your aunts back to Appling," she said sadly. "Until then, could you write me a letter? You can enclose it with your aunt's letters to my Mama."

"I ain't much on writing letters, Mindy," he said. "But if I was ever gonna write any words down on paper, I'd be writing to you."

Without any warning, she stood on her tiptoes and kissed his cheek. "Good bye, Leroy," she said softly, then turned and hurried up the path to the front porch. She paused just long enough to look back and give him a slight wave.

He touched his cheek where she had kissed him, then smiled, remembering her soft touch and the sweet smell of lilac that always seemed to be around her. *She's some gal. One thing's for sure, I'm coming back to get Mindy and I'm not waitin' till Aunt Gladys and Aunt Mary finish visiting with Ma.*

Leroy watched until she had disappeared behind the screen door, then he put his hat back on and climbed into the buggy. He hadn't traveled far when he saw Martin Reynolds standing on the far side of a sharp bend in the road. *Well, there's old Martin Reynolds and he looks madder than a hornet.*

"Mornin' Martin," Leroy said. "I'm surprised to see you here. Are you lost or something?"

"It's not morning anymore and I'm not lost," Martin retorted angrily. "Get down from that wagon. I've got a score to settle with you before you go back to Texas."

Leroy pulled Annabelle over to the side of the road under the shade of a spreading oak tree. He slowly climbed down, calmly placed his hat on the carriage seat next to the basket full of preserves, and then turned to face Martin Reynolds.

"You've been asking for it for a *long* time," Martin said.

Leroy grinned and chose his words carefully. "Mind if I take off my good Sunday coat?"

Martin shrugged. "I don't care what you do."

Leroy took off his coat, then moved toward the angry Martin Reynolds. Stopping just out of reach, he planted his feet firmly.

Martin lunged toward Leroy, his fists punching through the air between them. Leroy reached his arms up, protecting his face. Martin threw a punch toward Leroy's stomach but before it landed Leroy avoided the blow by leaning to one side. Martin swung at him again with his right hand but this time he was off balance. Leroy blocked the punch with his left arm, then with his free hand landed a powerful fist to Martin's face. He followed that with several punches to Martin's midsection. Martin's right leg shot up as he tried in desperation to kick Leroy in the groin. Leroy grabbed Martin's ankle while it was still in the air and twisted it as hard as he could. Martin cried out in pain and fell backwards onto the ground, knocking the breath out of him. When he was finally able to speak, he spat out the words, "You better get out of here. I swear I'll kill you next time."

Leroy took a quick step back. "You don't scare me, Martin. Besides, it's kind of hard to take you seriously, what with you layin' down there on the ground and me standing up here."

"Just you wait *cowboy*," Martin said. "Someday I'll teach you a lesson that you'll never forget."

Leroy shook his head, grinned and walked back to Annabelle who was waiting patiently with her eyes closed. "You slept through all the fun, girl," he chuckled, giving her a pat on her rump. "We can go on home now and leave Martin to fret."

"I'm warning you, you better stay away from Mindy!" Martin shouted as he ran behind the carriage shaking his fist.

Leroy was deep in thought all the way to Aunt Mary's house. He hated to leave Mindy in Appling while he was taking his aunts to east Texas. He was tempted to put them on the train and ride back for Mindy. Then he remembered that the train tracks weren't built all the way from Georgia to Texas. *Darn,* he thought. He began counting the months until he could see Mindy again. *Which is worse, leavin' Mindy here in Georgia with water moccasins or leaving her with Martin Reynolds?* He decided that Mindy could avoid the snakes easier than she could avoid Martin Reynolds.

CHAPTER 9

After Leroy and Clarence loaded the wagon there was barely enough room left for Leroy's aunts. Clarence drove the wagon, filled with trunks and hatboxes, from Appling to Augusta while Leroy rode his paint. He hated to leave the spirited mare, but Clarence promised to take good care of the horse until Leroy returned.

Leroy couldn't wait to get started. *The faster I can get my aunts to Texas, the faster I can get back here to see Mindy.* He intended to travel by rail as much as possible. For those stretches without a railroad, Mr. Lowry had assured him that he would be able to hire a wagon to transport his aunts and their baggage to the next railroad depot.

The Georgia Railroad train that ran between Augusta and Atlanta had several coaches pulled behind a large smoking engine. Bringing up the rear was a red caboose that had faded to almost pink under the hot Georgia sun. The coaches provided seats for passengers but there was no dining car on the train. With this in mind, Aunt Mary had packed a basket of biscuits, smoked ham and sweet bread for the trip and Aunt Gladys carried three jars of water in her satchel.

By the time Aunt Mary bought their tickets to Atlanta, Leroy had made up his mind. He would return to Appling as soon as he could and ask Mindy to marry him. He didn't tell anyone his plans, not even his aunts.

In Atlanta, Leroy's aunt purchased tickets for the next day's journey. Leroy had never traveled by train but by the time they reached Atlanta, he was ready to find another horse. The coaches were filled with travelers talking about the upcoming conflict between north and south. Most people were sure the war would only last a short time.

"Why, we can lick the Yankees in no time," an elderly gentleman sitting next to Leroy said.

Trying his best to ignore the man, Leroy opened the letter Daniel Lowry had given him before leaving on the journey home and carefully read his instructions.

Leroy,
You will purchase a ticket on the Georgia Railroad
from Augusta to Atlanta. When you reach Atlanta, you and
Mary and Gladys will travel on the
Atlanta & West Point from Atlanta to Montgomery, Alabama.
The Atlanta & West Point becomes the Montgomery & West Point
as soon as the tracks cross from Georgia into Alabama.
You should hire a wagon for the trip from Montgomery to Selma, Alabama.
From Selma, you can travel all the way to Meridian, Mississippi, on
the Alabama & Mississippi. The Southern Mississippi
Railroad will take you across the state into Louisiana.
The Mississippi-Louisiana will take you as far as Monroe.
You'll have to hire another wagon in Monroe in order to travel
across Louisiana. I have heard that the train tracks
have been built across the Louisiana state line into Texas, but I am
not sure what I have been told is correct.
This information you will have to learn on your own.
Leroy, you must be very careful when you and your aunts
aren't traveling by rail. I am most concerned about your safety
while you are traveling with the two ladies in a wagon.
I wish you and your dear aunts a safe journey and all of us look
forward to seeing you if you ever return to Georgia.
May God bless you and give you a safe journey to Texas.
Daniel Lowry

Leroy leaned his head back and stared at the train's ceiling. *Will this trip ever end?* Now that he had left Mindy behind in Appling, time seemed to go by slowly. He kept picturing Martin Reynolds sitting on the Lowry's porch swing with Mindy. *He's nothing but a dandy,* Leroy thought. *How long do you think he would last on the Texas frontier? Not long, that's for sure.* Leroy grinned as he pictured Martin in Texas surrounded by a band of Comanche.

"Leroy, Mary was able to purchase our tickets all the way to Montgomery," his aunt's voice brought Leroy back to the present. "Did you hear me?" Gladys leaned over to see what Leroy was reading.

"Yes, ma'am," Leroy answered as he folded the pages and replaced them inside the envelope. He didn't want his aunts to read Mr. Lowry's warning about traveling by wagon between rail stations.

His Aunt Gladys continued to speak, telling him stories about her family growing up in the Carolinas and describing Leroy's mother as a young and independent girl of nineteen who traveled west with her new husband. Leroy waited until she paused to catch her breath, then quickly covered his head with his hat and leaned against the window pretending to sleep. Slowly, he let his mind drift back to thoughts of the Comanche getting their hands on Martin Reynolds.

By the time Leroy and his aunts reached Montgomery, Alabama, he was more than willing to get off of the train and hire a wagon. Leroy had viewed the trip from Texas to Georgia as a great adventure. But the trip home had been, from the beginning, nothing but a burden.

"Montgomery has been the capitol of Alabama since 1846," Leroy heard his Aunt Mary say. "I believe your parents passed through here on their way to Texas." Leroy nodded absently. He had no interest whatsoever in the local history.

"We'll need to hire a wagon for the trip to Selma," Leroy said. He wanted to make arrangements for the wagon now so they could leave early the next morning for Selma.

"I'm very tired, Leroy," Mary said.

Gladys waved to one of the porters standing near the train. "Look, there's a hotel across the street. If we hire that man to help us with the trunks, we'll be there in no time," she suggested.

Leroy escorted his aunts to a two-story white washed building with a large sign hanging over the front door that read "Montgomery City Hotel." He then walked back to the train depot to ask about hiring a wagon. He was told that the Buckley Livery Stable had wagons with teams to hire, along with experienced men to drive the team. Leroy got directions to the stable and thanked the man for his help.

Hearing a man approach, the blacksmith looked up and stopped filing the hoof of a chestnut colored mare.

Leroy tipped his hat and said, "I'm looking to hire a wagon and team to drive to Selma."

The blacksmith nodded toward the stable and went back to working on the animal's hoof without ever saying a word.

Leroy walked toward the darkened stable. When he reached the door he heard a man say, "We got teams and wagons for hire, but you'll have to pay a driver 'cause somebody's got to get my property back to me."

Leroy looked carefully around the entry. The voice was coming from a small room just inside the stable.

"That'll be five dollars now to hold the wagon and team. I'll have the team hitched and ready to go at dawn."

"Yes, sir, I'll be right back," Leroy said.

"Gotta go git the money, boy?" the man asked as he rubbed his hand through his beard.

Leroy looked carefully at the unshaven man and slowly lowered his hand to rest on his pistol. "Yes, sir."

"My name's Chester Simmons. This here is my stable."

Leroy nodded. "I'll be back with the money directly." He turned and walked passed the blacksmith en route to the hotel to speak with his aunts. After making his way across the busy street, Leroy stepped up onto the sidewalk, opened the door of the hotel and looked inside. At the end of the lobby he saw a doorman helping Mary and Gladys with their hand baggage.

"Leroy," Mary smiled. "We have our rooms already assigned and this nice man has asked the cook to prepare us some supper."

Leroy removed his large cowboy hat and smiled at the clerk. Aunt Mary led the way to the dining room. Leroy waited until his Aunt Gladys walked past, and then followed them to a round table set with dishes and glasses. The soft glow from a hearth sent warm air from the back of the room.

"Have you arranged for a wagon?" Aunt Mary asked.

Leroy nodded. "It's gonna cost us five dollars in advance."

"Five dollars!" Mary said. "My Lord, that's an awful lot of money. Why so much?"

"We have to pay a man to bring the wagon back to Montgomery from Selma," Leroy answered. He looked toward the door that led to the kitchen, trying to see if the food was coming.

"After supper, I'll give you the money to pay the man," Aunt Mary said as she reached over to pat Leroy's shoulder. "Tell him to have the wagon ready early tomorrow morning."

"Yes, ma'am," Leroy said, still keeping an eye on the doorway in hopes that hot biscuits were going to be coming from the kitchen any minute.

After a restful night, Leroy rose early, checked his rifle and pistol, strapped on his gun belt and walked down the stairs to find his aunts. He remembered Mr. Lowry's warning. *You must be very careful when you and your aunts are not traveling by rail. I am most concerned about your safety while traveling with the ladies in a wagon.*

Montgomery, even this early in the morning, was busy with merchants getting ready to do business. Leroy noticed that many of the merchants lived over or next to their places of business. Every once in awhile he saw a pale light beginning to glow behind lace curtains covering the windows where people were beginning their daily chores. When Leroy arrived at the livery stable, the owner, Chester Simmons, was nowhere to be seen. Leroy waited impatiently while his thoughts went back and forth between worrying about Ranger duty in Texas and wondering what Mindy Lowry was doing in Georgia.

Sparrows were already singing happily near the stable by the time the driver showed up. After shaking hands and introducing themselves, Leroy and the hired driver began loading the wagon with the women's trunks plus Leroy's grip and saddle. The first hint of daybreak had given way to the half-light of dawn by the time they were ready to begin the trip to Selma.

"Make this trip often?" Leroy asked the driver

"'Bout once a week," came the reply.

Leroy looked up into the cool morning sky. "Looks like we're gonna have good weather."

"Yep," the man said. "This time of the year, we just have to worry about late season rains."

After helping his aunts onto the rear wagon seat, Leroy climbed up next to the driver and settled in for the trip to Selma. Leroy took time to look at the hired man. He was sure that the man was older than his father. He had the face of one who had worked the fields in the hot Alabama sun. Although Leroy remained cautious, the man seemed trustworthy.

They followed a road bordered by goldenrod and larkspur and shaded by large oak trees. As they traveled through the edge of town, past vacant lots and fields of weeds, they came upon a cluster of shanties. Leroy propped the rifle against the wagon seat in plain sight hoping to scare away any robbers. The last thing he wanted was to get into a gunfight with his aunts riding in the wagon seat behind him.

Leroy was relieved when they finally arrived without incident in Selma and boarded a train bound for Mississippi. He had kept a watchful eye during the entire wagon trip and now he was tired. Before the train had gone a mile, Leroy had tipped his hat over his eyes and was sound asleep. He awoke a few hours later to the sound of Aunt Mary complaining about the rum and tobacco smell that had invaded the crowded coach. He smiled, and while his mind's eye pictured Mindy's pretty brown eyes, he fell back to sleep.

Hour by hour, mile by mile, Leroy and his aunts got closer to Texas. Lunch on the train was often a cold apple and some dried meat on hard biscuits. Trying not to think about Mindy being in Appling with the slick city dude, Martin Reynolds, Leroy gazed at the pine trees as they passed through the states of the south. It wouldn't be long until he was back in Texas protecting the wagon trains and settlements from bands of Comanche.

Finally, and none too soon in Leroy's estimate, they crossed the Louisiana border into Texas. Leroy had sent a telegraph to his brother, Carter, and hoped that someone from the family would be there when the train stopped in Marshall.

CHAPTER 10

As the train slowly pulled into the depot in Marshall, Texas, the end of the Vicksburg, Shreveport & El Paso Railroad line, Leroy's heart felt a catch of excitement. He was finally back in his home state of Texas. When he didn't see either of his brothers waiting with a wagon and team, he let out a long sigh.

Aunt Gladys touched his arm and asked, "What's wrong?"

"I guess they didn't get the telegraph," Leroy replied sadly.

"We'll just have to hire another wagon and make the last part of the trip by ourselves," Mary said, her voice filled with resolve. "We've come this far. I don't intend to be disappointed that no one is here to meet us."

Still, it sure would have been nice for Carter or Clayton to help take Aunt Mary and Aunt Gladys on to Starrville, Leroy thought.

"Leroy," Gladys said as she tied her bonnet ribbon. "How much further to Starrville?"

"Aunt Gladys," Leroy's face was covered with a wide grin. "This is Texas and it's a mighty big place but we're almost home. As soon as I can hire a wagon we'll head toward the Earpsville Post Office. That's right on the way. Two more post office outposts and we'll be in Smith County. We'll have to cross the Sabine River between the Pine Tree and Gum Springs Post Offices but that won't be much of a problem this time of year."

Mary frowned and looked at her sister. "Crossing a river?" she asked. "I don't like the sound of that."

"Don't you worry, there's a ferry boat," Leroy said. "Believe me when I tell you that we've got a smooth trip from here to the farm."

Leroy left his aunts at a local eatery then went to the livery stable to hire a wagon. After he hitched a rented team and loaded his aunt's trunks, he swung his saddle and grip onto the wagon and walked to the Blue Willow Dining Room to enjoy a quick meal with his aunts before beginning the last part of the trip.

"The coffee's hot and the biscuits are as light as a feather, Leroy," Aunt Mary smiled. "This is the best food we've had since leaving Appling."

Leroy nodded. The mention of Appling made him think of Mindy. A slight frown crossed his brow when he thought of Martin Reynolds. Leroy looked forward to returning to Georgia, cantering across the fields to Mindy's house on a fast mustang or appaloosa and rescuing Mindy from Martin's grasp. *He'll never see the day when he marries Mindy,* Leroy promised himself.

When they reached the Sabine River, Leroy scanned the bank. An empty ferryboat was tied up at a dock made out of hardwood logs. *This ain't right,* he thought. *Whoever is working the ferry ought to be here tending to business.* Then he saw that a pair of vultures had landed near a pile of rocks about a hundred yards downstream. *That darn sure ain't right*, he thought.

"Wait here," Leroy said to his aunts as he reached under the wagon seat to get his rifle. He climbed down from the wagon while keeping his eyes on the area around the dock.

As he was making his way toward the vultures, a weather-beaten man suddenly jumped out from the brush holding a pistol pointed at Leroy's chest. He was dirty and appeared desperate. Leroy felt a chill in his bones. Although he was sure he could take care of this low life thief, he had to think of his aunts and their safety.

"Drop the rifle, boy," the man yelled at Leroy, waving his gun.

Leroy quickly glanced back at the wagon. He caught his breath when he saw that another man was standing near his aunts threatening them with a knife. He was responsible for the womenfolk. He wasn't about to let anything happen to them.

"Drop it and start moving back toward that wagon and I mean right now," the man shouted. "This here gun's ready to fire and I ain't choosy when it comes to what I aim at." He nodded toward the women.

Leroy did as he was told. He carefully dropped the rifle at his feet, raised his hands and scuffed his boot in the dust. *Gotta stall for time,* he thought.

"That's a whole lot better," the man laughed. "Now back up toward the wagon."

Leroy took slow, careful steps to make sure he didn't fall while keeping his eyes on the man in front of him. The man with the knife picked up Leroy's rifle and pointed it at him.

"We aim to see what's in them trunks." The man holding Leroy's rifle gestured towards the wagon. "Then we'll be on our way."

Leroy glanced at his aunts. He expected to see two terrified women but instead of fear he saw only anger on their faces. Mary gave Leroy a slight nod toward her lap. He watched her take off her glove and began to slowly work her hand into her drawstring bag.

While one of the men went to the back of the wagon to open the trunks, Leroy kept his eyes on the thief holding the rifle. It was aimed straight at his chest and the man's hand was on the trigger. Leroy knew that he could never draw and get off a shot before the man fired.

"Move over, Leroy," Mary said. "I want to get a good look at this thief so I can identify him to the sheriff in Starrville." When Leroy didn't respond, she whispered in a determined tone of voice, "Leroy, *please* move out of the way."

Leroy took two steps to his right thus giving his aunt a clear view of the thief.

"Well, Missy," the man holding the rifle said in an angry voice. "If I shoot both your eyes out, you ain't gonna be able to identify anyone, so I'd be mighty careful 'bout what I said if I was you."

"Just who do you think you're talking to?" Gladys asked. "My nephew is a—"

She didn't have time to finish the sentence. Mary pulled the trigger of her small Derringer. Leroy darted between his aunts and the man holding the rifle while drawing his Colt pistol and firing. Then he whirled around and aimed his pistol at the other robber.

The man knew that Leroy had the drop on him so he quickly threw the pistol down and held up his hands. He bit his lip and began to tremble. He waited for what he thought would be a gunshot through his chest. Instead, Leroy motioned to the man's wounded partner.

"Kick the pistol under the wagon and go tend to him," Leroy said. "But first tell me what happened to the operator of the ferry?"

"He's over there where them buzzards are, and if he's dead we didn't have nothing to do with it," the man answered in a quivering voice. "We found him all by hisself so we just tied him up and waited to see if anybody came by needin' to cross the Sabine."

"I guess we were the lucky ones," Leroy said. "If I didn't have these ladies with me, I'd take you boys into Starrville now, but I guess I'll have to leave the two of you tied to a tree 'till I can get back."

The man's eyes grew wide with fear. "Don't do that, fellow," he pleaded. "There's Injuns and no tellin' what else around here."

Leroy shook his head. "You'll just have to take your chances." Turning to Aunt Mary, he added, "That was some mighty fine shootin' even if you didn't hit anything. Why didn't you tell me you were carrying that Derringer?"

Mary was busy examining the hole in her new purse. "You didn't ask me, Leroy," she said in a matter of fact tone of voice.

Leroy smiled. "I don't know why it didn't occur to me. I guess I'm not used to ladies packing pistols in their purses and shootin' at fellows."

"It never hurts to be prepared for any eventuality," Mary smiled. Turning to her sister she frowned and asked, "Aren't you going to say anything, Gladys?"

Gladys's face was as pale as the clouds hanging over the Sabine River. She rolled her eyes into the back of her head and leaned against Mary.

"Leroy, hurry! Look in my carrying case and hand me the smelling salts. My sister has fainted."

Leroy, who was busy retrieving the dropped weapons, took in a deep breath and ran to the back of the wagon.

As soon as his aunt was revived and the robbers securely tied to a large tree, Leroy made his way downstream to see about the owner of the ferryboat. Expecting the worst, he was pleasantly surprised to see the man tied up and gagged, but very much alive.

"I thought I was gonna be supper for them vultures," the grateful man said after Leroy had removed the handkerchief from his mouth.

"Better lie still and catch your breath," Leroy said. He was already cutting the ropes that were binding the ferry operator's hands.

After Leroy had freed him, the man rubbed his wrists and looked up at Leroy. "My name's Graham, what's yours?"

"My name's Leroy Wiley. I live over in Starrville."

"I sure could use some water," Graham said as he began coughing. "Having a gag in your mouth sure does make a man thirsty." He cleared his throat, then added, "Darn them crooks, when the two of 'em jumped me, they made me lose my false teeth in the river."

"I'll get a canteen," Leroy stood and quickly walked back to the wagon.

"Is the poor man alive?" Mary called out.

"That he is, just minus his false teeth," Leroy answered. "Him being alive will help us get across the river cause I ain't never worked on a ferry boat."

"The poor man," Gladys whispered. "Wonder what happened to his teeth?"

After a struggle, Leroy managed to get the team to pull the wagon onto the ferry and they crossed the narrow Sabine River without any further problems. Leroy could hardly wait. He was almost home. He was grateful there would be a full moon that would help light the way from the Gum Springs Post Office, which was the last outpost between him and his farm in Starrville. A feeling of excitement swept over him. If his luck held, he figured they would arrive just after suppertime. The farmhouse would be filled with music. His mother always played the piano after supper. He began to whistle one of his favorite tunes.

"Aren't there no gals left in Texas, son?" His father asked after Leroy told him of his plans to return to Georgia. "This seems like a powerful lot of trouble for some gal you only just met. Now, if you'll just wait a few months, you'll be taking your aunts back to Columbia County and you can see her then."

Leroy didn't answer. His mind was made up. He was determined to marry Mindy, and Leroy was in no mood to wait. It had been love at first sight, from the time that he walked into the church and saw Arminda Suzanne Lowry play the harpsichord.

Taylor shook his head as he looked into Leroy's determined eyes. *That's one hardheaded boy,* thought Leroy's father. *She must be some special Georgia belle to git him back there this soon.*

"I'm afraid you're going to have to hold off going back to Georgia, at least for right now," Carter told Leroy. "Willis has been by the office several times asking when you were coming back. He said that you've been ordered to report to the Rangers as soon as you returned from Georgia."

"Now?" Leroy asked. "I'd hoped for enough time to go back to Georgia, maybe a month or so."

Carter shook his head. "Word is, the Comanche are raiding all over north Texas. The Rangers need every man they can get."

Leroy walked over to look out the window. The farmhouse faced east. Somewhere out there, a thousand miles away, was the girl of his dreams, Mindy Lowry. He squinted into the sun, which made him frown.

"What are you going to do?" Taylor asked.

Leroy took a deep breath. "I got no choice. I'll report for duty tomorrow, first thing in the morning." *Darn Comanche,* thought Leroy.

"Leroy, how the heck are you?" asked Willis. He turned and called out to several nearby Rangers, "Hey look, it's Leroy. He's back from Georgia." His deep voice matched his bulk. "How'd you manage to find us up here in Greenville?"

"You've gotten fat, Willis," Leroy laughed as he climbed down from his pinto. "As soon as I checked in at Mount. Pleasant they sent me here to keep you fellows out of trouble."

"That'll be the day," Jack Billings said. Jack was one of the most experienced Rangers in the company. Leroy both liked and respected him. Jack was over six feet tall, a bit on the thin side, but with big muscled arms and a thick neck. "Have some coffee while it's hot. I was just about to take it off the fire."

Leroy nodded.

"Tell us about Georgia," Willis said, his face melting into a broad smile. "Find any pretty gals?"

"Oh maybe one or two," Leroy grinned. He felt his face flush.

"Well," Willis waited. "Tell us about 'em."

"Nothing to tell," Leroy said as he sipped coffee from a tin cup. "Just a bunch of gals with shiny brown hair and big pretty eyes."

"As pretty as our Texas gals?" one of the Rangers asked.

Leroy raised his eyebrows and paused for a moment before giving the answer he knew they wanted to hear. "Naaah," he said. "Not nearly as pretty as the gals here in Texas."

"Sit down," Billings said, gesturing toward a fallen tree near the campfire. "I'll fill you in on what's going on. We've got a heap of trouble with the Comanche."

Leroy shook his head. "My brother said they were raiding again."

The other Rangers were silent. Leroy looked around. "That bad, eh?"

Billings nodded, narrowing his eyes. "Yep, as bad as you can imagine."

CHAPTER 11

Stephen F. Austin had formed the Rangers because Texas couldn't afford to pay and equip a regular army to protect the settlers along the Brazos River from the Indians and Mexican bandits. The Rangers were formally organized in 1835 and assigned the task of defending the Texas frontier.

The Texas Rangers were essentially a band of mounted riflemen. One company of twenty-five men was to patrol east of the Trinity River, another between the Trinity and the Brazos, and a third was assigned the territory between the Brazos and the Colorado.

Up to that time, the tribes of the Great Plains and the southwest had never been controlled. Before the white man arrived, they roamed at will. The Comanche, with their cunning, speed and courage, set the pattern for Indian warfare. Although no one could equal the Comanche when it came to horsemanship and path finding, the Rangers did their best to learn the skills necessary to defeat them.

Captain Garrison Davis commanded one full strength company of Texas Rangers reinforced with seven men from Smith County. They had been ordered to escort a small wagon train of pioneers to Fort Worth and from there on to a new settlement near Camp Cooper. *More than enough men to safely escort the settlers,* Garrison thought as he looked back at the Rangers riding behind him. Still, he realized that once they were in Comanche country, they would be under the constant threat of attack. The Comanche were determined to stop the pioneers from establishing any more farms or settlements in what they believed to be their tribal lands.

The Rangers made good time, riding through rolling prairie timbered with oak and sometimes covered with undergrowth. They
crossed several streams and saw no sign of the Comanche until they
came to a rise overlooking Mountain Fork Creek.

"See that smoke beyond the rise?" Captain Davis asked Jack
Billings. Davis stretched up in his saddle and pointed to a thin line of
smoke rising from below a distant hill.

Billings nodded. "I'll take four men with me while you circle
around to the south."

Davis pulled out a pocket watch and flipped open the cover. "It's
almost a half past eleven."

Billings looked up and noted the position of the afternoon sun.
"Yep. I'd say that's about right."

"I figure it's about one hour's ride," Davis said.

"Maybe less," Billings kept his eyes on the stream of smoke. "In
any case, that ain't no campfire."

"Pick your men while we give the horses some rest," Davis looked
around before adding, "just in case."

"If it's what I think," Billings said as he dismounted, "there's no
need to hurry." He turned to Davis and asked, "Isn't this about where
we were supposed to meet the wagon train?"

"Near enough. This bunch was supposed to go on ahead and
camp at the creek near Johnson's Station."

"Any other wagon trains due?"

Davis shook his head. "Not that I know of."

"Then you know what's probably burnin' over there?"

Davis nodded. He didn't expect to find anyone alive. He also
wasn't worried about finding Comanche anywhere near the wagon
train.

Billings told Leroy, Willis and two older members of the Ranger
Company to saddle up.

"What do you think we'll find down there?" Leroy asked Jack
Billings.

Jack took his time filling and lighting his pot shaped short stem
pipe.

While waiting for an answer, Leroy turned to look at the wisp of smoke floating over the far ridgeline.

"Looks like a wagon train was attacked by Indians, probably Comanche," Jack said. "I hope it's not the train we was supposed to meet up with. No telling 'bout that 'till we get to Johnson's Station."

Leroy frowned and continued looking toward the smoke.

"One thing you'll learn pretty quick is the difference between the Comanche and the other Indians in Texas," Billings pointed his pipe toward the smoke. Leroy looked in that direction, then turned back to face the older Ranger. Billings shrugged, then continued, "Here in Texas we got tribes like the Caddo and the Kiowa, then we got Comanche." Billings took a long puff on his pipe before asking, "You see that snake crawlin' 'round that rock over there?" He pointed to a small brown snake slithering around a cluster of rocks.

"Ah shucks," Leroy laughed. "That's just a gopher snake, Mr. Billings. He eats rats and other critters we don't need. He won't harm nobody."

"That's exactly my point," Billings smiled. "Growing up in Texas you might see a lot of harmless snakes like that gopher snake and they won't scare you very much, just like the Caddo and the Kiowa don't scare people too much, but when you see your first rattler, you know right away that he's dangerous. A rattlesnake means business. He'll kill you faster than you can shake a stick. Same thing with the Comanche." Billings nodded again toward the distant smoke. "I do believe those poor settlers just learned that lesson the hard way."

Leroy took a deep breath. "Looks to me like they ain't gonna be learning no more lessons."

"Nope," Billings said. "Let's go and get this over with. No need in putting it off." He looked at Leroy, then toward Willis and the other young Rangers. "If this is the first time you've seen something like this, it's gonna be hard. But it's something you're gonna have to deal with until we run every last Comanche out of Texas."

Leroy nodded and followed Billings over to the waiting horses.

As the settlers moved west, they lived by one rule, and that was to keep going regardless of sickness or injury. They would travel for fifteen to sixteen hours each day whenever they were threatened. When they stopped at night, they tried to defend themselves by pulling their wagons into a tight circle with the families clustered inside. Since the Comanche usually attacked just before dawn, the night ring was their best protection.

As soon as he looked down on the blackened, still simmering area, Billings knew that the attack had occurred before dawn. The wagons, or what was left of them, were still in their defensive circle. The tongue and ox chains were so close, he could picture what the barricade looked like.

"Where's the stock?" Willis asked.

"With the Comanche," Billings answered, "they were probably stolen during the night after they were unyoked and driven out to pasture."

"Looks like the gunfire from the wagons would have driven the Comanche off," Leroy said.

"Sometimes that happens," Billings said. "But not this time. There must have been too many Comanche or maybe they caught 'em by surprise, who knows?"

The Rangers rode closer to the grisly scene. Bodies had been dragged through the fire until they burst open. Some had been cut to pieces with either knives or tomahawks. Around the burned wagons they found trails of blood and torn bits of clothing. Leroy saw what looked to be a child lying face down under a heavy wagon tongue. He reached down to move one of the ox chains. When his fingers touched the chain he winced with pain. The chain, still hot, had burned his fingers. Billings walked over and kicked at the chain to expose a partially burned baby. Leroy drew in a quick breath and turned his head away.

"I told you it'd be hard," Billings said. "There's nothing much we can do except give whoever we find a decent Christian burial."

Leroy nodded. The horror he was witnessing made him open his mouth and breathe deeply. It was obvious that some of the settlers had been captured alive and tortured before they died.

By the time the rest of the Ranger Company arrived, Billings and the four other Rangers had finished carrying the bodies up to a small rise and started digging graves. Leroy poured some water from his canteen onto his handkerchief so he could wipe dirt and sweat from his face, then he wrapped the cool cloth around his blistered fingers. "At least they fought back," he said.

"Yep," Jack answered replied. "Maybe it gave 'em some comfort knowing that they were taking a few Comanche with 'em."

"Mr. Billings," Leroy said.

"Yes, son," Billings said in a weary voice.

"I know now what you meant when you told me 'bout them rattlesnakes."

"Then you've learned a lesson that someday just might keep you alive," Billings said. "Now let's get out of here. I wanna put the smell of all this death and destruction behind me."

Leroy knew that this wouldn't be the last time he would smell death as long as the Comanche were allowed to ride freely in north and west Texas. *Lord help us all,* he thought.

After the horses had been able to rest and graze, the Texas Rangers got ready to head toward Johnson's Station. Seeing the devastation of the wagon train had a sobering effect on all of the men.

"Okay, what happens next?" Willis whispered to Leroy.

Leroy frowned. "I've no idea 'cept we gotta follow orders. I guess that means tracking down the Comanche who did that." He nodded back toward the hastily dug graves of the settlers.

"You think we'll be able to take 'em on? Just us?" Willis asked.

Leroy hesitated, and then shook his head. "We'll have to, if that's what the captain orders."

"When I woke up this morning the first thing I thought of was home," Willis said. "Weren't we supposed to escort that wagon train somewhere, then go home?"

"Yep, that was what I was told. But now the situation has changed." Leroy looked at Willis. The disappointment on his face was evident. "I know how you feel. I got things I need to do, too."

Willis could hear the urgency in his friend's voice. "Like what?"

Leroy smiled and appeared to relax. "I gotta go all the way to Georgia to get me a girl and bring her back here to Texas before she marries some fool named Martin Reynolds."

"I thought you was just in Georgia," Willis leaned over to make sure no one else could hear their conversation. "Wasn't that why you took leave?"

"Yeah," Leroy answered. "I met her while I was visiting my aunts. I had to leave her behind so I could bring my aunts to Starrville. I'm trying to get some more leave, just enough, mind you, to ride like heck back to Georgia and ask her to marry me." Leroy gave Willis a big grin and added, "I'm pretty sure that she will unless Martin Reynolds gets in the way."

"Who's Martin Reynolds?" Willis frowned.

"Oh, just some dandy in Georgia," Leroy laughed. "I'd like to see him out here in Texas for just one week. If old Martin had to see what the Comanche did to those poor settlers, he'd go running back to Georgia so fast even the Comanche wouldn't be able to catch him."

"And he's there in Georgia with your gal?" Willis sighed. "Sounds to me like she could be Mrs. Martin Reynolds by the time you get back there."

"That's just what I'm afraid of, Willis," Leroy slapped his hand against his gun belt. "Oh, I think Mindy can see through the likes of him, but you know girls ain't too smart. They can be fooled, and Martin, with his lace cuffs and fancy duds, just might be the one to try."

"Lace what?" Willis laughed. "He wears lace on his shirt?"

"Yeah," Leroy replied. "You ought to see 'em. I plan to make sure those lace cuffs get a little dirty when I get to Georgia. If I ever do manage to get back there."

"You got problems," Willis said. "You need to ride east as soon as you can, but we're headed off in the opposite direction towards west Texas, hunting the Comanche. No tellin' when we'll get back home."

Leroy's heart beat faster. *Darn those Comanche, I could be halfway to Georgia by now if it wasn't for them.* A loud voice brought him back to the business at hand.

Willis gave him a quick jab with his elbow. "Captain's callin' everybody to get saddled up."

They walked through an open meadow toward their waiting horses. Passing a small stream, Leroy noticed the water rushing over rocks and spraying rainbows into the air. It reminded him of how Mindy's eyes sparkled in the sunshine. *Wait for me, Mindy,* he thought. *Don't make the mistake of your life and get tied up with the likes of Martin Reynolds.*

"Come on," Leroy heard Billings say to several of the Rangers resting under a big oak tree. "Get your horses cinched up and let's ride. We got to catch up with a band of murderin' savages carryin' those settler's scalps back to their teepees."

The Rangers mounted their horses and rode across a rolling plain with gentle rises and low hills. After learning that no wagon train had arrived at Johnson's Station, they continued on toward Bird's Old Fort. Long before they crossed Bear Creek, Leroy felt sweat rolling down his back. His eyes stared at the ground. He knew the captain would have to order them to stop soon. Both the horses and men were exhausted.

They came to a narrow creek and while the horses drank, Leroy and the other Rangers listened intently as Captain Davis and Jack Billings discussed how best to find the Comanche raiding party.

"If we go as far as Denton's Fort, then re-supply at the Lexington Post Office, we should be able to track 'em on into the canyons," Captain Davis said.

Jack Billings shook his head and placed both hands on his hips. "Captain, if we don't find the Comanche before they reach the canyons, we ain't never gonna find 'em. I tell you from experience once they get to them canyons we can go all the way to the New Mexico Territory and we still won't find no Comanche."

Leroy was beginning to think that the Comanche warriors were ghosts.

The Rangers rode from Johnson's Station to Denton's Fork and from there on to the Lexington Post Office as planned. Stopping only to rest the horses, their progress was continually slowed by streams and thick undergrowth. When they reached the spot where Silver Creek ran into West Fork Creek, Jack Billings picked up the trail of a band of Comanche.

"'Bout twenty of 'em," Billings called out to Captain Davis. "I figure they're a days ride ahead of us."

Davis nodded, then asked, "How many do you figure attacked the wagon train?"

"'Bout thirty," came the reply. Billings pointed to the tracks on the creek bank. "The ponies are unshod so there's no doubt that we're trailing Injuns, probably Comanche. No other tribes are gonna ride through Comanche country."

"We'll camp here for the night then go after them at sunrise," Captain Davis said. "I don't intend to ride any more today."

Billings turned to the Rangers and ordered them to start making preparations to secure the campsite.

"Jack," Leroy said as he began taking the saddle and bridle off of his mustang. "Where do you figure we'll catch up to 'em?"

Billings thought for a moment before answering. "If we do catch 'em, it'll probably be near Ash Creek. But I'm not sure we'll find 'em."

"How long do you think the captain's gonna hunt for 'em?" Leroy asked.

"Till he figures he ain't gonna find 'em."

Leroy shook his head and looked at the rolling country that stretched as far as his eye could see. *I wish we could just get this over with one way or the other. I'm ready to go home, pack up, and git to Georgia as fast as I can.*

CHAPTER 12

The Comanche Indians were known as the finest cavalry in the world. When fighting mounted Comanche the Rangers were nearly always at a disadvantage. Indian weapons were ideal for a fast paced battle on horseback. To protect himself, a Comanche warrior carried a shield made of buffalo hide so tough that a bullet would bounce off harmlessly, unless it struck the shield head on. When they attacked, a warrior used a bow with arrows tipped with flint. Each brave would carry up to a hundred arrows and could shoot them with a high degree of accuracy from a galloping horse. Each arrow hit with such a force that it could tear through the body of a buffalo and keep going out the other side. It was not unusual for a brave to shoot twenty arrows and cover three hundred yards on horseback in less than two minutes.

Leroy was riding with a company of Texas Rangers who were doing their best to track the Comanche responsible for the wagon train massacre. However, as sometimes happens when searching for the Comanche, the Comanche found them first. They attacked from behind, taking the Rangers completely by surprise. Captain Davis only had a few seconds to decide what action to take.

Jack Billings yelled to Davis, "Wanna try and outrun 'em?"

Davis was looking ahead desperately for any possible cover, but there was nothing in sight. "No!" Davis said as he turned his horse around to face the Comanche. "Let's take as many as we can with the first pass!" Captain Davis spurred his horse and led his men toward the Comanche.

"Oh, my Lord!" Leroy heard Willis say as they charged, guns blazing, at the approaching Comanche.

Leroy had no time to answer. Everything became a blur as they rode into the stunned Indians. The Rangers had never fought Comanche on horseback. As the Rangers rode amongst them, the Indians, one after another, fell from the backs of their unshod ponies. Six-shooters firing at close range tore into the flesh of both Indians and their horses. Their wounds were horrible. The Comanche, filled with panic, scattered and left a trail of dropped shields, bows and lances. When the Rangers were able to regroup, they counted twelve Indian bodies. Not a single Ranger had been killed or wounded. The Texas Rangers, armed with Colt six shooters, had won the battle and taught the Comanche a lesson.

Leroy, relieved that the battle was over, walked over to join Willis who was staring intently at one of the dead Indians. He decided to try and take his friend's mind off the sight of dead men.

"How long do you think it's gonna take me to git that Georgia belle to come back with me to Texas?"

Willis, in deep thought, didn't reply. He pointed to the Indian's shirt. "Look at that Injun's clothes, Leroy. I'll bet that shirt came off one of them bodies at that wagon train."

"It's not his duds, that's for sure," Leroy said. "Remember how the stuff was strewn around before the wagons were burned? I'll bet they took what they wanted before burning the wagons."

Willis shook his head in dismay. "Sad ending for those poor settlers. They were just trying to get some land of their own."

"Yep," Leroy said. "Trouble is, this fellow had other ideas."

Jack Billings called out, "Gather around and hear what the captain has to say."

It didn't take much time for Captain Davis to congratulate his men and order them to mount up. It was time to get back to east Texas.

Better make tracks, Martin Reynolds, Leroy thought. *Your time courtin' Mindy is about up.*

When Leroy arrived in Starrville after being released by the Rangers, he immediately began packing up his gear and gathering supplies so he could ride east to Georgia. He figured he had just enough time to get to Georgia and return to Texas before it got cold in November.

His parents were not happy about his plans. They wanted him to stay until it was time to take his aunts back to Georgia.

"I don't understand you, Leroy," Taylor argued. "This way you have to make two trips to Georgia."

Leroy reached over and gave his father's arm an affectionate squeeze. "I've met a Georgia belle that I want to bring here to Texas."

Taylor smiled and shook his head. "There's plenty of pretty gals right here in Texas. She must be something special if she's worth all this trouble."

Leroy grinned. "I promise you, she is."

"How long do you expect to be gone?" Taylor's voice was filled with concern. "From what I hear, war could break out any day now in Georgia and the Carolinas."

"I'll be back as soon as I can convince her to marry me," Leroy said.

"What?" Taylor frowned as he spoke. "You mean she hasn't agreed to marry you? Are you telling me that you're going to go all the way to Georgia without knowing if she's willing to marry you and come back to Texas? What makes you think she will? Why don't you write her a letter and find out before you go to all this trouble?" Leroy's father paused for a moment while waiting for his son's reply. When none came, he added, "You know Captain Davis was not real happy about giving you this leave. He told me that the Rangers needed every man they could get right now."

"I can't say for sure that she'll marry me," Leroy said as he threw his saddle across a big brown quarter horse. "But I don't have any doubts on my part, if that's what you're asking." Reaching down to give the horse a pat on its neck, Leroy decided it was time to change the subject. "This is one fine horse, Papa. Where did you get him?"

Taylor looked back toward the house before answering in a hushed voice. "I got a couple of horses from James Cave. He's been trading with some Mexicans. I swear that neighbor of ours is the best horse trader in Texas."

"Why are you scared that Ma might hear?" Leroy asked.

Taylor took a second long look at the front porch before answering. "Oh, she's got some idea that the Mexicans aren't on the up and up. James Cave's wife talked to your Mother about it. I swear that woman is like living with a preacher."

"Do you mean Ma?" Leroy asked while trying his best not to burst out in laughter.

"Heck no," his father said. "I mean Miz Cave. She watches over all of James Cave's business dealings and then she talks to Verlinda." Taylor paused and gave the kitchen another quick glance. "You know your Ma when it comes to right and wrong; there's no in between."

"The Rangers kind of feel that way too, Papa," Leroy gave the horse a second pat. "So tell Mr. Cave to keep an eye out as far as Mexican horse traders are concerned."

"Oh, if there was any doubt about those horses Miz Cave would have called you boys out to investigate," Taylor said. "I *swear* that woman should have been a preacher, least that's what James says, and I believe him."

Leroy smiled, waved to his mother who was walking down the path toward the barn and then said in a loud voice, "Nice horse, Papa. Mr. Cave and those Mexican horse traders sure know how to pick good horse flesh."

"Taylor Wiley!" Verlinda called out as she hurried down the path. "What did Leroy say about Mexican horse traders?"

Taylor flinched. "Darn it! I'll get you for that, boy! Just wait until that belle from Georgia gets here. I've got a thing or two to tell her."

Leroy laughed and tapped the quarter horse's ribs. The horse responded with a snort and began to trot, and then gallop, toward Tyler.

Leroy looked at the wall clock and thought, *if we leave here in the next couple of hours, I can make tomorrow's train before it leaves Marshall.*

"Let's go, Carter," Leroy said as he opened the door and walked out of Judge Smith's office. "I'm in a hurry and I'm hungry to boot."

"You're always hungry. By the way, do you need some money?" Carter asked as they walked down the side street toward his boarding house.

Leroy laughed. "I've probably got more than you have. I drew my Ranger pay and for once, I got a pretty good paycheck."

"Then leave some with me," Carter teased.

"Nope, I've got responsibilities. I have to provide for a wife from now on."

"You really believe she's going to marry you?"

"Never had a doubt," Leroy grinned. "You should see the dude she's been seeing back in Georgia. Silliest fellow you'd ever meet. Did I tell you he wears fancy lace on his shirt sleeves."

"What about the war?" Carter's voice changed to a serious tone. "Word is that the shooting could start anytime now."

"When I went back east to get Aunt Mary and Aunt Gladys that was the talk I heard at every stop but there ain't been no fighting yet. This might be a case of all talk and no bullets, if you know what I mean."

"I wouldn't be too sure," Carter said as he opened the door to the boarding house.

Leroy followed his brother into the furnished room he rented while working for Judge Smith. "Let me change clothes and pack a saddlebag. I'll ride with you to the train depot in Marshall." He tossed Leroy a rifle. "Load this while I get ready to ride."

"Thanks, Carter," Leroy caught the rifle and sat down on a straight-backed chair. "Your going with me helps more than you know. It keeps me from having to board Papa's quarter horse in Marshall. I'm going to need all the money I have to get Mindy back to Starrville."

Carter nodded. "Just get back here before the shooting starts."

CHAPTER 13

Leroy and Carter saddled their horses and rode east toward the railroad depot in Marshall. Unfortunately, when they arrived at the depot they learned there was trouble on the tracks east of Marshall. According to the stationmaster all traffic headed east was halted for at least a week.

Leroy thanked his brother for riding with him and decided to send his father's quarter horse home as planned. "It's not right for me to take Papa's horse all the way to Georgia," Leroy explained to Carter. "I'll have to leave the horse I'm riding in Appling because I'll want to bring Mindy back by train. I guess I'll just have to buy a horse here."

"Take this mustang," Carter said. "He's fast and he's strong enough to get you to Georgia without any problem. He came up from Mexico with some traders and I got him from James Cave. Sell him in Appling or leave him at Aunt Mary's farm, whatever you think best."

Leroy shook his head and laughed. *Wait 'till Ma hears that Carter's buying horses from Mr. Cave and the Mexican traders.*

"What's the matter?" Carter asked.

"Oh, nothing," Leroy feigned innocence while lowering his face in hopes Carter wouldn't notice his expression. "Nothing at all. I was just about to say thanks, big brother."

"Anytime," Carter reached out to shake Leroy's hand.

They left the Marshall City Hotel and walked in silence to the livery stable. Carter paid the boarding fee and then helped Leroy pack his saddlebags.

"Send me a telegram when you buy your train tickets in Shreveport and maybe this time I'll get it. If I hear from you, I'll try to meet you in Marshall. If I can't get away, I'll ask Clayton to drive a wagon and team to meet you," Carter said. "I hope everything goes alright for you with regard to my future sister-in-law."

Leroy nodded, saddled Carter's mustang, and headed east toward the Louisiana state line.

It didn't take Leroy very long to realize that summer was the season for growing cotton in the southern states. Cotton fields were everywhere along the route to Georgia. Leroy was surprised at the number of men working in the cotton fields, fields that seemed to fill the entire horizon.

At every stop along the way the talk was about one subject, and one subject only, the coming war with the Yankees. Leroy kept to himself as much as possible, but he listened and tried to remember what was said. He knew how much his family would enjoy hearing every detail of his trip. But most of the time he thought about what he was going to say to Mindy.

After an uneventful trip across the southeastern states, Leroy arrived in Appling on a beautiful Saturday afternoon. He had good weather and made this trip to Appling ten days faster than the previous one.

Georgia was experiencing an usually hot summer. Leroy's shirt was wet with sweat by the time he reached Appling. He washed up at the creek where he shot the water moccasin and changed his shirt before walking up the steps to stand nervously on the Lowry's front porch. He was disappointed when Mindy didn't open the door.

Mrs. Lowry smiled. She remembered Leroy and asked if his aunts had returned with him. Leroy told her that they were both still in Texas and assured her that they were having a pleasant visit with his family. Before Mrs. Lowry could ask another question, he asked to see Mindy.

"Mindy's not at home," Mrs. Lowry said. "She's gone on a picnic with Martin Reynolds." Seeing Leroy's disappointment, she added, "This being Saturday and all, the young people like to go on picnics."

"Yes, ma'am," Leroy replied, trying his best not to show his hurt feelings. "I'll call on Mindy tomorrow, if that's all right." *Tomorrow is Sunday,* he thought as he rode to the home of his Aunt Mary. *I'll see Mindy tomorrow at church. Am I too late?*

Aunt Mary's farm looked the same as it did the day he loaded the wagon with his aunts' trunks and hatboxes. A farm is a busy place throughout the year. The late summer season is not quite as hard as spring and fall, but the hogs, cows, and chickens always have to be fed. Clarence had taken good care of the barn and chicken house. Only the fence and gate needed to be repaired. Leroy made a mental note to see that the work was done before he left for Texas.

Leroy saw Clarence pushing a cart filled with hay into the barn. He waited until Clarence came out of the barn and began walking to the hen house to gather eggs.

"Hey, Clarence," Leroy called out as he rode through the gate.

The big man looked back and waved his hand. "What you doing back here so soon?" Clarence asked. "Now don't tell me, you're back to call on that pretty Lowry gal."

"Yep," Leroy answered as he climbed down from his horse. "I thought I'd try my luck and see if she'll go back to Texas with me."

Clarence sat the basket down and walked over to take the reins of Leroy's mustang. "Looks like he could use a good rubdown and some feed. You ride all the way here from Texas?"

"Yep," Leroy said. "I sure did."

Clarence laughed. "You're the same talkative fellow I remember from the springtime." He motioned toward the well. "There's a dipper and some mighty cold well water waiting for you."

"I could sure use a drink," Leroy replied thankfully.

"I'll see to the horse. He sure is a fine one," Clarence began taking off the saddle and blanket. "That paint you left here is doing fine and dandy." He handed Leroy his saddlebags. "You go get yourself washed up for supper." *They sure got themselves some good horses in Texas,* Clarence thought.

Leroy yawned. "I think I'll grab some shut eye. It's been a long day."

"I'll leave some ham and biscuits out for you." Clarence said as he led the mustang toward the barn. Leroy slung the saddlebags over his shoulder and walked toward his Aunt Mary's farmhouse.

Bright and early the next morning, Leroy woke up thinking about Mindy. He shaved, dressed, put on his Sunday-go-to-meeting coat and walked out the door to saddle his horse.

He was surprised to see Aunt Mary's carriage and mare hitched and waiting for him. He walked around the carriage and found Clarence bent over checking the wheel.

Clarence looked up and smiled. "Thought you might be needin' your Aunt Mary's fancy buggy to take some pretty gal for a ride."

"You might be right," Leroy grinned. "Thanks for your help."

"Don't you worry 'bout thanking me. Your aunts would want me to take good care of you," Clarence stood up, using both hands to brace his back. "That wheel sure does trouble me. But don't you worry, I think it'll hold up just fine for now."

Leroy reached out to shake Clarence's large hand, then turned to step up onto the wagon. "As long as it gets me to the church in Appling."

"Why you leavin' so early?" Clarence asked.

"I wanna be waiting when she gets there," Leroy grinned.

CHAPTER 14

Martin Reynolds was twenty-two years old and approximately six feet tall with rumpled sandy brown hair. He was a handsome young man with a background in law who looked forward to a bright future in politics. He worked for the local United States Congressman and intended to announce for a seat in the Georgia General Assembly. Two things were holding him back, the possibility of war with the Yankees and Mindy Lowry. A man wanting to make politics a career needed a wife and Martin had decided that Mindy would be a good choice for a politician. Martin was a secessionist and a strong believer in states rights. If war was declared, Martin looked forward to teaching the Yankees a lesson in manners. He believed that Yankees should remain north of the Mason-Dixon line unless traveling south for business reasons. After his encounters with Leroy Wiley, Martin had decided that he disliked Texans almost as much as he disliked northerners. His usual cheerful manner changed abruptly when he saw Leroy walk through the doors leading to the church sanctuary.

Leroy noticed Martin the moment he entered the building. *Might as well needle him a little bit,* Leroy thought. He flashed a mischievous grin and walked right up to the pew where Martin was sitting.

"Mind if I sit here?" Leroy asked as he stopped in the aisle next to the pew where Martin was sitting.

"Would it matter?" Martin replied haughtily. He folded his arms across his chest and kept looking straight ahead toward Mindy, who was softly playing an opening hymn.

Leroy chuckled, "No, I don't rightly think it would." He stepped into the pew and sat down, making sure that his body pushed Martin just enough to irritate him a bit more. "Everything going well, Mr. Reynolds?"

Martin stared at Leroy. This was crazy. Leroy was acting like they were old friends. "What's it to you?" His expression was cold and indifferent.

Leroy gave Martin a broad smile, then reached for the *Book of Common Hymns* and opened it while wearing a pious expression.

After the pastor inflicted the congregation with a long and boring sermon only made bearable by a few inspirational hymns, everyone slowly made their way to the church reception hall where baskets of fried chicken and sweet breads waited. During the entire service Mindy had kept her eyes on either the book of hymns or Mrs. Fogleman, who was directing the church choir. When the service ended Mindy was still not aware that Leroy had joined the congregation. Leroy waited at the door hoping to pay his respects to the Lowry family. After a few moments, he saw Mr. and Mrs. Lowry toward the end of the line of parishioners. Before they reached the door where Leroy was nervously twirling his hat in his hands, he felt a light touch on his elbow. He looked down and smiled into Mindy's big brown eyes.

"Well, my goodness! Whatever are you doing here?" she asked with a smile on her face. She was by far the most enchanting girl he had ever met.

To give himself something to do, he continued twirling his hat. She was just as he remembered, soft pale skin and curly brown hair. She was a tiny thing, all dressed up in a pretty light green dress.

He finally managed to speak. "I was hoping to see you. I sure enjoyed our time together when I was visiting my aunts."

She took a deep breath and smiled, "You mean to say that you came all the way from Texas to see me?"

Before he could answer, she politely excused herself and walked away. He watched her glide across the floor. She was so graceful. He frowned when he saw that she was walking toward Martin Reynolds.

Martin Reynolds, Leroy thought. *Standing there like a fool waiting for something to happen.*

Leroy was intimidated. He was out of his element. He was dressed in his best and only Sunday-go-to-meeting clothes and those clothes would have been fine anywhere in Texas, but in Appling, Georgia, the young men all dressed like Martin Reynolds. Leroy noticed the sharp cut of Martin's dark coat and smooth gray trousers. The lace cuffs hung from the sleeves of Martin's cotton shirt. *I ain't never wearin' lace shirts,* Leroy vowed to himself. *Not even to win Mindy's hand. Heck, I bet he wears lace drawers.*

"Leroy Wiley," Mindy's father said as he passed through the doorway. "What are you doing here in Georgia? Has something happened to your aunts?"

Leroy smiled and shook his head. "No, sir. They're fine. I'm just visiting. I thought I'd do a little traveling, and what with all the talk about war, I figured it was best not to wait."

"You're right about the upcoming conflict," Mr. Lowry said. "But I would think you'd want to be in Texas in case hostilities begin so you could join one of the Texas Regiments."

Leroy nodded in agreement. "Mr. Lowry, if war breaks out, Texas is exactly where I want to be."

"Then you might want to make your visit here a short one." Mr. Lowry shook his head and added in a tone of resignation, "The leaders of the southern states have convinced themselves that separation from the Union is the only way to save our way of life. Right now the power is in the hands of the secessionists."

"Let us hope it doesn't happen," Mrs. Lowry joined in, her voice filled with concern.

"Yes, ma'am," Leroy agreed.

"Come join us for our monthly Sunday supper here at the church," Mr. Lowry smiled. "I'd like to hear about your trip. Have you seen Mindy?"

Leroy deliberately looked away before answering. "Yes, sir. I spoke to her a few minutes ago."

"I'm sure she'll find us," Mrs. Lowry assured him. "Let's hurry, we should be seated before the pastor gives the blessing."

Leroy shared a table with Mindy, her parents and an obviously annoyed Martin Reynolds. It didn't take Mindy long to notice the tensions between Martin and Leroy. Martin sat at the end of the table listening but adding little to the conversation until Leroy began describing Texas.

"From what I hear the whole territory is so hostile no one lives there unless they have to. Anyone who lives in Texas has no where else to go."

"*And* Indians," Mindy frowned. "I've heard an awful lot of stories about wild Indians."

"A lot of fine people call Texas home," Leroy said proudly, glancing at Mindy before continuing his defense of his native land. "And it's a state, not a territory." He shot a look at Martin Reynolds. "I'll admit it takes courage to live out west, but it's that kind of courage that makes everything else worthwhile."

"What about the Indians?" Mindy asked.

"Oh, they're out there, that's for sure," Leroy smiled. "That's one of the reasons the Texas Rangers were formed. Our job is to protect the settlers from attack."

"Texas weather's unfortunate," Martin added with a sneer.

"Unfortunate? Mr. Reynolds," Leroy said while shaking his head, "you sure know an awful lot about a place you've never been."

"I can read," Martin answered. "Word gets back here after an Indian raid, not to mention all the Mexican bandits that are still stealing horses and robbing settlers."

Leroy's expression didn't change. *Well, he's got me on the part about the Mexican horse thieves,* he thought. He stood up, paid his respects to Mr. and Mrs. Lowry, and then smiled at Mindy. "I enjoyed having Sunday supper with you. I hope to see you again before I leave."

Mindy glanced at her parents, and then returned his smile. "I'll look forward to it."

Martin was on his feet before Mindy finished speaking. "If I may be excused, I'd like a word with this," he hesitated before adding, "gentleman from Texas."

Daniel Lowry raised his eyebrows, glanced at his wife, then nodded his head, not really sure what was going on.

As soon as they were out of earshot, Martin asked belligerently, "Just what are you trying to pull?"

Leroy waited until they had stepped outside into the warm afternoon sunshine before answering. Halting, he slowly put on his hat, adjusting it just so, and then turned to face Martin. "I'm not trying to pull anything. I'm here to see Mindy."

Martin shook his head. "She's my girl."

"I doubt that," Leroy replied.

"Stay away from Mindy," Martin warned.

"Only if she tells me that's what she wants," Leroy countered.

Martin was so angry his breath rasped loudly. "If you try to force your attention on her, I'll wait for you across the border."

"You'll what?" Leroy frowned.

"I'm warning you, stay away from Mindy or you'll have a choice. Either meet me in South Carolina, or go back to Texas." Martin moved closer. Leroy refused to step back.

"Why would I want to meet you anywhere, much less in South Carolina?" Leroy asked, his eyes fixed on Martin.

"It's against the law to duel in Georgia. We'd have to go to South Carolina to settle this."

"A duel?" Leroy laughed. "You want to call me out? If that's the case, I ain't worryin' none about going all the way to South Carolina. In Texas, if a man calls you out, then it's self defense, no matter what happens."

"In Texas, maybe, but this isn't Texas," Martin snarled.

Leroy turned to walk away, calling out over his shoulder, "I'll see what Mindy has to say. If she's really your gal, then there ain't no reason to go to South Carolina. But I don't think that's the case."

Martin's voice rose as he shouted at Leroy, "Mindy and I have known each other all our lives. You think you're going to ride in here and change that?"

"Yep," Leroy turned to meet Martin's angry stare. "I sure do."

The two young men continued to glare at each other as Leroy climbed up onto the carriage and gently tapped the horse with the reins. "Be seein' ya' around Martin."

When Leroy was gone, Martin took a deep breath, exhaled and walked back into the church reception hall to find Mindy.

CHAPTER 15

Leroy drove the carriage back to his aunt's home with his mind fixed on the future. *Living in Texas will take some getting used to on Mindy's part that's for sure. Texas is a whole lot different than Georgia,* he thought.

Clarence came to meet him at the hitching post. "I'll unhitch Annabelle, Mr. Leroy."

Leroy thanked him and watched while the large man with gentle hands patted the old mare. He thought about the possibility of war and wondered what would happen to the farm if Clarence left. Leroy hesitated, then asked, "What will you do if the war breaks out around here?"

Clarence smiled as he led Annabelle to her stall in the barn. "Oh, I'll stay and look after things. I ain't about to leave Miss Mary and Miss Gladys here by themselves. Besides, I ain't got no place else to go. I wish I belonged to a regular family but my wife passed away a few years back. Now all I've got is your aunts and I intend to take care of them. Don't you worry, I ain't about to let no Yankees come on this farm."

"I appreciate that," Leroy nodded. "Both my aunts think of you as family. And I sure wish you'd stop calling me Mr. Leroy."

Clarence's eyes grew wide. "I'd better not do that," he said, his voice filled with caution.

Leroy looked at the man and felt a moment of sadness.

He spent the rest of the evening thinking about Mindy. He wondered how long it was going to take to convince her to go with him to

Texas. *Her father could be right,* he thought. *War could break out while I'm a thousand miles from home. If that happens, Mindy would sure be better off in Texas.*

After a supper of cornbread, green beans, buttermilk and boiled beef, Leroy wrote a letter to his parents and enclosed a note to his Aunt Mary telling her that all was well at the farm. Early the next morning, Clarence knocked on his bedroom door and said in an excited voice, "Mr. Leroy, there's a man here to see you and he's bringing trouble with him." As Leroy opened the door, Clarence added, "All hell's done broke loose now."

Leroy quickly dressed, pulled on his boots and followed Clarence to the front door.

"Are you Leroy Wiley?" the young man asked in a serious tone of voice.

Leroy nodded but didn't speak.

"I am here on behalf of Martin Reynolds. My name is Barron James." The young man took off his top hat and carefully placed it under his arm. He waited for a reply. When none came, he continued, "Mr. Martin Reynolds is calling you out, sir."

Leroy looked at Clarence, then frowned and tilted his head slightly. "He's what?"

"He's calling you out," Barron James repeated. Leroy shook his head forcing an irritated Barron James to explain. "My cousin, Martin Reynolds, is challenging you to a duel."

Leroy could tell that Clarence was terrified. He turned back to face Barron James. "Well, why don't you get Martin and I'll whip his butt right here and now."

Barron James let out a distasteful sigh. "Mr. Wiley," he said in a condescending voice. "I'm speaking about a duel. Dueling is illegal in Georgia. Both you and Martin will have to go to South Carolina where the law will not punish whoever survives. That is, unless you wish to make a public apology and then immediately leave the state of Georgia."

"Since I don't plan to apologize to Mr. Reynolds and I'm not planning on leaving the state of Georgia anytime soon, I guess I better take

Martin up on his challenge. If he doesn't want everybody to know about it, I don't mind going to South Carolina."

"Because this procedure is obviously unfamiliar to you, I'll try to explain the process," Barron James continued.

"You do that," Leroy nodded, then turned to Clarence. "We'll sit out on the front porch while Mr. Reynolds's cousin tells me all about dueling. Can you bring us some coffee?"

"None for me, thank you," Barron James looked at Clarence. Clarence glared back at him, and then walked toward the back of the house to the kitchen.

"Dueling is a form of combat between two armed gentlemen. The duel is conducted according to a set of rules, called a code, and it is fought in the presence of witnesses. This challenge is the result of a number of insults by you, Mr. Wiley, against my cousin's personal honor. The man who is challenged has the choice of weapons. Duels are usually fought with pistols or swords. Do you have a preference?"

Leroy pointed to his gun belt hanging near the door. "That six shooter all right with you?"

Barron paused, took out a silk handkerchief and slowly wiped his brow before answering. "I'm sure that you are quite proficient. I'll inform Martin that you prefer to use pistols. Is sunrise the day after tomorrow convenient for you?"

Leroy sighed. "The sooner the better I guess."

"Your second?" Barron asked.

Leroy looked puzzled.

"Who is going to act as your second?"

When Leroy didn't answer, Barron said impatiently, "Your witness. Each duelist is supposed to choose a friend who is called his second. I will act as the second for my cousin. I also will make sure that a surgeon is present. I know of a forest clearing just over the South Carolina line in North Augusta. I suggest we meet there at daybreak. If you don't know of anyone who can act as your second, I'll ask—"

Leroy interrupted, "Clarence will be my second." He looked back at Clarence who was holding a tray with coffee cups. "If that's all right with you, Clarence?"

Clarence nodded. He was obviously frightened of Barron James.

"I've drawn a map to the location. If you are not present on the field precisely at six o'clock the day after tomorrow, we shall consider you a coward."

"Don't you worry, I'll be there at daybreak," Leroy responded as he reached for the large envelope containing the map.

Barron James nodded slightly, then placed his hat squarely on his head, turned on his heel and walked away.

"Jackass," Leroy said as he watched Barron mount his horse.

"Mr. Leroy," Clarence warned, "the gentlemen around here is plenty good when it comes to shooting. I wouldn't be too sure about doing this, if I were you."

"I'm pretty handy with a pistol myself, Clarence," Leroy assured him.

"Yeah, but there's rules that you gotta know, Mr. Leroy," Clarence shook his head. "Dueling ain't like nothing you've done out in Texas."

Leroy decided to heed Clarence's warning and speak with Mindy's father about dueling. He went to his room, filled the washbasin with cold water and washed up before saddling his horse for the ride to Mindy's house.

By the time Leroy was ready to leave, Clarence was busy with the farm chores. Leroy watched him spreading hay in a feeding field for the calves that had been born the previous spring.

"I'll be back to help you as soon as I can," Leroy called out. "I know how much work there is tending to a place like this."

Clarence smiled and waved his hand. "Go on, Mr. Leroy. I don't expect no help."

"Maybe not, but this is my aunt's place and she'd expect me to help out."

"You be careful," Clarence called after him. Leroy didn't hear the warning. His mustang was already galloping through the gate and turning onto the road that led to Mindy's house.

CHAPTER 16

"Dueling is the means by which two armed men settle an argument." Daniel Lowry crossed his arms and looked directly at Leroy. "Are you sure this can't be avoided? I don't believe you actually insulted Martin's honor. I'd like to speak with him before the two of you go through with this duel."

"His cousin, a fellow named Barron James, told me to show up at daybreak, the day after tomorrow, at a place somewhere in South Carolina."

"That gives me a day to talk some sense into him." Mindy's father shook his head slowly while deep in thought. "Martin's not used to handling firearms. He's just upset because he thinks Mindy is showing you too much attention."

"I didn't come all the way from Texas to have trouble with anybody," Leroy said. "But I did come back to see Mindy."

"Oh?" Daniel Lowry frowned. "Mindy didn't mention that she was expecting you to return just to see her."

Leroy lowered his head. "Yes, sir, I'm sure she didn't."

"Well, this situation has obviously gotten out of hand," Daniel Lowry reached for his hat. "I'm going to see Martin right now and put a stop to this foolishness."

"Mr. Lowry," Leroy said as he followed Mindy's father to the door. "In case Martin isn't agreeable, could you spend a few minutes and tell me what I'm going to have to do. I've never heard of dueling. Back in Texas, if a fellow gets into a gunfight, it usually happens so fast nobody thinks about rules."

Mindy's father took a deep breath, and then gestured for Leroy to sit down on the nearby sofa. "Usually, the two men stand back to back, then march an agreed number of steps in opposite directions. At that point, one of the seconds drops a handkerchief which is the signal for the duelists to turn and fire."

Leroy shook his head. "That's not exactly how we do it in Texas."

"I wouldn't think so," Daniel Lowry said. "Just the same, I'm sure you would be at an advantage. In fact, I think it might be a good idea if you put on a little demonstration for Martin." Mr. Lowry thought for a moment. "Leroy, when I return with Martin, I want you to be outside with your pistol. On the other side of the road in front of my house is a perfect place for you to do some target practicing. Have you done that before?"

"Many times, " Leroy grinned.

"I was sure that you had. Now, I want you to be very accurate and very fast. When we ride up, just keep shooting. Don't stop and speak to either me or to Martin. Do you understand?"

"Yes, sir." Leroy walked over and looked through the front parlor window to make sure he understood exactly where to go.

"You wait here. With any luck, I'll be back with Martin within the hour."

After Mindy's father rode off on his horse, Leroy walked outside to the porch and sat in the swing. A large light brown dog came up to him and sat down at his feet.

"You ain't much of a watchdog," Leroy smiled as he gave the dog a pat on his head. "Where's Mindy?"

"Right here," Mindy laughed. "Although I doubt that my dog will know where I am at any given moment."

Leroy stood. His face blushed as he smiled. "I was just making conversation."

"With the dog?" she smiled. "He's not much of a talker."

There she is with those big brown eyes, Leroy thought. *She gets prettier every time I see her.*

Mindy walked over near the swing. "Would you like some lemonade?"

"Maybe later," Leroy looked around, and then motioned to the swing. "Can you sit a spell and visit?"

"I can," she said as she sat down next to him in the swing. "Are you here to see Pa or me?"

"Him," Leroy said.

Mindy frowned. "Well, then, I'll just go into the house and let you wait here for him. I saw him ride off just a few minutes ago."

"Don't do that," Leroy said, taking her elbow. "I really came to see you, but something came up and I needed your father's advice."

"You're being very mysterious," she said as she smoothed her wide skirt then reached up to brush her hair back with her fingertips.

"I don't mean to be," he said softly. "Did I surprise you, coming back here so soon from Texas?"

She turned to face him. "I expected to see you when you brought Miss Mary and Miss Gladys home to Appling. When you turned up at the church last Sunday, I was surprised. Everyone was." She giggled before adding, "Especially Martin."

He ran his hand along the smooth surface of the porch swing. "I've been hearing all this talk about a war starting up. I thought I'd better come see you before the fighting started."

"War?" Mindy laughed. "There's no war here in Georgia. Oh, folks talk about war because they don't have much else exciting to talk about but I don't think anybody in Georgia really thinks the Yankees will fight our boys. They'd be whipped in no time and they know it."

"I'm sure you're right about that," Leroy said. "Still, in Texas, folks are starting to argue." Mindy was silent. Leroy kept talking because he was nervous. "Just the same, I thought about you an awful lot and I wanted to see you again."

Leroy was sitting so close she could feel the warmth of his body so she moved over next to the swing's armrest.

"Well, thank you. That's very thoughtful." Her eyes sparkled as she spoke to him.

"Mindy," came his quiet voice, "have you ever thought about living anywhere else besides Georgia?"

She turned to face him. Except for the few moments when she shared a picnic lunch with him, she barely knew him. *What a gentle smile he has,* she thought. "Are you sure you won't have that lemonade?" she asked.

He put his arm around her shoulder and looked into her eyes. "Maybe later. But first I want to talk to you."

For a brief moment, she turned her head to look at his arm, and then smiled. "Whatever you want to say, you better say it before Papa gets back."

"Mindy, whether you want to believe it or not, there's trouble coming. I don't have a lot of time. I've got to get back to Texas as soon as I can and I want you to go with me."

She pulled away from him. "This is very sudden, isn't it?"

"Not really," he smiled. "You see, I've been thinking about this for a long time, ever since I met you."

His arm was still on her shoulders, and in her heart, she wanted him to keep his arm around her forever. *He's so different from the boys here. What an exciting life he must live back in Texas.* Then she thought about the Indians. "What's Texas like?"

"Not a thing like here," he said. "Texas is much bigger."

She frowned. "How can that be?"

"It just is," Leroy smiled. He thought about all the things he planned to show her. "Wait 'till you see a Texas sunset. The sky's so big, you won't believe your eyes."

Before she could say another word, he pulled her close and kissed her. She quickly pulled away and her face darkened. "I'm not sure how to answer you. This is awfully sudden, Leroy."

"I know," he said softly. "But there's just not a lot of time to waste. Before I go back to Texas, I wanted you to know how I feel."

Leroy kissed her again and this time she didn't pull away. Mindy felt that time was standing still. She closed her eyes and didn't open them again until she heard horses riding up the path to the front porch.

Daniel Lowry could hardly believe his eyes. Instead of Leroy demonstrating his skills with a pistol, he was sitting on the front porch kissing his daughter.

Martin Reynolds jumped from the saddle and ran to the porch. Leroy stood up and stepped between Martin and Mindy.

"I'll ask you to step out in the yard, Leroy Wiley," Martin said, his voice full of anger. "There's no need to wait and fight you like a gentleman because you don't have the slightest idea how to behave like one."

"Martin!" Daniel Lowry called out. "I'll handle this. You go on home and Mindy, you go to your room." He stepped up on the porch and glared at Leroy. "I expect there's no way to settle this now without violence, but I intend to try."

Mindy lifted her skirts and walked quickly into the house. She tried to give Leroy an encouraging look but her eyes were locked on her father's stern expression.

"I'm awfully sorry, Mr. Lowry," Leroy said. He shuffled his boots nervously. "I should have spoken with you first about Mindy. I plan to ask her to marry me."

"You what?" Martin moved closer to Leroy.

Daniel Lowry put his hand on Martin's chest and pushed him back. "Martin, I need to talk to Mindy. Please go home. I'll speak with you tomorrow morning."

"I'll leave it with you," Martin said. He tipped his hat to Mr. Lowry, glared at Leroy and walked away.

Daniel Lowry waited until Martin was gone, then faced Leroy and asked, "What's the meaning of this?"

"I'm sorry, sir," Leroy said. "I meant to talk with you right after I had a chance to see how Mindy feels about going with me to Texas."

Daniel Lowry gave Leroy a disapproving look.

"Leroy, I don't understand you," Daniel Lowry said. "I thought we had a plan in place that would have discouraged Martin from going through with this fool hardy duel. Now, it appears to me that the only way to avoid bloodshed is for you to leave for Texas as soon as possible."

"Yes, sir," Leroy said. "I understand how you feel. I had planned on doing exactly what you told me but Mindy came out to the front porch after you left to get Martin. I should have sent her back into the house. But I didn't, and I want to apologize to you. I don't want to upset you none but running from trouble ain't in my nature. I think it would be best that I faced Martin Reynolds the day after tomorrow in South Carolina and ended this once and for all."

"I'm not about to allow you to kill Martin or for Martin to kill you. There's going to be more than enough killing once the war begins. If your serious about my daughter, I suggest you and Mindy talk this over and decide what she wants to do. Then, and only then, will this trouble with Martin be put aside. By the way, what makes you think she prefers you to a young man she has known most of her life? She just might want to stay here and make a good life with Martin, which, I must tell you, is what I would prefer her to do."

"Well, I prefer to decide for myself," Mindy said through the open door.

Daniel Lowry smiled and looked at Leroy. "She's a handful. I'm not sure you realize what you're getting into."

"Is it all right if Leroy and I take the carriage and go for a ride?" Mindy asked her father. "I'd like to have some time to speak with him." She looked at Leroy and grinned. "I want to hear more about Texas."

Daniel Lowry gave Leroy a disapproving look. Mindy reached up and gave her father a quick kiss on his cheek, then took Leroy's arm and said, "I promise we won't be gone very long."

Mindy directed Leroy to a gentle rise overlooking a small lake where she said they could be alone. On the way Leroy didn't say a word. He was too nervous to speak. *I want to ask her to marry me, but what if she says no?*

"This is a pretty place," Mindy said as she pointed toward a clearing that allowed for a view of a peaceful lake framed by pines and hardwood trees.

Leroy turned his head and smiled before saying, "No snakes 'round here I hope."

"If there are any, I know someone who can shoot them before they have a chance to bite me," she laughed.

"Just the same, we can sit in the wagon if you'd like." He looked into her soft brown eyes. He could see his whole world reflected in her eyes.

"I'd rather walk," she smiled. "If you don't mind."

He tied the reins to the wagon, climbed down then reached up to help Mindy. His hands almost circled her waist. Her feet landed on slick grass. She would have fallen if he hadn't held her tightly. Deep in his heart, he had made a commitment to Mindy. From the first moment he saw her, sitting so pretty at the church harpsichord, he knew she was the girl for him. *What are her true feelings for me?* Leroy wondered.

He knew that Martin Reynolds had been pursuing Mindy long before he had met her. But it didn't take him long to realize that in Mindy's heart of hearts, Martin Reynolds's affections were on the shakiest of ground. Now it was his turn to convince her not only to marry him, but also to leave her family and all that was near and dear to her. Did she love him and, what's more, did she trust him enough to move to the Texas frontier?

They walked through a thick sprawl of dandelion and chickweed toward the creek bed.

"Wanna wade in the creek?" Mindy asked. "I know a shallow part where we can splash and cool off."

Leroy paused near the trunk of a fallen tree. "Nope, I'd just as soon stay dry. But you can go ahead if you're of a mind. I'll keep an eye out for any unfriendly critters."

"Now what do you mean by unfriendly critters? Snakes or Martin Reynolds?" Mindy laughed.

"Probably both," Leroy grinned. He watched while Mindy unlaced her shoes then looked away while she pulled off long white stockings. He turned back when he heard her step into the cool rushing creek water.

Leroy took off his hat. His thick, sandy brown hair seemed perpetually out of place. He brushed his hair back with his fingers and smiled at Mindy. He had an infectious smile but until now he had always been too shy to smile at girls. With Mindy, things were different. He had never met a girl like her.

"You don't see any unfriendly critters do you?" Mindy asked as she made her way across the creek by stepping from one rock to another.

"Nope, the only critters I see are friendly," he pointed toward a nearby cluster of trees, their upper limbs swaying in the breeze.

"There's plenty of rabbits, squirrels and even some beaver nearby. Water draws 'em. But they'll keep hidden while we're here."

"Oh, I guess we're the unfriendly critters in their eyes," she laughed.

Leroy nodded. "They'd be right about that. Most people where I come from shoot 'em."

Mindy stopped and turned to face him. "I think that's sad."

"Not if you're hungry and need the meat," Leroy pushed himself up from the tree trunk and walked toward the creek. He waited for her to speak, expecting an argument. He was surprised to hear what she was thinking.

"Have you had to live in the wild back in Texas?" she asked. Leroy noticed a slight frown crossing her brow.

"Only when I was hunting or riding with the Rangers." He reached over to help her out of the water. "Part of being a Ranger is learning how to survive out in the woods if you have to. I've always liked camping and hunting so it's not much of a problem for me." He looked directly into her eyes before adding, "If you and I were to go to Texas, we'd be perfectly safe camping out if we wanted to."

She laughed, "I think I'd rather travel by train."

"You would?" he said as he leaned closer. He caught the scent of lilac bath salts.

Mindy looked up into his tanned face. He had the most engaging set of blue eyes that she had ever seen. "I wouldn't want to get caught out in a thunderstorm. Do you have thunderstorms in Texas?"

"They're the biggest and most excitin' thunderstorms you have ever seen. You'd like Texas. The sky is *so* big it just keeps going as far as you can see. There's Sunday suppers just like you have here in Georgia and sometimes on Saturday night we'll have a barbeque."

"We have barbecues right hcr in Appling," Mindy smiled.

"Not like in Texas," Leroy shrugged. "I'm not talking about hog bar-b-ques. I mean real barbecues with beef so tender it falls off the fork."

"What if I don't like barbecue?" Mindy frowned.

"Then I wouldn't like it either," Leroy grinned.

"Oh, Leroy," Mindy said. "You make Texas out to be the best place in the world. Martin Reynolds says that Texas is full of rabid animals and," she paused for effect before continuing, "Indians! Martin says that the Indians go around killing people for no reason. Martin says Texas is an awful place to live."

"Martin," Leroy's voice was so low it was almost a whisper, "doesn't know what he's talking about." He looked down so Mindy wouldn't see that he was mad. Then his mood quickly changed when he saw Mindy's tiny feet sticking out from the hem of her dress. He smiled.

"What's so funny, Leroy Wiley?" she stepped back.

"Oh, nothing," Leroy shrugged. "I was just picturin' Martin Reynolds in Texas. I don't think he would last very long out there."

To his surprise, Mindy laughed. "Martin gets lost going to Augusta." She turned to walk back to the creek. "I'd better find my shoes and stockings so we can go back. It's getting late and the wind's picking up."

"Wait, Mindy," Leroy said softly. "I wanna ask you something. Something real important that's been on my mind." She stopped in her tracks and turned to look him in the eye. "I can build things, and one of these days I'll build my wife a fine new frame house in the prettiest part of Texas."

Tying on her bonnet, she smiled to herself. *Now what is he trying to say to me?* She looked at him, her brown eyes wide but wistful. Her fingers twisted the strings of her satin and lace reticule.

"I'm sure not very good with words," he said. "Would you like to go with me to Texas." He noticed she had a quizzical expression on her face, neither sad nor happy. *She doesn't understand what I'm trying to say.*

Before he could go on, she asked, "Are you asking me to marry you, Leroy?"

His eyes were very serious. "I sure am. I've been thinking about nothing but you since I first came to Georgia. I want to spend my whole life with you—out in Texas." He watched her closely trying to understand her reaction. He was relieved when he saw her smile return. When she remained silent, he added, "Do you love me, too?"

She reached out and gently touched his hand before speaking. "I was waiting for you to say that you loved me, not ask me if I loved you."

"*Too,*" he sighed. "I asked if you loved me too. That should have told you how I feel."

"Forgive me but I don't read minds," she said. "I've always wondered what I would feel like at this moment, hearing someone asking me to marry him. I honestly thought it would be different." She turned to walk toward the bank of the creek. Leroy quickly followed her. "I thought some nice young man would tell me that he loved me and ask me to marry him, not just ask me to go to Texas with him."

A sudden smile lighted Leroy's face. He threw his arms around her as though to embrace the entire world. "You mean nobody else has asked you?"

"Leroy Wiley," she said as she tried to pull away. Leroy's strong hands held her tight. "It's not like I'm an old maid. I'm only seventeen."

"Well, you don't have to wait any longer," he could feel his face redden. "I'll make you happy, Mindy. I promise. Why, I'll even pick pretty wildflowers for you everyday. You'll love living in east Texas. It's the best place in the whole world." His thoughts were racing. "And I'll bring you back here to Georgia to visit your family every year or so."

Before she could answer, he pulled her close and kissed her for a long time. It was a sweet, gentle kiss; the kind a girl will remember for the rest of her life. *He's got a gentle heart and he'll take care of me,* she thought. *What an exciting thing to do—go all the way to Texas with a Texas cowboy!*

"Yes, I do love you," Mindy said. "And I'd love to see Texas." Then, remembering her parents, she added, "I don't know how you're going to tell my parents though. My father is awfully mad. And, oh my goodness, there's Martin. What's he going to do when he finds out? He's planning to run for the legislature."

Leroy said, "Don't you worry about Martin Reynolds. I can handle him. But I ain't looking forward to talking to your father."

"How long before we leave for Texas?" she asked, her tone very serious.

He hugged her for a few moments then loosened his grip on her shoulders before answering. "There's a war coming, Mindy, and it's coming fast. It won't be long before the whole eastern part of the country is fighting. I've got to get you and me to Texas 'cause once the shootin' starts, we won't be able to get out of Georgia."

"Leroy," she said softly, her cheek pressed against his chest. "I know that I love you and I want to be your wife, but I'm not sure we've had enough time to think things through. It seems like we're in an awful hurry."

"That's the way things happen in times like this," he said. "But I know that we're right for each other. I've had plenty of time to think about it, and we'll have plenty of time to make plans and get to know each other better while we're on our way to Texas."

She pulled his face down with soft hands covered in lace gloves. "Have you told your folks about this?" she asked.

"Yep," he nodded. "I told them you'd fit right in to Texas like fried chicken at a Sunday social."

"Did they agree? They haven't even met me."

"Maybe not, but I sure told 'em all about you." he stepped back. "You don't have to worry. You're gonna love my folks and they already love you. Wait 'till you meet my brothers!"

When she spoke, her voice was strangely flat, almost distant. "And if the war does come?"

"You'll be safe in Texas. Nobody thinks the fightin' will spread all the way out west," he said, his voice reassuring. "But if Texas decides to fight, then I'll have to defend my family and my home."

"That's what frightens me! If the Yankees start a war, I'll be all the way out in Texas, away from my family, and you'll be off fighting, probably back here in Georgia."

"You can trust me when I tell you that I'll never let anything bad happen to you," he assured her.

"I trust your heart," she said. "I believe that you love me and I know I love you. I just wish we had more time to make plans and have parties. People getting married are supposed to have nice parties."

He took a deep breath. "Before we go we can have a party here and I promise you we'll have the biggest Sunday social Smith County's ever seen."

After Mindy retrieved her socks and shoes, they walked arm and arm through colorful sweet gums covered in wisteria vines. Leroy looked up into the sky framed by fair-sized oaks and pines and one enormous magnolia heavy with white blossoms. *I'm gonna remember being here with Mindy for the rest of my life,* he thought. He helped her up onto the carriage seat and climbed up beside her. After one more very long kiss, they started their new life together. The Lowry's black buggy carried them down a shady lane, past fields filled with pink-white cotton in full bloom, to Mindy's house.

A very angry young man named Martin Reynolds was waiting for them at the front door.

CHAPTER 17

It was past eleven and already hot in Appling, Georgia. Martin grimaced. His face was covered with a sheet of moisture that began to tickle. He again reached in his coat pocket for a linen handkerchief just as the first drops of sweat fell from the tip of his nose. His hair, oiled and combed under his expensive hat, was wringing wet. He reached into his pocket for the heavy gold watch his grandfather had given him when he was a small boy.

Can't wait much longer. Martin frowned and gazed thoughtfully down the narrow road that led to Appling. *This is a most unexpected situation,* he thought as he tapped his hat against his pants in a purposeful gesture. *Who would have thought some cowboy from Texas would come all the way out here and try to steal Mindy? Good Lord! What in the world does he have to offer her?*

Martin sighed before speaking aloud. "Probably nothing but hard times. From what I hear, Texas is nothing but a God forsaken frontier."

Leroy and Mindy rode in silence in the Lowry's buggy. The horse trudged along slowly in the hot sun. Leroy looked straight ahead while Mindy's eyes were fixed on his handsome profile. *I wish he would say something,* she thought. She breathed a sigh of relief as they approached the fenced pastures that surrounded her home.

"Won't be long now," Mindy smiled. "I'm so hot and thirsty, I can't wait to sip some lemonade." She stiffened and lifted a gloved hand to shade her eyes and push a pair of soft brown curls away from her face. Squeezing Leroy's arm, she looked up at him with concern in her eyes. "Oh my goodness, there's Martin waiting on the front porch. I'll bet he's mad as a hornet."

Leroy tapped the mares back with the reins and made a clicking sound. "Well, let's not keep him waiting any longer than we have to."

"I would just as soon not have any trouble," Mindy said, concern in her voice. She stared at Martin who was walking toward the gate, then glanced at Leroy. *If Leroy is nervous he certainly doesn't show it, but Martin looks as if he is about to explode,* Mindy thought.

Leroy noticed the determined set of Martin's jaw. He said in a resigned tone of voice, "Sometimes a fellow can avoid trouble, sometimes not. I figure this ain't one of them avoidin' times. Looks to me like he's rarin' for a fight."

"There will be no fighting in front of my house. Martin, do you hear me?" Mindy shouted.

"I'd appreciate it if you'd go into the house, Mindy," Martin said, his red-brown hair dripping with sweat from the heat. "I'd like a word with this Texas *cowhand.*"

"I beg your pardon, Martin," Mindy said defiantly. "Leroy is a Texas Ranger and that's hardly a cowhand."

Martin gave Mindy a disapproving glance before turning his attention back to Leroy. "I'll meet you in North Augusta as soon as arrangements can be made."

I guess we're back to dueling again, Leroy thought. "Fine with me. Just send word with that cousin of yours. He can find me at my Aunt Mary's house."

Martin nodded, tipped his hat to Mindy and walked toward his waiting horse. Leroy and Mindy watched until he galloped over a low hill and disappeared in the distance.

Leroy noticed there was already a touch of autumn in the air. *Once I get this business with Martin behind me, it'll be about time to head west with Mindy,* he thought.

An hour later the mood had lightened considerably. They were in the little living room. Sitting one the piano bench, near an open window with a slight breeze lifting the lace curtains, Mindy glanced at Leroy and smiled. *Perhaps,* she thought wistfully, *it will be a good life in Texas—certainly a lot more fun than staying here with Martin. After all,* she reasoned, *Martin would be spending most of his time in Atlanta and I'd be left here alone in Appling. How exciting it will be to marry Leroy and travel all the way to Texas.*

"Let's get married next Sunday and leave for Texas bright and early on Monday morning," Leroy said. "You're coming with me to Texas aren't you, Mindy?"

"I'll go anywhere with you, Leroy." There was a twinkle in her eyes as she spoke. Then, her expression turned to one of concern. She frowned as she asked, "But what about Martin?"

"What about him?" Leroy was surprised and a bit hurt by her question, until he realized her concern was for him, not Martin Reynolds.

"I don't want to start our life together with violence. I'd like to be a wife before I'm a widow if it's all the same to you."

Leroy laughed. "Don't worry your pretty head about any fight between me and that fancy dude. He's a little hot under the collar but he's no fool. Handlin' guns is my business, not his." He slipped his arm around Mindy's shoulders before adding, "Now, let me tell you some more about Texas."

Mindy idly fingered the keys on her mother's piano for a few moments, then abruptly turned away and went out onto the sunlit porch. She sat down on the whitewashed porch swing and allowed her mind to drift. She thought of her mother and father. Sadness filled her heart knowing she would be leaving them. Then she thought of Martin Reynolds. Was she sure that she was making the right decision? When she thought of life with Leroy she felt intensely alive. Tapping her fingers along the porch swing, she tried to picture what life would be like for her in faraway Texas. Then she pictured Leroy riding away without her. Unexpectedly, she shivered. *I won't stay here with the likes of Martin Reynolds, no matter how scary Texas sounds.*

Mrs. Lowry carefully folded the camisole she had mended, picked up another garment, and looked carefully at the cream colored lace before speaking. "Mindy, I know you've made up your mind, but your father and I have your best interests at heart, not to mention your good name. Wouldn't it be better if you waited until next spring?"

"That's too many clothes," Mindy said, shaking her head while ignoring the question. "Leroy says we can't take more than what a wagon can hold and a team can pull."

Her mother stood still for a moment, looking over at her willful daughter and blinked back tears. "What about all your beautiful clothes? For goodness sake, at the very least you'll need pretty linens."

Mindy, seeing her mother's concern, reached out with both arms and held her tight. "Then we'll just have to visit in the springtime and get more things."

Mrs. Lowry turned and reached for an embroidered handkerchief. "What with the war coming, I'm afraid I'll never see you again. Everyone says we'll be at war by next year."

Mindy paused, not sure what she should say. "Don't worry Mama, if the war does start, I'll be safe in Texas. It'll be you and every-one here in Georgia that I'll be worried about. Leroy says Texas is too far west to be involved in the fighting."

Her mother nodded thoughtfully. "Then we'll all have to move to Texas and stay with you." Taking a deep breath she added, "If only it could be so."

"Please don't worry, Mama." Mindy knelt and placed her hands around her mother's tightly clasped fingers. "I know that you are wor-ried about me living so far away, but I know I'll be safe with Leroy and his family." Then she looked into her mother's tearful eyes. "I can't give you a definite promise, but I'll try my best to visit every year."

The noon meal was a silent one. Mindy's parents were busy with their own thoughts and Mindy kept her eyes on Leroy. Leroy, never much for idle conversation, spent most of the time looking at the center of his plate of uneaten food.

When he left the Lowry home, Leroy told Mindy once again that he loved her. For the moment, that was enough. She wouldn't see him again until she walked down the aisle to become his wife. Her world was about to change. At the last moment, before he climbed up into the saddle, she ran down the walk to the gate and called his name. He walked back to reassure her that everything was going to be all right.

She caught his face between her hands and kissed him fiercely. After tomorrow, he would be her family and Texas would be her new home.

"Don't ever leave me," she whispered.

"I never will," he promised.

Leroy reached his Aunt Mary's home with enough daylight left to help Clarence with some badly needed repairs to the barn gate and garden fence. Leroy had a talent for building and repairing any structure made of wood. He had inherited his father's love for carpentry. The skilled hands of Taylor Wiley had made all of the furniture in the Wiley's house. Three little boys had watched him and one son, Leroy, had pitched in to help mold and shape the soft pine, oak and maple into family treasures. Only Verlinda Wiley's upright piano had been bought, not built from scratch, by Taylor's hands.

Leroy finished working on the gate and called Clarence to show him the perfect swing of the balanced doors. Clarence smiled and nodded his approval. When the two men were gathering up the tools, Leroy suddenly stopped. After listening for a few seconds he lifted his hand and motioned to Clarence to be still. Leroy slowly made his way toward the open barn door.

"What you hearing, Leroy?" Clarence whispered.

"First thing a hunter learns is to pick out sounds that don't belong. I just heard a man moving around in the woods across the road."

"Who in the world would want to do that?" Clarence asked.

"Oh, I've got a pretty good idea," Leroy grinned.

"Ain't no Indians 'round these parts like there is in Texas," Clarence shook his head. "You probably just hearin' things."

"Nope," Leroy said as he strapped on his six-shooter. "Come with me, Clarence. I need you to help me set up a target. Let's show Mr. Martin Reynolds some Texas style shootin'."

"You sure it's him?" Clarence asked.

"Who else? Don't make no sense that anybody but Martin would be sneaking around watching me. I've got a mind to call him out and be done with it, but I don't want to upset Mindy and her folks." Clarence helped Leroy nail a makeshift target to one of the maple trees in Aunt Mary's front yard.

Clarence stepped back and watched as Leroy walked away from the target, then turned and drew his pistol. His draw was so fast and smooth Clarence couldn't believe his eyes. The Colt roared. The noise was deafening.

When the bullet hit the target dead center, Clarence yelled in an excited voice. "Leroy, iffen' a man blinked, he wouldn't see you shoot. I've never seen nobody handle a gun like you can. I sure would be afeared to face you in one of them duels!"

In spite of himself, Leroy grinned. Out of the corner of his eye, he saw a flicker of movement in the bushes across the road. He knew that he had an audience watching and although he pretended it was so, his performance was not for Clarence's benefit. Leroy stepped back, planted his boots firmly in the dirt and drew again, this time firing at a sycamore tree across the road. He then slipped his Colt pistol back in the holster and crossed his arms.

"You gonna come out and talk, Martin, or stay hiding in the bushes?" Leroy called out in a loud but steady voice. He waited for a reply but none came. *I guess he's a darn site smarter than I gave him credit for*, Leroy thought.

"They ain't nobody out there, Leroy," Clarence said. "You just imagin' things."

"Maybe you're right," Leroy said in a loud voice. "Let's go finish the chores and have some supper."

Crouched down low behind a thick cluster of junipers and rhododendrons, Martin Reynolds watched Leroy's exhibition and grimaced. As much as he would have liked to kill the lawman from Texas, he realized that at least for now, discretion was a darn site better than valor, not to mention healthier. Martin decided it was in his best interest to forget Mindy Lowry for the time being and go on with his life. *Wait until she gets to Texas and sees what she's gotten herself into*, he thought. *She'll come crying back to Georgia begging me to take her back.*

CHAPTER 18

Before the altar in the church where Mindy had been baptized, Leroy and the Reverend Cannon, waited as she walked down the aisle holding her father's arm. Mindy walked confidently beside her father with a smile that gave her round face a warm glow.

Earlier that morning she had awakened with an excitement and a readiness for the most important day of her life. Less than six months ago she had seen Leroy for the first time, the handsome Texas Ranger who rode into her life with a swagger and a mysterious smile. Now, before this day was over, she would be his wife.

Mindy wore a pale cream-colored dress fastened with thin blue and yellow ribbons tied into tiny bows. She carried a bouquet of summer flowers and ivy picked from her mother's garden and tied with those same blue and yellow ribbons. A lace veil framed her long brown hair. Leroy was sure that Mindy was the prettiest girl he had ever seen. He took her hand and his eyes never left hers while the minister gave a short sermon on the sacredness of married life.

The bride and groom exchanged promises to love, honor and cherish one another "as long as they both shall live." Mindy's father was proud and not a little surprised when she recited the vows from memory without prompting from the minister.

"She memorized the vows," Daniel Lowry whispered to his wife.

"I know," Mindy's mother said as she wiped tears from her face. "I heard her saying them over and over again last night in her room."

They joined hands and Leroy gave Mindy a wide gold band that had belonged to his grandmother on his father's side of the family. The initials M.W. were engraved in a flowing script inside the ring. Leroy thought it was fate that his grandmother's name, Margaret, and his bride's name both began with the same letter. *It's meant to be,* he thought as he slipped the ring on her finger. The ring fit perfectly.

The minister declared them husband and wife and concluded the ceremony by saying, "Those whom God hath joined together, let no man put asunder."

Leroy looked into Mindy's dark brown eyes, smiled, and gently kissed his new wife. He had no doubt that he had found the one girl meant for him and he promised the dear Lord that he would take care of her and protect her for the rest of her life.

Daniel Lowry leaned down and whispered a few comforting words to his wife. "She'll be all right. Can't you see how happy she is? Be happy for her."

With a bright Georgia sun warming the day, Leroy finished loading the wagon and lifted Mindy onto the seat. Her mother reached up and took her hand. As the wagon slowly pulled away Mindy held her Mother's hand as long as she could.

During the many long hours on the train, Leroy and Mindy made plans for their life together in Texas. Leroy was anxious to get back to the Rangers and couldn't help wondering what his company was doing. He had a nagging feeling that there was trouble in Texas and that the Rangers were right in the middle of it. He was just beginning to feel comfortable riding alongside the more experienced men when he had taken leave to fetch Aunt Mary and Aunt Gladys from Georgia. Adding up the time he had spent away on this trip, Leroy couldn't help but feel that he had been shirking his duties.

As it turned out, Leroy was right about trouble brewing in Texas. The Comanche Indians had risen up and were fiercely defending their tribal land against the white men. The Rangers were charged with defending the settlers and ranchers, which meant they were at war with the finest light cavalry in the world. Leroy had heard from older Rangers that a Comanche warrior could hang from the side of, or even ride under his horse while at a full gallop and still fire off a half a dozen arrows with deadly accuracy. As if this was not enough, the

Comanche were now beginning to arm themselves with rifles and handguns. Some of those weapons had been taken from dead settlers while others were being bought from unscrupulous traders.

Leroy was not fond of traveling by rail. The coaches provided seats for passengers but little else. After the food they had brought with them ran out, there was nothing to eat or drink other than what they bought at each stop.

He looked at Mindy for a long moment before speaking in a weary voice, "We'll both feel a lot better when we can get off of this train."

"I'm not complaining." Mindy looked out the window at the passing rainstorm. "It's better than being out there in the rain."

Leroy smiled. "I'm proud that my wife isn't a complaining type of gal."

"When we get to Texas I'll howl mighty loud every time you leave the house," she laughed. "And no drinking. My family has never allowed spirits."

Leroy raised his eyebrows. *I hope she understands that I'll be away from home for weeks and even months at a time with the Rangers, and what's this about no whiskey? A fellow has to have a drink now and then.*

"And no card playing," Mindy shook her finger at Leroy's nose. "Martin told me that just about every man in Texas spends all of his free time playing card games."

"Martin," Leroy said through clinched teeth, "ain't never been to Texas and doesn't know what he's talking about."

"Well, just the same," Mindy frowned. "I don't hold with card playing and drinking or missing church. That means we'll go to church on Sunday and Wednesday nights too."

"We don't have church on Wednesdays," Leroy said.

"Why not?" Mindy asked. "All the congregations hold Wednesday service in Appling."

"Because it's too far to ride into town during the week just for church service. Our farm is almost half a day's ride from the nearest church. I'm afraid you'll just have to get used to Sunday being the only church day. But don't you worry none, Mindy, 'cause if there's a church service going on, my Ma will be there and she'll make sure all of us are sitting there next to her in the pew."

Leroy and Mindy exchanged glances.

"What about Bible study?" she asked.

"Sunday mornings before church," Leroy answered. *She's just like Ma,* he thought. *How in the world did I find a woman who likes to go to church and don't hold with drinking or playing cards?* Leroy gave a deep sigh.

"By the way, can you cook?" Leroy asked.

Mindy shook her head. "Only sweets like fudge candy." *Oh, I guess I can learn to cook if I have to,* she thought.

Leroy took a deep breath, "Not even fried chicken?"

"Never had to cook except for fun," Mindy smiled.

I guess it's a darn good thing we're gonna be living at my family's house, Leroy thought. *I'd hate to live on fudge candy and sweets when she felt like cookin' for fun.*

"What are you thinking?" Mindy asked.

He grinned. "Just thinking about how much I'm going to like spending time with you, no matter whether it's in Bible study or under the covers in the bed."

"Leroy!" Mindy whispered as she looked around to make sure no one had heard what he said.

Leroy's grin spread from ear to ear. Mindy's face flushed bright pink and then her cheeks turned as red as the roses that grew around Tyler.

Mindy spent most of the trip asking questions about Leroy's family and their life in Texas. In an effort to keep his new bride happy, Leroy talked more on this trip than he had during most of his adult life.

CHAPTER 19

The train moved on through Georgia and into Alabama. After that nasty rainstorm in Georgia, the sun came out and the wind stopped blowing through the trees. Leroy looked out the coach window. He couldn't open a window because of the burning hot cinders that would blow inside. When it got to the point where he was about to go crazy for a breath of fresh air, Leroy reminded himself how happy he was to be going west with Mindy. *She's worth it,* he thought. *But I sure hope she learns how to cook.*

Leroy planned to rest for only a day in Montgomery but had trouble hiring a wagon to carry them and Mindy's heavy trunks to the next railroad depot in Selma. Selma was a full days drive, even with a good team. Realizing they would have to spend an extra day in the busy Alabama capitol, Leroy found a suitable boarding house that had clean rooms and served breakfast and dinner.

The best part of the stay in Montgomery was the time Leroy and Mindy had together. They walked hand in hand in moonlight as bright as dawn and listened to sparrows darting around low-hanging limbs of oak and maple trees. When he closed the door to their room to enjoy time alone with his wife, Leroy was the happiest he had ever been. He sneaked out right before supper to find flowers to give to Mindy. He knew how much she loved flowers. When he first met her in Appling, he learned that even weeds passed for flowers in Mindy's eyes. *Flowers,* he thought as he lifted Mindy onto the big feather bed, *makes a fellow's life a lot more fun.*

Leroy slept soundly, but by the time streaks of light began to appear in the eastern sky, he had already shaved and put on a clean shirt. *Time to get back on the road to Texas.*

When they crossed the Mississippi River, Mindy stared wide-eyed at the broad expanse of water. "I've never seen a river so big," she said. "Why, Leroy, the Mississippi is more than twice as big as the Chattahoochee."

Leroy nodded in agreement. "This makes the fourth time I've crossed the Mississippi and I still can't believe how big it is. On my first trip to Georgia I saw a big paddle-wheel steamboat hauling cotton down the river." Leroy shook his head as he remembered the big boat. "Sure was a sight to see. Of course, I've ridden all the way from the Brazos to the Trinity with the Rangers and we have big rivers in Texas too—a whole bunch of 'em, but nothing like the Mississippi."

The tired travelers arrived in Monroe, Louisiana, late one afternoon on the Vicksburg, Shreveport & El Paso Railroad, there Leroy purchased the tickets that would take them to the east Texas town of Marshall.

Leroy and Mindy had seen white columned mansions in the distance and fields filled with crops while crossing Mississippi and now in Louisiana they saw marshlands that gradually turned into gently rolling prairies that finally gave way to low, rolling hills.

Mindy struck up a conversation with a teacher who told them all about the traders and fur trappers who traveled along the water routes that covered the state. While Mindy listened to stories about the French settling Louisiana, Leroy's mind was already in Texas. By this time he had heard enough to know that the Comanche Indians were, as he suspected, running wild all along the Texas frontier.

Mindy noticed the moon hanging like a brightly shining crescent in the dark sky. Leroy put his arm around her and gave a reassuring squeeze even though he was deep in his own thoughts. She decided not to be intrusive.

"Almost home, sweetheart," he said, barely above a whisper.

Turning to him, she brushed the hair off his forehead with her gloved hand. "I can hardly wait to meet your family and see my new home."

He looked down at her, a mischievous grin suddenly filling his face. "I've changed my mind. I think I'll turn right around and take you back to Georgia."

"Not on your life," she giggled. "I'm here to stay. Besides, Martin would challenge you to another duel if you showed your face in Appling."

Leroy's voice quivered in mock fear. "Oh my goodness, I forgot all about the dangerous Mr. Martin Reynolds. I guess we both better go on to Texas where I'll be safe."

"Oh, you!" Mindy laughed. "You're impossible, Leroy Wiley."

"After we get to Marshall, I'll have to find a team strong enough to haul all of your trunks.

Mindy shook her head and said in a defensive tone of voice, "I'll need all the things I brought, Leroy. Besides, it would have made my mother very unhappy if I had left these important things behind. As it was, I didn't take all the tableware she packed for me."

Leroy didn't reply. He knew that after paying for their room and board in Monroe, all he could afford would be a farm wagon and a couple of plow horses. He hoped that they'd be strong enough to pull the wagon all the way to Starrville.

On the day Leroy and Mindy crossed the Louisiana Red River, the setting sun gave the water a crimson glow. Leroy stared out the window of the passenger coach. He had made a point of sitting at the most forward point of the rail car carrying them across the imaginary line that separated the states of Louisiana and Texas.

The train pulled into Marshall with enough time for Leroy to find the two of them a hot meal of cornbread, butter beans and smoked ham, before he got Mindy settled into a corner room at the Jefferson Hotel. Unfortunately, the livery stable was closed by the time Leroy made his way across town.

As he walked along the edge of town he passed a newly constructed gallows.

"Darn," Leroy said aloud. "It's gonna be a busy day for the hangman. They've built enough places to hang three men."

"You got that right," came a voice from behind him.

Leroy turned quickly, his hand gripping his pistol.

"Now, don't go drawin' on me," the old man stepped into what was left of the sunset. "I ain't harmful to nobody."

Leroy gestured toward the gallows. "When's the hanging?"

"Bright and early tomorrow morning," the man replied.

Leroy glanced back down the street, and then focused his attention on the gallows. This was the last thing he wanted Mindy to see. "I'm heading west toward Tyler. Is there any other way out of town?" Leroy asked.

"Nope," came the reply. "Not unless you wanna go way out of your way around the other side of town." The old man pointed beyond the gallows. "That's the only road west."

Leroy took a deep breath. *I better get to the livery stable first thing in the morning so I can get Mindy out of here before this starts,* he thought. "Thanks for your trouble," Leroy said.

The old man nodded and retreated back into the shadows where he'd been sitting on a pine bench. Leroy continued his walk, making a wide circle around the gallows. *They* would *build that right here where folks have to pass. I don't know what's so interesting about watching a man swing, but it sure does seem to draw a crowd.*

Leroy found some summer wild flowers, mostly larkspur and iris. With the flowers he made a nice little bouquet for Mindy in hopes of getting her in a good mood for later tonight. He paused by the saloon but decided not to press his luck. *If she smells liquor on me these flowers won't be worth a darn,* he thought.

Mindy opened her traveling valise, took out her brush and ran it through her hair. When she had finished brushing, she hunted for a ribbon to tie her hair behind her ears just the way she knew Leroy liked it. Walking over to look out the window she was surprised to see that it was already dark outside.

"Wonder where he is?" she asked as if someone was in the room listening. She sat in the narrow window seat and watched an old man carefully light the street lamps. One by one they cast a glow over shadows on each side of the wide main street. After a few moments she decided to pour a glass of water from the pitcher Leroy had left on the washbasin. Just as she filled the glass Mindy heard the sound of Leroy's boots outside the door. She smiled and quickly reached up to smooth her hair.

Leroy held the flowers inside the door and asked in a soft voice, "Where's my girl?"

"She went back to Georgia," Mindy giggled. "You took too long."

Leroy crossed the room and slid an arm around her waist while handing her the flowers. "These poor weeds are all I could find, but I promise to find you better flowers when we get to the farm."

Mindy sniffed the flowers before saying, "I think they're beautiful."

Leroy grasped her elbow. "Come over here with me, I've got plans for you."

"You've had those same plans every night of this trip," Mindy laughed. She allowed him to pull her along, paying no attention to anything but the comforting arm around her. "What are we going to do when we get to your house?"

"Same thing," Leroy grinned as he pulled Mindy down on the bed. "Just a little quieter, that's all."

CHAPTER 20

The next day, Leroy was waiting at the livery stable before sunrise. He found a blacksmith willing to rent a wagon and team for the trip to Smith County. Leroy knew that he could count on his brother, Clayton, to return the rig. Clayton would have to tend to it because he planned on riding west to join the Rangers as soon as he got Mindy settled. A quick stop at the general store finished off Leroy's savings. He bought a few yards of calico so his mother could make everyday dresses for Mindy, some smoked meat, tins of biscuits and cookies and two jars of well water for the last leg of the trip.

By the time he loaded the wagon and gathered Mindy from their hotel room, the streets were almost empty.

"Where is everybody?" Mindy asked. "It's like a ghost town around here."

"Oh, it's early yet," Leroy said, hurrying her toward the wagon. He knew everyone in town was standing around the gallows waiting for the hanging.

He helped her onto the wagon, then turned the team in the opposite direction of the gallows, clicked his tongue and snapped the long reins to start the horses on their way.

Mindy looped her arm through Leroy's and hummed a favorite tune while Leroy guided the team through side streets then out into an open meadow filled with long willowy grass. Halfway across the bumpy field she looked around and asked, "Leroy, where's the road?"

"Oh, we'll come to one eventually," he said cheerfully. "I thought you'd like to see the woods."

Mindy reached up and grasped her bonnet as the wagon bounced back and forth. "I can see the woods just fine from the road, Leroy."

He looked at her and grinned. "Being out here by ourselves I get plenty of chances to kiss you. On the road we'd be passing people—heck, this is more fun."

She looked around the meadow then behind them. "We're going in a big circle."

"Naaah," Leroy said. "I know exactly where we're going." I ain't gonna let you see no hanging. Not this day or any other if I can help it.

"Taylor!" Verlinda stopped working the butter churn and called out to her napping husband. "There's a wagon coming toward the house."

Taylor looked up, held his hand over his eyes, and then smiled. "I think it might be Leroy and his gal. Don't recognize the team, but it sure looks like our boy."

Verlinda stood up and hurried to the edge of the porch. "Call Clayton. We'll go meet them at the gate." At that moment the family hound came rushing out of the barn followed by Leroy's brother, Clayton. "Some watchdog we've got," Verlinda muttered. "If that was a pack of Indians we'd all be scalped by now."

Taylor tried to ignore his wife. "Clayton," he shouted. "Here comes Leroy and that pretty gal from Georgia!"

Leroy and Mindy laughed when they heard Clayton whooping and hollering so loud he could be heard all over Smith County.

"What a wonderful welcome," Mindy sighed, wiping tears from her eyes.

Leroy halted the team and wagon so Mindy could see the valley around the farmhouse.

"Look," he pointed toward the lake. "There's a place to picnic and," he paused to make sure she took in the entire area before continuing, "over there by the house is Mama's gardens. She's got a vegetable garden and a flower garden too. Of course, the flower garden ain't much to look at this time of year, but wait 'til you see it in the springtime." Then he pointed in the opposite direction. "Grazing in that pasture is the best dairy cattle in Texas. Not too many of 'em right now, but every year the herd gets a little bigger."

"I feel at home already," Mindy said. There was an excitement building in her. A feeling that she was exactly where she should be. Less than a year ago she had met him for the first time, handsome, strong, with that boyish grin and Texas swagger. Now here she was a thousand miles from the only home she had ever known. She was a married woman beginning a new life with the man she loved—and she did love him with all her heart. *This,* she thought, *is a good place to start our lives together and raise our children.*

Leroy swallowed hard. "God's been good to me, Mindy. He's given me you."

CHAPTER 21

"She's a right pretty gal," Taylor said to Verlinda. "Just enough red in that pretty brown hair to show a little spirit. She'll be good for Leroy."

"Don't judge a book by its cover," Verlinda warned. She placed her hand on her chin and thought for a moment before adding, "Still, I put a lot of store in Leroy's judgment."

Clayton was the first one to reach the wagon. He was tall and lanky, a little on the skinny side with a ruddy complexion and a big smile. He climbed up into the wagon and playfully shoved Leroy. Mindy noticed his easy manner and liked him immediately.

Leroy reached up to keep his hat from falling. "Clayton, this here is Mindy, the newest member of the Wiley family."

"Howdy, Mindy," Clayton grinned as he said the words. "We're all mighty glad to have you here."

"Thank you, Clayton," Mindy said as she held out her hand. "I'm proud to be here in Texas."

"You sure got good timing." Clayton turned his attention back to his brother. "Mama's been cooking all day."

"Biscuits or cobbler?" Leroy asked, a serious look on his face.

"Both," Clayton answered. Looking at the wagon full of trunks he asked, "What's all this stuff?"

Mindy frowned. She would have whispered to Leroy to hush but she was busy acquainting herself with her new surroundings. She was still a little fearful about Texas.

"I wish I knew," Leroy said. "All I know is that these trunks are full of things that are important to Mindy so that's all that matters."

Mindy's frown turned into a big smile. "I brought presents for everyone, including you, Clayton. Presents from Georgia."

"Leroy!" Verlinda reached the wagon and held out her arms to embrace her youngest son.

Leroy looked at Mindy, his face red, then climbed down from the wagon and allowed his mother to hug him. She held him for several moments before handing him over to Taylor.

"Papa," Leroy said as he shook his father's hand, then turned to Mindy. "I guess everybody's here 'cept Carter."

"He'll be here anytime," Verlinda smiled. "He's coming to take supper with us. Now," she smiled at Mindy and held out her hands. "Welcome, child! Leroy's father and I already feel as though you are one of our own."

Leroy raised his arms to lift Mindy from the wagon seat.

"You see," he said with a smile. "I told you that you'd like living in Texas."

Mindy's eyes grew wide as she took in every detail of her new home. *This certainly doesn't look a thing like Georgia,* she thought as her feet touched the thin grass covering the Texas soil. She could hear her mother's words spoken so softly the day she left Appling, *Remember, it's the people you'll be living with that matter most. Don't fret over the house or countryside.*

Well, Mindy thought while she hugged each member of Leroy's family, *everybody sure is friendly. Mama was right. What matters most is the people.*

After carrying Mindy's trunks up the steep stairs to the room his mother had prepared for the two of them, Leroy watched as his young wife pulled a new blue dress from the folds of packing cloth and held it up for his approval.

"I thought I'd wear this to supper. What do you think?"

He pushed back his cowboy hat and hesitated a second before he spoke. "I don't see the need to put on a different dress, but if that's what you want to do, I think that's right pretty."

She giggled, then twirled and pirouetted, pausing just long enough to look into the narrow mirror hanging on the wall behind Leroy.

"Oh, you. You'd say that if I held up a flour sack."

"On a gal like you, Mindy, a flour sack would be fine and dandy."

She reached over and gave him a playful shove. "Go on downstairs and tell your family I'll be there by the time the table's set."

Leroy hesitated, "I'd just as soon stay here."

Mindy pointed to the bedroom door and waited for him to leave.

"Don't take too long or I'll be back to check on you," he said as he closed the door.

The bedroom had a small bed that was made with bright quilts and pillows with embroidered flowers and green plants. Beside the bed sat a maple rocking chair and a cushioned footstool. *Thank goodness for the mirror,* Mindy thought.

She quickly brushed her curls until they were light and fluffy and carefully tied a wide yellow ribbon in her hair. Then she dressed in new undergarments, pulled out shinny brown shoes from the trunk and slipped the dress over her head. After taking one last quick glance in the mirror, she dashed out the door to join her new family at the supper table.

"She's a wonderful gal, Leroy," Taylor grinned, patting Leroy on the back. "I understand now why you hurried on back to Georgia like you did."

Leroy blushed. He avoided looking at his brother's silly grin. He knew what he was thinking.

Mindy carefully lifted her full skirt and hurried down the stairs to take her place at the table beside Leroy. The kitchen had two cupboards with doors and a long table made of sturdy Texas oak with benches on both sides. Leroy's mother had made rugs for the floor and cushions for the chairs that sat at each end of the table. The food smelled wonderful. Mindy suddenly realized how hungry she was and how long it had been since she had eaten.

"I hope I didn't keep everyone from supper," she said in a sweet voice. "I'm so glad to be here with all of you. I already feel like this is home."

"We were expecting Leroy's absent brother, Carter, Mindy. But I don't think we should let supper get cold waiting for him. You never know what might have come up at Judge Smith's office to keep him there late," Leroy's mother spoke as she reached for Mindy's hand.

The men stood while Leroy's mother took Mindy by the shoulders and looked her right in the eyes. "This is your home, child and we are all very happy you're here. After supper you can tell us all about your family back in Georgia. I just wish my sisters could have waited until you and Leroy got home. We tried to talk them out of it, but with all the talk about a war starting back east they decided to rush back to Appling."

"Never know what might happen to a farm when the men folk have to go off to fight," Taylor said, his voice filled with concern. "I know how worried Mary and Gladys were when they left."

The family made quick work of the fried chicken and vegetables; afterwards Mindy helped with the dishes while the men went into the parlor to chat. Leroy was anxious to catch up on Texas news with his father and Clayton but all they wanted to talk about was his trip to Georgia.

After briefly discussing the condition of the farm and news of family and friends, Taylor told Leroy that word had been left for him to report for Ranger duty as soon as he returned from Georgia.

"You're supposed to go out west to Fort Worth," Taylor said. "The Benson boy is waiting to go with you."

"Why is Andy waiting for me?" Leroy asked.

"He broke his arm about a month ago," Clayton laughed, "and his Ma won't let him go off by himself."

"Andy Benson always was a mama's boy," Leroy smirked. "We were all surprised when he joined the Rangers."

"What *really* surprised everyone was that his mama let him do it," Taylor laughed, and then his tone became serious. "What about Mindy?" he asked. "How's she gonna feel about you leaving so soon?"

Leroy cleared his throat before responding. "She knows I'm a Texas Ranger."

Taylor raised his eyebrows while filling his pipe with tobacco. "Still, it might not sit well with her. After all, you haven't even got the trail dust off of you yet."

After the dishes were dried and put away, Mindy and Verlinda went into the parlor with the intention of playing the piano and singing a few hymns before bedtime. Leroy had other ideas. He reached for the shawl Mindy had worn during the trip and wrapped it around her shoulders.

"If it's all the same to you, Mama," he said. "I'd like to take Mindy for a walk. We'll be back before bedtime."

Leroy's parents and his brother followed them out to the porch and waited while Leroy and Mindy walked down the path toward the nearby lake. Mindy blushed as Leroy kissed her cheek in full view of the house.

He looked at her for the longest time. When he spoke, his voice took on a serious note. "You remember I told you I'd have to go off on Ranger duty now and then." He hesitated. "I want you to be happy and getting you settled is important to me, but I've got to ride to Fort Worth in the morning."

She stopped and stared at him, a bewildered look on her face. "So soon? I've hardly had time to get to know your family. I need you here with me."

He stared back, his expression set, his jaw firm. "Mindy," he said in a calm voice. "It's the last thing I want to do, but I've got to go to Fort Worth.

"Where's Fort Worth?" she asked. "How far away is it?"

"Not far," he lied. "I'll be home in no time. Probably before you learn to cook."

"That's not funny," she said, looking up into his eyes. "Some honeymoon this turned out to be."

"I'll make it up to you," Leroy promised.

"When?" Mindy pulled away from him and folded her arms.

"Right now," he whispered in a mischievous voice. "Let's go back to the house."

She smiled in spite of herself. She realized that she loved this Texas cowboy more than ever. *Still, all in all,* she thought, *it would be nice if he gave up being a Texas Ranger and stayed here on the farm with me.*

CHAPTER 22

Leroy had no way of knowing what was waiting for him and Andy Benson. A dispute over watering cattle in Noland's River, south of Fort Worth near Wardville, had escalated into a shooting war. Two large Texas cattle ranches had each hired gunmen in hopes of settling the dispute in their favor. Some of the smaller ranchers and settlers were fighting back which put the Texas Rangers in the middle of a range war.

The next morning Leroy managed to get past a long, drawn out and tearful goodbye with Mindy. After stopping to tell Andy to pack up and get ready to leave town, he went to see his brother, Carter, who was working for a judge and studying to become a lawyer. The bell above the door jingled as Leroy opened the door to the law office.

"Leroy!" Carter called out. "I didn't know you were back from Georgia. Did you bring that Georgia belle with you or did she get smart and send you packing?"

Leroy grinned as he took his time taking off his wide-brimmed cowboy hat. "One question at a time. As you can plainly see, I'm back and, you know me. I wasn't about to come back empty handed."

"I definitely do know you," Carter laughed as he gave Leroy a bear hug. "So, when do I meet Mindy?"

"Anytime you can break free from this place," Leroy replied, his voice full of sarcasm. "Personally, I'd sooner serve time in the local jail than work here all day long."

Carter ignored the last comment. "Let's go get a bite to eat. Okay by you?"

"Sure," Leroy chuckled appreciatively.

Carter reached for his coat and hat while asking, "How are things going with the two of you?"

"Oh, I'd say I'm a pretty lucky fellow all things considered. Of course, she doesn't want me to go off on Ranger duty, but that's what I do. I'm a Texas Ranger and the sooner she gets used to the idea, the better."

Carter frowned and shook his head. His features were much softer than Leroy's. Leroy's firm set jaw and deep-set eyes had always set him apart from his brothers. Carter and Leroy walked side by side down the walkway covered with planks that led to the cafe door. What a contrast there was in the bearing of the two men; Carter was taller and slimmer than Leroy. He wore a tan coat over a gray vest and brown linen trousers. Leroy carried himself with a cowboy's slow easy going gait while Carter always resembled a man in a hurry to get to someplace important. Carter's hair was much darker than his younger brother's. Leroy's unruly sandy brown hair now hung almost two inches below his ears. Carter made a mental note to make sure Leroy visited the barber while in town.

Leroy had a confident manner about him. Although he was the youngest son, his parents always turned to him first whenever things needed to be done. No one in the family could explain why, but everyone knew it had been a fact of life at the Wiley farm since the boys were teenagers.

"From what I hear, you're going to have your hands full," Carter said. "You have the Mexican bandits causing trouble down south, while out west the Comanche Indians are still on the warpath and to top everything off, there's a range war going on between some cattle ranchers over water. The Judge told me that the reason the governor had to call up the Rangers here in east Texas was to try and settle the problem with the ranchers out west. We're pretty lucky things have settled down here in Smith County."

"Well, looks to me like there's enough trouble everywhere else to make up for this little peaceful part of Texas," Leroy said as they crossed the main street of Tyler en route to Mrs. Lloyd's Blue Plate Cafe.

The cafe counter was divided into two sections. The first displayed meat and vegetables, the second, the best pies and cakes baked in Tyler. Leroy moved along both counters stopping first to admire the pies and cakes before choosing a big plate of ham and sweet potatoes.

The brothers sat down at a corner table and waited to be served their food. Several patrons stopped by to speak to Carter while Leroy kept his eyes focused on the apple and mincemeat pies.

"I hope you got the money to pay for this," Leroy said as he gestured towards the food he had selected.

Carter laughed. "A fine mess we'd be in if I didn't. Don't Texas Rangers get paid these days?"

"Not a heck of a lot," Leroy shook his head. "And remember, I've been on leave. The Rangers ain't much for paying a fellow to go to Georgia and bring back a bride."

"How'd you talk her into coming with you?" Carter asked as the waiter poured two cups of hot coffee at their small table. "It must have been hard for her to leave her family. Who knows when she will have the chance to see them again?"

Leroy was silent for so long that Carter glanced at him, afraid that there was a problem. To his surprise, Leroy's expression was very serious.

"I can tell you this, Carter. I don't know what I would have done if she hadn't agreed to marry me. That gal has me twisted around her little finger. I probably would have dressed up in fancy duds and stayed with her in Georgia if that's what she wanted. In any case, her folks were right nice about everything, especially her father. He supported Mindy's decision and helped us every way he could. Her mother, on the other hand, wasn't too happy about Mindy marrying some cowpoke from Texas. You can kind of understand her feelings. She wanted Mindy to stay in Georgia."

"Sounds like everyone was friendly back in Georgia. They must have taken to you."

"Not everyone was friendly," Leroy laughed. "One fellow in particular wasn't at all happy 'bout Mindy and me. Seems he had other plans for her future."

"Well, it's obvious she made the right decision," Carter leaned back while the steaming plates of food were placed in front of the two brothers. "You sound like you're a happy man."

"I am," Leroy replied. "She don't hold with drinking or playing cards but I can live with that." Then he raised his eyebrows slightly before continuing. "At least while I'm here in Smith County."

"You rascal," Carter laughed. "You'll never change."

But he had changed. Leroy never spoke to anyone else about his feelings for Mindy. He was not ashamed of those feelings, but he felt they belonged only to him and Mindy. The minute he had left her standing on the front porch, waving goodbye, he had felt an unfamiliar pang of loneliness and longing to turn his horse around and stay home. *I'm not a farmer at heart. But I guess I could become one if that's what it takes to keep Mindy happy.*

Leroy and Carter finished their meal, then said their goodbyes outside the door of the cafe. Carter held out his hand and Leroy took it.

"Be careful," Carter said. "You've got a big responsibility now."

"Always have had," Leroy answered. "The Rangers are about all that stands between decent law abiding Texans and murderers, bank robbers and cattle rustlers."

"Don't forget about the Comanche," Carter reminded him. "Texas will be a better place when the law can put a rope around all of their sorry necks."

Before walking away Carter turned and asked Leroy, "Do you need a place to bunk for the night?"

"Nope," Leroy replied. "I plan to go by Andy's, then get on the road as soon as possible. We'll probably camp out by Kickapoo Creek, then get a early start tomorrow morning."

"Does Andy know he's leaving his mama today?" Carter laughed.

"Yep, told him on my way into town," Leroy said as he shifted his weight on one foot so he could knock some dried mud off of his boot. "He was kind of surprised I was back so soon. By the way, speaking of surprising folks, you were supposed to be at dinner yesterday. Mama was not a happy lady when you didn't show up. I figure Mindy and I got you out of a heap of trouble cause Mama was *so* happy to see us, she forgot all about being mad at you."

"Sorry, I just couldn't get away in time to make it to supper. I'll make it up to Ma next Sunday."

Leroy nodded. "Guess that'll do. Be on time for church next Sunday and even if I'm not back, you can meet Mindy."

Carter watched Leroy saunter across the street to his waiting horse. *He'd be a darn sight easier for a wife to live with if there was a little more give and a little less take to him. He's sure set in his ways.*

CHAPTER 23

Andy Benson's tall, big boned frame gave the illusion of a tough cowboy ready for a fight. But one glance at his easy going smile and large, sad eyes told anyone interested in fighting that Andy just wanted to 'go along and get along,' as the boys growing up with him in Tyler used to say. He was everybody's friend but females continually bossed him around. Andy was the youngest child of the town's school-teacher, Miz Mary, as the children always called her. On top of that, Andy had three older sisters, April, May and June, who made Andy's life miserable.

Leroy had often wondered why Andy joined the Rangers. Actually, Andy knew exactly what he was doing. As soon as he finished school, he took the *first* opportunity he had to get away from his sisters, not to mention his mother, the stern school marm.

Leroy hesitated before he knocked on Andy's front door. *What if one of his ugly sisters opens the door? I swear they are enough to scare a man half out of his wits.*

Leroy's worst fears were realized when, sure enough, the door opened and there stood Andy's three sisters. They all wore silly grins and were homelier than he had remembered.

"Good afternoon, ladies," Leroy removed his hat and gave the girls his best smile. "Andy around?"

"Come in, Leroy," April said, reaching for his hat.

Leroy made a vain attempt to hold on to his precious cowboy hat. *Darn it, that hat cost me a months pay.* "If you don't mind, April, I'll just keep my hat. I won't be troublin' you all very long."

"I do mind, Leroy," April said as she snatched the hat away from him.

Oh, well, what's a month's pay? Leroy thought.

"Leroy, stay for supper," June grinned, blushing as she spoke.

They ain't used to gentleman callers, Leroy thought. *Wonder why?*

"Of course he will," May added, as if Leroy had already agreed to extend his visit.

"Where's Andy?" Leroy asked in desperation. The last thing he wanted to do was face Miz iron pants, as Andy's mother was known to anyone who had spent time in her classroom.

"He'll be along anytime now," April said, then added, "Sit down."

"No need," Leroy started to explain that he was short on time when the largest sister, May, pushed him into a chair. "On second thought, don't mind if I do," Leroy said. He stifled a scream crawling up his throat. How he wanted to yell, "Andy!"

"We're having fried chicken livers and sweet onions for supper," June said with a smile.

Leroy barely heard himself speaking. He was mumbling something, but it was impossible to make out what he said. The sisters listened carefully; April leaned forward until her long nose almost touched Leroy's face. His vision blurred.

"Andy!" he called out when he finally emerged from his delirium.

During the entire meal, Miz iron pants berated Leroy and Andy for joining the Texas Rangers. Leroy wondered how any woman could be so fat when she never stopped talking long enough to eat. After Leroy choked down some fried chicken livers (Leroy hated chicken livers) mixed with red onions, Andy and Leroy waited patiently for April and May to serve up bowls of fruit cobbler. *The cobbler might save the day.* He was sure he could enjoy anything called cobbler.

"What kind of fruit is this?" Leroy asked as his lips curled up into a tight crease.

"Persimmon, of course," June replied with a huge, toothy smile. "That's our favorite kind of pie."

"Too bitter?" asked May.

Leroy managed to shake his head. "It's perfect," he lied, and then glancing at Andy, he thought, *don't you ever speak, you henpecked fool?*

"I've prepared extra linens in Andy's room for you, Leroy," Leroy heard iron pants say in a stern voice. "You'll sleep tonight and get an early start in the morning after the girls prepare breakfast."

Lord help us all, thought Leroy. "If it's all the same to you, ma'am, Andy and I will head on out for Fort Worth tonight. I had hoped to camp at Kickapoo Creek, then start from there at daybreak. Of course, I didn't plan on this good meal delayin' us."

"You'll do no such thing," iron pants said, her command voice evident. "You'll hurt the girls' feelings. They planned the entire evening for you boys. It is too bad Andy's cousins couldn't be here to join us."

April added in a cheerful voice, "Our cousins, Augusta, Savannah and Georgia are so much fun!"

"They're at a church retreat this entire week," May added, her voice filled with disappointment.

"But they'll be in town when you and Andy get back and we'll make sure you get to meet them," June said. "They are just like us."

Leroy looked directly at Andy. *Say something, you idiot,* he thought. *Get us out of here!*

"Yeah, Ma," Andy said indifferently, knowing better than to argue with her.

First words he utters all during supper and it's Yeah, Ma, thought Leroy. *Andy, you'll pay for putting me through this.*

As he walked into Andy's room Leroy paused to look at the maple bed with the covers turned neatly back, the bright colored quilt folded conveniently across the footboard. A deep frown began to form in his brow. How he missed his wife! *Everything is different now that I'm married to Mindy.* He looked into the small oval mirror that hung above Andy's chest of drawers. The mirror gave back a reflection and he didn't like what he saw—a man standing in a strange bedroom alone—without his pretty wife beside him.

After receiving hugs and kisses from April, May and June, Leroy made his escape from Tyler with Andy riding beside him leading a packhorse burdened down with everything ol' iron pants could put on the poor animal's back.

Leroy scratched his head and thought about the trip ahead. "We should make good time, Andy. Looks like good weather to the west."

"I wish I didn't have to pull this pack horse," Andy complained. "We probably won't need any of this stuff."

Leroy pulled the reins up, stopped his horse, and then turned to look Andy in the eye. "Why don't you stand up to them women? You're a man now, Andy."

Andy shrugged. "I didn't hear you say anything *but* yes ma'am back there."

"Andy, does that pack horse know the way home?"

"Sure she does. 'Specially this close to the house."

"Well, then," Leroy dismounted and walked over to take the reins from Andy. "You got a piece of paper and a pencil on you?"

"Yep," Andy said. "Ma packed writing paper in my saddlebag."

Leroy unbuckled the saddlebag and took out a writing tablet.

"Here," he said as he handed the paper to Andy. "Write what I tell you." Leroy paused, waiting until Andy was prepared to write. "You can start by writing these words," Leroy looked at Andy. "Dear Ma, we don't need this stuff, signed, your son, Andy."

"What?" Andy looked startled.

"This is your first step toward freedom from them women," Leroy said. "You write what I tell you, or I will do the writing for you and if I write it, I'll add a few more lines your mama won't like reading."

"Okay, Leroy," Andy sighed and began to write. "I might as well do like you say 'cause I sure don't want to pull this pack horse all the way to Fort Worth and back."

Leroy fastened the note to the saddlebags, tied up the reins, then turned the pack horse around and gave it a slap on it's rump. As the horse galloped away, Leroy declared, "Freedom from females telling you what to do, Andy! That's important for any man."

An expression of dread filled Andy's face. *There'll be hell to pay when I get home,* he thought. But then he pictured his mother's and his sister's faces when they read the note and in spite of himself, Andy began to laugh.

"I hope it's a long time 'fore I get back from Fort Worth," Andy said to Leroy. "Just so Mama can settle down."

"Ol' iron pants settle down?" Leroy said. "Naah, Andy. She'll still be waitin' for ya'."

Andy let out a deep breath. Without saying another word he gave his horse a gentle nudge with his boots. With the morning sun on their backs, the two young Texas Rangers rode west, toward Fort Worth.

CHAPTER 24

On the sixth of June 1849, Major Ripley A. Arnold established an army post called Fort Worth to protect settlers from the Indians. The soldiers left in 1853, turning the fort over to settlers themselves. By the time Leroy and Andy rode into Fort Worth, it had become a major trading post.

"Andy, let's get the horses taken care of first, then we'll go to the sheriff's office and find out what's going on." Leroy gave his tired horse a pat on the neck. "They need grain and a good rubdown."

"I'll take the horses to that stable over yonder and see if we can get them boarded for the night," Andy said, pointing to the far end of the street. "While I'm taking care of the horses you go talk with the sheriff. That'll save us some time."

Leroy nodded in agreement. "I'll see you directly," he said while climbing down from his horse.

"You boys have got here just in time to get slap dab in the middle of a range war over water," Sheriff Seth Braden shook his head as he motioned Leroy to take a chair. "How many Rangers are with you?"

"Just me and one other fellow. We're trying to catch up to a company of Rangers from east Texas," Leroy answered with as much confidence as he could muster, then voiced his concern. "When I joined the Rangers I thought my main job would be taking on the Comanche. I sure don't much like the idea of fighting other Texans."

"That may have been the case in the past and probably will be again in the near future, but the Comanche cleared out after that wagon train massacre. Last time I talked with the powers that be down in Austin they told me that at least for the time being the Rangers had orders to let the soldiers at Fort Belknap deal with the Comanche. The Rangers are supposed to stay around these parts and put a stop to all the fuss over the water runoffs from Noland's River."

Leroy walked closer to the worn map of Texas nailed to the office wall. He pointed to Noland's River. "Seems to me that there's enough water for everybody. What's the problem?"

"You'll find out," Sheriff Braden reached into the pocket of his waistcoat for tobacco. "If I was you, I'd hightail it over towards Wardville. Last I heard there was a bunch of Rangers camped where these two creeks join up with the river. " He pointed to an area south of Wardville on the map.

Leroy took one last look at the map. "We've been riding pretty hard, but as soon as our horses are rested, we'll hit the trail again." He turned to the sheriff who was busy rolling tobacco paper. "Any place cheap we could board for the night?"

Sheriff Braden smiled. "Ain't been paid yet?"

"Not for a while," Leroy chuckled as his face turned a bright shade of red. "But I reckon we can make out okay."

"Try the Widow Morrison's place, down the end of the street by the school house. She runs the school and keeps boarders at her place for the extra money."

Leroy nodded. "We passed the school when we rode into town. I'm mighty grateful for your help, Sheriff."

Sheriff Braden nodded his head, and then turned his attention back to rolling his tobacco. *Young fools,* he thought. *They oughta' find a better way to make a living.*

Leroy almost ran into Andy as he opened the door made of solid Texas oak.

"What's going on?" Andy asked. Before Leroy could reply he added, "The smithy's clearing out two stalls and putting down fresh hay but it's gonna cost us some money."

"I'll tell you what's happening on the way to the boarding house," Leroy reached over to give Andy a playful shove. "Right now, let's get some grub. I could sure use a piece of pie, any kind of pie, even your sister's persimmon pie would taste good right about now."

Andy grinned but said nothing. He brushed the dust from his eyes and looked around the busy outpost. Shadows were just starting to cover the trees. It was only then that he noticed that Leroy was walking briskly toward the horses, leaving him behind.

"Hold up, Leroy," Andy called out as he started down the walk.

Leroy mounted his horse and without saying a word, pulled the horse's reins toward the school house at the end of the street. "Let's go straight to the boarding house and see if we can rent a room for tonight," Leroy suggested. "We might be able to get a meal cheaper there."

After receiving a warm greeting from Mrs. Morrison, Leroy focused on the sweet smells floating through the house from the kitchen. He waited, hoping she was going to say that supper was ready to be put on the table.

The middle-aged woman stood, hands on hips, looking Leroy and Andy up and down. "You both could use a bath." She said firmly, and then added, "No time to heat enough water right now so you'll both have to sleep dirty and wash up good tomorrow morning."

"Sorry, ma'am," Leroy said humbly. "We've been in the saddle since dawn, with no time to wash up. We'll be glad to clean up as best we can. Just show us the way to the well water."

"There's a cistern out back," she smiled. "I've got a couple of clean shirts you can wear."

"Mighty thankful," Leroy said. "Andy and I appreciate your kindness and don't worry, we'll be paying for our keep."

"You can leave your horses in the barn," Mrs. Morrison tilted her head in the direction of a small barn behind her home. "There's hay and a watering trough out back."

"That will save us some money," Andy whispered.

Mrs. Morrison noticed the young men's preoccupation during supper. She sat at the supper table for a few moments in silence before finally asking for some information from her guests. "Where exactly are you boys from and what are you doing here?"

"We're Texas Rangers from east Texas," Leroy explained. "Andy, here, broke his arm and had to stay behind. I had to make a family trip back east to Georgia. Now the two of us are trying to catch up with the rest of our company."

"What kind of family trip?" she asked.

Leroy blushed. *Now why did she have to ask that?*

Before he could answer, Andy spoke up, "Leroy rode all the way to Georgia to marry a gal he met last year."

Leroy shot Andy a dirty look. They were Texas Rangers and private talk while on the job wasn't appropriate.

Mrs. Morrison gently placed her hand on Leroy's shoulder. "That's wonderful news," she said. "I'm sure she is a lovely girl."

Leroy didn't smile but his expression softened just a bit. "Thank you, ma'am," he said. "She sure is pretty."

After a supper of baked chicken and dumplings followed by blueberry pie, Mrs. Morrison led Leroy and Andy to a small guest bedroom filled with quilts and oak furniture that reminded them of their homes in Smith County. Leroy rested his head on a pillow stuffed with cotton and let his thoughts drift back to Mindy. Although he missed her terribly, a comfortable peace enveloped him for a few moments as his mind veered away from his life on the trail with the Rangers. He lay there without moving for a long time. The sounds of nighttime began drifting through the small window. Leroy raised his head to catch sight of a thin cloud covering the half moon. He could hardly wait until morning. It was time to get back to being a Texas Ranger.

Dawn came early. Leroy had finally fallen asleep, but it was a restless sleep. After breakfast, Leroy and Andy saddled their horses in the early morning light.

"I'll go settle our bill, Andy," Leroy said, leading his horse out of the small barn.

Andy nodded, reached for Leroy's horse's reins and pulled both horses toward the hitching post in front of the widow Morrison's gate.

Leroy was surprised to see that she was waiting for him at the front steps.

"There's a morning chill out here, ma'am," Leroy smiled and tipped his hat. "You could have waited inside. We wouldn't leave without paying for our keep."

Mrs. Morrison laughed. "I know that, you silly boy. After all, you're the law in this state." She reached out and took his arm. "Come with me into the kitchen. I've packed biscuit sandwiches and jelly cookies for you and Andy to take with you. You should be able to carry enough for dinner and supper on the trail."

"Thank you," Leroy said as he held open the front door, then stepped aside to allow her to go into the parlor. "Andy and me will remember your kindness for quite some time. Grub like this is mighty scarce on the trail."

"All I ask is that you both are careful and go home to east Texas in one piece."

"Thank you, Miz Morrison," Leroy replied as he handed her a dollar. "Will this be enough? I know we ate a lot last night and this morning."

She laughed, "Leroy, that's plenty." She usually charged guests twice that amount for one night and that didn't include supper.

After gathering up the food and thanking Mrs. Morrison one last time, Leroy reached for his hat and slowly walked to the door. It was time to ride south and find the Texas Rangers camped near Noland's River.

Leroy and Andy rode through rolling prairie past Caddo Peak to the small outpost of Wardville. Camped on the outskirts of Wardville was a group of homesteaders trying to fix a broken wagon so they could continue their journey west to the New Mexico Territory. The group included three families and a pair of guides armed with rifles for hunting and protection against the Indians.

Andy gestured toward a group of children huddled together looking tired and hungry. "Look at them young-uns, Leroy," he whispered. "They're in pretty bad shape."

"Everything okay here?" Leroy asked as the armed men walked forward to meet them. "We're Rangers on our way to Noland's River."

One of the men, who seemed older than the others, stepped forward. "We need to get this here wagon fixed." He turned and pointed toward the broken wagon propped up with logs. "The axle and one of the wheels have gone bad. We're trying to make do, but it's hard to fix the wheel without the right lumber and we sure don't have no iron to work with for the axle."

"Can you load up everything on the other wagons and leave it?" Leroy asked.

"Nope," the man answered. "That'd leave us short. We're barely making out as it is."

Leroy looked at Andy, and then took a long look at the hungry kids. Without saying a word they both reached into their saddlebags and brought out what food was left from Mrs. Morrison's breakfast table.

"It ain't much," Leroy said as he handed Andy the food and watched him carry the biscuit sandwiches and cookies to the hungry children. "But maybe it'll help."

"Much obliged and may God be with you," the old man called out to the Rangers. He then turned toward the waiting settlers. "Make sure the food is divided equal. It may be the last bites the young-un's get 'til tomorrow."

Leroy and Andy rode away without looking back but neither could wipe out the memory of the sad plight of the homesteaders. For a long time there was only silence between them.

Tough times, Leroy thought. *I hope they make it. They're gonna need a lot of luck to survive the badlands and the Comanche.*

Late that afternoon, Leroy and Andy rode through the rain drenched streets of Wardville. As they climbed down from their horses, Leroy couldn't help smiling at the site of his friend, Andy, dirty and tired, looking around the town for a dining hall.

"We sure are a sight, Leroy," Andy observed. "See any place to eat?"

"Nope, but I'll bet the sheriff will know where we can find some supper."

"I think we ought to ask the first person we see," Andy declared.

"We should be able to come up with some supper if we put our minds to it," Leroy laughed. "Us being Texas Rangers and all."

Andy gave Leroy a playful shove. "I wouldn't count on getting a meal just because we're Rangers. One of us better have some script."

Leroy returned the shove and said, "In that case, supper is definitely on you, Andy."

The sheriff of Wardville met the boys outside his office. As luck would have it, he was on his way to an early supper.

"You boys join me," he said with a hearty laugh. "I'm about to sit down at the best table in town and from the looks of you two, you could use some hot coffee and a good home cooked meal."

"I can taste it already," Leroy chuckled.

"Well, follow me to the eating place, then I'll show you where Captain Davis and the rest of the Rangers are camped. There's trouble brewing in these parts." Looking up at the cloudy sky he added, "You wouldn't believe this now, but it's over water. We've had a mighty bad draught these past few years. Everybody round here needs water for either cattle or crops. So now the ranchers and farmers are going at it over the water running off Noland's River."

Leroy shook his head. "That's what we heard. Don't make much sense, folks fighting over water."

"It does if there ain't enough to go around," the sheriff said as he slipped through an open door on his way into the dining hall. "Things have been pretty tough around here what with the draught. If it don't get better soon, I don't know how some folks are gonna make it."

A slim young woman with honey colored hair and wearing a blue gingham apron poured the coffee and set the dishes on the table. She hurriedly began carrying bowls of food to the hungry men. During supper, the sheriff, a lean man with strands of gray hair parted and falling over his ears, explained the conflict that was brewing.

"With the draught drying up all the streams, two ranches control all the water," the sheriff explained while pulling apart pieces of fried chicken.

"Why would anyone want to keep thirsty Longhorns away from water, Sheriff?" asked Leroy.

The sheriff pondered this question before answering. Leroy noticed that he was also carefully looking around the dining hall. Finally, the sheriff leaned close to the Rangers and spoke in a voice that couldn't be overheard. "Folks say it's because some ranchers, and I ain't about to say who, are bound and determined to run off the farmers and the smaller ranchers so they can lay claim to their land."

"That don't seem right," Andy said while putting a generous helping of jelly on a biscuit.

"You'll find out more when you join up with your Ranger Company," the sheriff paused and motioned for more coffee. "I'm sure Captain Davis was told who's causing all the trouble when the governor ordered you boys out here. I sure am glad you two boys are here because if the Rangers are gonna settle things they're gonna need *every* single one of you."

"Like you say, we'll find out what's gotta be done when we meet up with our captain," Andy said, a serious expression on his face as he looked at Leroy.

CHAPTER 25

When Leroy and Andy finally caught up with their Ranger Company, they found a group of shirt-sleeved men resting underneath elms and maples near the north fork of Noland's River, awaiting orders from the Ranger Headquarters in Waco.

Leroy was relieved to have found the campsite, whereas Andy was just happy to be near a campfire with a pot of hot coffee and trout cooking over a low burning flame.

Captain Davis greeted the new arrivals then filled them in on their present situation. As Davis reached out a big boned hand to offer Leroy a cup of coffee, he said, "The trouble centers around who has the rights to the water in the river and the surrounding creeks."

Leroy nodded. "That's what we've been told, sir."

"There's a couple of big ranchers around here who have forgotten how to treat their less fortunate neighbors. As soon as the fellows in Austin make up their minds and decide what exactly they want us to do, they'll send a rider from Waco and if I'm not mistaken, we'll have to teach a few ranchers some manners," Captain Davis frowned. He gestured towards the camp. "Leroy, you and Andy better get some rest. We don't know when we'll be going to work, but when we do, we'll be spending a lot of time in the saddle, that's for sure."

Leroy watched the captain walk over and lean against a big elm tree. His hat set firmly on his head, Captain Davis was the picture of calm self-confidence.

Joining Andy by the campfire, Leroy felt a familiar tap on his shoulder. He turned around and saw Willis wearing a grin as big as the hill country of Texas. "How's your wife?" Willis asked.

Leroy didn't reply, just returned the smile and sat next to Andy by the campfire.

As he traveled across much of Texas with the Rangers, Leroy discovered that just like in Smith County, ranching was the way most folks in Texas made their living. Cattle ranches were by their nature large because it required quite a few acres of grassland to feed a herd. Some of the newer homesteaders tried to make do with only five to ten acres while surrounded by ranches measuring hundreds or even thousands of acres.

"We normally don't have many city boys riding with us in the Rangers, but I just want to make it crystal clear to everyone why we're here," Captain Davis told his men as they sat around the campfire enjoying their evening meal. "Most of you know that the cattle follow a daily routine on the ranch. The cattle graze early in the morning, then find a shady place if they can, and rest during the middle of the day. In the late afternoon they go to the watering hole to drink. Cattle must have water or they'll die off pretty quick. Now we've got some homesteaders around these parts that the government has given land to, provided they agreed to live on it and raise cattle or farm some crops. According to the government they got every right to be here. That being said, someone forgot to guarantee them the rights to river water. The trouble started awhile back when the drought hit and it's gotten worse as the drought's continued drying up the small creeks running off Noland's River. Any questions so far?"

Captain Davis waited but no one spoke. He took a long sip of coffee and continued. "Two of the big outfits, the Bar N Ranch and the Double D Ranch, have cut off all the trails to the river. From what I hear, they intend to wait until the homesteaders get really desperate then buy them out, at darn low prices I might add."

"That don't seem fair," Willis said. "Most folks just scrape by as it is, they don't need big outfits trying to run 'em out."

"You're right, Willis," Captain Davis said with conviction. "And don't let anybody tell you otherwise. It's about survival for these homesteaders. If we don't get this problem solved before the calves come in the early spring, the homesteaders will be forced to fold up, take whatever they're offered and move on. Our problem is that the two big outfits I mentioned have gone ahead and hired some gunmen to take care of business."

The Rangers received their orders three days later. A Ranger Captain, sitting tall in the saddle and accompanied by Sheriff Briscoe, the local lawman, approached the campsite.

"This ought to be it," Captain Davis said when he saw the riders in the distance. He tossed his unfinished cup of coffee into the campfire, and then whistled. This was the signal for the men to form up at the campsite. Some had been fishing in the nearby stream while others tended to the horses. Once they were all gathered around the campsite, the Rangers patiently waited to hear their orders.

The Texas Ranger Captain from Waco greeted Captain Davis and nodded to the assembled Rangers. "My name is Evans and this is Sheriff Briscoe. I haven't ridden with you boys before but I'm sure our paths will cross eventually." He turned back to Davis. "Looks like you've got some new boys with you."

Davis smiled. "Young and eager."

Captain Evans smiled back, then shook his head. "If they're eager that means they haven't met up with the Comanche yet."

Davis looked at Leroy and the other young Rangers before saying, "They'll be alright. They rode with a friend of mine before he left to start a business in Mount Pleasant."

"Mallory?" Evans asked.

"Yes," Davis said. He pursed his lips and gave a short whistle before adding, "Another good man lost because his wife wanted him around the house with her rather than on the trail with us."

"That figures," Evans said. He turned to the young Rangers and added in a sarcastic voice, "Remember that boys. You better stay away from the womenfolk or you'll be leading a boring life when you're old. Once they get you in front of a preacher, it's all downhill."

"Well, here it is," Captain Evans said to Davis as he pulled out some folded papers from his saddlebags. His tone had changed from light hearted to serious. "These orders come from Austin. They want you and your men to settle this fight between the ranchers over water rights. Sheriff Briscoe is the local lawman and he'll fill in any necessary details." He handed Davis the orders. "This gives you the authority to back up the sheriff and do whatever needs to be done so that everybody has access to water."

After reading the papers, Captain Davis looked up and said, "As soon as we hear what Sheriff Briscoe has to say, we'll get ready to ride."

"I'll leave you boys with the Sheriff," Captain Evans announced as he walked towards his horse. "I've got a long ride ahead of me so I might as well get started."

"As most of you probably know, the Brazos River begins in New Mexico," Sheriff Max Briscoe began his briefing to the assembled Rangers. "It passes through western and central Texas on the way south to empty out into the ocean. It's all these streams and rivers like Noland's River that run off from the Brazos that keep the cattle and the settlers alive."

Before Briscoe could continue, Captain Davis interrupted with a wave of his hand. "We know the problem, Sheriff. Now solving it is another matter. We plan to pay a visit to both the Bar N and the Double D later today."

"I reckon that's where you ought to start," Sheriff Briscoe said. "I've got to get back to town." He hesitated, then turned back to Captain Davis. "I wish you luck 'cause I darn sure ain't had any with either of them outfits. In fact, the foreman of the Bar N blames me for not taking their side. Last time I rode onto Bar N land he told me that if I knew what was good for me, I'd turn in my badge and leave town. I tell you I've lived too long out here to be threatened by anybody."

"Nobody's gonna threaten a sheriff while we're around," Davis declared while jabbing a finger toward Sheriff Briscoe. "I just decided that our first visit will be to the Bar N." He turned to the assembled Rangers and added, "Let's see if we can talk some sense into these people and maybe give that foreman a lesson in respect for the law."

Captain Davis walked the sheriff to his horse while the Rangers prepared to ride to the Bar N Ranch. Leroy checked his horse's hooves and shoes, then joined Willis and Andy who were enjoying a last cup of coffee before mounting up.

As the Rangers rode toward the Bar N, Sheriff Max Briscoe headed in the opposite direction on his way back to town. The Sheriff was a lot more optimistic about bringing the big ranchers into line now that the Rangers had arrived. As he passed a grove of live oak and junipers, he was suddenly confronted by four masked gunmen who had used the trees and brush for cover. Max's fists clenched. "What the heck?" he yelled as he reached for his gun and whirled to face the gunmen.

Before he could get off a shot, a rifle butt slammed into the side of his head, throwing the sheriff from his horse. Briscoe broke the fall from his horse with both hands, dropping his pistol as he hit the ground. Blood spurted from his mouth and for a few seconds black and white stars seemed to cloud his vision.

"You've meddled in cattle business for the last time, Sheriff," came a voice muffled by a handkerchief covering the man's mouth.

"You should have hung up your badge and gun a long time ago old man," another man spoke, this time from behind the sheriff's horse.

Slowly, Max staggered to his feet. The men swarmed around him, punching him repeatedly in the head and chest. Again Max fell back onto the ground, his last conscious moment was filled with the image of a dirty rifle butt coming right at his face.

As the Rangers approached the Bar N's impressive stone entrance gate they were met with scattered gunfire.

"Hold your fire," Captain Davis called out to the Rangers behind him then turned back in his saddle to face the hidden gunmen. "We're Texas Rangers and we're here to see your boss man."

Leroy sat anxiously in his saddle. He glanced at Willis and then towards Andy and the other Rangers. "What ya' thinking, Willis?" he asked.

"Not much, other than I hope they don't start throwing lead at us again," Willis answered.

Leroy chuckled. "Those were only warning shots."

"What's so darn funny?" Andy demanded, leaning forward in his saddle in the direction of Willis and Leroy.

"Leroy says those were only warning shots," Willis explained.

At that moment, a bullet whizzed by Leroy's hat.

"Like heck they're warning shots," Andy shouted as he ducked down behind his horse's head.

"Take cover," shouted Captain Davis. Caught by surprise, he reeled his horse around to make sure his men were all right, and then quickly slid down from the saddle.

The Rangers hurriedly dismounted, and moved as fast as possible toward a cluster of nearby trees, pulling their horses behind them as they ran for cover.

"Git out of here, we ain't interested in what you got to say," shouted a voice from the far side of the gate. "Better git 'fore somebody gets hurt."

"We're not leaving until we talk to whoever is in charge," Davis yelled. "And if one of my men does get hurt, I swear that I'll see that every last one of you hang for it." Davis waited for a reply. None of the gunmen spoke so he added, "And if I have to bring the army in here to do that, well, that's exactly what I'll do."

Leroy looked around the gate and small stone entrance to the Bar N, quickly assessing the situation. "Captain," he whispered to Davis. "I believe I can work my way around back of 'em."

Davis shook his head. "Not likely. They've got us pinned down and there's not enough cover for even a Comanche to get past their gun sights."

"We gonna wait here until help comes?" Willis asked. "Maybe that sheriff will bring some deputies."

"The way I see it, we're on our own. The best thing to do is wait until dark and try to take 'em by surprise. Maybe then Leroy's plan will have a chance to work," Davis said.

"I got a bad feeling, Captain," one of the older Rangers said, his deep-set eyes staring intently at the Bar N. "They'll be expecting us to do just that."

Davis stared at the stonewall around the entrance to the Bar N. "Let's give it a couple of hours and see what happens. Everyone got a canteen?"

"If not, Andy and I have a couple extras we can pass around," Leroy volunteered. He looked at Andy whose mouth was contorted with a big yawn. "Andy looks like he's ready for a nap."

Several Rangers chuckled, while Andy turned beet red.

"Quiet," Davis said. He pointed toward a dark outline moving between distant trees and scrub brush. "Someone's moving in our direction from behind those trees."

Leroy slowly raised his rifle and took aim.

Halting, the man behind the trees took out a handkerchief, wiped the sweat from his forehead, dabbed his neck below his beard, and then waved the handkerchief in view of the Rangers. "We gotta talk," he said.

"Agreed," Davis called out. "Let's see you out in the open, no pistols, no rifles, then I'll meet you halfway."

"Who am I talking to?" the man yelled, still hiding behind the trees.

"Davis, I'm in command of a company of Rangers," the captain answered.

Leroy's mouth dropped open as he watched Captain Davis stand in plain view of the Bar N's gunmen. "We were sent here to put a stop to the trouble round these parts." Captain Davis watched as the old man slowly moved forward.

"I'm in charge here. The Bar N is my place."

"Your name?" Davis asked.

"Jack Miller." Davis watched as two men stepped from behind the trees and followed the old man as he moved forward.

Captain Davis met the men at the stone entrance gate. He reached out to shake hands, but Jack Miller ignored the gesture.

"This is my land. It was nothing when I came here," Miller said in a defiant tone. "None of you Rangers helped me then. I fought Indians, Mexicans and every kind of critter you can name. Nobody's got a right to tell me what to do now, especially not some worthless do-gooder sheriff."

"From what I hear, you're keeping the homesteaders from getting the water they need for their cattle. Is that true?" Davis asked. He noticed Jack Miller's face was so tanned by years working in the hot Texas sun that it had the appearance of leather. Miller's voice was crisp, sounding much stronger and younger than his years. The gunmen on either side of him kept their eyes on the Rangers.

"Ride on. This is none of your business," Miller said. "There's no trouble here that we can't handle by ourselves."

Davis shrugged his shoulders then spoke in a tone of voice that he knew Miller would understand, "I think we better hang around and make sure things are worked out fair and square." He motioned to the Rangers. Leroy stood up and began walking towards Captain Davis. One by one, the other Rangers left their cover and walked forward, standing next to their Captain.

Miller's brown eyes glared at the Rangers. Up to this point he hadn't realized how many Rangers he was taking on. A few Rangers he figured he could handle with the gunmen he had hired, but an entire company was a different story.

A man would have to be crazy to take on a whole company of Rangers, hired guns or no hired guns, that is unless I can even the odds a bit, Miller thought. He quickly glanced around then turned back to face Davis. *This ain't a good time to start anything.* "I don't want no trouble with the law," he said. "I'll see what terms I can work out with the squatters."

"You do that," Davis replied. "And while you're working out terms, we'll make sure the homesteaders, or squatters, as you call 'em, get their beef to water at Noland's River."

Miller said nothing for a moment. Finally, he spoke, "Captain, before you go meddling in my business, you might just keep in mind them Ranger badges ain't bullet proof."

With that, Davis turned on his heel and walked away, followed by the Rangers in his command.

"Well boys," Miller chuckled, the laughter not reaching his eyes. "Looks like we'll have to let 'em have the water for awhile until them fellows get bored and decide to go back to Waco or where ever they came from."

The gunmen smiled in agreement. Jack Miller wasn't the only one not anxious to tangle with a company of Texas Rangers.

About a half of a mile beyond the outskirts of the small town of Robertson, the Rangers were met by a deputy sheriff who was looking for Max Briscoe. By now the sheriff was long overdue at his office. Captain Davis immediately agreed to help search for the missing sheriff.

The Rangers rode back to the campsite where they had met with Briscoe earlier in the day. Once they were there, Davis spread his men out and began to search the entire area. The Rangers spent the rest of the day riding back and forth over hills and gullies.

Leroy and Willis were the ones who found Sheriff Briscoe. The two men watched as the dying sheriff's heavy breathing turned to sporadic gasps for air. With a harsh, wet sound, Briscoe coughed up a mouth full of bright red blood. He clasped both hands to his stomach, then with his chest heaving one last time, the sheriff died while blood continued to drip down his chin onto the dry grass. Willis knelt down beside the sheriff and felt for a pulse, then he looked up at Leroy and sadly shook his head. "He ain't hurting no more."

"I'll fire off a round so they'll know we found him," Leroy said. "It shouldn't take long for Captain Davis to get here."

Willis shook his head and looked up at Leroy. "All hell's gonna break loose now. Just when I thought them ranchers was going to listen to reason."

Hate bubbled up inside of Leroy at the thought of what had happened to the old sheriff. *Bushwhacked. That sure is a sorry way for a lawman to die.*

CHAPTER 26

While he stood at the gate waiting for the Bar N owner and his fore-man to show up, Captain Davis had the Rangers watching the front and side entrances to the bunkhouse and barn.

"They'll have to come out sooner or later," Leroy whispered to Andy.

"I'd just as soon it be later," Andy whispered back. "I'm thinking we're in for a fight."

Leroy frowned, took a deep breath and asked, "Well, ain't that why we came here?"

Three men stepped out onto the ranch house porch. Davis saw no one that he recognized from his visit the day before. As a cool wind blew off the nearby creek, one of the Bar N gunmen held his hands out and walked toward the gate.

"That's far enough," Davis called out. "We aim to come inside."

"What's the cause for you comin' out here again, lawman?"

"Just who am I talking to?" Davis yelled.

"Frank Miller, I'm Jack Miller's son. My Pa agreed to let them squatters water their stock, so what else do you want?"

"Now listen to me, Frank Miller," Davis walked through the open gate as he spoke. "I need to talk to your Pa. This is no longer just a fight over watering rights. Now we're dealing with the murder of a lawman."

"Nobody on the Bar N killed any lawman," Miller shook his head emphatically. "I'm sure of that."

"Well, I'm not," Davis replied.

Frank Miller's eyes were wide and he took a deep breath to calm himself. He was only in his mid twenties, but he had seen enough gun fights to know that one was coming in the next few minutes if he didn't give in to the Ranger Captain's demands. The Rangers were a formidable force, but the Bar N had enough men to at least give them a run for their money.

As if reading the young man's thoughts, Davis said, "Don't be foolish, boy. This is a fight you can't win. If you try, I promise you that you're going to die today and there isn't a thing you can do to stop it."

Miller started walking toward the Rangers, half expecting a bullet. "No one's gonna come in here on my land and tell me what to do."

Davis pointed to the house. "I'll give you ten minutes to talk to your Pa. Tell him that's all the time he's got."

Miller nodded, then turned and walked back to the ranch house. His father stood in the shadows of a heavy oak door that led to the inside parlor. After going over the options in his head, old man Miller pursed his lips and sighed. "I knew it would come to this as soon as those squatters were given free land."

Jake Wilson, one of the Bar N's hired guns, met Frank Miller's gaze. Miller shook his head and walked past him, stopping at the door to look directly into his father's face.

"Don't just stand there," Jack Miller said. "Get your ass in here so we can figure out how to get you out of this mess."

"They don't know who killed Briscoe," Frank said. "They're just guessing."

The older man pulled himself up to his full height. "They ain't gonna find out, either. I'll take Jake with me and go with them into town. When I get a handle on things I'll send Jake back to the ranch. If Jake tells you to high tail it, that's what you do. Go to Fort Worth, stay with your Aunt Margaret and keep out of sight. You hear me?"

For a minute or so the father stared straight into his son's eyes. His hands gripping the rifle so tightly that his knuckles turned white.

"I'd rather stay here," Frank said defiantly. "If trouble comes, I don't want to be in Fort Worth."

"You'll do as you're told," Jack said tersely as he brushed past Frank on his way toward the front door. "I'll be damned if I lose my son over the likes of Max Briscoe."

"Hold your fire," Davis yelled as he motioned to his men. "The old man's coming out. Looks like he's passing instructions to someone, probably his son."

"No need to draw a crowd," Jack Miller called out, his thin gray hair blowing in the wind as he made his way to a waiting horse. "I'm coming out unarmed."

"Good," said Davis to the Rangers gathered around him, "Let's mount up and get out of here."

"Captain, I'm bringing one of my men with me if that's okay with you," called Miller.

"Just as long as he stays out of the way and doesn't cause any problems," replied Davis.

During the ride to town Miller reasoned that they couldn't have any witnesses to Briscoe's murder. It was just possible that Frank could get by on this one without going to jail. *He's so darn hotheaded,* Miller thought, picturing his son. *I've got to keep him away from them Rangers.*

Sheriff Briscoe's office was just as he had left it, full of wanted flyers that hadn't been posted and paperwork needing his signature. Captain Davis sat uneasily behind the sheriff's cluttered desk.

"It's important that we get to the bottom of Sheriff Briscoe's murder," Davis said as he looked up at Miller. Leroy leaned against the far wall while keeping an eye on Jake Wilson.

"Captain, I understand you being upset because a lawman is dead but when you wear a badge things like that tend to happen to you. Besides, he was past his prime so what do you expect?" Miller replied. "They'll pin his badge on one of his deputies and next week no one will even remember his name. In any case, it's none of my affair. I only agreed to come here to avoid shooting at the Bar N."

"Until we find out who ambushed Briscoe you and your men are under suspicion. Briscoe told me you threatened him."

"I wouldn't say I threatened him," Miller reached out to steady himself. "I told the sheriff to mind his own business and stay away from the Bar N. That's my right, considering it's my land."

"Unless I'm mistaken, your land is part of Texas and that put it under Briscoe's authority," Davis frowned. He noticed that the hired gunman named Wilson had placed his gun hand on his pistol.

The old man shrugged, and glanced toward the door. "This is a waste of time. If you've got nothing else to say, I'm going back to my ranch."

"I'll be at the Bar N tomorrow morning," Davis said, looking down and stacking the papers neatly on the dead sheriff's desk. "I'll want to talk to all your hands, including your son."

Miller stiffened and raised an eyebrow. He glanced at Jake Wilson, then turned and left the office, leaving the door ajar. His lips felt thick and his mouth dry. *They ain't gonna git my boy,* he thought. *They might die trying but they ain't gonna drag him here and put a rope around his neck.*

After Miller and his hired gun had left, Leroy slammed the door shut.

"We've got nothing on them," Davis sighed, obviously frustrated. "Unless we can find someway to put enough pressure on one of the hands to talk. Meantime, let's saddle up and ride to the Double D."

During the ride to the Double D, one of the older Rangers, Cal Freeman, began telling Leroy and several of the other new Rangers about his days fighting the Comanche. The young men listened intently. They knew that it was only a matter of time before they would face the Comanche warriors again in battle.

"To us white men, things are pretty clear, from God to sin. Everything's good or evil. But to the Indian, things are different. The Comanche believes he's connected to everything he sees, the earth, the sky, the sun and the moon. Heck, even the animals have some sort of religious meaning. Everything's a big mystery."

Leroy looked at Andy, then Willis. "I sure understand the God and sin part, but I ain't so sure about the rest of it."

Captain Davis turned in his saddle and chuckled. "That's because you're not a Comanche."

"Just hope you don't git close enough to ask one of 'em about it," Freeman said. "If a Comanche gets that close, he's probably gonna kill you so there's no reason to make him any madder than he already is by asking a stupid question."

"From what I hear they stay mad." Andy offered. "I never hear 'bout the Comanche unless they're murdering folks."

Cal Freeman looked at Davis, then smiled. "I reckon that's what they do for a living."

CHAPTER 27

Sheriff Briscoe had spoken of the gunfighters and problems he was having with the Bar N, but he was murdered before he had the opportunity to brief Captain Davis about the Double D Ranch. The double D was over two hundred miles long and thirty miles wide. Molly Darden, the daughter of a hero of the Texas Revolution owned the Double D. The ranch had been left to her after her folks were killed during an Indian raid. The ranch was all that was left of her parents and the land filled her heart with memories. Although there were more than enough suitors who would have loved to marry the pretty Texas gal and take charge of the ranch, Molly had never married.

Molly pushed her hair back from her face as she met the Rangers at the Double D's front gate. She was a small woman who wore leather chaps and carried herself with all the confidence of a man. It was immediately clear to the Rangers and anyone else who met her, Molly Darden was in charge of things at the Double D Ranch.

"Mornin'," Captain Davis said as he removed his hat and got down from his horse.

"I'm Molly Darden and this is my spread," she said while extending a hand to Captain Davis. "I heard about Sheriff Briscoe. It's a sad day in Texas when a lawman gets murdered like that. He was a good man and he helped me when I needed it."

"Glad to meet you ma'am," Davis tipped his hat, then reached for her outstretched hand. He looked past her and took in the adobe style ranch house and large stone bunkhouse. He decided to get right down to business.

"We were sent out here to try and work out the water sharing problem, but the killing of Sheriff Briscoe takes priority over everything else. If you could just settle your problems with the homesteaders and point us in the direction of whoever killed the sheriff we won't bother you anymore." He turned and gestured to the waiting Rangers, most of the men had dismounted and were patiently holding the reins of their tired horses. "These boys and I would like nothing better than to finish up our business here and ride on back to east Texas."

"Well, I'm afraid I can't help you with what you describe as 'the water sharing problem', because there ain't a problem. This is my land and my water flowing through it and the Double D needs all the water it can get during the dry months." Molly crossed her arms, tilted her head at an upward angle, and looked Davis directly in the eye. "I don't hold with violence, but I'll do whatever I have to in order to protect what's mine."

"What about the homesteaders?" Davis asked.

"Give 'em an inch, they'll take a mile," she replied. "I agree with the Bar N on that." Molly shook her head decisively. "But like I said, I don't hold with killing, especially a lawman."

"That's good to hear," Leroy whispered to Willis. "I'll bet you that filly can hit what she aims at."

Willis was shocked to hear the lady use language like a common cowhand. He turned and answered Leroy in a low voice, "I don't plan to find out. She looks tougher than a woodpecker's lips."

It was all Leroy could do to keep from laughing out loud. "Where did you ever hear a saying like that?" he whispered.

Willis didn't honor him with a reply.

"How did you learn about Briscoe's death?" asked Captain Davis.

"Around here bad news travels mighty fast," Molly peered around Davis in order to take a long look at the company of Rangers. "If you want to find out who killed Sheriff Briscoe, then ride over and park yourselves at the Bar N. While you're at it, you might as well send for help 'cause it's gonna be a long wait. They ain't about to give any of their boys up without a fight. Old man Miller is tough as rawhide."

"You think one of their hands did it?" Davis asked, a deep frown forming across his thin eyebrows.

"Probably not one of the hired help," Molly walked over to size up Leroy and Willis who were standing behind Davis. "But if I made a guess, I'd say that old man Miller's son did it himself. He had a grudge against Briscoe, and I doubt he has the same attitude I have about not wanting to kill a lawman. I'd hate to have him draw down on me."

Davis stiffened. "The authorities in Austin want this problem ended peaceful and ended now."

"That's why they sent you?" Molly said in a firm voice.

"Yes," Davis replied. "My men will be escorting the homesteaders across Double D land as soon as we clear up Sheriff Briscoe's murder."

"I told you that you're at the wrong place to find out who killed the sheriff. You better ride over to the Bar N and confront Miller. Then," she chuckled, "if there's any of you Rangers still in the saddle, I'll show you where to cross to Noland's River. I don't intend to start no war with the governor in Austin."

"I appreciate your help," Davis tipped his hat again, smiled his most friendly smile, then turned and walked back to his waiting horse. *Well, that was a lot easier than I expected. I'm surprised she backed down so quickly,* he thought.

Before they rode off, Captain Davis addressed his men. "It appears that we're gonna be jumping from the frying pan to the fire. Mr. Miller might not be willing to put up a fight over homesteaders crossing his land, but you can bet he'll darn sure fight to keep his boy from hanging."

Leroy thought, *Can't say that I'd blame him, that's what my Pa would do.*

"Mount up, we're riding back over to the Bar N," Davis ordered as he grasped the saddle horn and pulled himself onto his big appaloosa stallion.

"Here we go," Willis said in a low voice to Leroy. "I guess this is where we start earning our pay."

The ride to the Bar N was uneventful. Leroy took note of a few patches of wildflowers so he would have something to tell Mindy when he returned home to Starrville.

None of the gunmen were standing guard at the gate so Davis led the Rangers up to the main house. Davis slowly dismounted and walked up the steps toward the front door. Just as his boot hit the porch, Jack Miller opened the front door and stepped out onto the porch holding a loaded shotgun.

"That's far enough," Miller roared, his voice filled with fire. "Nobody invited you here and you got no right to ride up to my door without being asked."

Davis motioned with his head and several of the Rangers, including Leroy, dismounted and walked up to the porch to back up their captain. "I mean to talk to your boy, Mr. Miller, either here or in town, it's your call."

"What do you want with him?" Miller held the shotgun close as he spoke.

"That's between him and me," Davis answered defiantly. He casually reached up to tilt his hat back. "It's a hot day, isn't it?"

"Always hot this time of year," Miller replied. He lifted his eyebrows and learned forward. "I'd appreciate your telling me what you want to talk to my boy about. He ain't done nothing."

"That remains to be seen. Bring him out here," Davis commanded. "Now."

Jack Miller turned around and called out. "Tell Frank to come to the door."

Two of the Bar N's hired guns stepped out on the porch. "He's coming."

Frank Miller, wearing his gun belt low, walked past his father and stood face to face with Davis. "I got nothing to say."

"About what?" Davis glared at the young man. "I've been told there was bad blood between you and the sheriff," Davis kept his eyes on the younger man's face. "That true?"

"Only when that old man meddled in Bar N business. You might say we had a falling out." Miller chuckled and turned to see the effect on his father. Jack Miller was not pleased.

"Did you kill Sheriff Briscoe?" Captain Davis spat out the words.

Jack Miller eyed his son closely, then looked at Davis. "He didn't do no such thing."

"I'm waiting for his answer, not yours," Davis replied calmly.

"I ain't about to disagree with my Pa," Frank Miller said sarcastically.

"Then you're coming with us," Davis jerked his thumb back toward the waiting Rangers. He turned to Jack Miller and added, "Get his horse saddled."

"I ain't letting you take him in," Miller said defiantly. "If you want bloodshed, that's exactly what you'll get."

Davis paused a moment before he spoke. "I intend to take him one way or another. The way I see it, your boy murdered a lawman so it don't matter much to me if I take him in dead or alive. Like I told you before, it's your call."

Leroy and the other members of the Ranger Company prepared to draw.

"Hold on now," Jack said angrily. "You ain't getting by with this."

"I'll go with 'em," his son stepped forward. "No need shootin' up the Bar N." He turned to Davis and asked, "Mind if I have a word or two with my Pa, then I'll go with you fellows quietly."

Davis hesitated. "Drop your gun belt where you stand. As long as you stay in plain sight, I'll let you have a minute but not more than that."

"That's a mistake," Willis whispered to Leroy.

"I think you're right about that, but it's not our call," Leroy replied in a low voice.

Jack Miller and his son walked slowly to the far side of the porch and began talking in whispers so that the Rangers couldn't hear. Davis watched them closely. Leroy and the other Rangers kept their eyes on the bunkhouse and the nearby barn.

"There's two of 'em coverin' us over yonder by the corral," Leroy whispered to Willis.

"I see 'em," Willis replied. "You can add three more hidden behind the bunkhouse."

Leroy slowly turned his body enough to get a clear view of the bunkhouse. *No need wasting time turning if I have to draw down on those buzzards,* he thought.

"That's enough time," Davis called out. To his surprise, Frank Miller turned and faced him with a smile on his face.

"Ready when you are, Captain," he said. Frank Miller resembled his father. Both men had ruddy complexions with wide set eyes and broad shoulders. The younger Miller's arms filled the sleeves of his work shirt. It was obvious that although he was the boss's son, he did his share of the hard work required to run a ranch the size of the Bar N.

Jack Miller stood still, glaring at Captain Davis. The old man nodded his head toward one of the Bar N gunmen and a saddled horse was brought around to the hitching post near the porch.

Captain Davis and one of the senior Rangers, Clem Roberts, rode in front, followed by Miller, who had half a dozen Rangers surrounding him. Leroy and Willis brought up the rear.

"Keep a sharp lookout for trouble," Roberts told Leroy as they rode away from the Bar N. "If you see anything that looks out of the ordinary, tell me or the Captain."

Clem Roberts had been a Texas Ranger nearly as long as Captain Davis. He was a slightly built man nearing forty with thin brown hair and a thick salt and pepper beard. He seldom spoke, but when he did, the young Rangers listened to his every word.

Half way to town the smooth, well-traveled road went through a wooded area with sloping hills on either side. Large boulders formed the base of the hill on the right, while smaller rocks rose up toward the crest of the steep hill on the left. Along this stretch the road became so narrow the Rangers had to ride in single file.

"If this ain't one heck of a place for an ambush, nothin' is," Leroy said to Willis.

Willis frowned. "That's for sure. I wonder why the Captain doesn't take the long way around. Even a half a day's ride would be worth it just to avoid this place."

Leroy sensed danger. He looked at the rocks then glanced forward to see how Captain Davis and Clem Roberts were reacting to the situation. Both were looking from side to side with worried expressions on their faces. Suddenly, Davis pointed to the rocks. Immediately Roberts whirled his horse around and reached for Miller's mount.

Andy stood up in his saddle in an attempt to see over the cluster of rocks. "Hey Leroy, I just seen…." His words drifted away in the wind as the crackling sound of rifle fire filled the small valley.

"Take cover!" Davis yelled. He turned in time to see Andy fall from his horse, clutching his stomach.

Leroy felt a sudden tightness in his chest as Andy hit the ground. He wanted to ride into the middle of the ambush to do what he could to help his friend, but every instinct told him that would be the wrong thing to do. *I'll get to him as soon as I can. I can't do him any good if I get shot too.*

As soon as the shooting started, Frank Miller bent forward, his head touching the horse's neck, and drove his spurs into the ribs of the fastest horse on the Bar N Ranch. He raced past the Rangers like he'd been shot from a cannon while gunfire erupted all around them. Captain Davis raised his rifle intending to shoot Miller before he got away but just as he was squeezing the trigger, a musket ball slammed into his chest. The Ranger Captain fell from his horse, mortally wounded.

"Good God Almighty!" shouted Clem, the most senior Ranger in rank after Davis. "We're all gonna die if we don't find cover."

Seconds later, a bullet blew the back of Clem's head off. The only cover was the cluster of rocks—the same rocks that the rifle shots were coming from. The Rangers tried to dismount and take cover behind their horses, but most of the horses bolted and ran. The men were only able to get two of the mounts on the ground.

Leroy realized that somebody had to do something to save the remaining Rangers or they would be killed. He saw that there was no way to get behind the hired gunmen, but if he could get to get the bushwhackers in a crossfire. Taking a quick look at the terrain, Leroy decided the only way to outflank the ambush was to ride back in the direction they had come from then make his way back along the ridgeline without being detected. As Leroy raced through a hail of gunfire, he saw Willis riding behind him.

"Leroy and Willis have run out on us," Jack Morris yelled from behind his fallen horse.

"Maybe they're riding for help," said another hidden Ranger.

Jack Morris was a big man, over six feet. He realized that his dead horse was not going to be enough cover to protect them from the rifle fire. He took off his big cowboy hat and raised his head just enough to see where the gunmen were hiding.

"They ain't got time to find anybody to help us," yelled Morris. He had poured water from his canteen onto a bright red handkerchief and was trying to wrap it around his head. "Billy, I'm grazed, most of the other boys are down with one kind of wound or another. I tell you, we can't hold out for long."

Before Billy or any of the other Rangers could answer, Jack's handkerchief proved to be a target. As he reached for his hat, a musket ball slammed into his forehead knocking him backwards onto the dusty trail.

"Good God Almighty!" Billy gasped as he was splattered in blood from Jack's fatal head wound. . The Rangers were being struck down one by one as rifle fire continued to rain down on them from behind the rocks.

Leroy and Willis quickly dismounted and started moving as fast as they could along the ridgeline in the direction of the rocks. They crouched low, carrying their rifles. Leroy led the way, rock by rock until they reached a hilltop overlooking the ambush site. Fire and smoke came from the rocks below. Leroy thought he counted ten men, Willis counted eleven.

"I swear I saw more than eleven of 'em, Leroy!" Willis said in an excited voice.

"Maybe the others took off with Miller. It don't matter right now," Leroy replied. "We ain't got time to worry 'bout how many of 'em are shooting at us." He checked his rifle and pistol, and then said, "Let's get this done."

"I may live to regret this, but I'm gonna be right behind you," Willis answered, shaking his head.

Leroy couldn't help but chuckle. "Just as long as you *do* live to regret it, Willis. Then you got no reason to complain."

Leroy and Willis rose up from behind a pair of boulders and began firing at the startled Bar N gunmen. Seeing Leroy and Willis, the Rangers who had survived the ambush rushed toward the rocks. Several gunmen tried to flee but were cut down in a hail of bullets. After the last gunman was taken care of, the two young Rangers rejoined their comrades.

"Captain Davis is dead, so is Clem," Willis sighed. "What are we gonna do now?"

"The way I see it," Leroy began speaking calmly in his slow east Texas drawl. "We've got to split up in order to see this through. There are only ten of us left who ain't shot up. Billy, you and the others need to get them that need help to a doctor. Willis and I will go after Frank Miller. He's the one who caused all this trouble in the first place."

Willis let out a loud sigh, followed by a groan. He reached up and pushed back his hat.

Leroy continued, ignoring his friend's reaction to his plan. "After you take care of the wounded, you high tail it to Ranger Headquarters so they can send some more men out here to finish the job."

"We'll get moving as soon as we can," Billy said while slowly moving to the middle of the road. He looked around in vain for the their horses. "After we gather up the horses, we need to take the wounded with us and ride. I want to be out of here before anymore of the Bar N gunmen show up."

Leroy nodded. With that, the Rangers prepared to move out.

CHAPTER 28

"How come you and me are the ones going after Miller?" Willis asked as they rode past scrub brush and some prickly pears that were badly in need of water.

Leroy grinned. "'Cause I knew you wanted to make a name for yourself so you could move right up through the ranks and make captain in a hurry."

"Right," Willis said while shaking his head. "All I know is that if you keep sticking our necks out like this, sooner or later someone is gonna knock 'em off."

Willis and Leroy rode in a steady gallop to the Bar N Ranch. They took cover in a cluster of cottonwood trees overlooking the impressive gate that led to the main houses. From there, they had a clear view of the ranch house.

"Think he's inside the house?" Willis asked.

"Unless he knew a shortcut, he ain't had time to git home and git what he needs to make a run for it," Leroy replied. "When he comes out, you can bet he won't be alone. The way I see it, old man Miller has to be worrying about getting him out of the state. He's probably planning to send his murderin' boy up to the Indian Territory or out west to the badlands in the New Mexico Territory."

"Then what do we do?" Willis asked.

"I've got a mind to do the same thing to them that they did to us," Leroy answered slowly. "I figure we ought to bushwhack 'em."

"Leroy," Willis said, his impatience showing. "Them fellows know the lay of the land. That's how we got into this mess in the first place. How you gonna figure out where to ambush 'em?"

"Shhhh," Leroy slipped down low behind the tree and gestured toward the bunkhouse. "They're coming out now."

"Darn it!" Willis exclaimed. "There's four of 'em."

"Three sorry paid gunmen and one coward that bushwhacks old men," Leroy said disgustedly. "If we can't take them out, we ought to find another line of work."

"Says you," Willis responded.

"Come on," Leroy said, his voice filled with concern. "We gotta git the horses and hightail it 'fore they see us."

Hiding behind trees and holding their horse's noses to keep them quiet, Leroy and Willis watched the Bar N gunmen escort Frank Miller away from the ranch. The four men headed due north. Leroy and Willis checked their saddle cinches and mounted their mustangs. Leroy was fairly confident that the Bar N gunmen would leave an easy trail to follow so he decided to give them a head start.

They followed Miller and the hired guns onto a rutted, narrow path that led to a shallow river crossing. Leroy wondered if the men were going to camp for the night or keep riding. *If they're gonna stop, it'll be here where they can get water,* he thought. Much to his chagrin, the gunmen rode on, pushing their tired, thirsty horses across the river. Leroy motioned to Willis to halt.

"Them darn fools might want to run their horses to death but not us. They ain't going no where we can't find 'em so let's rest a spell."

"All right by me," Willis agreed in a tired voice. He eagerly climbed off his mustang, gave the horse a pat on the neck and led him down the sloping riverbank.

Leroy took a few minutes and tried to come up with a plan. He knew that he couldn't afford to make a mistake. The gun fighters would probably stay with Miller until they got him out of Texas and beyond the reach of the Texas Rangers.

"But where?" he thought aloud.

"Where to hit 'em?" Willis asked.

Leroy wasn't aware he had spoken. "Huh?" He took his eyes off the drinking horses to meet his friend's gaze. "Yeah, that's exactly what I mean. We can't let 'em leave Texas."

"Leroy," Willis said. "Them buzzards are gonna go on north to the Indian Territory, not to New Mexico."

"What makes you think that?" Leroy questioned as he gently rubbed his mustang's front legs and checked to make sure the horse hadn't thrown a shoe.

"Just a feelin' I guess," Willis pulled a pouch of smoking tobacco from the inside pocket of his vest. "I know that's where I'd go if I was on the run. I'd go right smack up through the Territory into Kansas, maybe turn east toward Missouri," Willis looked at Leroy. "I'm just thinking."

"Well, Willis," Leroy chuckled. "Let's go find out where them bushwhackin' buzzards are heading."

He threw his leg over the mustang's back and pulled the reins left. Willis followed without saying another word.

"Tonight," mumbled Leroy as they rode up the gentle slope. "We'll take 'em out tonight, then we'll head north and deliver Miller to the United States Marshall in Fort Worth."

Leroy figured it was either the gusting wind or plain old fatigue that made Miller and the gunmen finally stop and make camp. They rolled out blankets and plopped their saddles down so they could rest their heads. One of the men watered the horses in a shallow creek, then set up a picket line that would allow the horses room enough to graze. The two young Rangers crept silently onto a small overhang and hid in a cluster of vines. They watched the gunmen make camp and build a big fire.

"Not a good idea when you're on the run," he whispered to Willis.

"That shows us they ain't got a clue they're being followed," Willis whispered back.

"Let's get back to the horses and plan what we're gonna do," Leroy carefully shoved his body back behind the bluff.

"Leroy," Willis said once they had made their way back to the horses. "Did you get a good look at them vines?"

"No," Leroy frowned. "Why?"

"Ain't there something said about leaves of three? Well, if there is, them vines had three leaves on each little twig. Ain't that supposed to be poison ivy or something?"

"Naaaah," Leroy assured him. "I didn't take a good look at anything but them buzzard's campsite, but I don't think we was hiding in no poison ivy or poison oak."

"Good," said Willis. "I don't wanna be scratching all the way back to Starrville."

"Forget about the poison ivy, let's concentrate on getting Miller," Leroy said. "Now, here's what I think we ought to do." He sat down and took a long drink from his canteen, then handed it to Willis.

"We'll wait until sometime before dawn, maybe around four o'clock. I'll sneak up on 'em, then you move in when I get their weapons moved to the far side of their camp. One of them low life rascals carries a double-barreled shotgun. That's the weapon I plan on using when we wake 'em up."

Willis shook his head, "How will I know when to cover you?"

"I'll give you a signal. I want you covering the three sleeping on the far side of the fire. I'll aim that shotgun right at Miller's head. None of them are gonna wanna face old man Miller if his boy gets killed here in Texas."

"They ain't gonna wanna face old man Miller regardless. I figure the old man will pay whatever it takes to hunt 'em down. That's why they'll put up a fight for that boy if we give them half a chance. You can bet on it."

"I am betting you're wrong and I'm right," Leroy grinned. "You better hope I'm right because I'm betting your hide and mine."

"Why did I let you talk me into this?" Willis sighed. "I should have stayed with the boys burying Andy and the others. As bad as that would have been, I'd still be breathing after I finished the job."

Leroy hadn't had time to mourn the loss of Andy and the other Rangers. He knew he'd have to deal with that later, but right now he had a job to do and besides, he was angry. He couldn't allow himself to be distracted until he brought Frank Miller to justice.

Willis watched as Leroy circled the campsite, then slowly crept up to each snoring man and gently removed his rifle and gun belt. It took almost a half an hour to completely disarm the sleeping gunmen. Willis held his breath, afraid that one of the gunmen would wake up and catch Leroy in the act. After Leroy lifted the shotgun from the last of the gunmen and moved around the campfire to where Frank Miller was sleeping soundly, he nodded to Willis and pointed the shotgun directly at Miller's head.

"All right, wake up you yellow bellies and don't make no sudden moves or old man Miller is going to puke when he sees what's left of his boy's brain," Leroy shouted. "That is, if he's got any brains, which I doubt."

The gunmen sat up at first confused and disoriented.

"Don't even think about doing nothin' stupid," Willis called out. "We've got you covered."

Miller began frantically looking for a way to escape. Leroy saw him squirming and looking around so he closed the distance between them and pressed the end of the double-barreled shotgun against the back of his head.

"You ain't gonna look too good without a head," Leroy said quietly. "Of course, you don't look too good anyhow."

In spite of the situation they were in, Willis couldn't help but chuckle.

Keeping his eyes directly on Miller, Leroy said, "If any of you are getting trigger happy, just remember what's gonna happen to Miller. It's only gonna take one barrel to kill him. That leaves me one more for anyone who wants it."

"You'll pay for this buddy," one of the gunmen said. "If we don't get you, old man Miller will."

"Old man Miller," Leroy said in a low, menacing voice, "is gonna have so much trouble coming his way that he ain't gonna have time to worry about me."

"You boys better git while the gittin' is good," Willis said. "We're runnin' outta time and patience."

The gun fighters looked at each other. It didn't take them long to realize that the cards were stacked against them. Slowly, keeping their hands raised, one by one they reached for their boots and got to their feet.

"Just leave them boots where they are," Leroy said.

"You can't make us walk out of here with no guns or boots," a tall, lanky gunfighter pleaded. "The Comanche have been raiding all up and down these parts."

"Walk for one hour, then turn around and come back," Leroy said. "We'll leave the boots along the creek bank."

"How we gonna find 'em?" asked the tall gunman.

"That's your problem, ain't it?" Willis said.

"The boots will be due north, on the other side of the creek," Leroy added.

"Damn you to hell," Miller hissed

"Now watch your mouth, Mr. Miller," Leroy said, his voice breaking into a chuckle. "I was gonna be right nice to you, being that you're probably facing the end of a rope when we get where we're going, but there's nothing that says I have to. If I were you, I'd move real careful and not cause me any worry or this here shotgun just might go off. If that happens, you've reached the end of the trail, no questions asked. Whereas, if you live to stand trial, well, there is a chance your pappy can git you off. Who knows?"

Miller began gathering his pants and boots while the three gunmen started walking away from the campsite. Willis watched their every move, ready to fire if any one of them made a wrong move.

After throwing the gunfighters weapons into the creek and hiding their boots, Leroy and Willis tied Miller securely to the saddle horn and began their trip to Fort Worth. They didn't tell Miller where they were going. He didn't seem to care. He just sat slumped over the saddle and mumbled one threat after another about what he was going to do with the two of 'em once his daddy caught up to them.

"He'll hire more fellows if he has to," Miller said nastily. "But one way or the other he'll git even with the likes of you."

Leroy and Willis tried to ignore him. They rode on in silence, sometimes talking about the land and the best way to traverse the difficult trail. They were determined not to make the same mistake the gunfighters had. The first rule they learned when they became Rangers was to always move with caution and expect the unexpected to happen anytime.

"Just when you think things are going well," Captain Davis had said many times, "that's when all hell's gonna break lose."

Leroy could hear the dead captain's words as they made their way under bright stars and a full moon. They rested the horses and took frequent breaks, but setting up camp was out of the question. They intended to ride on, as long as they could stay in the saddle.

CHAPTER 29

With Miller slumped over his horse, they rode across gentle hills covered with dry pale green and brown grass. Leroy and Willis had long since stopped talking to pass the time as the miles stretched by under a light blue Texas sky. The young Rangers took time to rest their mounts but not themselves.

As soon as Leroy saw the Comanche war party ride over a rise to their left he knew it was too late to avoid a fight. In single file, the Comanche warriors rode at an easy gallop. In less than a minute they had closed the distance between the three white men and appeared ready to charge.

"Hell's bells," Willis said. "How long have they been up there on that ridgeline?"

"They just showed themselves," Leroy answered, his voice filled with concern. "But I figure they've been following us for awhile."

"We can't out run 'em," Willis said as he looked at the long line of warriors. "Right now, neither the horses or us could out run a polecat."

"Well, we damn sure ain't in a position to fight 'em. There's at least fifteen of 'em which means there's probably ten more up ahead of us."

"Cut me loose goddamnit," Miller cried.

Leroy pulled out his pocketknife and leaned over to cut the ropes that tied Miller to the saddle horn. "If you wait a few minutes, those fellows will do it for you right after they use their knife on your scalp."

"Which will be just after they finish with us," Willis groaned.

"Let's go boys," Leroy pulled his hat low on his forehead.

Just as he was about to spur his mustang, a group of Comanche rode out from behind the trees to their right, arrows and rifles aimed at the three men. Leroy whirled from side to side in his saddle only to see more Indians blocking the trail ahead. One of the Indians motioned for the men to dismount.

"We're done for. You stupid sonsofbitches," Miller growled. "Texas Rangers my ass. You two don't know nothing."

Leroy could not remember feeling so low. He knew that right about now the Comanche would probably agree with Miller.

Slowly, Leroy climbed down from his horse. Willis and Miller followed his lead. The Comanche moved forward, pointing their rifles at the three men and motioning for them to drop their weapons.

"We should have made a break for it," Miller said. "We had nothing to lose."

"Shut up," Leroy ordered.

All of a sudden the Indians began shouting and waving their rifles and bows high above their heads. Suddenly, a dozen braves surrounded the three captives. The Comanche shoved, punched and kicked their victims until the men fell to the ground. Leroy had never felt so helpless in his life. Leroy knew that if he fought back they would probably kill him on the spot. Each kick and punch seemed to hurt more than the one before. Leroy tried to protect his head at the expense of his ribs and back. Out of the corner of his eye, Leroy could see Willis was being rolled in the dirt. Leroy had no idea what was happening to Miller.

As he drifted into darkness, a vision of Mindy appeared before him, clear as day, she was wearing a yellow dress with blue ribbons. His last conscious thought was, *is this what it's like to die?* Then he finally stopped feeling pain and drifted into a black cave filled with blinking stars.

"Leroy," he heard Willis mumble over and over again. "Leroy, you gotta come to."

Why, Leroy thought. He could barely move and when he did a sharp pain stabbed at his ribcage. Slowly, his blurred vision cleared. He moved his head so he could see what had happened to Willis and

Miller. All three of them were tied to trees not too far from a roaring fire. The fire was close enough for him to feel the heat of the flames against his legs and bare feet. He looked down and for a moment he wondered how he had lost his boots. Then, the memories of the day's events and the realization of what was probably about to take place swept over him. For a moment Leroy thought he was going to be sick.

"Not in front of these savages," he whispered to himself.

"Leroy, that you talking?" Willis called out.

Leroy could only manage a slight nod of his head. He could hear Miller moaning and crying. *Can't say that I blame him. As sorry as he is, he doesn't deserve being murdered by a bunch of darn Comanche.*

As far as Leroy could tell, none of the Comanche spoke English. He sure didn't speak Comanche so he remained quiet. It was a helpless feeling. He tried to think of any possible way to escape but he doubted that the opportunity would arise. He didn't know about Willis, but he was tied so tight, the ropes were cutting into his flesh.

Leroy's attention was suddenly drawn to a tall Indian warrior covered in war paint. He wore buckskin pants without a shirt and a vest decorated with what looked like some kind of animal bones. He walked straight to Willis. Leroy couldn't see what was happening. The tree holding Willis was slightly behind the rough pine that Leroy was tied to. He heard Willis grunt. Then the Indian stepped in front of Leroy. *I sure wish I could give that sonofabitch a push back into that fire,* Leroy thought.

The Comanche warrior moved close, his face directly in front of Leroy. Leroy braced for the worst. *Maybe he'll use a knife. At least that would be better than burning in that fire.*

Leroy decided he had nothing to lose. He glared at the Indian and waited to see what his response would be. Suddenly, Leroy heard a scream, he was sure the cry was coming from Miller but he was determined not to take his eyes off the Comanche in front of him. He continued to meet the warrior's eyes.

The Comanche dropped his head back, laughed, and then walked away. Leroy couldn't believe it; he thought the Indian was about to cut him to pieces. His relief was short lived when he saw that the Indians were preparing to roast Miller on top of the bonfire, his fear returned. *I'm probably next,* he thought.

To his credit Miller was putting up one heck of a fight. Not realizing how strong Miller was, the Indians had made the mistake of cutting his ropes without first securing his hands and feet. Indians were flying in all directions as Miller kicked and punched his attackers.

"Leroy," Willis called out. "This may be our only chance."

"What chance?" Leroy replied sarcastically. "These darn Injuns have me so hogtied, I can't move much less defend myself."

"Well, I can," Willis said, "wiggle around some, I mean."

"Can you get lose?" Leroy asked, a hint of desperation in his voice.

"I just might be able to," Willis whispered. "I'm trying my best."

Leroy's eyes were fixed on the crowd of screaming Indians while he prayed that Willis would be able to get out of the restraints.

"Hurry, Willis," Leroy pleaded. "For God's sake, hurry up! I don't know how much longer Miller can hold out."

Leroy felt hands frantically working to loosen the ropes that were holding his body against the tree.

"I don't rightly know how it happened, but I think the Injuns that tied me up were drunk," Willis, obviously short on breath, whispered from behind the tree.

"Darn it, Willis," Leroy moaned. "I don't care if they were drunk or not. What matters is that because you're free we got a chance to get out of here. It may be a slight chance, but it's all we got so shut up and undo these ropes."

Willis ignored Leroy and kept talking. "Boy, the Injun who tied you up really meant business."

Leroy rolled his eyes. Panic covered him like a cold wind when he saw two Indians running toward Miller, both carrying spears.

"Miller won't hold out much longer Willis. It's now or never."

Leroy almost fell forward when the ropes dropped to his feet. He whirled, met Willis eye to eye, then the two Rangers began to run. Leroy had never run like this before in his life. At one point he stumbled and fell to the ground, he immediately got up and continued to run. While gasping for air, they were determined to put as much distance between themselves and the Indian camp. As luck would have it, they came to a river. Without slowing down, the two of them jumped in and started swimming with the current downstream. They tumbled over rocks and Willis was sure he touched a couple of snakes, but the men kept on going. Leroy didn't know how long they fought the water but eventually, the river slowed and the two exhausted men crawled up a muddy bank.

"Dear Lord," Willis whispered while gasping for air. "I thought we were done for."

It took a moment for Leroy to gather enough breath to speak. "We would have been, if it hadn't been for you." He turned toward Willis. "I'll always be grateful to you for saving my life."

Even though he was still breathing hard, Willis managed a chuckle. "Heck, it probably won't be the last time and I'm betting you'll pay me back. Actually, it was the bad liquor them Injuns was drinking that saved us both." Then he paused a moment before adding, "What do you think they would have done with us?"

Leroy shook his head. "Same thing they were trying to do to Miller."

"God help him," Willis said. His voice was filled with genuine sadness. "No one deserves to die like that."

"It was our job to get him to Fort Worth. I feel mighty low."

"We took on a lot," Willis said. "I guess we did all we could."

"That ain't how old man Miller is gonna see things," Leroy sighed. "He's gonna look at the facts. You and I got out, his son didn't."

"I don't wanna think about it and besides that, we ain't out of this mess yet," Willis replied. "I wanna git on home to Smith County."

"We've gotta report," Leroy said. "That means we need to go on to Fort Worth."

"How?" Willis asked. "We got no horses, no boots, no food and nothing to carry water with either,"

"Want to go back and see if we can borrow some grub from the Comanche?" Leroy chuckled.

"Stop kidding around now, Leroy. I ain't in the mood."

After resting a few minutes, Leroy and Willis got to their feet and began walking. They tried to get their bearings by looking up at the stars sprinkled over the big Texas sky. Hungry and sore, they headed to the northeast in the general direction of Fort Worth. On foot and walking without boots, they were moving so slowly that Leroy's main concern was finding food and water.

The next morning dawned clear and crisp. Leroy woke up tired, aching all over and hungry. He didn't remember falling asleep.

"There's a stream over there," Willis pointed north.

Leroy raised his head and turned toward Willis. "How long have you been awake?"

"Not that long," Willis answered. "I woke up hungry and thirsty. I don't mind waking up hungry, I'm used to it but I'm not used to waking up with a parched throat."

"How far?" Leroy asked.

"Over that hill. I'd say about a half a mile."

"You went that far without waking me?"

"Yep," Willis said, his voice flat. "I was mighty thirsty."

"Let's go," Leroy pushed himself up and started toward the hill.

"Wish we had something to carry it in," Willis gestured toward the cloudless sky. "It's gonna be a hot one."

Leroy nodded and kept walking toward the stream.

Late that afternoon, they rested under a cluster of trees. The shade felt good and a cool breeze blowing from the north filled their shirts and fluffed their dirty hair. Willis had fallen asleep. Leroy swallowed hard. He still felt bad about Miller being murdered by the Comanche. *It was my fault that he was captured by the Comanche,* he thought. *I shouldn't have let it happen.*

Leroy promised himself if he managed to survive this encounter with the Comanche, he would never again allow himself to be captured alive by any Indian.

Scanning the horizon he saw three riders coming toward the trees.

"Indians, Willis," he whispered as he pulled his friend's arm. "Coming right at us, too." He quickly rolled over and hid behind the tree he had been leaning against.

"Willis, for God's sake," Leroy hissed. "Wake up."

"I heard you," Willis said as he crawled behind the nearest scrub bush. "Think they're Comanche?

"If they are, we're finished. They've seen us and they're heading this way."

"I never did have much faith that we'd make it," Willis sighed. "Odds were against us."

"Willis," Leroy's voice was filled with resolve. "They ain't takin' us back to no camp. If we gotta die, we die here. And we're gonna put up one heck of a fight before we go down."

Willis was straining to get a good look at the oncoming riders. "Wait, Leroy," he said. "Them Injuns are wearing soldier's shirts."

"That means they're either army scouts or Comanche who wiped out some yellow legs," Leroy said.

"They ain't Comanche," Willis shook his head. "They ain't yellin' and shootin' at us."

"We'll wait and see," Leroy replied. "There's only three of 'em so we have a chance. When they get near us, I plan on taking one of 'em off his horse."

As the riders approached, Leroy had a glimmer of hope when he saw they were riding on saddles, and their rifles were not in their hands but still in holders attached to the side of their saddles.

"They're scouts," Willis said hopefully. "Thank God."

Only then did Leroy stand. He followed Willis, who had already left the cover of the bushes and was walking toward the approaching Indians.

"What are you two doing out here?" called out one of the Indians. His English carried only the slightest accent.

"We're Rangers," Leroy answered. "We were ambushed." Although he had been told most of the tribes didn't like the Comanche, he decided not to elaborate.

"We can send help," the Indian answered. "But that's all we can do. We don't have any extra horses and it's too far to ride double."

"Where are you boys going?" Willis asked.

"Fort Belknap," the Indian answered.

When the Indian dismounted, Leroy decided he was probably a Kiowa scout. The man was well built and Leroy's height, just under six feet. The other scouts remained on their horses, watching Willis and Leroy without expression. Willis noticed that they all looked well fed.

"Can you keep going for a couple of days?" the Indian asked as he looked at Leroy's torn clothing and bare feet.

"If you can spare some food we'll make it," Leroy said.

The Kiowa hesitated.

Leroy added, "Anything will do. We're pretty hungry."

"I can leave you some beef jerky and a couple of canteens," the Indian said and without turning away from the Rangers, he gestured to one of the other scouts.

Willis walked over to the scout's horse and reached up to accept a small canvas bag and a US Army issued canteen. The horses had US Army brands and the saddles were light cavalry saddles. *Heck, the Army takes better care of them scouts than the state of Texas does us. We have to supply our own mounts and even our rifles and cartridges.*

"Much obliged," Leroy said as the Kiowa handed him a canteen.

"Walk due north," the Kiowa pointed to the sun. "One day's walk you should come to Carney Springs Station. They'll have horses and food for sale there."

As if we got money, Leroy thought. He grinned at the Indian. "We better get started."

At that moment, one of the scouts, who had been silent during the entire meeting, reached into his saddlebags and without saying a word, tossed Leroy a pair of buckskin moccasins. In spite of how Leroy felt about Indians at that moment, he could have hugged the scout. Willis stared at Leroy and then looked up at the mounted Indian, a hopeful expression on his weathered face. The Indian ignored Willis and tapped the sides of his horse, then rode away with the two other scouts.

"Gol-darn it!" Willis shouted. "Why didn't that sorry critter give me a pair of them stinking moccasins?"

Leroy laughed. "Looks like you're out of luck, Willis."

"My feet are hurting me so bad I can't stand it," Willis sat down, as mad as he could be. He felt like hitting Leroy upside the head when he saw Leroy slipping on the moccasins. *So much for saving his life.*

"Friendship only goes so far, Willis. You'll have to make do."

"Make do?" Willis snarled. "Make do with what? Blisters?"

"Willis," Leroy spoke, trying to console his friend. "I'm sorry them Injuns didn't give you no shoes but that's not my fault."

"I know. I just wish one of 'em would have had an extra pair for me."

"Maybe that Injun was the only one who carried an extra pair. I can promise you I'll never go anywhere without a pair of these here Injun shoes in my saddlebags. A fellow is out of luck if he loses his boots."

"You can say that again, Leroy," Willis groaned, his anger already gone.

"I said, a fellow is out of luck if he loses his boots," Leroy repeated his words.

Willis glared at Leroy. "I didn't really mean for you to tell me all over again."

Leroy grinned, then reached over to give his friend a playful shove before adding insult to injury, "Them Injuns sure know how to make a good pair of shoes. I ain't never had such a soft covering for my feet."

"Gol-darn them Indians and you too," Willis snarled.

The Rangers walked, rested, and then walked until sunset. That night they camped by a small creek where Leroy tried to make a spear out of a broken tree branch. The Comanche had taken his pocketknife so he doubted that he could make the spear sharp enough to kill any fish. After breaking several branches, he took the sharpest one and handed it to Willis.

"I'll build a fire. You try to get us a fish."

"With this?" Willis held up the broken tree branch.

"Willis, I'm sorry I don't have a proper fishing pole with me. Next time I'll try to remember to bring one," Leroy replied sarcastically. He was getting fed up with his companion's constant complaining.

"Why don't you try to catch some darn fish and let me make the fire," Willis asked. "You'd probably do better than me."

"Can't do it," Leroy said while holding up his hands. "I'm not about to get my brand new Injun shoes wet in that creek."

"Leroy, it ain't as if them shoes haven't got wet before. You know how Injuns are. They wade through creeks all the time."

Leroy lifted his foot to show off the worn buckskin. "They look in pretty good shape to me."

Willis turned his back to Leroy but before he began walking towards the creek he spoke to his friend, "I've got a gal waiting for me back in Smith County and before I left she said she'd marry me. I sure hope she ain't changed her mind. You know who I'm talking about, don't you, Leroy?"

"Sure I do," Leroy chuckled. "Everybody knows you're sweet on Patsy."

Willis turned to face Leroy. His expression was one of concern. "How'd you know that?" he asked.

"We go to the same church. My Ma knows everything that's going on," Leroy answered.

"Everything?" Willis said, raising his voice.

Leroy laughed. "Quit worryin' 'bout it. Patsy will be waiting for you and we'll have a big party when you get hitched."

Willis smiled. He looked up at a moon bright enough to mistaken for the sun on a cloudy day. He pictured Patsy's eyes twinkling with the same sparkle the stars had on this clear night. "If we can just make it back home," he sighed.

"Don't you worry none," Leroy assured him. "After what we've been through, things can't get any worse."

CHAPTER 30

Leroy and Willis made the exhausting walk to Carney Springs Station, a stop over on the Overland Trail without any further incident. They arrived dirty and hungry, hoping to be able to work for their food and maybe earn enough to purchase a pair of horses. Leroy was optimistic while Willis was worried.

Carney Springs Station was a small stone building with a large corral for horses on one side and a barn facing a smaller fenced area that held goats and a couple of milk cows. The men could hear chickens cackling from a hen house attached to the side of the barn. Willis pointed to a pen that held four fat hogs and a dozen or so pigs.

"Leroy," Willis said while licking his lips. "This here place is bound to have good eats. I can almost taste the fried eggs and ham."

"Listen," Leroy said in a serious tone. "If we play this right, maybe we can earn enough money to get home. Let me do the talking, okay?"

Willis rolled his eyes. "Don't you always do the talking?"

Leroy shook his head. "This time it's real important."

"Don't worry, I'll follow your lead," Willis whispered.

A strong man with a barrel chest gave Leroy and Willis a passing glance as he carried buckets of water to the horse trough. "You boys down on your luck?" he called out.

"What do we say to that?" Willis asked in a low voice.

"Hush," Leroy hissed. "We were jumped by some Comanche a ways back. We're Rangers. 'Been walking for a couple of days."

The man poured water into the trough as he spoke. "If the two of you ran into the Comanche, how come you're still alive?"

Leroy couldn't help but chuckle. "Luck I guess."

"The Comanche don't usually leave anyone alive to tell the tale." The man emptied one bucket and picked up a full one.

Leroy stepped forward and offered a hand. "Can I fetch some water for you?"

"These here troughs need about ten buckets each. Can you boys manage that?"

"We sure can," Leroy handed one of the buckets to Willis, then reached for the empty one

"My name's Hodges. I'm the station manager here. My wife is the postmistress. Her name is Sarah and I wouldn't make her mad, if I were you."

"Leroy Wiley, Texas Ranger," Leroy said as he reached to shake the man's hand. The manager's grip was bone crushing. "This man's name is Willis, he's a Ranger too."

"Rangers?" the man lifted his head and laughed. "The two of you got outfoxed by the Comanche?"

Leroy grinned. "You might say that."

"Well," Hodges looked Leroy and Willis over before adding, "You better hope it's the last time. The Comanche won't let you get away with all that hair if they catch you again."

"Mr. Hodges," Leroy said. "Willis and I ain't been Rangers long. We're still a little green, but we're learning fast."

Hodges nodded. "You'll figure things out."

"Got any work we can do?" Willis asked.

Leroy glared at him.

"Always plenty of work to do around here," Hodges answered. "Question is what do you fellows expect in return?"

"Supper would sure be fine with me," Willis declared.

Leroy pursed his lips and shot Willis a look that he was sure to remember for a long time.

For the rest of the month Leroy and Willis worked to build a flat stone retaining wall for Carney Springs Station. They dug and leveled a trench along the side of the house. After the trench was dug, they waded into the creek in order to find the flat stones that made the wall much easier to construct.

When they weren't working on the wall, they fixed gates, mended fences and early each morning they milked the cows and gathered eggs. Each night, after a hard day's work, they slept in the barn on blankets placed on beds made of hay.

Leroy sent a carefully worded report to the Ranger headquarters in Fort Worth with the first express rider who stopped at Carney Springs Station. He also tried his best to write a few words to reassure his wife.

Every time a stagecoach or express rider passed through the station, Willis asked Leroy the same question, "Anybody coming to git us?"

"No word yet," Leroy replied sadly. "I think we're on our own."

"As usual," Willis grumbled. "When you gonna ask Hodges 'bout our wages. How much longer 'fore we've earned a couple of mounts?"

Leroy lifted a post into a freshly dug hole, then answered in a flat tone of voice. "You interested in riding bareback cause the last time I checked neither one of us had a saddle."

"Leroy, I just gotta git home soon," Willis sighed. "Patsy's gonna git tired of waiting for me."

"Now, Willis," Leroy chuckled. "Who's gonna steal Patsy from you?"

"Any number of fellows who attend our church. Bob Williams and Earl Jones just to name two," Willis frowned as he spoke. "I've seen 'em both making eyes at her."

"I hear you two cackling," Sarah Hodges called out as she walked toward them. "I'll loan you them two geldings when and if that wall is finished but not a day before." She pointed to the wall and added in a strong voice, "I'm not giving charity to a couple of out of luck cowhands."

"Rangers," Leroy corrected.

"Makes no never mind to me," Mrs. Hodges said while waving her arms to emphasize her point. "Two hungry, dirty, down on their luck cowhands is what I see."

"Miz Hodges," Willis pleaded. "Ain't we earned enough for them mounts yet?"

She threw back her head and laughed. "Not on your sorry life, Willis."

Willis mumbled something Leroy couldn't understand, and then went back to work placing stones in the trench.

"And that there trench outta be a whole lot wider if it's gonna hold all them rocks," Mrs. Hodges observed, adding insult to injury. "If I was you I'd start all over again."

Leroy gave her a stern look. "Ma'am, that trench is plenty wide enough."

"How many stone walls have you built?" asked Willis in an exasperated voice while glaring at Mrs. Hodges.

"Not as many as I've seen fall down," she replied raising her hand to shield her eyes from the afternoon sun. "I'll bring you some coffee and cold water from the cistern. I made a pie for supper. You can each have a piece now if you'd like, but I warn you, it's still hot."

Leroy grinned. "Just the way I like 'em." He glanced at Willis who was wiping sweat from his brow with a dirty handkerchief. Willis nodded his approval.

Three weeks passed. Leroy and Willis had about finished building the flat stone wall when suddenly the wall started to give way at the center. After the wall finally collapsed all together, Leroy's temper got the best of him and he began throwing shovels, rocks and any other objects that happened to be nearby.

Without saying a word, Willis picked up a shovel and began digging a wider trench. A few moments Leroy joined him, adding a few words he knew Mindy wouldn't approve of.

Mrs. Hodges never uttered a word when she looked at the collapsed wall but her expression reminded the men that she had warned them before they wasted so many days of hard labor.

The food was good and Mindy's letters arrived on a regular basis. Those small blessings kept Leroy in good spirits but Willis became so depressed he was ready to walk back to Smith County. By the end of each day, the Rangers soaked their cut and bruised hands in warm water in an effort to work out some of the soreness. Towards the end of their stay, Mrs. Hodges felt sorry for them and offered the men some whiskey that she kept in a trunk by the fireplace. She poured the whiskey into small glasses and treated each drop of the amber colored liquid as if it were pure gold.

The day after the wall was finally finished and still standing upright, Mrs. Hodges brought the two old geldings to the tired Rangers. She had no saddles and Carney Springs Station's spare bridles were in bad shape. Willis worked most of the morning piecing the bridles together as best he could.

"If we run into any Comanche while we're riding these two old nags we're dead meat," Willis said.

"Heck, what else is new?" Leroy took one of the worn bridles from his friend's outstretched hand. "We've been in nothing but trouble ever since the ambush at Noland's River."

"You're darn sure right about that," Willis said.

"As much as I'd like to ride east toward home we better go north to Fort Worth and try to get some decent mounts, along with a couple of saddles and bridles," Leroy sighed.

"More work," Willis grumbled.

"We ain't got no choice, Willis," Leroy reached over to give his friend a pat on the back. "Let's leave at daybreak."

Leroy was not much for writing letters, but that evening, by the light of an oil lantern, he wrote a letter to Mindy telling her to expect him home by the end of the month. The task took him the better part of the evening. Willis watched patiently, rolling smokes and drinking his last glass of Mrs. Hodges's whiskey, savoring each drop.

"Glad somebody still has a gal to write letters to," Willis said. He leaned over the table to look at Leroy's handiwork.

Leroy smiled. He knew that Willis couldn't read or write, but he made a point of not embarrassing his friend. He covered up the letter, folding the pages carefully before sealing them with wax and leaving the letter for Mrs. Hodges to post with the next Overland rider.

Always an early riser, Leroy was dressed and drinking Mrs. Hodges coffee before dawn, while Willis snored loudly. *Too much whiskey,* thought Leroy.

"Better git him up and moving or he'll sleep all day," Mrs. Hodges tipped her head toward the haystack where Willis slept.

Leroy turned and faced the stout pioneer woman. "I didn't hear you come into the barn, Miz Hodges."

"You couldn't have heard me if you tried, what with all that snoring going on." They both shared a chuckle.

"I wanna thank you for all you've done for us, cooking and washing our clothes and all," Leroy said earnestly. "You remind me of my Mama. She's got your disposition."

"Poor you!" Mrs. Hodges laughed and then her face softened. "It's been a pleasure, Leroy. I hope to see both of you next time you pass this way. No matter what I said about Texas Rangers being like cowhands, I didn't mean a word of it. You fellows are all that stand between us and them darn Indians. I'm grateful to you for risking your life for us."

Leroy smiled and tipped his hat in appreciation for the kind words. Being a Ranger was very important to him. Feeling his face turning red, he looked away. Nodding at Willis, he said, "I'll throw some cold water on him."

Mrs. Hodges handed him a sack full of biscuits and ham, then stretched up as tall as she could in order to give him a quick embrace. "Stay well Leroy and keep Willis safe. May God bless both of you."

She pulled up her apron to wipe her face, and then walked out of the barn into the cool morning air. Leroy watched her walk away, her patched cotton skirt swaying to and fro.

CHAPTER 31

Leroy and Willis rode north toward Fort Worth. It was a slow, difficult journey due to the condition of the horses. By the end of each day both riders were tired and sore. It had been several years since either of them had ridden bareback. Leroy was thankful they were moving across flat terrain without many hills. They avoided gullies and made sure they didn't press the horses. Thanks to Mrs. Hodges's cooking, they had enough food to eat, but they only carried two canteens so they had to carefully ration their water.

After five days of riding they saw, in the distance, a column of Federal cavalry led by two Indian scouts. The young lieutenant in charge of the troops gave the order to halt, then sent the scouts ahead to bring back Leroy and Willis.

After Leroy explained, their situation, the lieutenant gave the two Rangers directions to Fort Belknap, which was located between their present location and Fort Worth.

"I'm sure you'll be able to obtain fresh mounts there," the lieutenant said. "We're chasing a band of Comanche that has been raiding the homesteads and smaller settlements around here or you men could accompany us to Carney Springs Station."

"We left there five days ago," Leroy informed him, glancing at Willis. "We haven't seen any sign of Indians since we left."

"Maybe so," the lieutenant offered. "But we received a telegraph at the fort two days ago that said otherwise. Besides that, the stage hasn't made it to the next stop. That's not a good sign."

"Lieutenant," Leroy explained. "A man named Hodges and his wife took us in and fed us when we were mighty hungry. I'd sure like to ride south with you to Carney Springs Station to see about them."

The lieutenant shook his head and pointed to the horses Leroy and Willis were riding. "Sorry but you wouldn't be able to keep up."

"We'd be obliged if you sent word as soon as you find out if the Comanche raided the station," Leroy requested.

"That may be a problem. I doubt if any of the telegraph lines in the area are still up and working," came the curt reply. "I have three other homesteads to check on after I see what's happened to Carney Springs Station. We'll report back to the fort as soon as we finish this patrol and if you're still at the fort when I get back, I'll be sure to let you know what I found."

The lieutenant signaled his men and the column rode off leaving Leroy and Willis feeling completely helpless.

The tired Rangers arrived at Fort Belknap three days later. By then word had already reached the fort that Carney Springs Station had been burned to the ground along with the stagecoach and the unlucky passengers.

"Any survivors?" Leroy asked.

"None," came the reply. The post commander's brow filled with wrinkles as he rubbed his chin in deep thought. Leroy and Willis waited impatiently to hear what he had to say. They had already explained their situation to him. "With the Comanche on the warpath, you men are needed with the Rangers. I'll send my top sergeant to get a couple of fresh mounts ready for you."

"Sir," Leroy said hesitantly. "We don't have saddles, grub or rifles. The Comanche took everything we had."

The post commander, a senior major, nodded in understanding. "I'll see to it. Every Comanche you boys kill is one less for me to deal with." He reached over to shake hands with Leroy and Willis before adding, "You'll have to wait a moment while I write you boys a statement on official paper explaining why you are in possession of US Government property, then the two of you can be on your way to Fort Worth. Good luck! I hope we meet again over a bunch of dead Indians."

Leroy nodded in reply, and followed Willis out the door.

"Them yellow legs are sure anxious to kill off the Indians," Willis said as they stepped out into the sunshine.

"Yep, that appears to be their plan," Leroy said. "Can't blame 'em though. They got their butts on the line out here." He turned and gave Willis a playful shove before adding, "just like we do."

Willis shook his head, reached into his pocket for his last bit of tobacco and started to roll a smoke.

The two young Rangers made good time during the remainder of the trip to Fort Worth. The US Army issued mounts were strong and fast and the Army saddle was the best Leroy had ever owned.

Willis was a happy man.

"Didn't we make out?" Willis said while patting the neck of his new horse. "I mean I ain't never had a saddle like this."

Leroy grinned. "I do believe I'll keep my brand new saddle unless some Comanche gets the better of me and that ain't likely to happen ever again."

"Says who?" Willis chuckled.

"Willis, you just got a taste of Comanche hospitality. Are you anxious for some more?"

"Heck, no," Willis answered. "Like you said, I'll go down shootin' or they'll get me while I'm running. I ain't gonna stay around and let 'em take me again without a fight."

The trail ran through a rocky area with scattered trees. The horses picked their way down a narrow path toward a sandy creek. Leroy gave his mount some slack, which allowed the horse to find the best way down a steep gully.

"These horses know what they're doing," Leroy remarked to Willis. "Whoever trained them did one heck of a job."

"They ought to be," Willis laughed. "After all, they carry those troopers all over Texas."

"Wonder why the Army puts that wide yellow stripe down them boy's pants leg? Looks like it makes 'em more of a target for the Comanche arrows," Leroy thought aloud. He ducked as the horse took him under the low branches of a willow tree. When Willis didn't bother to reply, Leroy continued voicing his thoughts. "Still, I ain't never seen any of 'em I wouldn't want to ride along side with," he twisted back in the saddle to look at Willis before asking, "Why are you so quiet, Willis?"

Willis took a deep breath, letting it out slowly. "I sure wish we was ridin' toward home, Leroy."

"We're working our way east by way of Fort Worth," Leroy laughed. "Now, some fellow might ask why we're going north instead of due east. Let's say we're taking a round about way home." Leroy made a circular motion with his arm.

Willis dropped his chin and said in a flat voice, "*Too* darn round about if you ask me."

Leroy and Willis arrived during a typically busy morning in Fort Worth. When the army abandoned the post in 1853, settlers moved into the buildings and began trading livestock and crops at the local market. The settlement steadily grew until it became the most important town in north Texas.

Leroy slowly dismounted, stretched his legs and back, then carefully slapped as much trail dust off his pants as possible. He took time to look up into a big sky full of gray clouds. "Rain?" he asked Willis as he gestured toward the heavens.

"Naaaah," Willis sighed. "Just some heavy clouds, this ain't the season for much rain."

"Willis, you'll always be a sodbuster at heart," Leroy grinned. "Ain't nothing gonna change that."

"If I could make a living at it, that's all I'd do," Willis frowned. "I wouldn't be riding all over Texas trying to get myself shot or scalped."

Leroy looked up and down the busy street. "Can you believe just a few years ago this place was an Army outpost? Heck, it ain't been that long either." Leroy thought for a moment before adding, "I think I read somewhere it was back during 1849 that the Army moved in here to give the settlers some protection from the Indians."

"They're still trying to do that," Willis shook his head.

"Without much success I might add," Leroy agreed. "That's where we come in, my friend and fellow Texas Ranger."

Willis chuckled. "You got a way with words, Leroy. I guess that's 'cause Miz Wiley was a school teacher."

Before Leroy could reply, a half dozen soldiers accompanied by two officers stopped them in their tracks.

"Hold up, you two!" an angry voice commanded. "What are you doing with those Army mounts and saddles?"

Leroy turned to meet the gaze of a red faced US Army Captain. The cavalry troopers all had their guns pointed directly at the Rangers.

"Keep your hands up high where I can see 'em," a burly sergeant yelled. "I don't trust horse thieves."

Leroy slowly pointed at the badge pined to his brown leather vest. "We're Texas Rangers, not horse thieves."

"Keep your hands up and away from your gun belt," the captain ordered. "Texas Rangers don't ride Army issued mounts. Where'd you get them?"

The guns remained pointed at the Rangers. Leroy's lips tightened into a hard line. "If you'd give me a chance, I'd be glad to tell you. If not, we can stand here all day out in the sun and argue about nothing."

"Nothing?" the lieutenant laughed, his voice filled with sarcasm. He turned to the captain and said, "He thinks stealing horses is nothing."

The troopers shared a laugh at Leroy's expense.

"You fellows better be careful who you call a horse thief," Leroy said in a stern voice. "That's about as low as you can git."

"You have an explanation?" asked the captain.

"Darn right I do," Leroy said. "If you'd let me reach into my pocket I can show it to you."

"As long as your hands keep away from that pistol, you can get whatever it is that says you're entitled to be in possession of those horses," the captain kept a steady eye on Leroy.

Leroy's hand moved slowly as he reached across to the inside pocket of his vest. He removed the paper and held it high. "You see this?" he asked. "It's from the commander of Fort Belknap. This paper says that he has supplied me and Willis with these horses and gear. It also says we was ambushed by some gunmen and while taking one of the outlaws to Fort Worth we were attacked by a Comanche raiding party."

The captain motioned with a slight nod of his head and the sergeant stepped forward and yanked the paper from Leroy's hand. Leroy stiffened and slightly spread his legs to keep his balance. *I'd like to hit that sonofabitch.* Leroy's eyes followed the sergeant as he handed the folded paper to the captain.

The captain quickly read the letter, then frowned at Leroy. "This is very strange," he said. "The name is correct and it's written on official stationary from Fort Belknap, but we don't give away Army horses and saddles to just anybody." He motioned toward Willis and the sergeant walked over and roughly felt through Willis's pockets until he found an identical letter the major had written for Willis.

After carefully reading both documents a second time, the captain looked up at Leroy and Willis.

"Lower your weapons," he said, his voice tinged with a hint of remorse. "It appears these men are in legal possession of government property. But I take it this was only intended to be a loan?"

Leroy raised an eyebrow, reached up and pushed back his hat before answering. "Heck, no. That major didn't say nothing about these horses and tack being a loan. This US government property, as you call it, was given to us free and clear and that's the end of it. If you got any problems, take 'em up with that major, not with me and Willis."

Leroy stepped forward and returned the captain's glare.

Willis thought Leroy's temper had gotten the best of him. He decided to step in and act as a peacemaker. "Seems to me we're on the same side," Willis pointed out. "That's what the major at Fort Belknap told us. He said that any Injuns we killed would be less Injuns for you fellows to fight."

The captain's gaze went from Leroy to Willis, and then to his men. His expression gradually softened. "I guess that just about sums up the situation," he said at last. "I'd keep these papers close if I was you." He handed the papers back to the sergeant. The sergeant, a big burly man with dark piercing eyes and a heavy beard stepped forward to return the documents to Leroy.

"The advice is appreciated," Leroy said, never taking his eyes off the sergeant, who continued to give him a hard stare.

As soon as the Federal troops had walked past them, Willis said in a voice filled with relief. "Good Lord, I thought they was gonna string us up without reading these darn papers from that major."

"They sure didn't wanna listen, did they?" Leroy said. As he watched them walk away, he added, "Horse's ass."

"You talkin' 'bout that captain?" Willis asked.

"No, I mean all of 'em and you can forget what I said about riding along side of them soldier boys. Right now I'd rather ride with the Comanche," Leroy replied, then turned his attention back to the main street of Fort Worth. "Let's find the headquarters and see if we can draw enough pay to get us home."

"I'm hungry, Leroy," Willis patted his stomach. "We ain't had enough to eat to keep a squirrel alive."

Leroy laughed. "Sure thing. Finding an eatin' place is our second stop. I believe I could eat a whole apple pie."

"I'll half that pie with you after I finish some chicken and dumplings," Willis said as he tied the horse to the hitching post and followed Leroy down the street towards the Texas Ranger Headquarters.

Leroy and Willis reported in, gave a detailed explanation of the events to date, and waited to see if they could finally go home. To their dismay, they were ordered to ride northwest of Fort Worth to help the undermanned Federal forces keep the Comanche Indians at bay.

"As both you boys well know, those darn Comanche are wreaking havoc all over north central Texas," the Ranger captain said as he swept his hand over a worn map of the Texas Republic. "The army is doing their best, but they're spread mighty thin. We've got some settlers along the Trinity River that have to be protected. That's where you boys need to go," he stabbed his finger against the map before adding, "Right there along the Trinity River valley."

It was all Willis could do to keep from arguing. He groaned to himself, then said, "Are we supposed to take on the Comanche all by ourselves or are we going to get a little help?"

A bit surprised by the young Ranger's remarks, not to mention his sarcastic tone of voice, the captain looked up, his thin hair falling over one eye, and frowned at Willis. Leroy noticed the captain had a nervous twitch that kept pulling up the right side of his face. The man was tall and thin with a face that showed a life of hard living in the harsh Texas sun. He wore a clean shirt that had been pressed and creased and his Ranger badge was pinned to a vest made of tanned cowhide.

"I'll go over to the bank and draw you men some pay. That way you can both get a hot meal and a good night's sleep before you head out in the morning. It's a shame what happened to you boys." Almost as an after thought he added, "Darn Comanche."

Leroy glanced at Willis, then followed the Ranger captain across the busy street to the bank.

That night Leroy and Willis shared a room at one of Fort Worth's many small boarding houses. Willis decided to spend the money *only* after he learned that the price included breakfast.

"It's still a lot of money and we didn't get paid much," Willis argued, shaking his head. "I can almost taste the biscuits and ham now, but still…"

"Where do you think we could stay around here without paying?" Leroy asked. "I'd like to spend an occasional night in a warm bed, if that's all right with you. Besides, I think we've earned it."

Leroy never mentioned Mrs. Morrison's boarding house to Willis. The last thing in the world he wanted to do right then was to face Mrs. Morrison and explain to her what had happened to Andy.

When they settled down for the night Willis continued to complain, "I wish I had never heard of the darn Comanche. We're back on the trail and we ain't getting any closer to Smith County." He waited for Leroy's reply. When Leroy remained silent, Willis added, "I wouldn't mind Ranger duty so much if I could just go home and make things right with Patsy."

Leroy was trying his best not to think of Mindy. What a difference she had made in his life. It was as if everything he was doing and all the hardships he was enduring was for her. *Just one day at a time,* he thought. *Willis has gotta learn that's the only way to get by.*

The next morning Leroy woke up early and walked over to the washbasin and began pouring water from a blue and yellow pitcher. He had slept badly and woke up with an ache in his back. He was pulling on his socks and boots while listening to Willis complain.

"I have to be home in time to harvest the crops, Leroy," Willis said. "How long do you think we'll be gone this time?"

Leroy dried his face with a hand towel before answering Willis. "Willis, how would I know? I'm just like you, I do what I'm told and draw my pay."

Willis was standing at the window looking toward the livery stable. He continued to complain while Leroy shaved and brushed his hair back away from his face.

Darn cowlick, he thought as he carefully placed his cowboy hat low over his brow.

Willis sighed. "You ever think about Andy?"

Leroy dropped the towel by the washbasin and looked down at the worn carpet on the plank floor. "Yeah, I try not to, but I think about Andy 'bout everyday. Andy dying like that bothers me a lot. He was a good friend. Maybe a little too much of a mama's boy, but he would have been a good Ranger, if he'd been given half a chance."

"Same thing can happen to us," Willis said, his voice flat.

Leroy unfolded a new shirt and began to unfasten the buttons. "It's part of the job, Willis." He glanced at his friend. Willis looked mighty low. Leroy decided to try and make him feel better. "Heck, nothin's gonna happen to you. I'm gonna make sure you stay alive, with plenty of hair just so Patsy can boss you around the rest of your life."

Willis allowed a small grin to crease his face. "I sure hope so, Leroy. She's the right gal for me. I just know it. Isn't that the way you felt about Mindy when you first laid eyes on her?"

Leroy thought for a moment. "Yeah," he finally answered. "I never had any doubts."

After breakfast, Leroy and Willis saddled their horses and rode out of town. The day was still overcast with gray clouds floating across the sky. Leroy tapped the horse's ribs and the frisky stallion galloped into the wind. Leroy was anxious to join up with the other Rangers, sensing danger on the dry open plains. They rode from sunup to sunset, resting the horses and walking them at regular intervals. They were pleased that the horses were strong, fast and sure-footed. Both men knew that their lives might depend on the Army issued horses they rode. By the time the men reached Camp Cooper they were in the heart of the Comanche raiding country.

"Horses like this can save a man's life," Willis commented. "If the Comanche comes after us while we're riding these mounts they'll be eating our dust."

Leroy nodded in agreement. When the blacksmith handed the reins of the reddish-brown stallion to Leroy at Fort Belknap, Leroy had asked the horse's name. "Spirit" the smithy answered.

Leroy liked the looks of Spirit. He had felt the horse's powerful legs and realized that they were suited not only for speed but for distance as well. The large muscles in the upper part of his legs would give the horse the ability to run with a minimum of effort. *Somebody sure picked the right name for you,* thought Leroy as he gave the horse's thick, arched neck a pat.

As the sun dropped toward the horizon Leroy and Willis began looking for a place to camp. Just before dusk they spotted a trail of smoke rising over a cluster of oak trees not too far away. Leroy slipped his rifle out of the scabbard and kicked his horse into a full gallop. Willis did the same. *This better not be an Indian campfire,* Leroy thought. *If it is the two of us are going to look mighty foolish.*

When they reached the crest of a hill they looked down on a homesteader's farm complete with a small, well built house, a large barn, a corral and a smokehouse. The smoke was rising from a chimney attached to the back of the house.

"That smoke's coming from the kitchen, Willis, and my belly tells me its suppertime," Leroy grinned. "Let's see if we can talk them into slicing the ham or chicken a little thinner so we can have a meal."

"I hope so," Willis said. "I'm about starved."

Leroy didn't hear Willis. He was already halfway down the hill riding toward the farmhouse.

He guided his horse down a path past a thicket of oak and pines into a clearing. The homesteader had cleared a large garden and placed a scarecrow in the middle complete with a broom face and faded bonnet.

When the Rangers approached the farm a man appeared on the front stoop carrying an old hunting rifle. He pointed the business end of the rifle directly at Leroy and waited until they were within range of the rifle before calling out in a firm voice.

"That's far enough. You got no reason to stop here, so ride on."

Leroy spoke to Willis in a whisper, "Don't take your hands off the reins. That fellow will shoot first and ask questions later."

"I ain't breathin' much less moving my hands," Willis replied.

"We're Texas Rangers," Leroy called out. "We're wearing stars pinned to our vest in plain sight." He waited for a reply. None came, so he continued. "The Comanche have been raiding not far from here."

The man laughed. "So they send two of you to protect us?"

"No," Leroy called out in a commanding voice. "We were part of a company but we got ambushed. Some of our boys were wounded, some others were killed."

"Who bushwhacked you?" the man asked. His matted brown hair hung almost to his shoulders. He was a small man with big shoulders that seemed too wide for his body. His pants had more patches than cloth and were cut high over his work boots. The Rangers knew not to challenge the man. They waited for permission to ride forward. He was protecting his family and still unsure if he wanted to let two strangers on horseback ride up to his front door.

"First a bunch of gunmen who worked for them big ranches down by Noland's River. After that fight we met up with a Comanche raiding party," Leroy called out as they *slowly* approached the house.

"You're lucky to still have your hair," the man whistled. "The Comanche don't normally leave anyone alive."

"My name's Leroy Wiley. I'm from Starrville. That's in Smith County over in east Texas." Leroy nodded toward Willis. "This here is another Ranger from east Texas named Willis. I've known him all my life and he's a stubborn fellow, but a God fearing one."

The man frowned, lowered the rifle just a little, and said, "One of you come forward and let me get a good look at your badge."

"Be glad to," Leroy said. "Willis, go show the man your fine Texas Ranger badge made from a gen-u-wine Mexican peso."

"He'll probably shoot my head off," Willis whispered. "Looks to me like that's where he's aiming that rifle."

"Why do you think I'm asking *you* to walk up there?" Leroy said through clinched teeth. "But don't worry, I promise you I'll take him in if he blows your head off."

Willis climbed down from his horse, held one hand up while he slowly unbuckled his gun belt and let his six-shooter fall to the ground.

"He's telling you the truth," Willis said as he slowly walked forward. "We're lawmen, Texas Rangers. We're out here to protect you and your kinfolk. I promise we ain't planning on doing you folks any harm."

The farmer lowered the rifle, reached out to shake hands. "I can see that. Come on in and share some vittles with us."

Willis turned to Leroy and grinned. "Bring my gun belt, Leroy, and tie the horses up over at the water trough."

"Yes, sir, Captain," Leroy said, his voice full of mischief. "Anything you say."

The farmer opened the front door that led to a large room that served as the family parlor and kitchen. Leroy noticed the windows were covered with heavy wooden slats hinged to act as protective shutters. A long table dominated the room with benches on each side. The farmer obviously sat at the head of the table where the best chair in the room, a rocking chair, was pulled up to the edge of the table.

"Ruth," he said as he led the men through the door. "These men are Rangers who have ridden out this way either chasing the Comanche or running from 'em. I ain't sure which, but I've invited them to take supper with us."

His wife stood at the back of the room with her arms around their two children. A small baby rested in a cradle nearby. She was a small, frail looking woman with an easy smile. She had red hair. Leroy enjoyed looking at gals with red hair, but it always bothered him to see red haired women on the frontier because he knew that Comanche warriors loved to hang red hair from their spears. He had heard that any captives unfortunate enough to have red hair were always the ones who were scalped first.

Leroy and Willis removed their hats, scraped their boots outside the front door and stepped inside.

"Mighty pleased to meet you, ma'am," Leroy said. "My name is Leroy Wiley. This here is Willis. We're both from Smith County."

The woman nodded, but didn't respond. The children giggled. Willis giggled too.

"Come sit," the farmer said. "My name is Elijah. These are our children, Sara and Ryan."

"Mind if we wash up first?" Leroy asked. "I'd like to get the trail dust off before we sit down at the supper table."

"Of course," Elijah replied. "I'll take you out back." He looked at his son, "Ryan, see to the horses before supper."

The boy smiled and slowly walked past Leroy and Willis in order to get a good look at both their badges and gun belts.

"Supper will be hot soup and chicken and dumplings, more dumplings than chicken, but it's all we got," Elijah said.

"Elijah, don't forget I baked a cobbler," Ruth called out through the back door.

Leroy looked at Willis and grinned.

After supper Elijah and Ryan took Leroy and Willis to the barn where they spread clean hay for bedding. Ruth sent two quilts and feather pillows. When Leroy rested his head on the soft pillow he thought he had died and gone straight to heaven.

"These pillows sure makes the saddle easier on my neck," Leroy said to Willis. "I wake up with a hitch in my neck just about every morning after using my saddle for a pillow."

"Being around this family makes me homesick," Willis sighed. "A good hot meal for supper and now these quilts covering us along with the softest pillows I've ever seen. Only when a woman is running things does a man have a home like this. That Ruth gal sure keeps a fine house."

Leroy thought of Mindy. "Not too much longer, Willis," he said. "We'll be home soon. I feel it in my bones."

"How did you ever convince your new wife to let you ride off like this?" Willis turned over to face Leroy. "Being a new bride and all, I'd think she'd want you home."

"Mindy knows that being a Ranger is what I do," Leroy said in a firm voice. "I told her that while we was back in Georgia."

"Well, she's in Texas now, and you're a married man. She ain't gonna put up with this much longer."

"She's happy with my folks," Leroy tried to sound convincing.

"Yeah?" Willis said. "Things might be different by the time you get home after this long trip."

"I hope not," Leroy sighed. "She's a good gal and I don't want no trouble."

"Leroy," Willis said after a few moments of silence.

"Yeah?" Leroy answered, obviously wanting Willis to hush and let him to get a good night's sleep.

"Will you stand up for me if Patsy says she'll marry me?"

"Sure I will," Leroy said. "You tell me when to be at the church and I'll be there in my Sunday best."

Willis smiled and closed his eyes so he could better remember Patsy's sweet face.

CHAPTER 32

One of the first lessons Leroy learned when he became a Texas Ranger was to always have a healthy respect for a Comanche on horseback. They rode like the wind and killed without mercy. By the time Leroy joined the Texas Rangers in 1858 the Comanche had come to the realization that their only hope for survival was to put an end to the wave of settlements surging across west and north central Texas. With this in mind the Comanche set out with a vengeance to eliminate any and all settlements in or near their traditional tribal lands.

Leroy and Willis joined an under strength Texas Ranger company camped near the Brazos at Clairemont. After waiting in vain for more Rangers to arrive, the men rode northwest hoping to drive the Comanche back into the Palo Duro Canyon. The Comanche wintered and often kept their squaws and extra horses hidden in either the Paulo Duro or Tule Canyons. The Palo Duro canyon, over one hundred miles long, just over twenty miles wide and more than eight hundred feet deep, had proven to be a safe haven for the tribe. The colorful and unusual shaped walls of the canyon were formed by water erosion from a fork of the Red River and provided crevasses and caves that could hide both men and horses. Short, thick prairie grass covered the canyon's rim, which acted as a buffer and helped to conceal the canyon's actual size from any riders who viewed the canyon from a distance. Over the years, the Comanche had found numerous routes into and out of the canyon that were unknown to anyone else.

"To heck with this," Willis gestured to Leroy while they were walking their horses. "We keep heading west and to my mind, that sure ain't getting us any closer to home."

"What's the matter, Willis," Leroy laughed. "Don't you trust Patsy?"

Willis took a quick look around to see if any of the other Rangers could hear. He leaned toward Leroy and whispered, "You're darn right I do, but right now she ain't obligated to me. Speaking of being tied to one another, how long 'fore that sweet Georgia belle goes back to that fancy dude in Georgia? She ain't gonna stay on a farm in Starrville forever without a husband."

"She'll wait," Leroy laughed. "I'm sure of that. You don't know her, Willis." Leroy felt a pang of homesickness and attempted to shake it off by changing the subject. "Look at that," he gestured toward a broad vista. "Seems like the land just keeps going on and on."

"Yeah, and it's dry as can be," Willis responded. "A man would have a heck of a time raising any crops around here."

Ahead of the Rangers stretched a treeless open plain dotted here and there with scrub brushes and small mesquite trees. Willis pointed out the deep erosion in the sandy soil while Leroy noticed a pile of dead trees and branches stacked near a cluster of rocks that obscured the trail.

"Lieutenant," Leroy called out to Clay Hopkins, the Ranger in command.

Lieutenant Clay Hopkins was only a couple of years older than Leroy. He was walking at the front of the column just ahead of Leroy and Willis. He turned, pushed back his hat and smiled. "Ready for a break?"

"Always." Leroy laughed. "Even though we've been walking our mounts they still seem mighty tired. I bet they'd appreciate a break as much as we would."

"I was hoping for a little shade," Lieutenant Hopkins pointed towards the rocks. "Maybe we'll find some over there." He looked up into a clear, cloudless sky. "We won't find much shade around here during midday though."

Leroy handed his horse's reins to Willis and quickened his pace in order to catch up with Hopkins.

"It's not so much them rocks that bothers me," Leroy nodded toward the rocks and brush. "It's all them dead tree limbs and brush piled up. Somebody might be trying to hide something or keep us from seeing what's up yonder."

Hopkins stopped in his tracks. "I'd better send out a scout."

"That would be me," Leroy volunteered. "That is, me and Willis."

Willis groaned. The Rangers around him couldn't keep from laughing.

"Now, Willis," Lieutenant Hopkins turned to face him before saying what was on his mind. "You know that Leroy only has your best interest at heart. Besides, he likes your company." Hopkins tried to keep a straight face, but in the end he couldn't keep from grinning.

"Well, I can't say that I'm all that fond of his company," Willis snarled while keeping his eyes fixed on his friend's back. "Especially when he's trying his best to get me scalped."

"Oh, come on Willis," Leroy motioned for his friend to join him. "Let's mount up and go see if the Comanche have another party planned for us." Leroy held out his arms in a comical gesture to the rest of the Rangers. "Recently, Willis and I had a most exciting time visiting with a Comanche raiding party. He ain't forgotten their hospitality yet."

"You're darn right I ain't forgotten," Willis said as he climbed on his horse. "And neither have you, Leroy."

The Rangers laughed while Willis continued to frown.

Leroy's expression turned serious as he turned back and spoke to Lieutenant Hopkins, "We'll ride up and see what's beyond them rocks. I'll signal if it's clear. If you see us hightail it out of there, I would strongly suggest that you and the boys run like the devil himself is after you."

Hopkins pursed his lips. "Thanks for the advice, Leroy. I'll consider it." He motioned to the men to move off the trail. "You men take cover."

"There ain't much cover to take," one of the Rangers called out.

"If the Comanche comes after you I'll bet you find some," Willis assured him.

"Let's go," Leroy grinned at Willis.

Willis let out an audible sigh and tapped his horse's neck with the reins as the two Rangers rode forward. Leroy pulled his rifle out of the scabbard. Willis decided to keep both hands on the reins in case they had to make a run for it. If things took a turn for the worse, Willis didn't plan on spending any time trying to aim and shoot at a bunch of charging Comanche warriors.

Leroy kept his eyes on the dead tree branches stacked in front of the rocks. When they were in range, he aimed his rifle and fired into the branches. When nothing happened, he reloaded the rifle and fired again. This time, his shot was answered with an arrow that whizzed by his head so fast he almost missed seeing it. Another arrow fell short or it would have killed Leroy's horse. Leroy whirled around in the saddle, and began signaling to Lieutenant Hopkins. When he was sure the lieutenant had seen his signal he yelled at Willis and turned his horse around. Realizing that the Indians would probably out number them, Leroy decided to ride in the opposite direction, away from the other Rangers hoping to divide the Comanche war party. Willis followed his lead. Leroy was grateful they were still riding the mounts that they had gotten from the United States Cavalry.

Lieutenant Hopkins had the Rangers mounted and ready to make their escape as the sounds of screaming Comanche warriors and galloping horses filled the air. Leroy turned to see whether the raiding party had split up to follow both groups of Rangers, but to his dismay, the entire war party, more than twenty Indians, was racing after him.

Leroy saw where a series of gullies formed a small canyon ahead and decided to try to make a stand on the high ground. It wasn't much of a chance but it was the only one they had. He doubted that he and Willis would be able to outrun the Indians even with their new mounts. Willis stayed by his side. Leroy pointed with his rifle toward the rise above the small canyon. *If we can make it around the rim, we might be able to pull up and get off a few shots.*

When they reached the rim of the canyon, Leroy half fell off his horse and ran for cover. He dropped to one knee and began firing.

Willis pulled his rifle out of the scabbard and joined him. The Indians suddenly found themselves caught in crossfire. Instead of making their escape, Lieutenant Hopkins had circled around behind the Indians. He, along with the other Rangers, was coming on strong. This maneuver caught the Comanche totally by surprise.

Leroy and Willis each fired several rounds with their long rifles, then took out their pistols and continued to fire.

"We ain't gonna hit anything from this distance with these handguns," Willis snarled.

"That's all right," Leroy said as he squeezed off another shot. "Maybe we can distract them a bit."

Lieutenant Hopkins watched as the Comanche warriors turned their unshod ponies to face the Rangers. "Keep up the fire boys," Hopkins yelled. He was doubtful that any of the men heard him but it felt good to be giving encouragement.

Leroy whirled around to see where their horses had gone. He was surprised to see both animals standing right where he and Willis had dismounted. Apparently the horses had been trained to stand still whenever their reins were dropped.

"God bless whoever trained them horses," he said to Willis.

"God bless Hopkins and the boys for riding back to help us out," Willis shot back, his voice filled with relief.

"Come on, Willis," Leroy yelled as he threw a leg over his waiting horse. "We'll miss all the fun."

Willis shook his head and said nothing. He wanted nothing to do with the Comanche, dead or alive.

The Rangers lost only two men. Four Indians lay wounded. Two were dead.

"Leave 'em be," Hopkins said. "Their own can come for 'em or not. In any case, it's not our business."

"It would be our business if any of them fellows could still handle a bow," Leroy whispered to Willis.

Willis pointed with his rifle to the wounded Indians. "Look at 'em, they're dying anyhow, Leroy."

"I don't hold with leaving 'em alive no matter what," Leroy said in a low voice, making sure only Willis could hear his opinion. "The

Comanche will see this as us being weak and they don't respect weakness."

"Who cares what they think," Willis argued. "We ain't gonna be talking to 'em 'bout nothing anyhow."

"You got a point there," Leroy chuckled.

"All right, listen up," Hopkins called to his men. "We've got to take care of the men we've lost, Pete and Cory," he paused and swallowed hard before adding, "I intend to give 'em a decent burial, but not here." He paused again. "You all know why. Them darn Comanche would dig 'em up as soon as we leave."

One of the Rangers stepped forward. Sam Jeffers was a stout man with arms that bulged against his shirtsleeves. He pushed back his stained cowboy hat and leaned down to lift up the body of his friend, Pete Wilson. "I'll tie him across his saddle," he said in a flat voice. "One of you boys pick up Cory and let's get out of here."

Leroy walked around one of the mortally wounded Comanche warriors and took a long look at him. When the Indian's eyes met Leroy's, they had a glassy look to them. The Indian obviously expected no mercy. Leroy figured the Indian expected someone to do to him what he would have done to a wounded Ranger. Leroy kept his eyes fixed on the Indian until he mounted his horse and rode away.

Later that day, they found a place to bury the two fallen Rangers. It was on a rise covered in rich grassland that overlooked a clear stream and was shaded by a lone oak tree. Knowing the two men, it seemed like a perfect place. Pete loved to fish and Cory could always be found under the spreading branches of any tree that offered shade from the hot Texas sun. The Rangers left no marker for fear the Indians would see it from a distance. Lieutenant Hopkins asked Sam Jeffers to say a few words.

Leroy and Willis joined the rest of the Rangers and listened intently as Sam spoke words from his heart. Leroy felt a cool breeze lift his hair. Willis wiped his eyes with a worn handkerchief. Lieutenant Hopkins swallowed audibly, trying to push a big lump down his throat.

"Fellows," Sam spoke in a deep voice. His slow Texas drawl was filled with emotion. "We all know this can happen to any one of us.

Ever' time we leave our loved ones, we know there's a good chance we won't ever see them again. I didn't know Cory too well, but I was as close to Pete as any man can be to another. He was good to the bone. He loved Texas and he loved his wife and kids." Sam twisted his stained hat around in his hands as he tried to find the right words to say. "I know he's in a better place and I'll be asking each one of you to give a dollar or two to his widow when we git back home. The good Lord gives and he sure does take away." He paused and took a deep breath. "That's all I can think of to say."

"Well done, Sam," Lieutenant Hopkins said. "You've said all that needs to be said for Pete and Cory."

The Rangers, one by one, put on their hats, mounted their horses and silently rode back to Fort Worth.

CHAPTER 33

Leroy and Willis drew their pay at Fort Worth and enjoyed the best meal they had eaten in months. While in Fort Worth, Leroy bought Mindy some calico material and ribbons. For his mother, he purchased a pair of Sunday slippers and for his father a supply of pipe tobacco. He wanted to buy something for his brothers, but there was no room left in the saddlebags. Willis, always frugal with his money, looked all over Fort Worth for a silver wedding band that he could afford for Patsy. Willis then decided to cover his bet by purchasing a bottle of tonic from a traveling salesman. The salesman, a man named Mr. Reed, promised Willis that the tonic was guaranteed to repel mosquitoes and attract women.

The men made their last stop while in Fort Worth at the Silver Star Saloon. Leroy convinced Willis to have a few drinks in order to make the first day of their ride home relatively painless. When they finally left the saloon they were definitely feeling no pain. Although neither man would admit it, the main reason they were drinking so much was that now they had to face up to the fact that their friend, Andy, was never going home. After leaving the saloon, both men headed home with heavy hearts.

Willis managed to sing a few songs along the trail, but Leroy dozed in the saddle and hoped the horses would continue heading east toward Smith County. Having had more than enough of Indians, gunfighters and living on the trail, at least for the time being, Leroy was anxious to enjoy some time with his wife.

The pinewoods and grassy flatlands of east Texas were a welcome sight. Starrville, a farming community had been Leroy's home since he was a small boy. He had no memory of living any place other than his parent's farm.

After deciding that Leroy should be the one to tell Andy's mother and sisters the bad news, Willis and Leroy separated on the outskirts of Tyler. Leroy decided to stop in town to speak with Carter before going on to Andy's house. Willis, on the other hand, planned to ride straight to Patsy's farm and ask her to marry him. Willis had little to offer except his love and devotion and a willingness to do whatever it took to provide Patsy with a good home. During the ride to Patsy's home, Willis rehearsed his speech.

"Patsy," he began. The horse made a snorting noise that distracted him and made Willis forget what he planned to say. "Hush, now!" he said to the horse. He cleared his throat and started what he was sure would be the most important speech of his life.

"Patsy," he said in a clear voice. "I know I ain't got much to offer, but you will never find anybody who will love you more than I do. I will work hard to provide what I can. I won't ever let you go hungry or cold. I'm a God fearing man which means I ain't gonna have nothing to do with any other woman no matter how pretty she is or how old you get. I promise you we'll be together as long as the good Lord lets us."

He paused and reached down to pat the horse. "How's that?" he asked the gelding. "Pretty darn good, eh?" He cleared his throat. "What am I gonna say to Patsy's daddy, Ernie?" He stopped, climbed down from the horse and led him to a shade tree. "We'll sit a spell while I think about what to say to Ernie. He ain't as easy to talk to as Patsy and he ain't nearly as pretty to look at either. In fact, Ernie always looks like he's about to hit me right in the mouth. I can't never remember seeing Ernie happy 'bout nothing." The horse nodded his head in agreement. Willis took off the horse's bridle and saddle to allow him to graze and drink from Muddy Bottom Creek. Willis sat under the branches of a poplar tree and looked over the horizon. "If she don't see her way clear to marry me, so help me, I'll shoot myself." Willis leaned over to check on the horse. "I don't know why they named that creek *Muddy* Bottom Creek," Willis said as if the horse understood every word he was saying. "It runs clear as can be unless we've had a lot of rain."

As he rode into town, Leroy momentarily forgot his troubles when he saw Carter crossing Tyler's main street. Carter's new gray suit showed off his broad shoulders and narrow waist. The warm Texas sun had lightened his curly brown hair. A smile as wide as the Trinity River spread across Leroy's face as he galloped toward Carter. Carter turned, just as Leroy jumped off the horse and grabbed him in a bear hug.

"Good grief," Carter laughed. "What are you doing back so soon? I thought you were leaving Mindy here so she could find some farmer who would stay home with her and not go riding off with the Texas Rangers."

"That'll be the day!" Leroy grinned as he released his brother. "Let's go surprise her and the folks."

Carter was a little embarrassed by his brother's display of affection. *Something's wrong,* he thought. Carter shook his head. "I've got a steady job, Leroy. I can't take off anytime I feel like it and pretend to be saving Texas. Where's Andy? Didn't he ride back with you?"

Leroy's face darkened. He bit his lips, swallowed hard and tried to speak. After a moment, Carter repeated his question. "Leroy, where's Andy?"

Leroy shuffled his feet, stuffed his hands in his pockets and shook his head.

Carter took a deep breath, held it for a moment, then asked, "He's dead, isn't he?"

Leroy nodded.

"Oh, my Lord," Carter sighed, thinking of Andy's mother and sisters. He reached out and put an arm around Leroy's shoulders. "What happened?"

Leroy took a deep breath. "We were ambushed down by Noland's River."

"Indians?" Carter asked.

Leroy shook his head. "Gunmen from one of the big ranches. Remember, we were sent down there to try and settle the water problems between the homesteaders and a couple of big cattle ranches. It's a long story."

"I'd like to hear it, but I know you're not up to telling me now," Carter began walking toward the Rosewood Café and pulled Leroy with him. "Let's get something to eat."

Leroy nodded and walked beside Carter.

"Who's going to tell ol' iron pants?" Carter asked.

"You're looking at him," Leroy replied.

Carter lifted his head and started to argue.

"I rode out with him," Leroy said. His voice was flat. "Andy would want me to be the one."

Carter opened the door to the café and stepped aside, allowing Leroy to walk through the door first. He decided not to ask Leroy any more questions. *He'll tell me when he's ready.*

During the meal, Leroy picked at his food, talked about Mindy and asked about his parents. He didn't mention Andy, the fight at Noland's River, or the Comanche Indians. Leroy felt that the hard things in life were better kept deep inside.

Carter paid the check. The brothers walked outside as the sun dipped toward the horizon. Slivers of golden light had begun to blend with shadows. Shopkeepers were closing their doors and hurrying home for supper.

"I'll go with you," Carter said softly.

"Nope," Leroy sighed. "It's something *I* gotta do."

"Then I'll be here waiting for you. You can bunk here with me or we'll go out to the farm."

Leroy gave Carter a surprised look. "It's the middle of the week. It's too late for you to ride out to the farm and get back here tonight."

"Then I'll spend the night at the farm and get up early tomorrow," Carter gave Leroy a reassuring smile. "While you go see Andy's mother, I'll tell Judge Ben I might be a little late tomorrow, then why don't I ride ahead to make sure the folks don't go to bed before you get there?"

Leroy nodded, and walked over to the hitching post to untie his horse.

For the rest of his life Leroy would remember the pain and sadness he brought to Andy's home that night. April, May and June wailed and cried while their mother sat stoically in her favorite chair clutching one of Andy's shirts. The parlor was the same as Leroy remembered when he stayed with Andy the night before they left to join the Rangers, but now there was a different feel to the room. Leroy looked at the soft chairs on each side of the dark green loveseat and the tables covered with lace cloths.

"I'm so sorry," Leroy said over and over again.

Andy's mother simply rocked back and forth, nodding her head with tears streaming down her face.

"He died a brave man," Leroy said, trying to give comfort to Andy's family. He wanted Andy's mother to be proud of him.

Leroy was surprised that neither Andy's mother nor his sisters asked for any details about Andy's death. He waited for a few long moments and, believing that he had done all he could, he slowly turned to leave.

As he reached the front door he heard Andy's mother call out to him, her voice filled with grief, "Just like with his father." She paused, gathering her strength before continuing. "I have no grave, no place to leave flowers." She slowly turned her head and looked at Leroy. "His father died in Mexico during the war and was buried someplace I've never heard of, and now my only son is buried in some God forsaken part of Texas that should have been left to the Indians."

"No, ma'am," Leroy swallowed hard, then managed to speak in a breaking voice. "Andy is resting in good Texas soil that reminds me a lot of east Texas. He's resting alongside men he was proud to fight and die with. I know that because he told me. He told me how proud he was to be a Texas Ranger. What Andy was doing was mighty important to him and to us all. Long after we're gone, folks are gonna remember what men like Andy gave up to make Texas a decent place to live."

Andy's mother dropped her head and began sobbing. "Leroy, come here to me."

Leroy left his hat on a chair and moved slowly to the fireplace where Andy's mother sat in her rocking chair. He knelt on one knee and placed his hand on his former teacher's arm. "Believe me when I say how awful I feel for you and Andy's sisters."

"Leroy, there's another war coming and it's going to bring so much sadness to mothers, fathers and brothers and sisters too. Make sure at least one of you Wiley boys stays at home on the farm. Don't let your mother risk losing all her boys." Leroy started to speak but she touched his lips with her hand. "Promise me, Leroy. You're the youngest, but it'll be up to you. After all, you have a wife to look after."

"I thank you for thinking of my mama during your time of loss and I'll do what I can to keep my brothers at home."

"What about you?" she asked. She dropped her handkerchief and Leroy bent forward to pick it up.

"Well, since neither of my brothers can hit anything they shoot at, I better leave them at home to take care of the folks," he watched her mouth form a slight smile. "If the war does start, and I ain't too sure Texas will be in it, you understand, but if any Yankee tries to come down here to Texas and fight, they'll be plenty of boys ready to run them back where they came from."

"But not my Andy," she sobbed.

"No, ma'am," Leroy squeezed her arm. "Andy has already given his life for Texas. He ain't hurting no more."

Leroy kissed Andy's mother's hand and then hugged April, May and June. Not another word was said. He let himself out, closed the door and sat down on the front porch and remembered his last days with Andy.

While Leroy was paying his respects to Andy's mother and sister, Carter walked briskly to the livery stable and saddled his horse for the ride to the Starrville farm. He arrived in time to tell his parents and his new sister-in-law that Leroy was on his way home. After telling his mother and father where Leroy was and about the death of Andy, Carter climbed the steep steps to the room he once shared with Leroy. He knocked on the door and asked Mindy to come downstairs.

"I'll be down in just a few minutes, Carter," Mindy said as she brushed her hair back and reached for a wide yellow ribbon.

Carter waited patiently for her at the bottom of the narrow staircase.

"At last," Mindy smiled as she cheerfully walked down the stairs. She reached out to take Carter's hands. "I thought he'd never come home. Did he say where he's been all this time?"

"No, Mindy," Carter sighed. "But I can tell you that he's had a tough time."

"He's not hurt is he?" Mindy frowned and stepped closer to Carter in order to see the expression on his face. What she saw worried her. She glanced at her mother-in-law who gave her a reassuring smile.

"Oh, no," Carter said. "Nothing like that. But his friend, Andy, was killed while they were trying to put down a range war. When I left Tyler, Leroy was telling Andy's family the bad news."

"That's awful!" Mindy said. "I wish I could have been with him when he told them. I'll pack a basket for her and Andy's sisters. Don't forget to take it with you when you ride back to Tyler."

Carter nodded, then walked over to sit with his parents and wait for Leroy. Mindy followed him.

"I plan to talk to Leroy about all this running around he does with the Texas Rangers," she crossed her arms defiantly. "I'm sure he was right there when his friend was killed. Why, it could have been Leroy."

Oh, no, thought Carter. *Here comes trouble.*

CHAPTER 34

Leroy smiled when he first caught sight of the farmhouse. He could see light coming from the kitchen where his mother had placed an oil lamp on the kitchen table. He could hardly wait to see Mindy and hold her in his arms.

"The dog's barking and I hear a rider comin' down the path," Clayton said as he came into the house.

"It's our wayward brother," Carter turned around and gave Mindy a big smile.

Mindy ran for the door, swung it open and ran out onto the porch.

"Leroy!" she called to him as she ran down the steps. Mindy's heart started to pound.

"Hello gal," Leroy smiled as he jumped down from his tired horse. He gave her a long hug and kiss, then started to unlatch his saddle-bags. "I got something for you."

Mindy smiled and reached for the package wrapped in brown paper. "I love surprises!"

"Hold on," Leroy laughed. "Wait until we get into the house before you start unwrapping things."

"I've never been able to wait for surprises," Mindy laughed, then stopped and gave him a slight frown. "Just exactly why were you gone so long, Leroy Wiley?"

Leroy lifted his head and smiled. "It's a long story and I'm not going to waste any of our precious time together on it. Besides, you can listen when I tell Papa. He always wants to know all about what happened on the trail."

He slung his saddlebags over his shoulder, put his arm around Mindy and walked toward his mother's waiting arms.

After supper he told his parents and brothers how Andy died in the battle with the gunmen. He glossed over his run in with the Comanche Indians, carefully omitting the part about being held captive. He knew that wouldn't sit well with either his mother or Mindy.

"Son, it looks like there's a war coming at us," Leroy's father said. "What do you think the Rangers will order you to do?" He paused to light his pipe before adding, "Stay here in Texas, or go fight alongside the Confederate states?"

Leroy's eyes drifted over to Mindy. She was frowning and clutching her handkerchief. Leroy shot his father a worried glance and tipped his head toward Mindy.

Taylor nodded that he understood, but to Leroy's dismay, Clayton added to the problem when he said, "Papa, I bet you that Leroy will be the first one to sign up to go fight the Yankees."

Leroy glared at him, but Clayton continued, oblivious to Leroy's discomfort. "At church last Sunday the talk was all about the war starting up anytime now." He turned to Leroy, "When do you think the Rangers will leave to fight the Yankees?"

"I don't have the slightest idea," Leroy said. His words were spoken through tight lips. When Clayton began talking about the fellows he knew who had already left Smith County to start their training, Leroy grasped Mindy's arm and said, "Let's go for a walk, Mindy."

Mindy reached for her shawl and without saying another word, they left to enjoy the beautiful autumn evening.

"Looks like about a thousand stars up there," Leroy motioned to the sky lighted by a bright harvest moon. Mindy leaned closer and wrapped both hands tightly around his arm. Leroy noticed she was wearing a pretty green dress with cream-colored lace tucked into the neckline and sleeves. He sensed what she was thinking. "Mindy, if the war does start up I guarantee you it won't last more than a few months. I doubt I'll even leave the state of Texas."

"War is all folks talked about for the past year in Georgia and now that's all I'm hearing here in Texas," Mindy said in an obviously unhappy tone of voice.

"Let's talk about moving into our own place," Leroy leaned down and kissed her. "I'm pretty good with building things. I figure we can save enough to start building our house by late spring."

Mindy's eyes sparkled. "Where?" she asked, happy to change the subject. "You've shown me some pretty places on Papa Taylor's farm, but I'm not sure where you want to build *our* home."

"Over there about two miles is the prettiest valley with a creek running slap dab down the middle of it. I'll take you there tomorrow morning after breakfast," Leroy pointed toward the gentle hills west of his father's farm. "It's always been one of my favorite places."

"I wish we could go there right now," she smiled. "I can't wait to see it."

Leroy leaned down to whisper in her ear. "I've got a better idea as to how we can spend the rest of tonight."

She blushed, but to his delight, she gave him a big smile while at the same time giving his arm an affectionate squeeze.

The next day, while Leroy was saddling a gentle mare for Mindy to ride, Willis marched into the barn and announced the date for his wedding. Leroy slapped Willis on the back and offered him his heartiest congratulations.

"She's a fine gal, Willis," Leroy said with a smile. "Too good for you, that's for sure."

"I ain't about to argue, Leroy," Willis said. "But she's agreed to marry me on Saturday and I'm here to ask you to stand up with me."

"You know I will," Leroy said. "Mindy and I will be there, so will the folks."

"I had planned on asking Andy," Willis looked down, his expression changing from happiness to a sad, melancholy look. "I sure do miss him."

Leroy swallowed hard, thinking of the day before when he had to tell Andy's mother she had lost her only son. "I know what you mean." He brushed away some small rocks with the toe of his boot. "But we've all gotta move on."

"That's what Patsy said to me," Willis sighed. "So I'm getting married before it's too late."

Leroy raised an eyebrow and looked at his friend. "Why do you say that? Just because Andy got shot doesn't mean that'll happen to us."

"I know," Willis said, his voice cracking. "But you never know, do you? Next week we might be riding back to Comanche country. Doesn't that beat everything? We just got home and word is they're sending us out again."

Leroy frowned. "Where did you hear that?"

"I rode over to Mount Pleasant to see if I could draw some more pay," Willis looked around the barn delaying what he had to tell Leroy. "Sure would've been nice to have some money, what with me getting married on Saturday."

Leroy remained silent. He knew Wills would get around to sharing the bad news soon.

"Anyhow," Willis continued. "I wasn't able to get no more money."

Leroy began to walk the mare out of the barn. Willis reached out and caught his arm. "Orders have come from Fort Worth for us to ride up north and put a stop to the bandits and rustlers coming down from the Indian Territory. There's been a lot of trouble near the Red River. They say not even Red River Station is safe what with all the thievin' going on."

Leroy sighed. "Any idea when we leave?"

"Maybe next week," came the reply. "Could be *early* next week."

"Darn it," Leroy shook his head. "We'll be out there fighting them rustlers from the Indian Territory while they're forming up a regiment here to fight the Yanks. We can't be in two places at the same time."

"I don't wanna be in either place," Willis said. "To heck with all this fighting. Unless they pay me money, I'm staying home."

"They'll pay us, Willis," Leroy said. "I'm counting on my Ranger pay to be able to build me and Mindy a little ranch house over by Spring Creek."

"That's your Pa's land?" Willis asked.

"Right at the edge of it. He gave me enough acres to get started when I married Mindy."

Willis let out a deep breath. "I don't expect that Ernie will give me any land when Patsy and I get married. We'll be lucky if he shows up for the wedding. But no matter whether we like it or not, me and Patsy are gonna be living with Ernie and farming his land for a long time." Willis paused, then added, "I swear that man looks like he wants to take a swing at me every time I'm around him."

Leroy gave Willis a pat on his shoulder. "As long as you and Patsy are happy, I wouldn't worry about Ernie." Leroy's mind was already on Mindy and what he would say to her if what Willis was telling him came true. He forced a smile as he watched Mindy making her way to the barn. "Here she comes, Willis," Leroy whispered. "Not another word about the war or Ranger duty, you hear me?"

"I hear what you're saying," Willis replied. "You can count on me."

Mindy's riding skirt, vest and Cowboy hat made her look like a real Texas rose instead of the pretty Georgia peach he had married. Her soft brown hair hung in curls around her shoulders.

"I'm ready to go riding," she called out to Leroy. She gave Willis a slight frown. "I didn't know you were going to be here today, Willis. Are you coming with us?"

"No, ma'am," Willis smiled and tipped his hat. "I stopped by to ask Leroy to stand up for me Saturday when I marry Patsy."

"Oh!" Mindy ran to Willis to give him a big hug. "Willis, I'm so happy for you." Turning to Leroy she added, "I'm sure he said yes."

"I did indeed," Leroy laughed. "I have every intention of being at the church bright and early to see Willis become a married man. Living with Patsy is bound to improve his disposition. It may take awhile, but I know she'll get the job done."

Willis felt his face fill with color. "Ah shucks," he dropped his chin and smiled. "I still can't believe she's agreed to marry me."

Leroy reached over to look at the time on Mindy's watch pin. "I probably still have time to talk her out of it. It's over forty-eight hours until she says I do."

Mindy gave him a gentle shove, "Oh, you!" She turned to Willis and added sweetly, "Willis, he docsn't mean a word of it. He's almost as happy as you are."

"I sure am happy, Mindy," Willis gave her a big smile. "And if Leroy and I don't have to leave next week to fight them darn outlaws I'll be even happier."

Leroy drew in a quick breath.

"What?" Mindy cried. "Leroy, what's he talking about?" She put her hands on her hips and stepped forward, her hat just inches from his chest. "Leroy?" she waited for an answer while looking up into his eyes. No answer was forthcoming so she turned to Willis, "Can you please tell me what my husband is keeping from me, Willis?"

Willis, realizing he had made a big mistake said, "I better be going. I promised Patsy I'd be at her house by dinnertime. She's making fried chicken and dumplings." He stole a quick look at Leroy. Leroy glared back, his eyes narrowed and his jaw was set in stone. "I'll see you Saturday morning, Leroy." Willis spoke as he made a hasty exit from the barn.

If Mindy hadn't been standing there, Leroy would have given Willis a piece of his mind or at the very least a look that would have sent chills down his friend's spine.

When Leroy pushed his hat back and reached out to take Mindy's hand, she stepped away from him and crossed her arms. "I don't believe I'm in the mood to go riding with you, Leroy Wiley!" She said with all the anger she could muster.

"Now wait a minute, Mindy," Leroy pulled her back into his arms. "I don't know what Willis is talking about and he probably doesn't either."

"If that's the case, you can promise me that you won't be leaving this farm next week," Mindy reached up to grab her hat as the wind blew it from her head. Leroy grinned and rescued the hat before it hit the ground.

"Not used to cowboy hats are you?" he lifted her chin for a brief kiss.

"Well, they certainly aren't like wearing a bonnet, that's for sure. Besides, this hat belongs to Clayton and it's too big for me." She quickly refocused her attention back to the problem at hand. "Leroy, surely you aren't going to leave home again so soon, are you?"

"Sweetheart I don't know," Leroy sighed. "I have to go whenever I'm called to duty. I don't have a choice. We've talked about this, haven't we?" He kept Mindy's chin turned up to face him.

She nodded. He brushed a tear away and continued to speak in a gentle voice. "I love you, Mindy. Now let's go see where I'm going to build your new home."

She smiled, hugged him close and sighed, "Just stay with me as long as you can, Leroy. I'm afraid once the war does start you'll be gone a lot longer than two or three months."

"Naaaah," he whispered. "Not a chance."

On Wednesday of the following week, Willis left his bride and joined Leroy, who had packed his saddlebags and said a long goodbye to Mindy. They met up with Travis as they rode northwest through misty rain toward Van Zandt County. They were to be joined by three more Rangers at Canton and from there, they rode to Cooke County and the Red River. Crossing a series of creeks running off of the Sabine River during a pouring rainstorm didn't make for a pleasant ride. Willis was in a dark mood, while Leroy's state of mind wasn't much better. The last look he had of Mindy was when she came out on the porch wrapped in a blanket to keep out the early morning chill. Her eyes were red and puffy from crying. It was a sight that he was afraid would be repeated many times in the next few years if war broke out.

The Rangers rode through rolling country timbered with oak and pine trees until they reached Canton where they planned to spend the night before riding on to Cooke County. Once they arrived in the town of Canton, they found a room at a small hotel that was large enough for the three men to share.

Leroy had to convince Travis to share the room because of Willis's snoring. Almost six feet tall with red hair and a boyish face, Travis was the practical joker in this group. The first time they had ridden together Leroy had laughed for two days after Travis had put a king snake in Willis's bedroll.

"It'll sure save us all some money," Leroy told Travis during a late supper of biscuits and beef stew. "Wait till you see the room, it's huge. There's a bed and two sleeping cots in there."

"If I get the bed, maybe you've got yourself a deal," Travis said while Willis was at the stove getting a second helping of stew. "Otherwise, I'm getting my own room, no matter how much it costs me."

Leroy frowned. "Willis and I gotta save our money, Travis. Every dollar we save, helps."

Travis grinned. "I sure am glad I don't have to pay for a wife. I can spend my money on whatever I want. I don't have to scrimp and save like you fellows do." After making sure Willis couldn't hear, he added, "Let's put Willis on the far side of the room. He snores so loud on the trail, it keeps the coyotes away."

Leroy shook his head. "Not really, they howl right along with his snoring. I think the noise he makes sets them off."

"I swear I never noticed that," Travis laughed. "I try to get as far away from him as I can and still be near the campfire."

"Here he comes," Leroy whispered as Willis returned to the table carrying a heaping bowl of stew. "Let's go in together and get a bottle of whiskey. A few drinks always puts me to sleep."

"That's a deal," Travis said.

"Willis," Leroy said, using his most convincing voice. "How about going in with me and Travis and buying a bottle so we can have a drink or two after supper?"

Willis frowned and shook his head. "I made a promise to Patsy." His eyes narrowed as he stared at Leroy before adding, "And so did you."

"I didn't promise Patsy a darn thing," Leroy replied, struggling to sound serious.

"You know what I mean," Willis looked at Travis. "He promised Mindy he wouldn't drink or play cards." He pointed at Leroy with his spoon. "You told her that, remember?"

Leroy reached for his hat. "I don't remember exactly what I told her, so while I'm on the trail, I'm gonna have a drink now and then."

Turning to Travis, he said, "Let's go. We'll meet you back at the hotel, Willis."

Travis reached for a biscuit from Willis's plate. "I'm sure glad nobody tells me what I can or can't drink or smoke or whatever."

"Just you wait," Willis said as he snatched the bread out of Travis's hand. "Your time's coming."

Travis followed Leroy out the door while Willis finished his supper. The two Rangers headed directly to the only saloon in Canton, *The Texas Yellow Rose.*

"Travis, I know what you meant when you told Willis that you were glad nobody could tell you not to drink, but what exactly did you mean by 'whatever'?" Leroy asked. The grin on his face went from ear to ear.

"If there's any pretty gals in that saloon you'll find out soon enough," Travis tipped his hat back on his head and grinned from ear to ear.

CHAPTER 35

Leroy was normally an early riser, up and about before anyone else, but this morning he awoke to a loud pounding on the door. It took Leroy a moment to get his bearings. He slowly sat up, reached for his pistol and slid the blanket off his legs.

"Who the heck is it?" Willis asked, keeping his voice low.

Leroy gestured that he had no idea. He got up, pistol in hand, and slowly walked to the door wearing only his drawers. Travis slipped his pistol out of its holster and joined Leroy, taking up a position on the opposite side of the door. The pounding continued. Leroy motioned to Willis, who was still in the bed. Willis called out in an angry voice, "Who the hell is it and what do you want?"

"It's Marshall Thompson," came a loud reply. "Open this door right now!"

Leroy knew the door wouldn't stop a shotgun blast, so he carefully swung the door open while standing to the side. Seeing Marshall Thompson walk through the open door, he lowered his gun and stepped out of the way. Thompson, well over six feet, seemed to fill the room.

"You boys sleeping all day?" Thompson asked while looking around the room.

Willis fell back on the bed and rubbed his hand over his eyes.

"Not likely," Leroy said. He pointed to the small window. "The way I see it, the sun's barely up."

"Well, get dressed and meet me in my office," Marshall Thompson said as he turned and walked back out the door. "The

Rangers have been called up to put down a Comanche war party. They've hit settlements in Buchanan, Palo Pinto and Young counties."

The Rangers watched as Thompson slammed the door on his way out.

Leroy turned to Willis. "That man makes a lot of noise, don't he?"

"Where's Buchanan, Palo Pinto and Young Counties located?" Willis asked.

"Not in east Texas, that's for sure," Travis answered while pulling on his pants.

Leroy took a deep breath and faced Willis. "Don't start complaining, Willis," he said. "I ain't in the mood to listen."

Willis pulled the pillow on top of his face. "Somebody might as well shoot me now and save Patsy the trouble."

Leroy couldn't help but grin. He buttoned his shirt and sat down to pull on his pants and boots.

When the three young Rangers came down the steep stairs that led to the hotel lobby they were surprised to find Marshall Thompson waiting for them. "Let's get something to eat," he said, leading the way into the hotel dining room.

"I hope he's paying," Willis whispered to Travis. Leroy turned and glared at both of them.

"Pour the coffee, sister," Thompson said while motioning to a waitress wearing a fresh white apron over a blue calico dress. "Hurry up! And remember I like lots of jelly on my biscuits."

The waitress frowned and pushed a wisp of brown hair back into place. "How could I forget?"

Thompson laughed and turned to Leroy, "She really is my sister. We've been fighting most of our lives. Hurry up with that coffee, Ellen."

Leroy sat down on a maple bench and made room for Travis and Willis. Marshall Thompson had taken up the entire bench on the other side of the table.

"I hope she doesn't poison us along with you," Willis said.

"Oh, she means well," Thompson laughed. "Never mind Ellen."

At that moment his sister returned and poured each of the
Rangers a full cup of coffee then gave her brother half of a cup.
"Sorry," she said. "I've got to make more coffee."

"Well, see that you do," Thompson snarled. "And hurry up, will
you?"

Leroy noticed that Ellen left with a big smile on her face.

"Let's get down to business," Leroy said after pouring cream and
sugar into his coffee.

"I sent a telegraph to Ranger headquarters in Waco yesterday
telling them that you boys had reported in here. Last night I received
a reply ordering you boys to ride out to Camp Cooper as soon as possible."

"Camp Cooper?" Leroy tried to picture a map of north Texas in
his mind. "We've been near there, but Willis and I were in such bad
shape I'm not sure if I remember exactly where Camp Cooper is
located."

"Due west of here," the Marshall said. "Should take you a couple
of days of hard riding to get there, so if I was you, I'd get started right
after breakfast."

Willis groaned.

The Marshall continued, "The three Rangers you were supposed
to meet are over at Miz Dowd's boarding house. You can go wake
them up yourself after we're finished here."

When they arrived at Camp Cooper, they were told there had
been yet another change of orders. They were told to rest up, and then
ride to the north central Texas town of Denton to put a stop to some
cattle-rustling going on near the Red River Station.

"Good news, if you ask me," Travis said as they walked out into
the sunshine.

"I ain't asking you, Travis," Willis replied grouchily.

"I am," Leroy reached over to give Travis a shove. "Can you give
me one reason why you think this is good news?"

Travis turned around and hooked his thumbs into his gun belt. "I
can give you boys not one, but two good reasons." He hesitated to
make sure he had their full attention before adding, "First, Denton

ain't that far from Greenville. From Greenville, it's only a couple of rabbit hops to Smith County."

Willis squinted in the sun and looked Travis in the eye. "Didn't you say there were two reasons?"

"I did," Travis laughed. "Rustlers, as sorry and ornery as they might be, ain't the Comanche. I'd rather face a rustler fighting to keep his neck out of a rope than a Comanche on the warpath any day."

Leroy grinned. "Travis, you have made your point and you're right as can be. Even Willis will agree."

Willis chuckled. "For once, Travis knows what he's talking about."

Travis frowned. "One of these days, Willis, I'm gonna punch you right in the mouth."

"That'll be the day," Willis called out as he walked away.

Travis looked at Leroy. "I swear, that is the most aggravating fellow I ever did *have to* spend time with."

Leroy tilted his head toward Willis. "That he is, but he's one hell of a man to have by your side when you're in trouble."

Travis shook his head and thought for a moment before agreeing with Leroy. "You're right about that, but he's still hard to put up with sometimes."

"Don't worry, Travis," Leroy said. "Willis is one of them fellows who manages to grow on you."

"He *ain't* growing on me," Travis replied while shaking his head.

The Baker Brothers had been stealing horses and cattle in north Texas for years. They learned their craft from their daddy who learned the trade from his daddy prior to the tribes arriving in the Indian Territory from the southeastern states. Joel Baker, the youngest, was only fourteen years old when he was caught by the Choctaws while trying to steal a few head of cattle from their herd. The Choctaws whipped Joel until there was almost no hide left on him. They did this to teach him and the rest of the Baker clan a valuable lesson, leave the Choctaw herds alone. From that day on, Joel and the other members of the Bakers gang harbored a hatred for Indians tempered by a healthy respect for Indian justice.

After their run in with the Choctaws, the Baker gang began riding into the north Texas plains to steal cattle and horses for their spread near Sivell's Bend in Fannin County. It didn't take long for the Baker's to begin doing business with the Choctaws, but Joel always kept his distance from the Indians—any Indians.

The local sheriff suspected the Bakers were behind all the rustling, but didn't have any proof. Six Rangers, including Leroy, Travis and Willis, began patrolling the Red River basin hoping to catch the Bakers red handed and bring them to justice.

After three weeks of patrolling, the Rangers were tired and frustrated. The rustlers always seemed to be one jump ahead of them. As time passed with no resolution of the problem, the Rangers began running into angry farmers and ranchers with spreads near the boundary of Grayson and Fannin Counties where most of the cattle had been stolen.

One rancher threw his worn, sweat-stained hat at Leroy and yelled, "My best stock, including my prize bull disappeared last night! Why can't you boys put a stop to this rustling?"

"Mr. Canfield," Leroy picked up the man's hat and dusted it off before handing it back. "I understand how you feel." He gestured to the Rangers gathered behind him. "We're the ones out there all night in the rain trying to catch up with them sorry buzzards."

"Yeah," said Travis, echoing Leroy's words. "We've covered almost every square inch between here and the Red River looking for 'em. It's like we're chasing ghosts."

"If you don't find those rustlers soon, me and my neighbors are going to take matters into our own hands," the farmer said. His face was red with anger. "I'm to the point of riding into the Territory and stringing up some of them thievin' Indians. A lot of us think they're the ones stealing our stock. No white man can disappear like them Indians. I've heard tales of cattle disappearing during the middle of the night while men were keeping watch on their herd. It's plum spooky I tell you."

Leroy couldn't help but raise his eyebrows after hearing this story, but on the other hand he had to admit that he couldn't figure out how the livestock kept vanishing without a trace. Meanwhile, he tried to placate Mr. Canfield and the other farmers without much success.

When the angry farmers had finally ridden off, Leroy turned to Willis, "The last thing we need is a bunch of farmers going up into the Territory and causing trouble. Before you know it, the tribes up north will be crossing the Red River and doing as much killing as the Comanche."

"You're right," Travis said, "We darn sure can't let that happen."

That night the Rangers gathered around a campfire to cook a supper made up of dried beef and beans while they tried to come up with a plan to catch the cattle rustlers. It was finally decided that they should split up. Travis and Leroy would ride north into the Indian Territory in an effort to learn where the rustlers were taking the cattle, while the rest of them continued to patrol along the Red River.

After the meeting broke up, Willis pulled Leroy aside. His face showed disappointment. "Leroy," he whispered. "Why are you splitting us up? I thought after all you and I have been through you'd want me riding with you."

Leroy sighed. He looked Willis directly in the eye. "I would rather have you by my side during trouble than any man I know." Leroy hesitated a moment before continuing, "Willis, you know what I went through with Andy's mother and sisters," he slowly shook his head back and forth. "I still haven't gotten over it. I'd sure hate to be the one to face Patsy and have to tell her something awful had happened to you."

"Leroy," Willis pleaded. "You can't think like that. You'll wind up getting both of us killed. The best chance I have of going home to Patsy is being with you and you know that as sure as shootin'." Willis leaned closer and said in a voice so low he knew no one else could hear, "Travis might think he knows what he's doing but half the time he's just putting on a show. He's a green kid, greener than early spring grazing grass."

"Well, he's gotta learn sometime," Leroy argued. "We had to learn, now it's his turn."

"Take me with you," Willis said. "Or I guarantee you it'll be a big mistake that both of us will regret."

"Heck, don't you think I know it," Leroy said as he leaned against the broad trunk of a large oak tree and crossed his arms.

"That settles it," Willis turned to walk away. "I'm going with you. I don't care if Travis comes with us or not."

"Darn," Leroy muttered to himself as he watched Willis lay out his blanket and saddle and then settle down for the night. "I gotta watch out for Willis or Patsy will kill me dead if anything happens to him."

He smiled as he pictured Patsy on her wedding day. She had borrowed a dress from Mindy and looked almost as pretty in the soft yellow dress. "*Almost* as pretty, cause no woman on God's good earth is as pretty as my Mindy," Leroy whispered.

"What did you say?" Travis asked as he walked toward the picket line to check on his horse.

"Oh," Leroy pushed himself away from the tree and laughed. "Just talking to myself. You'll start doing that too when some pretty gal has you wrapped around her little finger."

Leroy was up before dawn. He checked the horses, then gathered enough wood to build up the fire to cook breakfast. Willis was the next man to put the night's rest behind him and he began helping Leroy with the camp chores.

"See if you can catch us some trout in that stream, Willis," Leroy said. "Heck, anything would be better than beans for breakfast."

"Another day on the trail," Willis snarled. "I woke up as sore as can be."

Leroy pointed toward the creek. "That cold water will get your blood moving and work the soreness out."

He looked at Leroy and frowned. "Oh, yeah. There's nothing like wading out in cold water in the morning, and then wearing damp pants all day," Willis said sarcastically.

"Then take your pants off, Willis," Leroy laughed. "I'm the only one awake and I won't mind."

"Leroy," Willis said in an irritated voice. "How come you always want me to catch fish especially when I ain't got nothing to fish with?"

"That's because I'm partial to fried fish," Leroy laughed.

"Then you get your butt out in that cold water and catch them yourself," Willis snatched the firewood out of Leroy's arms. "I'll tend to the fire and wake up those sleeping babies over there." He tipped his hat toward the still sleeping Rangers.

Sleeping babies? Leroy laughed at the thought. *Hell, Willis, we ain't exactly old men.* Leroy pursed his lips. "Okay, I'll catch the fish. I brought along some string that I can use for line and I'll make my own hook. Just break off some of that smoked bacon while I cut me a pole from that willow hanging over the creek bank."

"I can almost taste the trout now," Willis chuckled.

"You just get the fire going," Leroy pointed toward the campsite. "And build a big-un 'cause I'm going fishing and I ain't coming back empty handed."

Leroy pulled out his knife, cut off a thin branch and began fashioning it into a fishing pole. By the time Willis had returned with a handful of cracked bacon, he had the string tied to the end of the pole. Leroy smiled as he pulled out a hook from his vest pocket and tied it securely to the string.

"You brought a fishing hook?" Willis said shaking his head. "I can't believe you remembered to put a hook in your vest pocket.

"Willis, you know how much I like fresh game and fish while we're on the trail but we usually don't have time for it," Leroy held up the pole for approval. "Because I knew we were gonna be 'round the Red River, I decided to come ready to catch me some fish."

Willis reached for the pole and gave the hook a yank. "Good luck!" He walked away and continued to pick up pieces of wood. "'Cause I'm plenty hungry."

Within an hour the sleeping Rangers woke to the smell of trout cooking over a blazing campfire. Willis poured coffee while Leroy made sure the fish didn't burn. The day had started off, as Leroy liked to say, 'as good as life can get on the trail.'

The Red River got its name from the red clay and sediment that clouded the river and gave it a rusty color. In addition to serving as the boundary between Texas and the Indian Territory, the muddy river had several forks that began in the Texas Panhandle and the New Mexico Territory and ran all the way to Arkansas where it divided

Texas and Arkansas near Texarkana. After flowing through portions of Arkansas and Louisiana, the Red River joined the mighty Mississippi on its way to empty into the Gulf of Mexico. During the dry season the river was little more than a stream divided by jagged islands of dry clay running down the middle of the riverbed.

Leroy's horse stumbled once, otherwise, they crossed the river without any problems. Halfway across the river Willis pointed out a few undesirable critters as he liked to call them, crawling along the bank on the Texas side.

"Them's cottonmouths," Willis pointed to the snakes and called out a warning to Leroy and Travis. "They're as mean as rattlers, maybe meaner."

"I'm not about to find out," Travis whistled. "I try to stay away from anything that crawls." He tapped his horse's ribs lightly to urge him through the current.

"It gives me the creeps going into the Indian Territory," Willis said. "There's a reason folks call it the badlands. I'd just as soon keep my distance from Indians."

"We gotta find out what's happening to the stolen cattle and horses," Leroy said. "The way I see it, we got no choice but to go up into the Territory and look around for 'em."

"Leroy," Willis said. "I hate to bring this up, but we ain't got no authority once we're up in the Territory."

Leroy threw his head back and gave a hearty laugh. "Now you tell me. You should have mentioned that while we were on the other side of the river." His mustang began climbing up the gentle sloping bank on the Indian Territory side of the river.

"What good would it have done," Willis replied as his horse made it's way up the bank. "I know that wouldn't have stopped you."

"You know me well," Leroy laughed.

"Maybe *too* well," Willis yelled as Leroy's horse picked up his pace to a gallop.

While the Rangers were crossing the Red River, the Baker gang was delivering seven milk cows to some Wichita Indians in Fannin County. The milk cows had been brazenly taken from Ray Canfield's barn. When Canfield's wife and daughter went to the barn to do their milking chores they discovered that all the stalls were empty. Canfield was furious. He immediately grabbed a switch to beat the family dog only to discover that the hound had also been taken.

"It's not safe to sleep around here anymore," Canfield raged during a breakfast that was served without any milk. Canfield spit out his morning coffee. "It's no good without milk."

His wife, who had listened to Canfield complain all morning, decided she had heard enough of his ranting and raving for one day. "What do you mean it's not safe to sleep here anymore? It *never* has been safe. Why don't you men do something about it? If it's not rustlers and outlaws, it's the Indians."

Hearing his wife say what he believed to be true, Canfield saddled a horse and rode off towards his neighbor's farms and ranches intending to gather enough men for a raid across the border. Somebody was going to pay and Canfield wasn't overly particular about making sure the guilty party was the one on the receiving end of the punishment.

While making their way into the badlands, Leroy, Willis and Travis ran into three Kiowa scouts who were stationed at Fort Sill. The scouts spoke English and had heard talk that a gang of white men was trading stolen livestock with all the local tribes except for the Comanche, who would still rather kill you first and *maybe* trade with you later. The scouts offered to let the Rangers ride with them to Fort Sill where they could speak with the Federal authority stationed there. Leroy thought they had nothing to lose and Travis readily agreed. Only Willis thought they were wasting their time. Fort Sill was located in the southwest portion of the Territory, an area that had been given to the Chickasaws.

"We're gonna ride all the way to Fort Sill and talk to a bunch of Yankees and learn nothing," Willis complained.

The Kiowa scouts looked at each other and smiled.

When neither Leroy nor Travis spoke, Willis continued, "If they gave a hoot about catchin' them rustlers they would have already done it."

Leroy glared at Willis, nodded his head slightly toward the Kiowa scouts and rode on. Willis realized Leroy wanted him to shut up around the Indians. *Darn Indians speaking white man's language,* Willis thought. *That leads to nothing but trouble.*

At Fort Sill, the Rangers received a less than friendly welcome from an over worked US Army colonel and an uninterested Indian Agent. Before the meeting ended, Leroy was ready to shoot the Indian agent.

"Ten minutes after I sat down with that man I could tell he's about as crooked as anybody I've ever met," Leroy confided to Willis and Travis after leaving the Indian agent's office. The office also served as a storeroom for supplies that were to be given to the Indians during the winter or 'hungry season' as the Indians called the time when cold weather gripped the Territory.

"What was his name?" Travis asked.

"Baker," replied a still angry Leroy. "The man's name was Baker."

While riding out of the fort, the Rangers passed the building where the Kiowa scouts were billeted. Leroy decided to see if the scouts knew anything that might help him track down the outlaws. The scouts told him that they knew some Indians who traded with white men for cattle with different brands, a sure sign that the cattle were stolen.

Two of the scouts agreed to take the Rangers to a Choctaw trader in Durant, a small trading village not too far from one of the crossing points of the Red River. Willis was less than enthusiastic about riding anywhere with a couple of Indians, but Leroy assured him the scouts weren't about to scalp them in the dead of night. Ever since the Comanche had captured him, Willis had a fear of being scalped by Indians while asleep. Travis settled the matter when he asked Willis if he had ever known anyone or anything that could sneak up on Leroy. Everyone knew that Leroy was one of the lightest sleepers in the Rangers. Willis still wasn't happy, but in the end he agreed to ride with the Kiowa scouts.

That night, they camped near Durant. Willis spent the entire night propped up against a tree, rifle in hand while Leroy and Travis slept by the campfire. The Kiowa scouts slept nearby. Early the next morning, just as Leroy was preparing breakfast, the two scouts walked into the camp, leading their shod Army horses.

"He says they're ready to go, Leroy," Travis said, pointing to one of the Indians.

"I heard him, but I ain't had breakfast yet. Hell fire, what time did they get up?" Leroy growled as he poured his coffee on the fire and started packing up the supplies. He looked at Willis who was still propped against the tree, clutching his rifle while snoring as loud as usual.

Travis chuckled and pointed toward Willis. "Anybody could scalp him now."

"His hair too thin," one of the Kiowa scouts said, his voice flat. "Not make good scalp."

Leroy couldn't help but grin. *Wait until Willis hears that.*

The Kiowa scouts looked at each other, shrugged their shoulders, and started to mount their horses. Leroy, realizing that they were about to be left behind ran over to shake Willis awake while Travis finished packing up the camp.

The scouts took the three Rangers to see Walking Moon, one of the elders of the Choctaw tribe. Leroy noticed that Walking Moon didn't acknowledge the Kiowa scouts or allow them into his lodge.

While Leroy was inside the lodge, Walking Moon explained in no uncertain terms that he would buy beef wherever he could in order to keep his people from going hungry. He wasn't about to help the Rangers track down the source of his livestock. Leroy tried to explain that the beef was stolen

"This is white man's problem," he snarled at the Rangers, "not mine."

Finally, Leroy asked to see some of the Choctaw's cattle, hoping to salvage something from the trip. Walking Moon thought about the request for a moment then moved his head back and forth slowly.

When he was sure the Choctaws couldn't hear what he said, Leroy told the scouts about Walking Moon's refusal to allow him to inspect the herd.

"Go see the cattle anyhow," one of the Kiowas suggested. "The Choctaws keeps their cattle by Stony Creek so they can drink clean water."

Leroy looked around, none of the Choctaws looked friendly.

"Where's Stony Creek?" he whispered.

"Not far," the Kiowa replied.

"Will you take us there?" Leroy asked.

The Kiowa, a tall Indian with two scars running down the right side of his face, frowned, "No, but you can find the cattle if you ride west of here. The creek runs into the Red River."

Leroy decided not to push his luck and ask why the Kiowa had taken the Rangers to Durant, but wouldn't take them to the herd. *Maybe the Indians just don't like to mix,* he thought, remembering how unfriendly the Choctaws had been towards the Kiowa scouts.

An hour later the Rangers found the Choctaw's herd. The cattle were guarded by several braves riding unshod Indian ponies. Leroy took a good look at the horses. He decided the last thing he wanted was to have to hightail it back to Texas with the Choctaws right behind him. *I bet those ponies are as fast as greased lightning. We could never out run 'em even if we had a head start, which we won't have if they see us,* Leroy thought.

Leroy left Travis and Willis holding the horses out of sight while he prepared to sneak up on the herd. Making sure he was downwind from both the Indians and the animals, he slowly crawled through the tall grass in order to get a look at the brands on the cattle. Sure enough, the cattle were stolen. Some were even wearing Ray Canfield's Rolling C brand.

Leroy knew it was no use confronting the Choctaw elder. He had too many mouths to feed and he had already made it clear to Leroy that he didn't care where the beef came from.

The Rangers felt that the Federal authorities at Fort Sill should take care of this matter, but the colonel commanding Fort Sill had his own problems. The Federal Government was worried that if war broke out between the states, the Indians in the Territory would fight against the Union, so no one wanted to antagonize the tribes. The colonel was also aware that as soon as hostilities occurred, there would be plenty of

Southern troops riding up from Texas to take the fort. With all the problems on his plate, stopping cattle rustlers was not high on his list of priorities.

"It's gonna be up to us," Leroy said to Travis and Willis.

"What else is new?" Willis asked, his voice filled with sarcasm.

"Leroy," Travis held his hands out in protest. "Just how are you planning to catch a bunch of rustlers running cattle up here from Texas? I'd like to get back home before winter sets in."

"I figure we gotta set up a trap," Leroy said, his hand rubbing back and forth across his whiskers as he spoke.

"Travis, he's thinking of something and I can guarantee you it's gonna get us in a heap of trouble," Willis said, shaking his head. "I can always tell when he's up to no good."

Leroy ignored Willis and Travis while he worked out a plan. He gazed through the trees toward the valley where the Choctaws were keeping watch over their cattle. That evening, at twilight, the three Rangers rode west along the bank of the Red River until Leroy found the spot where he planned to wait for the rustlers.

"Look at this place, Willis," Leroy said as he pointed out the slow-moving, shallow river. "This has gotta be where the rustlers run the stolen cattle across the Red River."

"Leroy, there's gotta be at least a dozen other places just as good along this river," Willis argued.

"There's only three of us, that means we have to pick out one place and stay put at least a couple of nights and see if them sorry rustlers don't come this way. If I was them," Leroy took a moment to look at the river, "I'd want to cross right here where the water's shallow and the bank isn't steep."

"Just like I said," Willis sighed. "This is a darn good spot, but it ain't the only one. We can't cover 'em all."

"Let's just give this crossing a couple of nights," Leroy said. "If nothing happens, we'll move on to another place." He hesitated, looking around the river crossing. "I've got a feeling that this is the place."

Willis groaned. "Another night out in the rain."

"It's not raining, Willis," Leroy grinned.

"Not now, but look at them clouds," Willis pointed to the darkening sky. "Just give it time, Leroy. By midnight we'll be as wet as them darn snakes swarming out there in that river."

Just as Willis predicted, by midnight the sky was dark and veined with lightning. A steady downpour drenched the Rangers who were huddled with their horses. Leroy and Travis wore slickers while Willis wrapped a blanket around his shoulders.

"No fire and no coffee," Willis snarled at Leroy. "This is one hell of a fix if you ask me."

Travis chuckled at Willis's discomfort.

Willis glared at him. "You got nothing to be happy about, Travis."

Travis tried not to laugh.

Leroy kept watching the dark river crossing. There was no moon to light the night sky but the streaks of lightning fired up the area enough to see anything that moved. Leroy turned and asked Travis to keep watch. "I'm going to try to get some sleep," he said.

Travis nodded.

"Oh, heck, I'll keep watch," Willis said. "I'm the only one without a slicker. I'm so wet I can't sleep anyhow."

"What happened to that slicker you bought from that undertaker in Fort Worth?" Leroy asked.

Willis shook his head before answering. "I left it with Patsy in case she had to work the fields in the rain. Patsy didn't have nothing, not even a warm coat."

Leroy felt a pang of sadness and guilt thinking of Patsy working outside while cold and wet. Mindy had brought enough clothes from Georgia to keep every female in east Texas dressed but most of them were dresses and petticoats that weren't exactly suited for work clothes. He made a note to remember to ask her if she had an extra cape for Patsy. Leroy liked Patsy. She was a God fearing woman who would make Willis a good wife.

"Oh, hell," Willis whispered. "Will you look at that?"

Leroy's attention was instantly riveted towards the Texas bank of the Red River. Dark shadows were moving down the riverbank. A burst of lightning had stampeded about twenty head of horned cattle.

Riders were trying to turn them without much success. Leroy saw one-man fall from his horse into the water; the horse regained his footing and ran on with stirrups flying loose and flapping against his ribs.

"Good God Almighty," Willis said. "They're caught in a stampede."

"Those rustlers will play hell turning that herd," Travis said. "Let's go see what trouble we can give 'em." He gave Leroy and Willis a mischievous smile.

"Forget about that," Willis nudged Leroy. "Why don't we just wait right here until they're all tuckered out, then we can bushwhack 'em."

Leroy carefully considered his options. He looked up into the dark sky. It was pitch black with no stars, just clouds and the occasional burst of lightning. He turned to Travis. "Let's follow 'em and see where they're taking the cattle. I'd like to know where they're going and what we're up against."

"Agreed," said Willis.

"Okay by me," Travis nodded in agreement. "I just thought if we hit 'em now, we'd surprise them and what with all the confusion because of this storm and the stampeding cattle, we could take them out without too much trouble."

"That's not a bad idea, Travis," Leroy said. "But we need to find out a little more about their operation. I don't know anyway to do that other than we follow them and see where they take us."

"The storm will cover their tracks," Willis pointed out.

"What helps us is that they've got their hands full and won't be watching for anyone following them in this rainstorm," Leroy wiped his face with a handkerchief. "Let's mount up."

The three men made their way back to their horses. The wind was whipping through the trees making the horses restless. Leroy didn't blame them. It was a scary night to be out in the open grasslands. The horses kicked up mud and water as they rode through the heavy rain. The Rangers stayed well back, watching the rustlers while they worked to get control of the cattle.

Leroy had no idea how long they rode that night. All he knew was that he was exhausted from lack of sleep and his body, down to his wet socks and drawers, was cold from the hours spent in the wind and rain. At least the wind was at their back and not blowing into their faces. He thought about Willis giving that slicker to Patsy. *Darn fool, bet he'll think twice before he does that again.*

The rain stopped as streaks of dawn began to cut through the dark sky and a heavy fog filled the air. Leroy was grateful for the fog. It would give them enough cover to follow the rustlers without being detected.

The Rangers watched as the rustlers turned the cattle into a narrow, boxed canyon a few miles from the Choctaw herd. One of the rustlers rode on while the others stayed with the herd.

"That leaves three," Willis said. He was lying beside Leroy in the tall grass along the canyon's rim. Travis stayed with the horses out of sight from the canyon entrance.

"It's not much of a canyon," Leroy said.

"They probably won't be here long," Willis said, pointing to the men who had dismounted. "They haven't taken the saddles and bridles off of their horses. Think they're waiting for somebody?"

Leroy answered Willis's question with one of his own, "Why else would one of 'em have ridden off? He must have gone to get the sorry buzzard who is buying this stolen stock."

"Heck, Leroy," Willis muttered. "We're in over our heads here. Let's send Travis back to Fort Sill for help."

Leroy shook his head. "You saw how much help that Yankee officer was gonna give us—none. It's up to us to deal with the rustlers."

"This may not be the only bunch doing the rustlin'," Willis argued.

"You got a point there, Willis," Leroy grinned. "But that just means we've got to take 'em out one at a time." He reached over to give Willis a slap on the back. "Go get Travis. We're gonna need him. Let's take this bunch down before the other one gets back, in case he's not alone."

Willis didn't reply. He began to crawl backwards, carefully making his way away from the canyon rim.

"Hurry, Willis," Leroy whispered. "I got a feeling we ain't got much time."

CHAPTER 36

The Rangers approached the outlaws from three different directions, crawling in the grass and hiding behind rocks, trees or whatever cover they could find. When Leroy was sure Travis and Willis were in position to fire, he stood up and raised his rifle.

The outlaws were busy gathering wood to build a fire when Willis and Travis saw Leroy stand. The two Rangers quickly got into position and aimed their rifles. Before they could open fire, one of the outlaws spotted them. The man yelled out a warning and dived to the ground while grabbing for his rifle. Leroy fired sending a shot through the chest of one the outlaws before he could reach cover. Travis ran forward and fired at the outlaw lying on the ground, hitting him in the shoulder. The third outlaw, Joel Baker, dropped his rifle and raised his hands. Within a matter of minutes, two of the outlaws had been captured while the third lay on the ground mortally wounded.

"We ain't saying nothing," Joel Baker shouted to Leroy as he was being hogtied. "You can all go to hell before I tell you anything."

Leroy drew his pistol and aimed it at Joel's head. "You're too young to die, fellow. I'd think twice about telling me where to go and whether you'll talk or not."

Joel spit at him. Leroy dodged the spit, then gave Joel a kick to his gut. Joel coughed and moaned but didn't cry out.

"This your brother?" Willis asked Joel as he held up the dying man's head.

Leroy noticed Joel's face drain of color.

"He's dying boy," Leroy said. "But at least he won't be dancing at the end of a rope like you will. It's a hard way to die. I'd think about that if I was you."

"Hey," the other outlaw called out. "What about me? I'm bleeding all over the place. You've got me tied up so tight I can hardly breathe."

"You got something to say?" Leroy asked.

"No, I don't guess I do unless you can see fit to loosen this rope and doctor my shoulder," the outlaw answered. He looked over at Joel and gave a slight nod of his head. He wanted to reassure his younger brother that help was on the way. He knew his cousin, Sam Baker, should have already reached Fort Sill. If they could only delay for a couple of hours, maybe they could overpower the three Rangers when his cousin came back. Hopefully, he'd have a bunch of Choctaws with him.

"Well, what do we do now?" Willis asked, looking first at Travis, then at Leroy.

"I say we leave Travis here while you and I wait for the one who took off," Leroy said. "When he comes back we'll bushwhack him."

"Him?" Willis said. "You know as well as I do he ain't coming back alone."

"Willis," Leroy rolled his eyes and shook his head. "Why can't you ever look at the bright side?"

"Because there ain't no bright side, Leroy," Willis retorted, reloading his long rifle.

"Travis," Leroy called out. "Will you be okay here by yourself?"

Travis answered in a nonchalant voice, "I don't know why not. I'll move these two out of sight and wait."

Leroy motioned for Travis to step away from the outlaws. He nodded and walked over to Leroy and Willis.

"I don't know what we're gonna face when that other fellow comes back." Leroy paused, then continued, "But you're gonna be in the hot seat here. Willis and I will do our best to cover you but keep an eye open and be sure you're ready, okay?"

"I was born ready," Travis nodded, then grinned confidently.

Leroy smiled, gave Travis a slap in the back and joined Willis who was already walking back to find the horses.

"Born ready?" Willis grumbled. "Hell, that's a kid carrying a six gun."

"A kid who's faster than you or me," Leroy replied. "And he ain't much younger than the two of us."

"Don't seem so," Willis said.

"As long as we all keep getting older, Willis," Leroy laughed. "You ain't got anything to complain about."

"Oh, yeah?" Willis asked. "I sure would like to see my Patsy now and then."

"You'll see her soon enough," Leroy gave him a playful shove.

Leroy and Willis decided that their best chance to ambush anyone approaching the herd was to split up. Leroy found a good place to hide and watch the trail from Fort Sill, while Willis was supposed to wait on the eastern side of the canyon in case someone came from the direction of the Choctaw camp. After two hours of waiting, Willis decided to join Leroy. To Leroy's dismay, Willis rode up in full view of the trail.

"Get down and hide that darn horse, Willis!" Leroy yelled. Realizing that Willis probably couldn't hear him, Leroy motioned to Willis with his hat. "Willis!"

Willis saw him and rode toward the ledge where Leroy was crouched down. "Willis, go warn Travis. I just spotted somebody over yonder and from the looks of it, we're about to face about twenty or thirty men."

"Gol-darn it," Willis yelled. "Let's get out of here *now!* Them outlaws know they're gonna face a rope so they'll put up one hell of a fight."

"Get down to the canyon and warn Travis. We're running out of time," Leroy said, his voice filled with urgency.

Willis slapped the reins against the horse's neck and galloped toward the canyon. Leroy slipped back into his hiding place just as the riders appeared over the crest of a hill. Leroy frowned. *What the heck are they doing out here?* A column of Federal cavalry rode toward a nearby stream. Leroy watched as the troops stopped to water their horses. Leroy climbed out of the hiding space, got on his horse and made his way as quickly as possible towards the troops. He intended to ask them to either help with the ambush or to get the hell out of there before they scared off the rustlers. He waved his hat to make sure they understood he was friendly and not posing a threat. *Never know when one of 'em might be trigger- happy.*

A Federal officer accompanied by two sergeants walked forward to meet him. The captain was a clean-shaven, small fellow. He looked friendly enough, but the sergeants, both wearing salt and pepper beards, were pointing their rifles directly at Leroy. Several troopers fell in behind the captain and the two sergeants.

Leroy tipped his hat, dismounted and said, "I've got a couple of rustlers tied up in that small boxed canyon over yonder. I figure there's at least one, maybe more on the way back here, and there could be some Indians with 'em."

"Slow down mister. I'm Captain Nolan. My men and I are from Fort Sill. Now, just exactly who are you?" the captain asked.

"My name is Leroy Wiley. I'm a Texas Ranger. Three of us tracked these buzzards here from across the Red River," Leroy explained.

"In case you hadn't noticed, this isn't Texas," the captain shook his head. "You have no jurisdiction on this side of the river."

It was all Leroy could do to keep from telling the man off right then and there. He took a deep breath, squared his shoulders, and spoke slowly. "I know where the boundary between Texas and the Indian Territory is, but we've got to put a stop to the cattle rustlers on the Texas side of the river." Leroy paused to see the officer's reaction. Captain Nolan pursed his lips but before he could speak, Leroy continued, "I sure could use some help."

The captain motioned the sergeants to follow him. They turned and walked away from Leroy towards a cluster of rocks. At that moment Leroy felt like shooting all three of them, beginning with the captain.

After a few minutes that seemed to Leroy to drag on for hours, the captain came back and said. "We're headed to Stoney Creek. Someone attacked the Choctaws and ran off part of their herd last night. Still, I believe I can spare a few men to help you with your problem." He turned to one of his sergeants. "Sergeant Henderson," he commanded, "take four troopers and assist this Texas lawman."

Henderson saluted, then motioned to four troopers standing nearby with their horses.

Leroy smiled, his expression one of relief. "I can't thank you enough, Captain. I think you can see that we need to put a stop to this before it gets out of control." *I guess Canfield and the other ranchers decided to take matters into their own hands.*

The officer nodded. "Sergeant Henderson will arrest the cattle rustlers and turn them over to you at the Red River."

Leroy waited for the sergeant and troops to mount, and then led them back toward the canyon. *I hope we're not too late.*

Once they reached the canyon Leroy stopped and spoke with Sergeant Henderson, "Okay with you if we hit 'em here? We'll have clear shots from that ledge. I was hiding up there when I saw your column."

Henderson nodded, and then followed Leroy around the ledge. The path became steep and rocky. The horses struggled so the troopers dismounted and one of the men led their mounts to an area hidden from sight of the trail.

"Do you want them dead or alive?" Henderson asked when they finally got into position.

Leroy laughed, "You're the kind of fellow I like to work with. I suppose we ought to take 'em alive if we can, but I ain't too worried about it."

Henderson leaned over the ledge then said in a flat voice, "Well, make up your mind because riders are coming this way."

Leroy's heart began to beat faster. He strained his eyes and looked at the trail ahead.

"Here," Henderson said as he handed Leroy a spyglass. "This will let you get a good look at 'em."

"Two, no wait, there's three of them," he carefully handed the extended spyglass back to the sergeant.

Sergeant Henderson raised the glass to his eye. "I don't believe it!" He turned to Leroy. "One of them is Sam Baker, the Indian agent from Fort Sill."

The Indian Agency was established in 1824 as part of the War Department. The agency's mission was to help the Indians manage their land. Sam Baker, like so many agents who worked for the United States government's Bureau of Indian Affairs, was a thoroughly corrupt man. It was the agent's job to provide for the Indian's welfare and administer government programs such as the distribution of cattle and grain to help the Indians survive on the reservations. Instead, agents like Sam Baker took advantage of their position to steal from both the Indians and the government they were supposed to serve.

When challenged by Leroy and the troopers that were with him, Sonny Baker, Sam's brother, whirled his horse around and tried to escape. *They're on foot,* Sonny Baker thought. *By the time they get mounted, I'll at least have a head start. Maybe the Choctaw's will help me hide until the army gets tired of looking for me.*

Leroy raised his rifle and squeezed the trigger, but the rustler was already out of range. Sonny Baker laughed and whipped his horse. His laughter was short lived. As he rounded a bend in the trail, there was Willis standing with his rifle raised and ready to fire. Before Baker could decide what to do, Willis pulled the trigger. This time, Sonny Baker wasn't out of range.

While Sonny Baker was making his unsuccessful bid to elude justice, his brother Sam Baker and their partner Clem Robertson were riding into the canyon. When they saw the unguarded cattle, they both realized their chances of getting away weren't very good. In their haste to dismount, both men fell. They staggered to their feet and hid behind a small cluster of rocks. Travis spotted the two fleeing men and immediately opened fire.

Clem made a dash for the middle of the herd, stumbled and fell forward against the one bull stirring in the mix of cows. The bull raised his head, snorted, and began trying his best to stomp the daylights out of the intruder. Clem screamed out in pain and reached for his handgun. Before Clem could get off a shot, Travis had him in his gun sights. He aimed for the rustler's chest. While Clem was trying to avoid the charging bull, he stumbled again and lurched forward just as the musket ball blew out the back of his head. Clem Robertson was dead before he hit the ground. Seeing what had happened to Clem,

Sam Baker dropped his rifle and began crawling away as fast as he could. He was passing between two large rocks when Leroy's boot slammed into his ribs.

"Well now, Mr. Baker," Leroy said, his voice filled with sarcasm. "Where do you think you're going? You weren't planning on leaving these poor lost cattle up here in the Territory? It's doubtful them dumb animals can find their way back to their home in Texas unless you're willing to help."

Sam twisted his head and looked up at Leroy. "Go to hell," he spat while still trying to recover from the kick Leroy had given him. Leroy gave him another strong kick to the ribs, then picked him up by his shirtfront. Sam stumbled all the way back to the campsite. Travis was waiting. His mouth formed a smile as big as Texas. "Where's Willis?" he asked.

"Probably napping," Leroy replied. "This here is a very important man, Travis. He works for the United States Government."

"I think the government of Texas might have something to say about that," Travis chuckled as he grabbed Sam's arm. "Let's go join the rest of the rustlers."

Leroy thanked Sergeant Henderson and the troopers for their help and told the sergeant that he planned to take the rustlers back to Texas for trial. Henderson asked the Rangers to wait until Captain Nolan got back since one of the prisoners was the Indian Agent at Fort Sill and as such a government responsibility. Leroy agreed. He owed the captain that much for sending Henderson and the troopers to help round up the outlaws.

When the captain returned he insisted on taking Sam Baker into custody. Leroy told Willis and Travis he would have preferred to take the man back to Texas with the other rustlers, but it wasn't worth arguing with the Yankee officer.

"We'll be arguing soon enough," Willis said as they watched the troopers form up for the ride to Fort Sill. "To hell with him. I'd just as soon the Indians and the Yankee soldiers kill each other off and leave us alone."

Leroy turned his attention to the problems at hand. They not only had prisoners and bodies to take back to Texas but also a small herd of livestock. Leroy wasn't thrilled about driving cattle back across the Red River all the way to Fort Worth.

The next day they met some Wichita Indians willing to help drive the cattle. With their help the Rangers were able to cross the Red River near Taoyaya while losing only a few head of cattle in the process.

Over the whispered objections of Willis, Leroy agreed to go with the Wichita Indians to their camp and spend the night before continuing on to Fort Worth in the morning. Just the sight of teepees surrounded by Indians and their horses made Willis so jumpy that Leroy told Travis to keep an eye on him.

"It ain't that far to Smith County you know," Willis said to Leroy.

"Willis, will you cut it out," Leroy snapped. "I know exactly how far it is to Smith County, but we've gotta take these prisoners to Fort Worth and turn them over to the US Marshall. Maybe he can figure out who these cattle belong to."

"You telling me we got to take these darn cows with us? I thought we could leave 'em with these Indians and let the Marshall come get 'em," Willis slammed his hat against his knee.

Leroy looked at Travis, silently conveying his frustration.

"He sure does miss Patsy, don't he?" Travis said while grinning from ear to ear.

Willis glared at Travis. "You watch your mouth. I'm doing my part."

Leroy, realizing how upset Willis was about spending the night with the Wichita Indians, decided to cut Willis some slack. He folded his arms across his chest and walked over to where Travis stood, red faced and feeling bad about getting on Willis's nerves.

"Hey, Travis," Leroy said while giving a slight nod of his head toward Willis. "How about checking on the horses?"

"The horses are fine, Leroy," Travis said. "The Indians have 'em all watered and fed."

Leroy let out a deep breath. He tried once more to make Travis understand. "Still, it might not be a bad idea to make sure none of our horses threw a shoe while crossing the river."

Travis frowned. "Well, heck. If they threw a shoe there's nothing we can do about it here. These Indian ponies are unshod."

"Travis!" Leroy got about an inch from the younger man's face. "Get the heck out of here so I can talk to Willis!"

Travis raised his hands in mock surrender. "All you had to do was say so, Leroy. I can't read your mind." With that, he stomped away from Leroy and Willis.

Leroy rubbed the back of his neck before turning to face Willis. His neck was so tight it felt like it was tied in knots. "What's the matter with you? You with me or not?" His eyes were locked on Willis.

Willis walked to the opening of the teepee. "Let's take a walk. This place smells like Indians," he said quietly. Leroy joined him.

"I reckon that's because this place sleeps about seven or eight Indians every night," Leroy laughed. "They've doubled up so we can sleep in here out of the rain." Leroy pointed to the dark clouds gathering in the west. "It's a heck of a lot better hospitality than our prisoners are getting. They're tied up out there by the campfire for the squaws to stare at."

Willis took a deep breath and sighed. "When are we going to be able to go home, Leroy?"

"Two, maybe three weeks," Leroy said. "That's what I figure."

"Let's leave the cattle here. That way we can get to Fort Worth a heck of a lot faster."

Leroy shook his head. "Can't leave the cattle here and get these Indians involved."

Willis nodded. "Sometimes when I think of Patsy working the farm I wonder what I'm doing here."

"I feel the same way, but I need the money," Leroy ducked under the flap of the teepee and knelt down on a bed of pine needles. "Mindy and I plan on building our own place. That won't happen unless I have the extra pay coming in from the Rangers." He turned and looked up at Willis. "Let's go find Travis and see if these Indians have any firewater."

"They don't call it firewater," Willis grinned. "I heard that big Indian chief plain as day. He told the squaws that three white men would be staying in the village so they better hide the whiskey."

"Whatever they call it," Leroy laughed. "I'm all for it."

The young Rangers spent the night in the Indian village. They cooked their own breakfast. When they had finished eating Willis tied Joel Baker's hands to the saddle horn. Joel's brother had died during the night. Leroy figured the man bled to death. *Nothing we could have done would have saved him,* he thought. *I'll write up the report when I get to Fort Worth. He probably lucked out. It's a lot easier to die in your sleep than at the end of a rope.*

With the help of the Wichita Indians the Rangers drove the cattle to the stockyards in Fort Worth. Afterwards, they paid the Indians for their help with a dozen head of cattle, then turned Joel Baker over to the United States Marshall.

While Leroy sat in the Marshall's office writing up his report, Travis and Willis got the horses stabled and searched for the most inexpensive lodging they could find. Both men were surprised that the main topic of conversation around Fort Worth was about the election of Abraham Lincoln as President of the United States. Travis pointed out to Willis that the front page of the newspaper was full of calls for secession from the Union.

Travis picked up a paper someone had left in a chair at the hotel and began reading it to Willis. "It says here that the radicals, whoever those fellows are, want Governor Sam Houston to pull Texas out of the Federal Union and join the Confederate States. But it seems that Houston doesn't want to do that, so these radical fellows want to hold a convention and have the counties vote to leave the Union."

"I don't wanna hear nothing about it," Willis snarled. "They're just asking for trouble and I don't intend to get into a fight just because somebody in Louisiana or Mississippi says I gotta." He waved his hands in the air in frustration. "Let's go get Leroy and have supper."

Travis laughed. "You think Leroy will have the money to pay for us to eat?"

"If he don't, we're in a heap of trouble," Willis said. "Cause I'm hungry and I don't have any script and I'm pretty sure you don't either."

Travis suddenly stopped and grabbed Willis by the arm. "Look! There's a card game going on in that saloon. Let's go see if we can win a hand or two. That hotel nearly wiped me out the last time I was in town. My luck is bound to change."

"Well," Willis leaned over and looked through the swinging doors, "I'm mighty tempted but we better not."

"Why not?" Travis asked.

Willis rolled his eyes. "Travis, what the heck would happen if we lose?"

Travis frowned. "Heck, it don't matter none, 'cause between us we ain't got enough to get into a game anyhow."

"Then why the heck did you mention it?" Willis asked, obviously annoyed.

At that moment Leroy stepped step out of the Marshall's office and crossed the street. Travis and Willis quickened their pace in order to catch him. They had to wait until several wagons and a fast moving stagecoach had passed before getting Leroy's attention.

"Good news, boys," Leroy grinned. "There was a reward out for both the cattle and the Baker boys. By turning them in we should have been entitled to two hundred dollars in reward money."

"Gollee!" Travis slapped his hands against his gun belt. "Now we can get into that card game, Willis!"

Willis ignored Travis. His eyes were locked on Leroy. He learned toward Leroy, squinted his eyes and asked in a guarded tone, "What do you mean when you say that money *should* have been coming to us?"

"I mean," Leroy pushed his cowboy hat back, "that if we weren't Texas Rangers we would have gotten two hundred dollars in reward money for delivering the stolen cattle and what was left of the Baker gang to the Marshall. But it just so happens," Leroy hesitated as Willis leaned even closer, "that we aren't allowed to take the reward money because we're Texas Ranges and we work for the state of Texas."

"Then I quit," Willis said. "Just show me where I have to go to turn in my badge."

Leroy reached out to grab his arm. "Wait, Willis. You still won't get any of the two hundred dollars."

"And why not?" Willis asked indignantly.

"Because you were a Ranger when we took down the Baker gang. The way the Marshall explained it to me was that the reward was offered to what he called laymen, not lawmen."

"Are you telling me that only a preacher could get the reward money for turning in that sorry Joel Baker?" Willis asked.

"Willis," Leroy chuckled. "The US Marshall told me that a layman, and I'm using his exact words, means 'one who is not' a lawman. I had to ask him to explain it to me twice but that's the rule. In this case, only someone who is not a lawman can collect the reward money for turning in them murderin' rustlers."

"Two hundred darn dollars," Willis sighed deeply. "We'll never earn that much working for the Rangers. Heck, half the time they don't even pay us."

"There goes the card game," Travis said. "Now, how are we gonna get something to eat?"

"I just may have the answer to that," Leroy grinned.

"I hope you have something more than answers 'cause words ain't gonna fill my stomach," Willis grouched.

"The Marshall gave us thirty dollars for bringing in the cattle. Seems like some of the ranchers put up some reward money, and they didn't put no strings on their reward. So we can eat." Leroy reached into his pocket and pulled out two twenty dollar gold pieces and ten dollars in script.

Travis frowned. "Two twenty dollar gold pieces and one ten dollar script doesn't equal thirty dollars, Leroy." Travis slapped his knee and turned toward Willis, "We got fifty whole dollars. Let's go play cards."

"Nope," Leroy pursed his lips and crossed his arms over his chest. "You fellows ever hear of a finder's fee? I found out about the money so I'm charging a small fee for my extra work."

"The heck you are," Willis said. "That's our money fair and square and I mean all of us, Leroy. Me and Travis have a stake in this, too."

Leroy winked at Travis. Travis gave him a grin of recognition.

Travis pointed to a dining hall across from the saloon. "Let's talk about it over a hot meal."

Leroy nodded. "I'm sure a big slice of apple pie will make Willis feel a whole lot better about not getting a share of that two hundred dollars."

"Not likely," Willis grumbled as he followed Travis and Leroy. The Rangers made their way across the busy street and hurried into the best dining hall in Fort Worth.

After a good meal followed by drinks at the Longhorn Saloon, the Rangers climbed the steps to the top floor of the Fort Worth Hotel to enjoy a good nights sleep. Leroy and Travis made beds on the floor and let Willis sleep in the narrow bed. Leroy hoped that allowing Willis to sleep in the only bed in the room would put him in a better mood.

"Leroy, I want to thank you for letting me sleep in the bed, but I'm still feeling mighty low about not getting any of that reward money."

"How much is left of the fifty dollars, Leroy?" Travis asked.

"Not enough to play cards so go to sleep and forget about joining that poker game," Leroy tipped his hat down over his eyes. He heard Travis chuckle.

"How'd you know what I was thinking?" Travis asked.

"Travis," Willis leaned over the side of the bed to make sure Travis was listening, "if you'd spend more time thinking about important things instead of card games and saloon gals you'd be a lot better off."

"Says who?" Travis retorted as he tossed a pillow at Willis.

"Willis speaks from experience, Travis," Leroy laughed. "He's a one woman man and she's got him wrapped around her pretty finger."

"Look who's talking?" Willis said.

"I just ain't found the right gal," Travis said. "But I plan on spending as much time as possible looking for her."

"Travis, maybe you ain't been looking in the right place," Willis said, his voice very serious. "You spend too much time 'round them saloon gals."

"You might ought to wait until the war starts," Leroy said. "I bet we wind up fighting in Georgia and there sure are some pretty belles in Georgia," Leroy whistled.

"Darn this war talk," Willis said. "It'd be just my luck I'll be sent off to fight in this here war before I can get home to see Patsy."

Silence filled the room as the men drifted off into their own thoughts. Willis fell asleep while worrying about Patsy, while Travis drifted off picturing himself dressed in a soldier's uniform riding a spirited horse into battle. Leroy stayed awake for a long time. He could almost feel Mindy's body pressed close against him, her hands gently touching his face or softly running her fingers through his hair. He raised his head and looked out the small bedroom window into a black sky filled with the light of a thousand stars.

I sure do miss that gal, he thought. *Just you wait and see, I'm gonna build her the prettiest little house in Texas.*

The next morning, the United States Marshall sent a deputy to find the Rangers and to tell them that their orders had arrived by telegraph.

"The telegraph said for you boys to go back to the Wichita tribe's camp at Tawakoni. The message goes on to remind you fellows that the Wichita Indians are friendly," the US Marshall said with a smile. "I was raised near there and I swear it's the best part of Texas."

"That's all well and good, Marshall," Leroy replied. "But what are we supposed to do once we get there?"

"It says here," the Marshall leaned back in his chair and picked up the telegraph. He fumbled around his desk looking for his reading glasses. Leroy rolled his eyes but remained silent. After a few moments the Marshall gave up searching for the glasses and held the paper at arms length. He squinted as he tried to read the telegraph. "As I was saying, it says here that you boys are supposed to join up with some other Rangers from Mount Pleasant and await further orders. It also says you won't have to wait very long. So I guess that means you better saddle up as soon as your horses are ready to ride."

He looked at the three confused young men, raised his thick eyebrows and shrugged. "The telegram don't say no more, just that they want you back in east Texas, which I believe is good news since the three of you happen to be from that part of the state."

Leroy looked at Travis, then Willis, "Make much sense to either of you?"

Travis shook his head. Willis silently stared out the window.

The Marshall took a sip of coffee and continued. "As I said, that's my old stomping grounds. I can tell you that the Wichita and Tonkawa Indians roam free around the prairies and woodlands of that area, but they don't cause no trouble. They live in tepees and pole houses made mostly from skins, grass and brush. They do some hunting and they raise the best corn in the state. You boys won't have no problems with 'em. Just tell 'em you're waiting to join up with some more Rangers."

Hell, we know all that. We've been there, Willis thought. *You ain't the only one from that part of Texas.*

Leroy thanked the lawman and reached for the telegram. "We do as we're told," he said to Willis and Travis as they left the office.

"At least it gets us a little closer to home," Travis said. "That's good enough for me."

"Yeah," Willis agreed. "But for how long?"

"You fellows ready to ride?" Leroy asked.

Willis and Travis nodded and without another word they walked to the corral and saddled their horses.

CHAPTER 37

"I tell you what I am ready to do," Willis whispered. "I wanna get away from these here Indians."

"Which Indians do you mean?" Leroy asked as he carefully looked around.

Willis shook his head in dismay. "Does it matter? Heck, I mean all of 'em."

"We're supposed to wait till the captain gets here with further orders," Travis said. "The telegram said he'll be here any day now."

"Any day?" Willis sighed and turned to Leroy. "How much longer? I'm beginning to smell like 'em."

"That's because you're eating the same grub," Leroy grinned. "Right now we both could sneak up on any Indian and they'd never pick up our scent, even if we were up wind of 'em."

Travis began to chuckle. "That's real good news. Next time I meet a pretty gal, I'll just explain to her that I smell like an Indian because I've been eating and sleeping with 'em. She'll wanna get *real* close to me after she hears that."

"I just wanna go home," Willis said, his arms crossed over his chest as he spoke.

Leroy's patience was wearing thin. "Heck, who doesn't? But the fact is, we gotta do what we were ordered to do. At least we're finally back in east Texas, and not all that far from home."

"I'm gonna try to take a nap under that big oak tree over there. Look at it, Leroy. It's about a hundred feet tall. It reminds me of that bunch of laurels and water oaks on Patsy's family's farm. Them trees grow little acorns that feeds all the hungry critters," Willis sighed. "Try to keep an eye out for me, will you?"

Leroy gave the tree a look then said, "Your scalp's safe as long as mine is."

"Thanks," Willis replied sarcastically. "That's just what I wanted to hear. I appreciate you reminding me that we're stuck here with a bunch of Indians."

Leroy watched as Willis walked towards the grove of shade trees. He thought for a moment about warning Willis about the snakes that might be settled in by the water. *Just to shake him up a bit,* Leroy thought. But before he could speak, Travis pointed towards the squaws who were hard at work preparing the afternoon meal.

"Three squares a day," Travis said to Leroy. " I can't say too much about the food. The squaws do the best they can with what they got, but that ain't much."

Leroy rested his hand on his loaded pistol, never forgetting that these Indians lived in a dark, dangerous world not understood by any white man. He glanced over at Willis who was already fast asleep, then rolled his eyes and scratched his bristly chin. "That fellow can sleep anywhere," Leroy said while shaking his head in dismay.

Leroy and Travis decided to take a walk through the camp. They watched some kids playing a game with a ball made from hides and sticks sharpened and covered at one end with a web made from horsehair.

"Looks like a lot of fun," Travis said as Leroy walked over to a large campfire.

A fine figure of a woman was stirring the contents of a big pot hanging over a flickering fire. Even though it was a warm day, Leroy moved closer to the fire. To Leroy, a fire, no matter how small, represented comfort and nourishment.

The Indian girl wore a dress of tan leather and a pair of dark brown moccasins covered her feet. She had tan colored leather straps covered with beads holding her hair in braids. Leroy gave her his best smile and she looked back at him, her eyes cold. She was red-blooded and round where she should be, but slim like most Indian girls her age.

"Howdy," Leroy said, his voice gentle and friendly.

She turned her face away and gave no reply.

"Well," Leroy sighed. "It was just a thought."

He thought she might want some company, but he thought wrong. Growing up on the frontier had taught most Indians that it was best to keep to themselves as much as possible and avoid any contact with white men.

"Darn it," he said while watching the Indian girl walk away. "I sure do miss Mindy."

Travis laughed. "No doubt about that." He tilted his head toward the Indian girl. "The kids wouldn't have anything to do with me either."

"It's high time the boys from Mount Pleasant got here," Leroy complained.

"Think we ought to ride toward Mount Pleasant?" Travis asked. "Maybe there's been some kind of mix-up."

Leroy took a deep breath and sighed. "Let's wait a day or two and if they're still not here, then we'll talk it over."

Travis motioned toward the creek bank. "That's about as long as Willis will wait anyhow, unless we hog tie him to one of those trees."

"Agreed," Leroy grinned. "He sure is impatient these days."

Travis laughed. "I think I know why."

They walked back to watch the Indian boys running back and forth across a grassy meadow.

As the sun dropped through the clouds toward the horizon, all work in the camp came to a stop. Bellies were filled with stew made from root vegetables, some kind of meat which remained a mystery, followed by a few hours of relaxation after a hard day's work by everyone but the visiting Rangers.

While they bedded down for the night the Rangers could hear stories being told by one of the elders of the tribe, followed by songs that were sung in the Indian's language. The Rangers couldn't understand a word but Leroy smiled at Willis, "That old guy just finished telling a few lies that everyone seemed to enjoy. Heck, even Indians enjoy a good yarn now and then."

When Willis didn't reply Leroy leaned over to see if he was already asleep. He was surprised to see his friend deep in thought, no doubt missing Patsy. Leroy tipped his hat over his eyes and tried to sleep.

Early the next morning the Rangers were awakened by the sound of horses riding into the camp. Leroy's heart jumped when he saw three tall Indian braves walking toward him.

"Bacon and eggs, Willis," Leroy said as he poked his still sleeping friend with the toe of his boot. Travis was already awake. He looked up and gave Leroy a nudge.

"I see them," Leroy said in a quiet voice.

"Them Injuns ain't never seen no bacon and eggs, Leroy, so cut it out," Willis snarled and turned over, pulling his blanket with him.

"Well, the breakfast committee is fast approaching so if I was you, I'd get ready to greet 'em," Leroy said in a low voice as he slowly got to his feet.

It wasn't so much the words Leroy said but his tone that told Willis something wasn't quite right. Leroy's words were light but his voice was filled with tension.

Willis rolled over and slipped his hand over the gun tucked under his bedroll. "What do you think they want with us?"

One of the Indians motioned to the campfire and said in halting English, "Come, you eat. Other Rangers are coming. Maybe you leave today."

"How long before they get here?" Leroy asked.

The Indian gave a shrug and stepped aside waiting for Leroy and Willis to move toward the campfire.

"Think it's the captain?" Willis asked as he stood and brushed the dust off his clothes.

Leroy nodded in the affirmative but didn't speak.

The Rangers rode into the village just before noon.

Captain Bailey ordered his men to dismount, loosen their horse's cinches, and rest while he expressed his appreciation to the leaders of the Wichita tribe.

Willis nudged Leroy and whispered, "One pack mule, that's all they brought. We're gonna be hungry before this duty's over."

Leroy grinned, "Just think of it this way, if your horse gives out, there's an extra mount. Remember what the old timers used to say about mules?"

"What?" Willis asked with mock interest. "I can't wait to hear this."

"The old boys used to say if you start out riding a horse, you'd end up walking. If you start out riding a mule, you'll end up riding."

"I never heard that," Willis said, keeping his voice low.

"Pa said that's what the old guys said when they were going west on the Santa Fe Trail."

"We're probably going to be riding all over Texas chasing some darn Mexicans or worse yet, a band of Comanche on the warpath."

"Only time will tell, Willis," Leroy chuckled. "We'll know soon enough. Here comes the man that gives the orders."

Captain Zack Bailey, followed by a few young Rangers, walked toward Travis, Willis and Leroy.

"We gonna head home now, Captain?" Willis asked before the Ranger Captain could speak.

"Afraid not, Willis," Captain Bailey pursed his lips and gave a slight nod of his head.

Willis gave Leroy a disappointed look.

Darn it! What now? Leroy thought. He realized that Willis was upset and gave his friend a sympathetic pat on the shoulder. Willis looked at him and frowned.

"It seems the Lipan Apache are running wild again. We've got orders to round them up or chase 'em back to west Texas where the army wants 'em to stay put." Captain Bailey motioned for the Rangers to gather around him.

West Texas! Willis thought. *Not again!*

Zack Bailey was a big man, about six feet and packing well over one hundred and seventy muscular pounds. His features were strong and weathered by the hot Texas sun. His face was accented by a set of dark brown eyes. The first thing people noticed about him were his thick shoulders and muscled forearms earned from working his family's farm in Van Zandt County. His carriage gave the impression of sternness and cold reserve but nothing could have been further from the truth. Zack had a boyish, winning personality that made him one of the favorites among the leaders of the Texas Rangers.

"Other than the usual questions of how many days we'll be in the saddle and how far are we going to have to ride, anyone have anything else they want to ask?"

Willis cleared his throat and then said, "When do we get paid?"

Everyone laughed including Captain Bailey. The captain reached out and gave Willis a playful shove before replying. "I plum forgot about that question, Willis. The answer is, as usual, I have no idea. I'm sure your pay will be forwarded to Tyler. My boys will be paid when we get back to Mount Pleasant."

The captain waited for the others to speak, when no one had anything to say, Bailey continued. "You men from Smith County have been ordered to ride along with us in order to bring our company up to full strength. If we're going to do our job we're going to need every last one of you. Most Apache tribes are out west in the New Mexico Territory but we've got this band of Lipan Apache here in Texas. Let me warn you, any Indian tribe with the name Apache attached to it is trouble. About the only thing a Comanche is scared of is an Apache." Bailey paused and then added, "Rest up men, we ride at daybreak."

Captain Bailey was commanding a newly formed Ranger company from Van Zandt Counties. This had Leroy worried because Captain Bailey was the only experienced Ranger riding in the group. None of the other Rangers had ever gone up against the Comanche. Leroy had a healthy respect for the Comanche and if the Comanche were afraid of the Lipan Apache that was enough for him. Leroy kept his concerns to himself not wanting to spook the other Rangers.

The Rangers separated. The men who had ridden in from Mount Pleasant went to unsaddle and care for their horses while Leroy and Willis walked over to the creek by themselves to discuss their new assignment.

"Look, Willis," Leroy said as he tapped the side of his boot against a rock. "I don't want to go after them darn Apache any more than you do but it means we'll draw some more pay when this is over, so look at the bright side."

"The bright side you talk about is Indian fighting and that is about as welcome to me as that nasty stuff you're trying to get off your boot. I can't spend no extra pay if my scalp is hanging in some Apache teepee."

"I've learned a valuable lesson while being in this Indian camp, Willis," Leroy grinned.

"What's that?" Willis asked.

"To watch where I'm walking when I'm around a bunch of hungry hound dogs." Leroy checked the other boot before adding, "You know what was in that stew you were eating last night, don't you?"

"Stop!" Willis said as he held up his hand. "I had two bowls of that stuff."

"Okay," Leroy said in mock surrender. "But I thought you might have noticed that one of the hounds was missing? Remember that yellow one with..."

"I'm getting out of here," Willis said as he hurriedly walked away. "And I ain't eating nothing else 'cept what the boys from Mount Pleasant have in their saddle bags and on that *one* darn pack mule."

"Oh, come on, Willis," Leroy teased as he followed his best friend back to the camp. "Them squaws have worked all day making a special stew. They're having some kind of big pow-wow tonight."

"To heck with them darn squaws," Willis huffed as he stormed off. His mouth felt like it was filled with cotton and his stomach began heaving.

Leroy laughed as he listened to Willis complain. "Them squaws would poison a man by feeding him hound dog stew without giving it a second thought. Heck, them Injuns will eat anything."

Later that night, after a hushed darkness had fallen over the Indian village, Leroy spread out his bedroll and positioned it so he could look up into a clear sky filled with stars as bright as Mindy's eyes. He always thought of Mindy before falling asleep. His wife had made his life complete and although he was not a praying man by nature, he asked the Almighty to help his wife understand his long absences and help her to be happy living with his family on their farm in Starrville.

"I've loved that gal ever since I laid eyes on her," he whispered.

"Well, I feel the same way 'bout Patsy," Willis chimed in, obviously still awake.

Leroy looked over to where Willis had settled down for the night. "I thought you'd be asleep by now," Leroy said. "A man with a near empty stomach falls asleep pretty quick."

"I reckon I'm getting used to my stomach being empty," Willis groaned. "I only get good vittles when I'm home or visiting at your house."

I should have known he wasn't asleep, Leroy thought. *I didn't hear him snoring.*

Willis turned over and covered his face with his well-worn Cowboy hat.

CHAPTER 38

While they were saddling up at sunrise the next day, Captain Bailey told the men that the renegade band of Apache they were after had wiped out a patrol of US Army cavalry and raided several farms in west central Texas. Hearing that the Apache would take on the United States Cavalry impressed Leroy and only served to increase his concern about taking on the Apache with so few experienced men.

The piney woods gradually flattened into wide plains as the Rangers rode toward the territory traditionally occupied by the Lipan Apache. At noon, while both the horses and men rested, Captain Bailey filled the men in on the latest news regarding the secession movement in Texas. These young men were all aware that sooner or later they would leave their part time Texas Ranger duty for full time service in the Confederate Army. But first, there was a small matter of finding the renegade band of Lipan Apaches.

After nearly a week in the saddle the Rangers reached what had once been the settlement at Round Rock Post Office. The structure had been destroyed and all the occupants killed. Captain Bailey had been warned about this and prepared his men for the worst. Fortunately, fresh graves had been dug and the three families who had lived at the settlement had all been given a Christian burial.

"They were after the horses," Leroy said to Willis as they watched Captain Bailey and two Rangers walking around what was left of a fenced in corral. "Probably held about a dozen horses, maybe less. But whatever the number, the Apache have them now."

"Too bad they had to kill everybody to get 'em," Harry Simpson said as he kicked a few pieces of burnt wood and ash out of his way.

"Well," Bailey said as he surveyed the destruction. "That's their way and that's why we're after 'em. The Apache don't make a habit of leaving anyone behind to tell what happened." He turned to Leroy and Willis who were still mounted. "Boys, this is nearly a week old but just the same, I want the two of you to scout the area ahead and report back."

Leroy looked at Willis. He nodded in agreement and the two Rangers turned their horses. Before they rode off, Bailey cautioned them, "Not too far out, I want to ride on as soon as we rest and water the horses."

Leroy and Willis rode about a half a mile west of the settlement. They had reached the top of a knoll nestled between a cluster of rocks and hardwood trees when Leroy spotted a narrow path that opened into a small clearing.

Although Leroy doubted that any Indians were still in the area, he motioned to Willis to keep silent and cover him. Willis carefully slipped his rifle out of its scabbard and dismounted. While following the path, Leroy saw a piece of cloth dangling on the lower branch of a tree. He knelt and stared at the ground. *Unshod ponies mixed in with a few horses wearing shoes. This is where they stopped after burning the settlement.*

He put the strip of calico into his pocket and kept walking slowly until he came to a clearing that gave him a good view of the path ahead.

Even though he hadn't heard Willis coming up behind him, he felt his friend's presence. "The trail goes cold here, nothing but hard rock ahead as far as I can see. If I was a betting man, I'd put my money on them darn Indians going straight west, then turning south to avoid Comanche country," Leroy added.

Willis pointed to the calico hanging out of Leroy's pocket. "Think they took some hostages with 'em?"

Leroy shook his head. "I don't know. Probably not, it would slow 'em down too much. This cloth could be torn from a shirt or apron worn by one of the bucks. My bet is that they took this here cloth from one of them settlers," he paused, then added, "before them settlers lost their hair." Leroy looked at Willis and pointed back toward the settlement. "That's something the captain will have to figure out."

Later, back at the camp, Zack Bailey took the cloth from Leroy and sniffed it.

"You think it's from a hostage?" Leroy asked, pointing to the cloth.

Bailey frowned and shook his head in disgust, then said in a weary voice, "Probably." The Rangers waited for him to elaborate but all he said was, "Mount up."

As the Rangers tightened their horses cinches and climbed into their saddles, Bailey said, "Leroy, take the lead and show us that path."

Leroy, who was checking to make sure his pistol and rifle were loaded, holstered his gun, then slid his long rifle into place and climbed onto his horse.

For more than a week the Rangers tried to find any sign of the renegade Indians. It was during this time that Captain Bailey began relying on Leroy to act as a scout for the company.

Leroy enjoyed the duty and always took Willis along. He knew that Willis, despite all his complaining, was the best man to have with him if the going got tough. He had once confided to Mindy, "I know I can always count on Willis. Nobody watches my back like he does."

The Rangers were several miles behind Leroy and Willis when the wind changed and Leroy pulled his horse up and whirled around in the saddle to face Willis. Willis was already beginning to gag. He managed to ask, "Is that what I think it is?"

Leroy took a deep breath and answered, "Yep, nothing else smells like human flesh when it's rotting."

"It's gonna make me puke," Willis said as he pulled his handkerchief over his nose and mouth. He would much rather breathe his own sweat and the dust collected on the handkerchief than smell the putrefied flesh.

Leroy motioned to an area of thick underbrush. "It's coming from over there." He ignored Willis who by this time was leaning over in the saddle attempting to empty his stomach.

Leroy cocked his rifle and dropped his horse's reins. Leroy had trained the fast little mustang not to move when the rcins were dropped to the ground. Leroy climbed down from the saddle and headed slowly toward the thick underbrush.

Willis wiped his mouth and pulled out his rifle. He stayed mounted and eased the horse forward.

Leroy had just stepped through the dry bushes when he saw what was left of two hands tied against a small tree. The greenish skin on the arm was hanging from the bones. The woman had been dead for at least a week, but Leroy took a slow, careful walk about the area before speaking to Willis.

"It's a woman," he said as he knelt down. "She's been dead for awhile so it's a pretty safe bet that whoever did this is long gone.

"Jesus," Willis said, his voice filled with disgust mixed with fear and pity. "Her own mother wouldn't recognize her."

Leroy stood. "Let's go get Captain Bailey." He paused and looked back at what was left of the woman's face. "They stuffed her mouth with dirt, Willis," he said. "Why the heck did they do something like that?"

"'Cause they're a bunch of sonofabitches, that's why," Willis said angrily. "They ought to swing from the nearest tree when we catch up with 'em." Willis shook his head before adding, "Every last one of 'em."

None of the Rangers came near the body of the young woman. Most of them walked through the surrounding underbrush looking for any signs that would tell them how many Apache they were going to have to go up against.

"They ain't gonna find nothing," Willis grumbled to Leroy. "We could be facing ten or thirty of 'em."

"Apache or Comanche, makes no difference," Leroy agreed. "They ain't leaving no trace."

"Unless you consider her," Captain Bailey joined them. Bailey was taller than either Leroy or Willis. He took off his hat and wiped his brow with his sleeve. "She's about the only thing they left, once they were finished with her."

"That's where the calico came from," Leroy pointed to the body. "How do you think she died?"

"Hard," said Bailey, his voice filled with rage. "Damn hard."

"Looks like they choked her to death," one of the Rangers said. "Look at the rope hanging from her neck."

"No," Zack Bailey corrected the young Ranger. "The rope is there because they dragged her behind one of their horses. They raped her but I'm not sure if that happened before or after they dragged her here."

Leroy said, "I'll bury her now, if that's okay with you, sir."

Bailey nodded. Leroy waited for him to speak but the Ranger captain remained silent.

"Give me a hand, Willis," Leroy said, his voice flat.

"Why did you have to volunteer us?" Willis whispered as they walked away to bury the dead girl. "Darn it, Leroy, I'm still sick from the smell."

"Get over it," Leroy replied. "This was once a girl just like Mindy or Patsy. I aim to do what's right by her."

Leroy walked over and began taking off the ropes that bound the woman's arms and neck. The Rangers had no shovels so Willis began to gather stones to cover the body.

"Ain't gonna make no difference," Willis muttered to himself. "She'll be dug up in no time by a pack of hungry critters."

CHAPTER 39

A few days after covering the dead woman's body, Leroy and Willis were once again scouting ahead when they came upon a deserted campground. The woods around them were quiet except for an occasional rustling of branches due to a brisk wind. Leroy scattered the ashes with his boot, and then reached down to feel the ground.

"Let's go, Willis," he said as he hurried back to his horse.

"We going back to report?" Willis asked.

"Not yet," Leroy answered. "Looks like they split up here."

"Leroy!" Willis started to warn his friend but Leroy was already riding away, his horse keeping a steady gallop. "Darn, he's just asking for trouble," Willis said to himself. "We ought to go back and get the others."

An hour later, Leroy and Willis had stopped to walk their horses when they both heard a sound that made the two Rangers freeze in their tracks. Leroy raised his hand and motioned for Willis to keep quiet and listen.

I knew we should have gone back, Willis thought. He wondered how far behind the rest of the Rangers were. *Maybe they aren't too far back. We've been walking the horses for a while now.*

For a few minutes there was dead silence, then suddenly there was another sound. Leroy dropped the reins and started moving in a circle, his breathing quickened and his entire body began to tingle. He could actually feel the presence of another man and this time, it wasn't Willis. Leroy locked on the direction of the noise but it was too late.

Out of nowhere he heard the sound of rushing feet coming from behind him.

"Look out," yelled Willis.

Before either Leroy or Willis could draw their pistols, the Apache charged. Both Rangers were attacked at the same time. Leroy had barely enough time to turn and face his opponent. The Indian held a tomahawk high above his head and was about to smash it into Leroy's face. Leroy managed to deflect the tomahawk with his rifle, but was thrown off balance by the tremendous force behind the blow. The Indian used his free hand to grab Leroy around the neck and pull him to the ground. As they both sprawled on the ground Leroy thought that there was no way one man had this much strength. Leroy could feel the man's ribs as they grabbed at each other and rolled around in the dirt. He had no time to check on Willis as he tried to get the best of the wild-eyed Apache. Meanwhile, Willis was in the fight of his life.

Two Apache braves had rushed Willis before he could draw his pistol and get a shot off. Willis was as strong as an ox and in a fight it was said he gave as good as he got. But this time he was outnumbered and Leroy was in no position to help.

Willis landed a powerful blow to one of the Indian's stomach. The man buckled at the waist but before Willis could finish him off the other Apache grabbed him from behind and yanked his head back. Willis reached out to grab the man's arm before an ugly looking knife slit his throat. He had a grip on the man's arm but the Indian was strong and the knife slowly started to move toward his throat. Willis felt his strength leaving him as he slipped to his knees. *I'm done for,* he thought.

He could almost feel the knife slicing through his skin. Then two quick shots exploded next to his head. Leroy had managed to subdue his attacker by hitting him in the head with a rock while they were rolling around in the dirt. As soon as the Apache let go of his knife and fell to the ground, Willis whirled and saw his friend covered in blood and dirt and bleeding from an open gash on the side of his head. His left arm hung limply at his side. Leroy held a pistol in his hand; smoke still coming from its barrel. In spite of his shaky hands

Leroy's shots were true. Both Indians were lying on the ground in a pool of their own blood.

Leroy gingerly touched the wound on his head while Willis tried to get his breath. He rolled back on his haunches and held himself up with both hands resting on his legs.

"My God," Willis managed to gasp while spitting blood and dirt from his mouth.

The two young Rangers didn't realize it, but they had just made a mistake that would nearly cost them their lives. They had turned their backs on a live Apache. The Indian had managed to crawl to within reach of Leroy's legs. Before Leroy could react, his feet were pulled out from under him and he crashed down landing on top of the Indian. He cried out in pain as the Apache punched him in the ribs. Leroy tried to get to his feet but the Apache was quicker. One more blow brought Leroy back to his knees. In desperation he reached for a handful of dirt, turned and threw it with all his might in the face of the Apache. The Indian was momentarily blinded and Leroy knew that this would be his only chance.

Willis tried to find his weapons but his guns were buried under a combination of dirt and two dead Indians. He grabbed his rifle but it was covered in blood and slipped out of his hands. By the time he picked up and wiped off the bloody weapon Leroy and the Apache were engaged in such a fierce struggle it would have been impossible to get off a shot without a fifty-fifty chance of hitting Leroy. Willis cursed and circled the two men trying to find a way to help his friend.

"If I can't shoot the sonofabitch I can at least knock him out with the butt of my rifle," Willis said. He was not speaking to anyone in particular but his voice was deadly serious.

Leroy lunged forward, his right hand feeling for the Apache's throat while the Indian's fists were constantly pounding him. The two men fell to the ground with Leroy on top of the Indian. Leroy squeezed his hands and kept choking the Apache in spite of the fact the Indian's fists were landing painful blows to his face and chest.

After what seemed like an eternity to Leroy, the Apache heaved himself up rigid, then crumbled back to the ground. Leroy fell down beside him gasping for air. He looked up to see Willis standing over him, the butt of his rifle aimed at the Indian's face.

"Damn you," Willis snarled. "If you're still breathing I'm going to send you to hell where you belong."

Leroy, still gasping for air, managed a crooked grin. "Don't worry, Willis. He's already there. This time he's dead."

Leroy rolled away from the Apache and stayed there for a few moments, his eyes closed. Willis stood over the Indian in case the devil came back to life.

Leroy and Willis met Captain Bailey and the other Rangers at dusk. They were both still bloodied and dirty from the hand-to-hand fighting with the Apache.

After the Rangers set up camp, Leroy and Willis lingered over some hard earned coffee and stale biscuits longer than usual. They were both still exhausted. After they had reported to Captain Bailey, the other Rangers gathered around and demanded to know every detail of their fight with the Apaches.

"We're gonna be sore in the morning," Willis groaned while rubbing his arms. "I think I might have a couple of cracked ribs."

"I hurt in more places than I thought possible," Leroy agreed. "It's gonna be hard to climb into the saddle at daybreak."

"The captain ain't waiting around for us," Willis said. "We'll just have to hurt, that's all we can do."

Leroy tried to raise his left arm. I think my shoulder is out of place. That darn Injun was strong as an ox, not to mention mean as a bull with a burr up his butt."

Willis looked at Leroy's face twisted in pain as he tried to move his arm. "Let me get my handkerchief off and I'll tie it around your neck," Willis said. "It'll help brace your arm."

"Nope," Leroy replied through clinched teeth. "Let's wait and see how it is in the morning. I'll sleep on my right side so I don't bump it in the night."

"It's probably broke."

Leroy gave a deep sigh, "Thanks, Willis. That's just what I wanted to hear."

After a restless night Leroy and Willis were not in any shape to keep up with the other Rangers. Reluctantly, Captain Bailey decided to leave the men behind. "We've got a job to do," he said to Leroy and Willis. "It puts me between a rock and a hard place." He shook his head before continuing, "I need both of you men, but I've got to move on and neither of you can ride well enough to keep up with the rest of us."

"With all due respect, I disagree," Leroy said. "Willis and I want to do our part to kill them murderin' savages."

Willis glared at him. *What is he thinking? The captain's offering us a way out of this mess and Leroy wants to go on and find more Indians to fight. Hell, we was both almost killed.*

As if Leroy could read his friend's mind, Leroy shot Willis a look that warned him to keep quiet.

Bailey thought for a few moments before he finally spoke, "No, you boys head home and get patched up." Then he added, "I'll see that you'll draw full pay for the time the rest of us are on duty. You did your part and would have been with us until the Apache were caught and brought to justice if you were able. Both of you were busted up in the line of duty and that counts for a lot."

"Thank you, sir," Willis hastily spoke before Leroy could argue. "Like you say, the two of us are in pretty bad shape."

"We are not," Leroy said, frowning at Willis.

Captain Bailey held up both hands before speaking. "The matter is decided, Leroy. I'm sending Travis with you. Right now I'm not sure that either of you men could defend yourself." He turned and walked briskly away.

As soon as Bailey was out of hearing distance, Willis asked, "What's got into you?"

"I want to see the sorry sonsofbitches who murdered that poor girl pay for what they did," Leroy swallowed hard. "I wanted to be there."

"Well, that's too bad," Willis said. "As it is, we'll be lucky to get back to Smith County in one piece." He shook his fist at Leroy. "In case you hadn't noticed, the two of us couldn't fight off a couple of ladies from a Sunday social, let alone the Apache."

Leroy sighed and turned away so he wouldn't have to look at his fellow Rangers as they rode away in search of the Apache.

"I wanted to be there," he repeated his words as if he could make them come true.

"If I live to be a hundred I won't be able to understand you," Willis shook his head. "What difference does it make? If Captain Bailey catches up with the Apache them sorry savages are as good as dead and," Willis paused for effect, "dead is dead. Ain't no difference in the end, Leroy."

Within the hour Leroy, Travis and Willis were riding, ever so slowly, east toward Smith County. The Rangers spent hours in the saddle passing flat and hilly ground covered in prairie grass. The wind blew gentle waves in the light green and brown carpet of dry grass. The wind blew so gently that the Rangers barely felt the breeze on the hot, dry day. While Willis and Leroy let their minds drift toward east Texas, Travis took note of the various animals feeding on leaves, roots and seeds of prairie plants.

"Look fellows, there's a prairie chicken," Travis pointed toward a small buff colored animal covered with brown stripes.

"That critter is called a prairie dog, Travis," Willis grumbled. "Prairie chickens are a whole lot smaller. I know because prairie dogs cause farmers a lot of trouble. Them critters not only eat the grass, they eat the roots, too."

"That looks like a bird, Willis," Travis said. "That makes it a chicken, not a dog."

"Critters like that make holes that break horse's legs," Leroy said as he raised his pistol and aimed at the animal. "I don't care if it's a chicken or a dog, it's about to be a goner."

"Oh, don't shoot it, Leroy," Willis said. "It's a waste of good bullets that we have to pay for ourselves."

Leroy looked over to Willis and grinned. "You got a point there, Willis. Not to mention that we may need every shot next time we are socializing with the Comanche or the Apache. But since we are riding back toward Smith County where there ain't too many unfriendly Comanche or Apache, I think I'll take me a practice shot at that ugly critter."

Leroy carefully aimed, squeezed the trigger on his Colt, and watched in dismay as the small bird's feathers puffed up around the neck and it began leaping about in a circle.

"You missed," laughed Willis.

"I ain't so sure," Leroy frowned as he watched the bird's tail spread out, then droop toward the ground.

"Well, if he's hit, it don't seem to bother him much," Willis reached over to give Leroy a friendly poke in the arm as the prairie chicken took off in flight.

"Say, fellows," Travis laughed as he spoke. "I've been meaning to ask you how you got tangled up with the Apache. Seems to me you two needed me along to watch out for you and keep you out of trouble."

"Huh?" Willis asked as he leaned over in the saddle to look Travis in the eye. "Just what good do you think you would have done back yonder while Leroy and I was fighting them wild eyed Injuns?"

Travis began to laugh. "I can shoot better than you and unlike Leroy, I can hit what I aim at."

Leroy let out a long breath and shook his head. "You're all talk, Travis. If them Apache were close enough for you to shoot at I'll bet you'd have been shaking so much you wouldn't have been able to hit nothing."

Travis stretched up high in the saddle and looked around the Texas prairie. In the middle of splashes of yellow, orange, red and purple wild flowers he saw movement. "Wait a minute, fellows," he said in a low voice. "I think I see an armadillo."

"Where?" Willis asked.

"Over there, right in the middle of those scrub brushes," Travis answered as he climbed down from his mustang.

"I don't see nothing," Willis said. "You just think you saw an armadillo. Them critters don't venture this far north. They stay down near the border, don't they, Leroy?"

Leroy joined Travis and stared intently at the distant horizon. "I ain't too sure where they usually hang out, but I think Travis just may have spotted one over there."

"Look," Travis lifted his rifle. "It's an armadillo. He's in plain sight now."

"Well, Travis," Willis said. "Now is the time for you to show me and Leroy just how good you are with that brand new rifle you're toting around."

Travis looked up at Willis. "I'm the best sharpshooter you'll ever ride with so get off that horse and maybe you won't scare off my armadillo. Right now I believe I've got a clear shot at him."

"Ha," Willis laughed as he swung his leg over the saddle. "Let's see just how good you really are. Ever-body knows them armadillos can't run fast. In fact, they tend to be right slow."

"It's about two feet long and probably weighs about fifteen pounds, Travis," Leroy said. "That's a darn big target if you ask me."

"Be quiet and watch a master at work," Travis whispered as he carefully took aim and fired. "You boys might learn something." At the sound of the rifle fire the armadillo ran around in a circle then curled itself into a tight ball. Having missed with his first shot, Travis quickly reloaded and fired a second time. The second shot sent dirt flying against the armadillo. It reacted by rapidly digging a hole into the ground for cover.

"You missed! Both times!" Willis roared. "Look at him, he ain't hurt."

"He's got a darn tough shell, maybe the shot bounced off," Travis took aim again.

"Don't embarrass yourself again, Travis," Leroy laughed. "The way I see it, the safest place in Texas right now is where that armadillo is hiding."

"Bounced off?" Willis continued to laugh. "Travis, the first shot didn't even raise dirt and the second one missed by a foot." Willis pointed toward the armadillo. "Heck, he ain't even running from you."

Travis squinted and watched the armadillo hug the ground. He felt Leroy's arm on his shoulder and listened as Willis and Leroy laughed at his expense. "You fellows might laugh, but I swear," Travis said. "That's the luckiest armadillo in the whole state of Texas!"

Willis and Leroy continued to laugh as the three young Rangers mounted their horses and rode away, looking for a good place to bed down for the night.

"I hear tell them armadillos have claws as long as a man's fingers," Willis said. "And they got darn sharp teeth, too." He paused as he looked at Travis and Leroy. "But they sure can't out run or bounce off no bullets."

Travis pursed his lips and looked away. "If the two of you don't mind, I don't wanna hear nothing more 'bout armadillos."

Leroy looked at Willis and grinned.

CHAPTER 40

"Miz Wiley," Patsy called out as she climbed down from the wagon loaded with seed and food supplies from the Starrville Mercantile Store. "I'm here to call on Mindy, if that's okay with you."

Verlinda Wiley stopped churning butter, stood and wiped her face with the corner of her apron. "Why of course, Patsy. Please come in and have a glass of cider. Mindy made a pitcher this morning." As she walked down the steps to give Patsy a hug Verlinda noticed Patsy's boots were worn and scuffed.

"Where is Mindy?" Patsy asked in an anxious tone. "Has she heard from Leroy? I'm so worried about Willis."

"Now settle down, child. Mindy's out riding with Clayton," Verlinda replied in a soothing voice. "Clayton had to chase down a lost calf and Mindy went along to help him. That girl rides better than anyone I've ever seen except for Leroy." She took Patsy's arm and walked her through the front door. "Can you sit a spell?"

"No, ma'am," Patsy frowned. "I'd like to visit, but I've got so much work to do before supper. If Mindy's not here, I better be on my way. Please ask her to come by the farm if she hears from Leroy."

"Come inside for just a minute," Verlinda protested. "I'll pour that glass of cider I promised you and cut out some pie for you to take home. "I don't suppose you've heard from Willis?"

"No, ma'am," Patsy frowned. "That's why I've come to see Mindy. I'm sure Leroy and Willis are together and Willis can't write letters." Patsy lowered her eyes as she spoke. "I was hoping Leroy had written to Mindy."

"We have no idea where the boys are," Verlinda said. "I know for a fact that Mindy hasn't heard any news. That son of mine never has been one to write letters. But the next time you are in Tyler, ask Carter to help. He can ride over to Mount Pleasant and see if there is anyone at the Ranger headquarters who might have an idea where our boys are and when they might be home."

"I'm so worried," Patsy's hand quivered when she held the glass of cider. "We need Willis on the farm, Miz Wiley. This is such a busy time of year."

Verlinda sliced some pie to send home with Patsy. "I wish you could wait until Mindy returns. She's going to be so disappointed if she doesn't see you.

Patsy walked around the kitchen, pausing to touch the cotton curtains Verlinda had made for the windows. "I hope to sew some curtains for our home as soon as Willis draws his Ranger pay. It should be almost fifty dollars considering all the time he's been gone."

"I know what you mean, Patsy," Verlinda said. "We could sure use the money here, too."

"Well, hello there, Patsy," Taylor said as he walked into the kitchen. "Verlinda, I didn't know we had company."

"If you had been working on that barn door like you were supposed to, Taylor," Verlinda raised her eyebrows as she spoke, "chances are you would have seen Patsy's wagon out front."

Taylor frowned. "I fixed it yesterday."

Verlinda reached for a basket to pack some jelly and smoked ham for Patsy. "I don't read minds, Taylor."

He nodded to Patsy. "You know she was a school teacher. She ain't easy to live with sometimes."

"Yes, sir," Patsy smiled. "Leroy and Willis both told me that a long time ago." Patsy's face reddened. "I meant they told me that you used to be a school teacher, Miz Wiley, not that you were hard to live with."

"Oh, never mind what Taylor and the boys say about me, Patsy. I know they don't mean no harm." Verlinda had a faraway look in her eyes as she walked toward the front door and stared out into the pasture. "I wish that boy would write more often," Verlinda said. "You'd think once he married Mindy he'd want her to know that he's safe."

A big smile crossed Taylor's face. "Patsy, don't expect to keep up with your husband the way Leroy's mother keeps up with me. She watches every move I make."

Verlinda whirled around and looked him square in the eye before speaking to Patsy. "Somebody has to or nothing would get done around here."

"I better be going," Patsy laughed. "I wouldn't want to be the cause of a family fight."

"We never fight," Verlinda said with a wink. "Oh, we may argue a bit until Taylor realizes that he's wrong, but we never fight."

Taylor let out a deep breath but kept quiet. He lifted Patsy's basket and walked her to the wagon.

"Now don't you worry your pretty little head none about Willis," Taylor said as he placed the basket under the wagon seat then reached for Patsy's arm. He leaned over and whispered, "You know that if Willis is with Leroy he's gonna be just fine. Ain't nobody mean enough to hurt them boys. They got a tough streak in 'em."

"I know that Mr. Wiley," Patsy said, her voice filled with sadness. "But they're over in Comanche country. I just know it."

"Well, the way I see it, that's bad news for the Comanche," Taylor said as she took her hand in both of his.

Patsy smiled, tied her bonnet, and picked up the reins. Her dark blonde hair was pulled up and tied underneath. "Let's go Sally Sue," she said to the mare hitched to the wagon.

Taylor watched Willis's young wife as the wagon made it's way back down the road toward Starrville. *That mare's got all she can do to pull that wagon. Patsy ought to have a team pulling it,* Taylor thought. *I think I'll ask James Cave if he's got a horse he'll sell cheap.*

Verlinda joined him and they watched the wagon until it was only a shadow on the horizon. "That girl is as skinny as a bean pole," Verlinda said. "I worry about her."

"Their place is built from scrap lumber," Taylor worried aloud. "When Leroy gets back I'm going to send him and Clayton over with a load of wood." He pointed to the cluster of trees. "Those pines could use thinning out."

Verlinda slipped her arm through his and whispered, "Don't you be cutting down big pine trees, Taylor. Leave that to the boys."

"Are you worried about me?" he grinned and leaned over to kiss her cheek.

"No, you old rascal," Verlinda teased. "I just don't want you trying to cut down or split any pine trees. There's plenty of work for you to do without getting in harm's way." She turned to look across a broad pasture before adding, " I wonder what's keeping Mindy and Clayton. It's time to warm up supper."

CHAPTER 41

By the time Leroy and Willis arrived in Smith County they were feeling better. They had taken their time on the ride home and the slow pace helped their bruised bodies to heal. After a rousing welcome from their families both men enjoyed a few weeks of uninterrupted time spent with their brides.

Leroy picked up their Ranger pay in Mount Pleasant, and then rode out to give Willis his hard earned money.

"This is more than I expected," Willis said when Leroy finished counting the money.

"It's sure more than I thought we'd get. Think they made a mistake when they figured what was coming to us?" Leroy asked.

"If they did, that's their problem," Willis said. "I ain't giving none of it back."

"Me neither," Leroy laughed. "Heck, my pay is pretty much spent already. What's left goes to the folks for keeping Mindy." His voice suddenly became sad, "I ought to have a place of my own."

"Being able to buy things Patsy needs for the house makes it almost worth getting shot at," Willis said to Leroy, and then added, "Patsy wants to fix things up nice for us so we can start a family."

"That sounds like a mighty good idea." Leroy gave Willis a playful shove, causing Willis to grimace in pain due to his sore muscles. "Now that we have some time to ourselves, how about helping me start on my house?" While Willis was considering the idea, Leroy decided to add an incentive, "I'll pay you what I can."

"I know that," Willis laughed. "But you don't have to pay me nothing. You'd help me if I needed it. Besides, while we were gone your Pa bought a horse from Mr. Cave for Patsy so she could plow and haul supplies. That counts for a lot in my book."

"He told me it was a wedding present," Leroy said.

"Miz Wiley already gave us stuff," Willis shook his head. "The horse was something extra and it sure meant a lot to Patsy."

"Well," Leroy grinned. "When can we start on my house? It'd make Mindy happy to see us clearing land. I've got the plans all worked out in my head."

"Got the lumber?" Willis asked.

"Almost enough," Leroy answered. "Right now, I got enough to get us started."

"When are you aiming to start this fine house for Mindy?"

"That depends on Carter. He's supposed to come out to the farm as soon as he knows if Texas is going to leave the Union." Leroy looked off into the distance. "I got a bad feeling about what Carter's gonna tell us."

"When are you expecting Carter?" Willis asked.

"Any day now. To tell you the truth, I've been expecting him for over a week," Leroy answered. Taking in his friend's downcast eyes, he added, "Come by the farm tomorrow and I'll show you what I've got in mind for my new place. Mindy loves the spot where I'm gonna build it. I tell you, its real pretty land."

Willis smiled. "Maybe someday you can help me build a place for Patsy."

"That I will gladly do," Leroy said. "But right now I've got to head back to the farm before Mindy sends the Rangers after me."

Willis shook his head. "Now, Leroy. You know that ain't about to happen."

The next day dawned clear with a gentle southwest wind. Leroy had hoped for just such a day because he had promised to show Mindy the land where he intended to build their home.

Mindy stood at the bedroom window looking at the first rays of light breaking through the cloudless sky.

"I didn't know you were awake," Leroy said as he walked through the door carrying a cup of coffee.

"For once I thought I'd have breakfast with you," she turned and faced him with a big smile. "You're always gone by the time I wake up."

Leroy took a sip of coffee before replying, "Me and Clayton usually have breakfast at dawn with Papa. There's nothing like early mornings in Texas. The sky is usually light blue or gray with pink streaks running through it."

"Oh, Leroy," she laughed. "It's the same in Georgia and probably everywhere else."

"Nope," he said as he sat the cup on a nearby table. "Not like in Texas."

He pulled her close and she rested her head against his chest.

"Want me to help you get dressed?" he asked, a look of mischief on his face.

She pulled away from him and giggled. "That probably wouldn't be a good idea because Clayton and Papa will be wondering what's keeping you from helping with the chores."

"Mindy-girl," he said while unfastening the tiny buttons on her gown. "I think they can start without me this morning."

CHAPTER 42

"Leroy," Willis called out as he quickly climbed down from his horse. "Did you hear? The boys are all forming up in companies and getting ready for the war."

"Yeah, I know all about it. But from what I hear there hasn't been any fighting yet, so I guess it's mostly talk by a lot of fellows with more time on their hands than good sense. While you're here, come help me draw some water for the chickens," Leroy suggested while he carried a pair of buckets towards the cistern.

"I'd rather go see Mindy and see if she's baked some biscuits or sweet bread." Willis took off his hat and tapped it against both pants legs to get rid of the trail dust. "I've been in the fields since daybreak trying to get all my work done before the first frost."

"Come on and help a friend draw some water," Leroy laughed as he handed Willis an empty bucket.

"This bucket's 'bout rusted through," Willis said, holding the bucket high in order to take a good look at the rusted bottom. "I'll bet you it leaks."

"Probably, but if you run fast enough you can get most of the water to the chicken coop," Leroy gave Willis a playful shove toward the cistern. This time Willis showed no sign of pain. His body had finally healed.

"It's fall Leroy, them chickens don't need water like they do during the summertime when it's hot." Willis continued talking, oblivious to the fact that Leroy wasn't contributing to the conversation. "I ain't too happy hearing all this war talk," Willis frowned. "Patsy says there ain't nothing good gonna come of it if we go out and start fighting." Willis reached for the rope and dropped the bucket into the cistern.

Leroy remind silent.

"Still," Willis said. "Nobody in my family has ever been called a coward, so if the boys around here go, I guess I'll be with 'em."

Leroy glanced over his shoulder and saw Mindy skipping down the back steps of the house. "Hey, Willis," he said in a hurried tone of voice. "Whatever you do, don't say anything about the war to Mindy. She's mighty worried about her family back in Georgia."

"Sure thing," Willis whispered, and then turned to tip his hat to Mindy. "Hello Mindy, got any biscuits or sweet bread baked?"

Mindy reached an arm through Leroy's and smiled. "Willis, you know I do. Mama Wiley and I bake every morning and it's dinner time."

Willis looked up at the midday sun warming the east Texas landscape. "No wonder my belly's calling out to me."

"Come on, Willis," Leroy laughed. "Let's get some water to the chickens, then wash up for dinner." He took time to steal a quick glance at Mindy. "You sure are looking fine today, Mindy-girl."

She smiled and pulled a knitted shawl tightly around her shoulders. "Don't be too long. Mama Wiley was taking up the fried chicken when I came out to find you."

"We won't be long, Mindy," Willis called out while dropping the bucket into the deep, cool cistern. "Darn it, I'm hungry. Them chickens could have waited to get a drink until after I ate some fried chicken."

Leroy laughed. "I don't think them chickens care about keeping you from eating their kinfolk."

Willis took a long look at the chicken coop, and then said, "I never thought about that."

"Won't Patsy be wondering where you're at?" Leroy asked as he put down an empty bucket by the cistern.

Willis began pouring water into Leroy's bucket then dropped the bucket attached to a rope back into the cistern. "Naah, I told her I was riding over to your place."

"Then she'll be expecting some of my Ma's chicken and biscuits," Leroy said as he picked up the full bucket of water.

Willis filled the rusted bucket to the brim and watched the water seep out the bottom onto the dry soil. "Darn it," he called out as he lifted the bucket and began to run. "If I get any water to them chickens it'll be a miracle."

Leroy laughed. "Run, Willis, run! If them chickens don't get water they won't make good broilers which means the next time you come a calling the table might have nothing but beans and cornbread on it." He continued laughing as he watched Willis run while trying to hold the bucket away from his boots. The whole time water was leaking out of the bottom of the rusted bucket.

After the midday meal, Willis looked at Leroy's father who was sitting at the end of the table patiently filling his pipe. "Mr. Wiley," Willis said. "Have you heard about the boys from Smith County meeting out at Flat Rock Camp? I hear they're getting ready to fight in the war."

Leroy tried to kick Willis's boot under the table but missed and hit the table leg instead. He looked at Mindy. She was staring intently at Taylor. Leroy frowned at Willis but Willis wasn't paying attention.

Taylor Wiley glanced toward his wife, and then smiled at Mindy. "Oh, I've heard about some boys doing some drilling, but from what I hear most of them just want to get out of farm work, clerking at the general store, or sweeping floors at some business in Tyler. I don't believe they know anymore than we do," he puffed on his pipe to get the tobacco burning before finishing his sentence, "and we don't know anything for sure except that people in Virginia, Georgia and Mississippi are doing a lot of talking and stirring things up."

"Now, Taylor," Verlinda said in her usual firm teacher's voice. "You read the letter my cousin, Emily, wrote from Augusta. It arrived last week. Things are getting mighty serious back east."

Leroy was watching Mindy the entire time. She was sitting on the edge of her chair, her hands clasped together. Leroy reached over to cover her small hands and gently pulled them apart.

"Leroy," she whispered. "What about my family? Wouldn't they be better off here in Texas? Maybe you ought to go get them before..." Her voice trailed off.

He leaned over and gave her a reassuring smile. "If we hear that fighting has started near Appling, I'll head east and bring 'em back here before the Yanks can march into Georgia."

"Enough talk," Taylor said. "Verlinda, pour me another cup of coffee. I'll bet Willis and Leroy would like a hot cup too."

Verlinda, realizing exactly what Taylor was doing, joined in to help get Mindy's mind off the problems her family would be faced with if the war broke out between the North and the South, "Mindy, you pour the boys coffee while I pack a box of chicken and biscuits for Willis and Patsy."

Willis smiled, "I appreciate that, Miz Wiley and Patsy will too once I get that box to her."

"Better pack it in a flour sack, Ma," Leroy said. "Willis is riding that half broke quarter horse Mr. Cave gave him."

"Mr. Cave still giving you horses to break, Willis?" Taylor asked.

"Yes, sir, I break 'em and give 'em back to him so he can sell 'em. He buys 'em from some Mexican fellows who come up here from south Texas. After I make sure them horses are good and broke, he sells them to the army."

Verlinda raised her eyebrows and looked sternly at Willis. "James Cave is still in the horse trading business?"

Taylor coughed. "Now Verlinda, it's no business of ours what our neighbor does with his time."

Leroy chuckled. "Willis is sure riding one high stepping mount. I can picture some Mexican vaccaro getting thrown about ten feet in the air the first time he tried to ride him."

Willis leaned across the table and spoke in a low voice. "I need that horse training job, Leroy. And it don't matter to me who Mr. Cave buys and sells 'em to."

Verlinda sighed. "I'm going to have a talk with Mrs. Cave." She nodded her head with resolve as she packed biscuits and jelly into a bright yellow flour sack. "We'll see what she knows about this horse business. Just last week she told me that James was no longer doing business with those Mexican horse traders."

"Now, Mother," Taylor began.

Mindy decided this was a perfect opportunity to interrupt. "Mama Wiley, you better hurry so Patsy won't be worried about Willis."

Verlinda turned and gave Mindy a long stare. "You're absolutely right, Mindy." She looked at Willis. "Hurry up and finish your pie and coffee, Willis."

"No need to remind him," Leroy laughed. "He's finished off the pie and there's not much coffee left in the pot."

Willis gulped the last of his coffee and stood. He smiled while Verlinda handed him the flour sack filled with food.

"Now be careful with these vittles, Willis," she said.

Willis hesitated for a moment, then said in a husky voice, "Thank you, Miz Wiley. You know how much this means to me and Patsy."

Leroy, sensing Willis's discomfort, quickly added, "Let me help you with that overstuffed flour sack."

He reached over to give Mindy a kiss on the cheek and whispered, "I'll be right back. Or better yet, why don't you bring a glass of cold water out to the porch swing?"

"It's November, Leroy. It's too chilly to sit out on the porch drinking cold water, but I'd love to sit in the swing and talk for a spell. Let me get a warmer wrap. I'll be just a minute or two."

Leroy followed Willis through the door. As soon as they stepped off the porch Leroy glanced back toward the house before he spoke in a hushed, but very irritated tone of voice, "Willis, I swear, didn't I tell you not to say a word 'bout the war." He shook his head in dismay, "Heck, we don't even know what's happening back east. They could have signed some sort of treaty by now. It takes awhile before we hear any news coming from Washington City. Besides, out here we do pretty much as we please, no matter what the Yankee government thinks."

"I swear, Leroy, I didn't mean no harm," Willis said as he climbed up on the powerful quarter horse. The horse snorted and pawed the ground. "He's ready to run," Willis laughed trying to change the subject. "I hope I make it home with this flour sack in one piece."

"Tie it to the horn," Leroy said as he handed the sack to Willis's outstretched hand. "And you better tie it good." Watching his friend struggle with the sack filled with food, Leroy decided the knot would probably not hold. "Wait, Willis! I'll get another sack to tie from the other side of the saddle."

Leroy hurried back to the kitchen door and disappeared inside. Willis looked up to see a rider approaching from the direction of Tyler. "Wonder who that is?" he said aloud. "Well I'll be darn, its Carter." He turned and shouted back to the house, "Leroy, Carter's coming and he's riding that big buckskin mighty hard."

Leroy, followed by his mother and father, stepped out onto the porch. He was carrying a half filled sack of food. Seeing his brother riding toward the house hell bent for leather, Leroy frowned. He looked at his father whose brow was also creased with worry.

"Go see to Mindy," Taylor said to his wife. "The boys and I will be back in the house directly."

"Mindy's about to come out here to sit with Leroy," Verlinda said. "I think she'll be alright."

Taylor let out a deep sigh, and then turned his attention back to his son who had jumped down from his horse and was making his way toward the porch.

"What's all the excitement about Carter?" Taylor called out.

"Governor Houston has called a special session of the legislature for the end of January to decide whether or not Texas is going to leave the Union. From what I hear, there's not much doubt what the outcome will be." Carter looked at Leroy and Willis before he turned back to face his father. "In just a few months we could be in a war."

Taylor shook his head. "When did you say the legislature is going to meet?"

Carter walked back to his horse and pulled a telegraph from the saddlebag. " I don't know the exact date but Judge Smith's been summoned to an important meeting in Austin. He left an hour ago. When he gets back he'll know a lot more of the details."

"Damn," Taylor said, his mind deep in thought.

"Taylor Wiley, what in the world did you just say?" Verlinda put her hands on her hips and leaned toward him.

Taylor, realizing what he had said, turned to his wife, "Verlinda, this is important."

"I know the news is dreadful, but that is no excuse for cussing in front of me and your sons, not to mention Willis, who I know for a fact was raised in a very religious home."

Taylor rolled his eyes before speaking, "Verlinda, please go stay with Mindy before she comes out here."

Verlinda reached over to give Leroy's arm a gentle squeeze. "I'll be in the kitchen with Mindy."

"Thanks, Ma," Leroy said. "I'd appreciate that."

"Read the telegraph, Carter," Taylor said.

"It says here that after the election of Abraham Lincoln so many people in Texas want to leave the Union that Houston's got to call a convention or else. He's fought secession as long as he can."

"Whether or not we leave the Union will have to be decided by the people at the ballot box," Taylor said.

"The leaders of the secession movement have the people behind them, so taking a vote will almost be a moot point," Carter said. "It looks like in a few months we could be in the thick of the fighting."

"Probably not here in Texas, but you boys might have to go fight the Yanks back east or up north," Taylor shook his head. "I sure hate to see that happen."

"Well, we know how Smith County will vote," Leroy said. "Nobody around here wants Lincoln to be our president."

"It's a sad thing because we fought so hard to be part of the United States and now we're going to fight just as hard to leave it," Taylor sighed. "We probably would have been better off staying an independent Republic."

"I'm going home," Willis spoke for the first time since hearing the news from Carter. "I need to talk to Patsy."

"Willis, wait a minute until I tie these vittles up for you," Leroy said as he hurried toward the quarter horse.

"Give my best to Patsy," Leroy said as Willis pulled on the reins and rode toward his farm.

Carter stepped up on the porch to speak to his father. "You realize that war would mean that Leroy and I *will* have to join up with the other Smith County boys and leave Texas until the Yankees give up."

"I know," Taylor said. "I was hoping that one of you boys could stay here to help with the farm work. The women and I will have a hard time managing without some help."

Carter nodded in agreement. "Clayton's the one who should stay. I'm not much of a farmer and neither is Leroy. Besides, we all know that nothing, not even Mindy, will keep Leroy from fighting for Texas."

Taylor smiled. "He'll probably keep you and a lot of other boys from Smith County alive."

"I couldn't agree with you more," Carter said.

"Carter," Mindy said as she hurried out onto the porch. "Has the war started?" The words seemed to tremble out of her lips.

Leroy reached out and pulled her close to him. "The governor was only talking about the possibility of Texas leaving the Union, Mindy." Leroy looked over Mindy's shoulder toward Carter.

"Carter?" Mindy said. "What's everyone saying in Tyler about the war? Is there any news about Georgia??

Leroy frowned at Carter. Carter took the hint and stepped up on the porch.

"Judge Smith received notice to go to the capitol and attend a convention of delegates sometime after the holidays," Carter paused and glanced at Leroy. "That's about all I know, Mindy."

Mindy placed her hands on her slim hips and glared at Carter. "Phooey," she said in an angry tone of voice. "You know a lot more than that or you wouldn't have ridden all the way from Tyler like you did."

Leroy and Carter exchanged glances before Carter answered. He chose his words carefully. "No need getting all upset over nothing, Mindy. The governor's called a meeting to decide whether or not Texas will leave the union. No matter what they decide, they'll have to put it to a vote. All this takes time."

Mindy looked up at Leroy. "If the fighting starts back east can you go get my folks and bring them here?"

Leroy smiled, "Sure I can if your Pa will agree to leave Georgia."

"Why don't you write your family a letter, dear?" Verlinda said. "Tell them how you feel and ask them to consider a long visit to Texas. Your folks are more than welcome to visit and wait out the war here with us."

Mindy nodded and gave Leroy a small grin. "If anybody could get them here safe and sound it would be Leroy. He's not afraid of anything."

"Maybe not, but I have a powerful amount of respect stored up for the Comanche." Leroy leaned against the porch railing and tipped his hat back. "As far as the Yanks go, well, they don't worry me much."

"They worry me," Carter laughed. "There's too many of 'em."

Without saying a word, Mindy turned on her heel and went back into the house.

Leroy frowned and tipped his head in Mindy's direction. "Wait 'till she's in the kitchen or upstairs, Carter, before you express any more of your concerns. She's just about decided I should stay here and work the farm all the time."

"That's not a bad idea, son," Verlinda said.

"I'll second that," Taylor tapped his pipe on the arm of the rocker. "With Carter living in town, we need you to hang your hat around here more often, Leroy."

"I think I'll ride back to town in the morning with Carter and see what's going on," Leroy said. "The news from Austin ought to be the big talk all around Tyler."

Carter untied his horse and followed Leroy. The brothers walked in silence toward the barn. Leroy lifted the saddle and blanket off of the horse and then turned to face Carter.

"I figure we'll be at war before long," Leroy said in a matter of fact tone of voice. "Ain't no doubt about it."

"Sooner than later would be my guess," Carter replied. "I don't envy you when it's time to leave Mindy."

Leroy continued walking toward the pasture where the family's horses were grazing. He leaned the saddle and blanket against a fence and looked over the stock. As he reached to take the bridle from Carter he asked, "Think Papa would mind if I took the red roan?"

"Heck no," came the reply. "If you want a strong horse, he's the one."

"I sure like the looks of him," Leroy pointed toward the horse. The roan was almost chestnut colored with white and red hair covering a large portion of his body. Leroy took note of the solid, powerful legs with stockings on the hind legs.

"He's the one I want," Leroy laughed. "But Papa might not let me ride him off to fight in a war."

"When the time comes," Carter sighed. "He'll let you have any horse that has a chance of bringing you back alive."

"Agreed," Leroy said as he opened the gate and walked into the pasture. Once inside, he paused for a moment and grinned at Carter, "Which one do you want?"

"I'll stay with the buckskin I bought from Judge Smith," Carter reached up to give the canvas colored horse a pat. "He's the best horse I've ever owned."

"I like him too," Leroy gestured toward the horse. "I like the black tips on his ears and his matching black legs. The dark hooves just set him off. He reminds me of a horse one of the Rangers down south rides."

"Enough talk about horses," Carter said, his voice filled with resignation. "In the morning you and I can ride back to Tyler. Maybe then we'll have some more answers."

The following Sunday after church services Leroy and Carter asked Willis to meet them in town the following Tuesday. When they met in front of the Starrville Post Office, Carter gave Willis the bad news.

"Leroy and I didn't want to say anything to you in front of Patsy," Carter said with a tone of resignation, "but all of the fellows from Smith County have been asked to report to the Mount Carmel Post Office on Saturday to start training for the army."

"I appreciate what you did but she figured it out," Willis said.

Leroy couldn't remember seeing his friend look so sad.

"You know something?" Carter said as he leaned against the hitching post, his voice quivering with frustration. "Everybody is all excited about going to war, but all I feel is sadness. I'm not sure that when it's all said and done any of us will ever be the same."

"I wish I could stay here with Patsy," Willis said. He lowered his face. "Just when things have started going good for us, I gotta leave the farm and go off to fight some darn war. How's she gonna manage?"

There was silence for a few moments while each young man pondered his own future.

"Well," Leroy took a deep breath, his voice cold and detached, "as much as I hate to leave Mindy, I'd just as soon spend a couple of months whipping Yanks as busting sod." He looked at Carter and Willis before adding, "I've been giving it a lot of thought and I think we're gonna remember what we do during this war for a long time, maybe the rest of our lives."

"I've got a feeling you're right," Carter said.

Willis remained silent.

A gust of wind came up blowing dust and scrub brush past them. Leroy tugged on his hat and grinned, "Ah shucks, Willis. Quit worrying. We ain't gonna be gone long."

CHAPTER 43

The newly formed east Texas Confederate regiments were camped at the Mount Carmel Post Office. Several officers had already been chosen and drills were beginning when Leroy, Willis, Travis and Billy rode into camp.

Billy climbed down from his horse and lifted the animal's hoof to remove a small pebble. "You all go on ahead," he said. "I'll be along in a few minutes. Ever since we crossed Sandy Creek I could tell his foot was bothering him."

"We'll wait for you," Leroy said with a grin. "We wouldn't think of joining the Confederate Cavalry without you, Billy."

"Thanks," Billy laughed. "I wouldn't want to miss out on all the fun."

"Leroy," Willis sighed. "Remember what your Pa told us? He said that a mighty storm was bustin' out all over the country and it was going to end up in nothing but bloodshed and chaos. That don't sound like fun to me."

"Yep," Leroy said, his voice almost a whisper. "But that don't change nothing. We fight for Texas, no matter what."

"I'm ready," Billy said as he mounted his gelding. "Got the pebble out of his foot." He looked around at the other Rangers. "Let's go."

The young Rangers received a hearty welcome from their friends and neighbors as they rode into camp. Carter, who had arrived the day before, motioned for Leroy to follow him to a nearby cluster of pine trees. "They've already voted on the officers," Carter said. "For what it's worth it looks like we've got some good men in charge."

"What do we do now?" Leroy asked while sizing up a group of officers standing nearby.

"No one seems to know," Carter shrugged. "It's a given that the state will vote for secession, so we're putting together Texas regiments for the Confederate Army."

"Who is we?" Leroy asked.

"The state government in Austin. A West Point graduate named Horace Randall is going to be our commander. That's him over there." Carter pointed to a slender man wearing a United States Army uniform. "Our regiment is going to be called the 28th Texas Lancers."

"I like the sound of that," Leroy grinned. "Let's go tell Travis and Billy."

"What about Willis?" Carter asked.

"Oh, heck," Leroy said as he walked toward the assembled group of men. "He doesn't care. He doesn't want to be here anyhow. Willis will just find something to complain about. I swear, he'd gripe if they hung him with a new rope."

"I don't blame him," Carter said as he followed his younger brother, shaking his head. "I wouldn't be too thrilled if they hung me with a new *or* an old rope. But when it comes to Willis, some people never change," he said with a smile.

"Well, boys," Travis said as he pointed toward a group of young men from Smith County. "There's our fellows lined up over there and there's Willis, all by himself. "Do you think we ought to make sure he's included in this new Confederate Cavalry Regiment?"

Leroy and Carter laughed, but didn't reply.

"Looks like we're forming up by counties. There's Clay Martin from Van Zandt County over yonder by the trees," Billy said.

"Sitting on his butt in the shade," Leroy said with a chuckle, and then added, "as usual."

"Let's go see what we're supposed to be doing," Travis suggested. "I'm still not too sure I want to be here. I came along 'cause you fellows were signing up, but I wonder if we should just sit tight with the Rangers awhile longer and see what happens."

"Now, Travis," Leroy said sarcastically. "We all know how much you enjoy being out on the trail."

"Says you," Travis shook his head. "Ever since I joined the Rangers I've either been freezing to death or hot as heck. Not to mention getting shot at on a regular basis."

"You're probably going to be shot at on a *more* regular basis if you join the army," Carter said, his voice taking on a serious tone.

"We ain't got no choice," Leroy said resignedly. "So we better make the best of it. By joining up now, at least we get to choose our outfit. The Cavalry is the best outfit in the army. I don't want to be stuck in an Infantry regiment having to walk from one end of the country to the other."

"I ain't too sure about the whole thing," Willis said joining the group. "But I agree with what you say about not wanting to walk any more than I have to."

"You fellows line up over here for inspection," one of the officers called out.

Leroy took a deep breath, gave Carter a nudge, and said in a low voice, "Here goes nothing, big brother."

Carter winced. "I'd just as soon go back to the judge's office and spend my time working there. At least I'd know what I am supposed to be doing."

The men were lined up according to the counties where they lived. The Smith County boys formed a company, as did the volunteers from each of the surrounding counties.

Most of the men had already signed muster rolls. Leroy followed Carter and signed his name. He looked around for Willis. Knowing that Willis could neither read nor write Leroy wanted to make sure he signed for his friend, too.

Willis was nowhere to be seen.

Leroy stretched up, looked around, and then questioned Carter, "Where the heck is Willis?"

"I saw him walking over there by the creek a moment ago. He better hurry. They've got just about everyone from Smith County signed up."

"Everybody except for that darn fool, Willis," Leroy shook his head. "Wait here and I'll get him."

"What do I tell him if he suddenly shows up?" Carter called after Leroy.

"Sign his name for him on that list of volunteers. You know how he hates to make his mark," Leroy answered, never breaking stride.

Carter shook his head. *What the heck have we gotten ourselves into? Even if it lasts only a few months, you can bet those months will be long and bloody.*

Leroy hurried along the creek through a grove of sugar maples, all the while looking for any sign of Willis. He finally found his friend leaning against the trunk of a cottonwood, obviously depressed.

"Come on, Willis," Leroy prodded. "Most of the boys have already made their marks or signed their names, including me and Carter. Now, all the Confederate Army needs to go off and whip the Yanks is *you.*" Leroy gave Willis a playful shove.

Willis ignored Leroy's attempt at humor. He continued to gaze out over the sparkling water to the far side of the creek where a company of Texas volunteers was already drilling.

"I got a bad feeling about this," Willis said with a deep sigh. "Your Pa told me plenty about war."

"Ah shucks, Willis," Leroy gave his friend a big smile. "Old fellows like to brag and tell tall tales. The fact is, we gotta go whip the Yanks to make sure Texas stays just like it is." Leroy leaned close to Willis before continuing, "full of pretty gals and the fun loving Comanche."

He reached over to tug his friend's sleeve. "Come on, Carter's waiting for us over by where we sign up. They ain't gonna wait forever so let's high tail it back over there now."

Willis looked into Leroy's eyes. His face was lined with a deep frown. Leroy was momentarily taken aback.

"Willis," he said. "We've been through too much together to turn into old women. We're Texas Rangers. We ain't supposed to be scared of nothing."

Willis looked back at the creek and paused before answering, "It's not that I'm scared, which I probably should be, but I'm too dumb to realize it. I just don't want to leave Texas and go fight somewhere far off."

Leroy picked up a small pebble and bounced it over the calm water. "The way I see it, the last place I wanna fight is here in Texas. I'd rather tear up somebody else's farmland and leave ours alone."

Willis turned to face Leroy. He waited until he had Leroy's full attention before adding, "Just bring me back alive, Leroy. If I get through this it will be because I was able to stay close to you."

Leroy shrugged. "Heck, Willis. I'll tell you the same thing I told Carter. We'll either live or we won't. There's not much I can do about it." He looked at the sad expression on the face of his best friend. *Can't let him feel that way.* "There ain't a Yankee been born that can whip a Comanche or an Apache, and as of now, we still have our hair, which means we've whipped 'em both." Leroy continued, his voice filled with resolve. "I figure fighting them darn Indians is the best training a fellow can git." He gestured toward the men across the creek marching back and forth trying to learn how to stay in step. "Fighting Indians and learning how to stay alive is a lot better training than marching back and forth while someone's yelling at you."

Leroy didn't wait for an answer; he turned and walked back toward the camp. He didn't bother to look behind him; he knew Willis would follow. He pointed to the row of tents and said in a voice he knew was loud enough for Willis to hear, "Look at them tents, Willis. For now that's home sweet home." With that, he heard Willis utter a few choice cuss words. *Well, Willis is griping again. It's gonna be a long couple of months before we whip the Yankees and come back home.*

CHAPTER 44

Texas did vote to leave the Union and the men of the newly formed regiments were granted leave to settle their affairs and say their good-byes. Leroy, his brother, Carter, and his best friend, Willis, rode home in silence. Not a word was spoken as they crossed over small rolling hills filled with switch grass.

Carter left them at the edge of a longleaf pine forest where the road curved toward Tyler. He still had some unfinished work at Judge Smith's office.

Leroy paused long enough to pick up some plants with pretty leaves. He always tried to bring a wild flower or blossom home to his wife but this time of year, greenery was his only option.

This ain't much, but it'll have to do, he thought as he pictured Mindy's smile. He took a deep breath, gave a short whistle, and rode toward the farmhouse.

"Where's Mindy?" Leroy asked his mother and father after giving them both a hearty hug. "Can you put these in a jar of water for her?" he asked as he handed the greenery to his mother.

"Where she is everyday about this time," Verlinda smiled. "Out riding that new paint Taylor got for her. That gal sure can ride a horse. She sits mighty pretty on the back of that little paint. She'll be along anytime now." Verlinda picked up a glass jar and began filling it with water from a nearby pitcher

Leroy smiled and nodded in agreement.

Moments later, the front door slammed as Leroy hurried outside, jumped off the front porch and ran to the barn to saddle a fresh horse.

His parents watched with big smiles on their faces.

"I better tend to his horse," Taylor said. "The poor fellow looks pretty tired."

"The way that boy feels about his wife, he'll ride that pasture horse hard 'till he finds her," Verlinda said. She wiped her hands on her apron and then went back inside the house.

"Better bake two pies," Taylor called out as the door closed. "Leroy will eat one all by himself." He heard his wife's laughter as she began working in the kitchen.

The familiar gentle hills and woods filled with pine trees were always a welcome sight to Leroy, but not as welcome as the sight of his wife sitting on top of a brown and white paint horse. She was stretched up as high as she could trying to see who was riding toward her.

Leroy called out to her and waved his hat. Even from a distance he could see her smile. In the long months ahead that turned into years not a day would go by without his minds eye seeing her smile and hearing her laughter.

Instead of galloping forward to meet Mindy, Leroy sat still for a minute just watching her. While he tried his best to watch every move she made, he reached down and gave his horse a couple of pats on its neck. "Seeing her like this is going to have to last me a long time, fellow."

When they met, they leaned across saddles and kissed. Mindy turned her face up to look at him and with the sunshine giving her a golden glow he thought she couldn't possibly be any prettier. Neither spoke for the longest time. They both just sat there on their horses looking at each other.

Finally, Leroy gave her a mischievous grin and asked, "How about joining me at our favorite picnic place?"

"Race you to it," she replied.

"No fair," he laughed. "I happen to be a pretty good judge of horseflesh and that is one fine pony you're sitting on Mindy-girl."

She nodded in agreement. "He's the best horse I've ever ridden. I think he understands where I want to go before I do."

They laughed and instead of racing they rode hand and hand to their special place under a canopy of big laurel and water oak trees where Leroy had played as a boy and where he had first taken Mindy after her long trip from Georgia.

He lifted her down from the saddle and held her for the longest time. She reached up to gently caress a bruise on his face he had gotten while training at the Mount Carmel camp.

"What in the world happened to you?" she asked.

"Took a silly fall from my horse," he lied. "Willis and I were showing off."

"Serves you right," she giggled. "Both you and Willis ought to know better."

"I want you to sit right here for a minute and let me have a look at you," he smiled. "I plum forgot what you looked like."

"You haven't been gone that long, Leroy Wiley," she laughed. "Although sometimes I thought the nights would never end. That's when I miss you the most."

"I know," he said softly. "I know all too well."

Mindy leaned against him, "I could stay here forever, just the two of us."

"I'll go along with that. Of course, we'd get mighty hungry after awhile because there's nothing much around here to eat except some berries during the springtime."

Their eyes met and Mindy giggled, "Why do you keep smiling at me? Do I look funny?"

Leroy threw his head back and laughed. "I keep smiling at you because you are the prettiest gal in Texas. Everybody who sees you knows that." He paused for a moment then added, "Mindy, you're so pretty you put the spring flowers to shame."

Without answering she held out both arms and they embraced. Only when they heard the bell calling them to supper did they leave their special place.

After church the following Sunday, Leroy and Mindy shared dinner with Willis and Patsy. It was a wonderful afternoon. They enjoyed Verlinda's fried chicken, biscuits and boiled potatoes, topped off with plenty of apple pie.

After dinner they sat outside on the porch. Mindy and Patsy shared the porch swing while Leroy and Willis sat on Taylor and Verlinda's rocking chairs.

When Leroy slipped back into the kitchen for another slice of apple pie, Willis decided to tell Patsy and Mindy about their adventures with the Apache Indians.

It didn't take long for Patsy to realize that Willis was scaring Mindy to death. Patsy tried her best to stop him, but Willis continued with his vivid descriptions of the fight he and Leroy had with the Apache warriors.

"What were you and Leroy doing fighting Indians all by yourselves? Where were the other Rangers?" Mindy demanded to know.

"Well, you know Leroy. He was never one to run away from a fight or ask for help if he doesn't feel he needed it," Willis explained.

Patsy noticed Mindy's hands were clasped tightly in her lap. She said, "Oh, Mindy, don't you mind what Willis says. He's a man after all, and he wants us to believe he's caught the biggest fish in the river or killed the wildest Indian. Leroy probably tells people the same kind of stories."

"No, he doesn't," Mindy said, her voice almost a whisper. "He doesn't tell me anything he does while he's on Ranger duty and now he's about to go off to war."

"That's because we're always about to get kilt, or we're out in the bad weather going hungry. I'm always cold and hungry because we usually can't build a fire," Willis added.

Patsy frowned at the thought of Willis going hungry. "Why can't you take the time to build a fire when you set up camp, Willis? It seems to me that you would do that, even if you were tired."

"Oh, heck," Willis explained. "It has nothing to do with being too tired. It's just that we're usually in Indian country and we don't want 'em to find us during the night. Give 'em half a chance and they'd scalp us while we're asleep." Willis paused and shook his head. "Nobody can see or hear them savages when they sneak up on you. They're like ghosts."

Mindy's hand shot up over her mouth and she said in a high pitched voice, "Oh, no!"

Leroy finished his second piece of pie and poured a glass of apple cider for Mindy and Patsy before leaving the kitchen. When he got back out to the porch, Mindy was nowhere to be seen and Patsy was tearing into Willis.

"What's the matter?" Leroy asked while looking around the yard for his wife. "Where's Mindy?"

Patsy glared at Willis before answering. "Leroy, Willis told Mindy about your fight with those awful Indians."

"Darn it!" Leroy said as he struggled to place one of the glasses on a small table. "That happened a long time ago."

"Don't cuss, Leroy," Patsy said. "Willis didn't mean it and in any case, you shouldn't be so quick to use bad words."

Leroy ignored Patsy's constructive criticism. "Willis, what did you tell Mindy?"

"Not much," Willis said, never taking his eyes off his wife's red face.

"Not much?" Patsy said, her voice full of anger. She looked up at Leroy. "He told Mindy about the fight you two had with three wild Apache Indians. The two of you were all alone and nearly killed. Leroy, what in the world were you and Willis trying to prove?"

"Now, Patsy," Leroy tried to explain but she cut him off in mid-sentence.

"Don't you speak to me that way, Leroy Wiley. I've known you too long. There's no doubt in my mind that the only reason Willis was in a fight for his life with three Indians was because of you."

"It was only two Indians, Patsy," Willis lied in a vain attempt to make everything right. "Leroy was fighting with one Indian and I was fighting with the other two. But, they were Apaches, and them Apaches are much worse than the other kind of Injuns, except for the Comanche."

Patsy's mouth flew open. "Oh, my Lord help us all!" she cried as she jumped up and ran down the steps of the porch.

"Willis," Leroy spoke through clenched teeth. "Can I see you out back for a minute or two?"

Willis fingered his sweat-stained cowboy hat but kept silent.

"What's going on here?" Verlinda bound through the front door. "Mindy just ran inside crying. I tried to stop her when she flew past me in the kitchen, but she just shook her head and kept running." Leroy's mother glared at her youngest son. "What has upset Mindy? You are home one day and the next thing I know your wife is running to her room in tears! Didn't I raise you better?"

Taylor followed his wife out to the porch with a quizzical expression on his face. "Son, do you realize Mindy's upstairs crying? I can hear her wailing all the way downstairs in the kitchen. Carter and Clayton are both out by the barn but I bet they can hear her too."

Leroy looked helplessly at his parents, then at the back of Patsy's bonnet and finally to Willis. "I'll be right back," he said. Before going back into the house he turned to Willis and said, "Don't leave, Willis. I got a thing or two to settle with you."

Willis stood and began walking toward Patsy. "Maybe we ought to get on home, Patsy. It's getting late."

"No, sir," Patsy said without turning to face him. "We'll wait right here until Leroy gets back. He asked you to wait, and that's what we'll do."

Leroy's mother sat down in the swing and asked Patsy to sit with her. Verlinda placed her arm around the young woman's trembling shoulders. "Now, Patsy," she said. "Please tell us what has upset both you and my daughter-in-law."

"Well," Patsy began to speak slowly. "It all started when Willis.."

Taylor reached over and tapped Willis on the arm. "Come with me, Willis. Let's go visit with Carter and Clayton. I'm sure they'll be glad to see us. They're not supposed to be working on Sunday, but we've got a sick yearling on our hands."

Leroy slowly climbed the stairs and hesitated before opening the bedroom door. He took a deep breath and collected his thoughts.

"Mindy," Leroy said as he gently opened the bedroom door. He was still carrying her glass of cider. When she didn't answer he said softly, "Mindy, I brought you some cider."

She was lying across the bed, her face buried deep in the pillows. He crossed the distance between them and sat the apple cider down on a small table.

"Don't sit that glass down on Mama Wiley's oak table," Mindy fussed, her face still covered by the pillows. "It'll leave a water mark."

Leroy smiled. "Are you peeking at me?" He sat down on the bed and began to rub her back.

"I know now why your face was all beat up," she said without looking at him. "You didn't tell me the truth, Leroy. What else are you not telling me?"

He leaned forward until his face was very close to her hands. "Mindy-girl," he said with a gentle voice. "Willis and I got into a little scrape with a couple of Indians while we were acting as scouts for the Ranger Company. That's all there was to it."

She turned her head to face him, "But you were almost killed!" she said with tears streaming down her cheeks.

"No, we weren't," he said while stroking her hair. "And the other Rangers were right behind us," he lied.

He waited for a response but none came. Instead she threw both arms around his neck. "I don't want to lose you," she sobbed. "It's bad enough that you're going to have to go fight the Yankees, but fighting with dangerous Indians too! It's not fair."

"Ah shucks," he whispered while stroking her hair. "Them Indians weren't much trouble and I can pretty much guarantee you that them Yankees won't be much of a problem either."

"But one of them hurt you and Willis said the two of you were almost killed," she held on to him, her slender fingers clutching his shirt.

"I'll admit it was rough, but I'm here now and that Indian is back there on the trail dead." He paused and kissed her face. "And Mindy, that Indian isn't going to hurt any more women and kids either."

She nodded her head and he felt that he was slowly but surely calming her down. "We have to go back downstairs and visit with Patsy and Willis," she whispered. "It's very rude to stay up here when company has called on us. Didn't Mama Wiley teach you that?"

Mindy pulled away from him and began to wipe her face.

"Nope," Leroy said, his voice so low she could barely hear him. "We're gonna stay right here awhile. Willis and Patsy can visit with the rest of the Wileys." More than anything else he wanted to comfort her. He held her close and slowly began to untie the laces that held her dress.

"Leroy!" Mindy exclaimed. "It's broad daylight!"

"I know," he whispered.

Less than a month later, on a day Mindy described in her diary as "clear with the air smelling so good it made her feel glad to be alive," Leroy hitched a wagon and took her to their special picnic place. He spent the entire day with her, sharing funny stories about him and his brothers while they were growing up. When he described the Sunday church service where he slipped two frogs into the building and turned them loose while the congregation was singing hymns, she laughed until tears streamed down her cheeks.

"Oh, Leroy," she laughed. "What happened?"

"Well," he said as his eyes dropped and focused on his dusty cowboy boots. "The frogs made their way up to the choir and one of 'em hopped on the foot of my mother's friend, Miz Wilson, who was a pretty big lady I might add. That woman raised such a ruckus that all the other ladies in the choir started yelling and stomping around which scared the other frog. He jumped right into the lap of the preachers wife and," he paused to watch Mindy because her eyes twinkled whenever she laughed, "Miz Fitzgerald, that was her name, Miz Elmira Fitzgerald, wasn't exactly a skinny lady either, so she jumped up and the whole church started rocking back and forth until all the ladies ran out the door."

"Did they find out it was you who let those frogs loose?" Mindy asked, her hands clasped to her face.

"Oh, yes," Leroy said, shaking his head. "My behind can swear to that fact."

Mindy giggled. "How did they find out?"

"Well," Leroy pursed his lips and pretended to be very serious. "I was suspected right away. I knew I was in big trouble when I saw the preacher walk straight to my mother and start talking to her. She looked like she was facing the Almighty."

"And?" Mindy prompted, leaning closer to hear every word.

"Carter decides if he's going to be a lawyer he has to tell the truth, so he fesses up. Naturally, he blamed me."

"Which was right!" Mindy lifted her chin in a very serious manner.

"It was," Leroy said. "I was guilty as charged and I paid the price."

Mindy leaned closer. "Did Papa Taylor give you a whippin'?"

"No," Leroy replied. "I wasn't that lucky. He always pretended to whip us when Ma told him to, but he never did. He only got mad if one of us got hurt and that was because it scared him to death."

"So Mama Wiley paddled you?" Mindy asked. Her dark eyes growing wide.

"Did she ever," Leroy declared. "Whenever she picked up a switch, she meant business. I couldn't sit down for a week. But that wasn't the worst part."

"Oh," Mindy giggled. "Tell me more."

"I had to go say I was sorry to every lady in the church choir. Mama spent the better part of a week carrying me all over Smith County. I honestly think," he leaned closer to Mindy before adding, "I ate more apple pie that week than any other week in my life because every one of those ladies gave me a big slice of pie after I said I was sorry. So you see, Mindy-gal, it wasn't all that bad."

"Oh, you!" Mindy laughed as he gently pulled her down and started kissing her.

She wanted to protest. After all, they weren't in their bedroom and even though this was their special place, they were outdoors in front of God and everyone. She touched his shoulder with a firm hand thinking that she would push him away, but his kisses left her breathless. Instead of pushing him away, she pulled him closer.

The next morning as dawn broke Leroy and Carter saddled their horses, tried their best to swallow a few bites of ham and eggs, and then said sad goodbyes to their parents and their brother, Clayton, who was remaining behind to help bring in the crops before he too would go off to fight in the war.

"I'll be following you as soon as the crops are in," Clayton said, almost breathless with excitement. "I already signed up along with the other boys who have to stay home for now. But it won't be long. Gosh," he turned to his father, "I hope it's not all over by the time I can leave."

"Unfortunately, son," Taylor said to Clayton, but his eyes were squarely on Leroy, "I don't think you have anything to worry about."

"I pray to God it ends before my boys reach the battlefield," Verlinda said, her hands holding her apron over her face.

Carter walked over to comfort his mother. Leroy remained at his father's side.

"You know I'm counting on you, Leroy, to keep yourself and your brothers alive and well," Taylor said seriously.

Leroy nodded.

Carter decided to try to lighten everyone's mood. He said with a half-hearted smile, "Does anyone around here remember that I'm the oldest brother in this family?"

"Yeah, but Leroy's the meanest brother in the family," Clayton said as he gave Leroy a playful shove.

"Clayton," Carter said with mock sternness. "That's not a polite thing to say about your younger brother, even if we both know it's true."

Realizing how hard this departure was on their parents, Leroy and Carter gave each other a silent signal, a slight tip of their heads, that only they and their brother, Clayton was aware of it. The brothers picked up four pillowcases packed with food and walked quickly to their waiting mounts. As soon as they tied two pillowcases across each saddle horn, they both climbed onto their saddles and gave Clayton a wave.

"Send word as soon as you can," Clayton called out, "With any luck, I'll join your outfit before all the shootin' starts!"

Mindy remained upstairs in their bedroom. As he rode away, Leroy took one last glance at the farmhouse and saw his wife wrapped in a quilt staring out the window. He knew her eyes were full of tears.

He reached up, tipped his hat to say a last goodbye to his wife, and then said in a *very determined* tone of voice to his brother, "Race you to the war, Carter!"

EPILOGUE

Over seventy thousand Texans would fight for the Confederacy, most of them would fight beyond the borders of Texas in faraway states such as Virginia, Georgia and Tennessee. The battles would be fierce but no worse than the Rangers had endured while fighting on the Texas frontier between the Rio Grande on the south and the Red River, the northern boundary of the state. The men would return from fighting the federal forces to face the finest cavalry soldiers on the western frontier, the warriors of the Comanche Nation.